A MATCHBOX
FULL OF PEARLS

KAMILLE ROACH

First published in 2021

Copyright © Kamille Roach 2021

Visit: kamilleroach.com

ISBN: 9780645390407

Edited by Karin Cox www.editorandauthor.com

For my mother, Brenda, a true earth woman who made the whole world possible.

Prologue

September 1971

She glimpses a pale face on the other side of the water's surface, high above. Her foot brushes and drags against the riverbed. The current rolls her bodily, and there's a moment's panic—her new world, full of pitch-black water. Heavy liquid, pushing up her nose, into her ears, her mouth tight against the invasion. Where are the lights, the stage, the adoring faces? Where is the band? The music? Was it real—the music? They said it wasn't real. She saw things she couldn't touch. She saw the beauty they couldn't see. Why is it so cold?

A surge pulls her along as her lips release, her mouth and lungs fill, and she surrenders, tugged into the heart of the current. Then it happens. The world lights up, the orchestra plays, the audience claps. She walks out onto the stage.

PART ONE

Chapter 1

I wake to two tidy deaths. The first is unfolding before me through the window of a suburban Carlton house-sit.

In the garden, a pigeon coos to itself, geek eyes, shades of grey, bob-bob head. In the grass, a cat the colour of autumn mist stalks.

'It's a cat, stupid!' I hiss futilely at the glass.

I return the phone to my ear. My old boss, Mary, replies from halfway across Australia, 'Huh?'

I made the mistake of answering the phone. I thought it was the café where I work. There's a long pause while she waits for me to react to her news that my foster mother has died of a brain aneurysm. Typical of Blossom to die quietly and alone.

'I have to save a pigeon. Seriously the dumbest birds.' I notice my reflection in the window glass, all wild hair and oversized T-shirt, skinny legs sticking out beneath. It hits me that I've barely changed in the two years since my eighteenth birthday.

'Mary, thanks for calling.' I sound lame, knowing there are right words for this, but not knowing what they are.

'I know you and Blossom weren't close, Lola, but ...' Mary hums, like she's working something out. I feel sorry for her, having to be the one to call. 'You'll come back for the funeral?'

Outside the window, above the temporary pigeon, a crimson rosella gnaws myrtle flowers. Its belly is intensely vivid, and then it flips over, all violet back, cheeks, wings, grasping claws. There are no rosellas that colour in the west.

A tug happens deep in my gut. Western Australians are as bound to the landscape as children to their parents. But I've been adrift from one house to another, unfamiliar faces, frozen box dinners.

'Yeah, course,' I mumble.

Outside, water drops heavily from the leaves and branches. The pigeon flutters, settles. The cat creeps closer, grey hunting grey. I wave frantically through the window. The pigeon tilts its head.

I wish Mary would just hang up, but something sits there between us like an over-boiled egg.

She sighs. 'The thing is, Blossom left something important. Couldn't give it to you when she was alive.'

'Like what?'

'Just come back, Lola. Okay? You need to come home.'

'I don't have one.'

'Yes, you do.'

'I need to go.'

'You'll book a flight?'

I swallow hard. 'Yeah. I will.' I sense a little lift. Maybe it will feel like a homecoming. That anchored feeling people talk about that pulls them back to a place like two magnets. 'Today.'

'Good-good. Walshy can pick you up.'

'He's back?' I hold my breath to hear better.

'Been back from Carnarvon a few weeks. Seems better. Meat on his bones.'

'Does he want to see me?'

Mary makes an exasperated sound. 'Of course! Why not?'

Where do I start? Because he didn't want me? Because he went up north and refused to let me come? He said he had to go to a place without edges. Alone.

'Gotta go. I'll ring when I know my flight.' I press end.

Movement catches my eye. The rosella dangles upside-down to reach the end of the branch. With a violet flash, the branch springs up, bounces empty. The cat sinks into its haunches, eyes fixed on the pigeon.

I run down the hall, through the laundry, bumping into things. I wrestle with the lock and burst onto the lawn just as statue cat launches.

'No!' Clapping, I run towards them, wet grass between my toes. 'Git! Git!'

The grey mass wrestles. The cat's jaw is clamped on the pigeon's neck and his paw pins a pathetically flapping wing.

I rush at them, growling.

Pricked ears swivel, and the feline bounces sideways with a look of contempt, scampers up the fence and is gone.

'Monster!'

The pigeon shivers, dappled red on the grass. Its wings and head are the wrong angle, like unfolded origami. I try to pick it up, but its neck flops. The heat of the dying bird sweats in my hand, blood sticking tiny feather threads to my skin. 'Damn you!' I shout.

I hear a scratching and fingers curl over the top of the fence like pale, fat claws. An older lady's head appears—neighbour, cat owner, nosy old cow.

'What's the fuss?'

'Your damn cat keeps killing the birds!' I hold up the corpse for her to see.

'Penny is well fed, young lady. She doesn't kill birds.' She tuts and disappears.

'Bloody does so, you old witch! Should be shut inside!' I find a place beneath the camellia bush to lay the dead pigeon. I stomp back inside.

These days, I am requested by name from the Melbourne house-sitting agency because I make no noise, have no friends over, and leave everything untouched. The ghost who takes out bins and walks dogs. Two years of sleeping in a 'spare room', always half-packed for a quick departure.

Two years of comfortable anonymity.

After a hasty flight booking, I inform the housesitting agency of my sudden holiday.

'You'll give us a call when you're back? You're a great house sitter Miss Harris.'

I race around the house to return it to pre-Lola condition before dressing in a long brown skirt and antique lace camisole I found at the Queen Victoria Market. I pull a big brown jumper over the top and wonder how hot it is in Perth.

I get an excited tingle. I'm going to see Walshy. Today.

Outside, taking out the rubbish, I pause at the fence, and then empty it over the top into the neighbour's yard. Then I lock the back door and hide the key beneath a potted plant. Grey feathers litter the back lawn.

In the taxi to the airport, I close my eyes. I see Walshy as if it were yesterday. Standing in the middle of the river, sun beating down on his wavy hair, his muscular, ropy arms, his legs with a graduated farmer's tan, his gappy, forever-young grin.

A boy who taught me to survive.

A man who taught me how to love.

Chapter 2

On the plane, while heaving my bag into the overhead locker, I notice a stocky, bald man staring from the centre aisle.

'Thought you weren't gonna get that in for a sec.' He smiles, his eyes flickering over me. 'Was gonna offer to do it for ya. Travelling alone?' His gaze snags on my bust.

I note his beer belly, well-worn stubby shorts, long-sleeved rugby jumper.

I take a deep breath and let it out slowly, as I've been encouraged to do by school counsellors, foster parents, bus drivers, an old lady on a train. 'Nah, got my tits here to keep me company.' I turn and sit down near the window. Behind me, someone snorts.

My row of seats scores another occupant: a blonde lady who looks like she belongs in business class. She moves across beside me and points to the window.

'Air hostess said the middle is empty. Is that okay?' She has a private girls' school voice.

'Sure.' I move my backpack.

She shifts over and settles in. Her earrings are huge sparkly diamonds or cubic zirconia. She smiles, revealing a perfect row of teeth. 'Going to Perth for a holiday?'

'York. I used to live there.' I gather up my hair and stick it down the back of my jumper, where it will stay for about three seconds. 'There's a funeral.'

I lift my knees and wrap my arms around them. I don't want to look at her in case my eyes get watery; or in case they don't.

'Oh, sorry. Family?' She touches my wrist, and it feels too sudden to be touched by someone. Her hand is cool, her fingernails long and pink.

'Foster mother. Since I was nine. She was ill.'

'That's sad.' She shakes her head and crosses her arms. 'Do you know your birth parents? Hope you don't mind me asking. I've always been interested in this kind of stuff.'

'No. I've had lots of parents. It's a long story.'

I watch her waiting but keep my mouth closed.

'Oh, right. What was your foster mother like?'

I think something will come out of my mouth, but my brain is as vast and blank as a rainy Victorian sky. 'Um, quiet.' She waits.

'Sorry for your loss. You must feel a bit adrift. I can't imagine not having a huge family that harass each other all the time.'

'No. I'm used to it.'

I stare out the window. The tarmac is dark and smooth. It's odd to be this close. Just bitumen, nothing mysterious. At the edge of the runway, white birds and ducks waddle over the grass. I wonder if they'll rise up into the turbines and blow an engine at take-off.

A gust of rain smears the window. I pull the magazine from the seat pocket in front of me.

The front cover is Broome, Western Australia. Vivid colours: red, blue and white. Hot blue sky, the whitest fleece of cloud. I run my hand across the picture, half expecting heat. Even the electric-red pindan soil is cool on the glossy page.

Walshy's been to Broome. He said we'd go there one day, that I'd love it. But that was a long time ago.

Engines roar and the force of acceleration pushes us deep into our seats. After a few minutes of climbing, the plane evens out, horizontal. Below us, Victoria is a slice of verdant beauty wreathed in either rainforest or snow or smoke depending on the season. In the dry, it burns like a bastard.

Inside the magazine, an article on South Australia explores the Great Australian Bight: whales spouting; empty, scrub-covered land. The land glares up, the sun glares down, stunting trees with drought and wind. Everything there scrapes for water, except a few coastal pockets where optimists tend vineyards.

Our flight path soars over the southern end of Western Australia and then north to Perth. We'll see the long, white beaches of Esperance.

Walshy has told me all about these places. He used to camp a week here or there, all by himself. Just chucked his swag into the back of his ute and drove off. He was more comfortable with the wild than people. Silver-white saltpans that burn your eyes. Gorges where you can skinny-dip in the jade-coloured water and never tell a soul. Dingoes that howl like wolves. Camels leftover from the gold rush, which tromp through fences to quench their thirst at cattlemen's water troughs.

I used to listen to him talk about it. I loved the way his face lit up, his hands moving, all animated. He told me that up north was where the most miracles happen. The sky swells thick and purple. Veins of electricity snake to the earth. Great, flat red plains run like blood or sprout carpets of wildflowers. Papery everlastings, tiny but victorious, spring a soft stubble over the ochre. In the wet, the drumming rain coaxes hidden leather-skinned frogs to the surface. Crawling insects take flight, drop wings. Birds screech from the skies to nest in dead trees. It can be silent as a whisper, loud as a roar. You can imagine dinosaurs, the Dreamtime.

I could listen to him talk about it for hours.

A voice rolls through the plane's speakers, permitting us to take off seatbelts. I lean back and close my eyes.

Chapter 3

I was five when Coral, another foster mum, hung herself. Her husband was in jail for fraud, and then her boyfriend, Heartbreak Eyes, left her.

There's me: squatting in the backyard of a little house in Merredin, where I'd lived for almost a year. Sun sweats my T-shirt to my back. My small hands clutch a bottle of pink nail polish and a brush. Heartbreak's shadow falls over my hands and my ants, which are toenail-sized, black and shiny with a bite that hurts for an hour. I'm dabbing their backs with pink.

'What are you doing?' He has a ninety-year-old's smoky voice box.

'Seeing if the polished ones come back out of the nest.' I dot another ant, but it's too much polish and jams up its legs. The ant staggers in a circle like a wounded soldier. 'Shit.'

Ants are one of the most effective species on the planet. They're on an underground mission. The nest starts with a sand pyramid coated with fine, silty silica from down deep. I want to know how far they go and why the polished ones don't return.

I squint hard. The sun sits behind Heartbreak's hat, obscuring his face.

'Don't tread on them. It's an experiment.'

He shuffles back and looks down, hands finding his hips. There's a polished ant in his boot print. Its legs are mashed in all directions. One leg, thick as an eyelash, is completely separated from the thorax.

'Sorry.'

'Doesn't matter. I think they kill the polished ones anyway. 'Cos they're different.'

He pinches his jeans just above his knee and squats, exhaling heavily.

'I'm going away.'

The ground recedes and surges, so I close my eyes for a second. This always happens. Just when you get used to someone, they go away.

I watch an ant, its regular six-legged canter, the way its body stays lined up like a cannon on a trailer. You can trust ants. They're predictable. Put a stick on their path and they'll stop, search it, find a way around.

'Coral won't be happy no more.'

'She ain't happy now.' He growls and spits to the side, pull things from his top shirt pocket and then rolls a smoke between his stained fingers without looking. He takes a long breath. 'She wants you to go to school more.'

'Fuck that.'

He chuckles and cuffs me gently behind the ear. 'School gives detention for swearin', Lola.' He rocks back on his heels, lights the rollie's end with a match and drops it. Taking a long drag, he tilts his head back to study the horizon. His hair is black oil, skin tawny, eyes a summer sky. His eyelashes are thicker than Coral's, even when she wears makeup. He exhales blue smoke and spits a thread of tobacco off his tongue.

Heartbreak Eyes—Coral's name for him. At first, I didn't want him. It was nice having Coral to myself for a while. Not that her husband was home much before he left. 'He's wheeling and dealing,' she told me. I still had to share her with the other hairdressers and customers at the salon. Then Heartbreak Eyes came over and she told me to go and play, distracted again. But soon, we cooked together and sat around a campfire off the back veranda, waiting for damper. We'd eat in front of an old black-and-white movie, honey dripping down our wrists. When Coral giggled and snuck off to her room with Heartbreak Eyes, I didn't mind. They came back later to have hot chocolate with me.

Heartbreak sighs. 'You're a smart kid.'

An ant touches the end of my big toe with its antenna. It's so fine I can't feel it. *Just bite me*, I think. *Then I'll have something to cry about.*

He squeezes my shoulder. 'Bye, Lola. Be good.'

I twitch like a dog with a fly. I want to say something mean, but nothing comes out. Coral says I've got to watch my temper. Heartbreak stands up, drops the smoke, and stomps on the end. He strides away.

That horrible feeling happens, the one where the earth opens up and I fall and fall. Then the anger comes. I need a superpower, a laser I can zap him with. I imagine a big smoking hole in his back as he walks away.

I pocket his dead match.

Heartbreak's Holden HG ute grumbles awake and pulls away. I screw the lid back on the polish and head for the house, trudging up the three steps to the back door like a soldier from the desert.

First, I see tiny pearls on the hardwood floor, and then something in front of the big window. Coral's bare feet hover two or three feet off the ground, her skirt, caught in a breeze from the open window, flaps against her freckly calves. Her body turns slightly where it hangs by a rope from a ceiling beam.

I've been told I never actually saw Coral's body, that the door was locked. But I remember the pearls.

Death confetti.

Chapter 4

Someone shakes me awake. It's diamond earrings. She smiles apologetically. 'Meal's here. Didn't want you to miss out.'

I sit up and wipe drool from my mouth. Aeroplane noise drones. Rattling trolley. Small talk. Music. The engine rush encloses us. I pull down the tray table and nod yes to the chicken option. 'Thanks.'

'Would you like juice or soft drink?'

'White wine.' I reach for my wallet, noticing the tiny newspaper clipping folded behind my bank card.

The hostess smiles through plum-coloured lipstick. 'Just need to see some ID.'

I already have it out. She takes it, peers, and then nods and hands it back. 'Terrific. You don't look twenty! You'll love that when you're thirty! There you go. Dry white.' The trolley rattles forwards.

'That must get annoying.'

I shrug. 'I'm used to it.' The edge of the clipping is still sticking out. I pull it out. It is deeply creased from being folded.

Historical murder turns thirty-five! Plans for murderer's room to be a new tourist attraction at York's historical Lion Inn. Lovely Lorrelai, *exotic dancer turned murderer, drowned her lover's wife in 1971 and was awarded a life sentence!*
Devonshire teas available!

The name 'Lorrelai' is underlined in biro.

'Funeral notice?' Private school smiles sympathetically, her eyes sparkling with curiosity. I silently count how much time I'll be stuck with her. Three hours and forty-five minutes.

I'm feeling generous, or maybe I just don't care, so I hand her the clipping. 'No. I used to work at the Lion Inn. My foster mother sent it to me. Last thing I got from her.'

She reads it. Frowning, she hands it back. 'Lovely Lorrelai?'

With a shrug, I smile and refold the clipping back into my wallet.

'Oh, while you were asleep, I remembered. York was on the news the other night — serial rapist on the loose.' She pulls a face. 'Sorry. Probably shouldn't have mentioned that … with your funeral.'

My heart rate rises suddenly, and I stare at her. 'I don't watch the news. A serial rapist? How'd they know it was the same guy?'

'Left a doll. A toy. Isn't that crazy? Apparently, this is the third time.'

My ears ring and my skin shrinks a little.

Diamond earrings sits forwards like a journalist who's found a source. 'Did you live there when the other rapes happened?'

I sandwich my hands between my knees to warm them. 'Yeah. The other two were in Northam. But that was years ago.'

'Horrible.' She makes a noise, shivers, and then sits back in her seat.

* * *

Eight years ago, there was a rape in a backyard. Lisa Lee, twelve years old, grabbed while looking at the stars through her backyard telescope. Lisa's parents had been inside, watching television.

It had happened the night of the school social dance in Northam. I'd been there to catch up with my caseworker, Sarah. She had stopped outside the hall where the dance was held, so I could watch the kids all dressed up and filing into the hall before she dropped me back to York, where Blossom was waiting, for once. She usually would have left for the weekend.

I remember the news reported that Lisa hadn't even seen her attacker, and she had been throttled so she couldn't scream. He left something on the lawn near the telescope. A huge doll in a box with a pink ribbon tied in a bow. It was reportedly an expensive one, with a porcelain face, real hair and leather shoes.

At the time, police seemed optimistic the doll would lead them to her attacker. They were wrong.

Then something else emerged. The attacker had left something on Lisa which implicated someone from the school social.

16

Glitter.

* * *

I drink the wine first for maximum impact, and then I eat half the food. It's all I can manage on top of the butterflies.

My companion isn't eating at all. She holds out her hands, takes my tray and puts it on the spare seat. 'I love your style. Is it boho?'

'I suppose. I shop at Goodwill and markets.'

'Oh, it totally works on you!' She waves one hand around me like I'm a model or a mannequin. 'Wild hair. Off the shoulder brown jumper —'

'The seam's gone.'

' —vintage. Sorry, what?'

I shake my head, and her eyes are drawn there instead.

'Naturally curly?'

'I definitely wouldn't do this on purpose.' My hair has always mystified people. They act like I'm supposed to explain it. I find these conversations cryptic. How do women instinctively know the right banal compliments to exchange? 'Your earrings are nice.'

She smiles, showing me I've said the right thing. 'Fake.' She winks, snaps a pair of big white headphones over her ears, and takes out a book.

Relieved, I turn back to the window. The sky is darker, a deep ocean blue, clouds feathering beneath us.

I never thought of Blossom as a mother, more of a housemate. When I saw her that first time, in the meeting room of the children's home, she looked like a middle-aged man. She wore a green t-shirt and work shorts, had a fat belly, sagging boobs with no bra and a tattoo on her forearm. There was dirt on her boots. Mud left scuds on the industrial green carpet. I'd focused on the dirt.

'Ah, yeah.' She had swallowed and nodded. 'Hello.' Her eyes played around the room like she wanted to look at me but couldn't.

My smiling caseworker looked from me to her and back, playing stare ping-pong. 'Blossom would like to look after you. She has a huge garden, and she lives in a tiny country town called York. She says the garden is bigger than the house.'

The garden convinced me. Even with the risk I'd be used for child labour, I went with her.

Blossom walked me to a bus stop, and we got on without exchanging a single word. After two hours, the bus rolled along the jacaranda and eucalypt-lined streets of York. The town was surrounded by bush and paddocks dotted with sheep. The bus stopped, waiting to cross the wide Avon River, with its sign romanticising a famous bushranger, Moondyne Joe, who'd had a cave and corral nearby in 1861. I pondered what a corral might be.

Soon, the bus expelled us with a hiss, and Blossom pointed to a fenced house half a block ahead. It looked promising. Old wood and corrugated iron, a shabby jigsaw decorated with faded paintings and poems. The garden was thick and tangled, bees zooming from bloom to bloom in a mess of flowers.

'It used to be a backpacker hostel,' said Blossom, only the second time she'd spoken. 'It was tradition for travellers to leave a plant or picture or …' She pointed to writing on the walls.

I walked upstairs onto the veranda that skirted the house. The boards creaked.

The Flower House
Here we are under messed-up stars,
A big, big sky overhead.
We found this place with its flowers and snakes,
And an old, creaky, stained-up bed.
Here we lay, lovers in sin,
And all we can afford is bread.
Who knows where you'll see us next,
Hope we don't wind up dead.
– Flo and Pete

I imagined, suddenly, a bare mattress on the floor and mosquitos humming round my head.

Around the veranda, a glorious mess reigned. Banksia, grevillea, Geraldton wax, roses and liliums. I knew all the plant names from the gardener in state care. It was safe and quiet in gardens. Good things happened, like bulbs sprouting, worms silently digesting soil. I turned a slow, full circle.

'The Flower House,' I said.

Blossom had two chickens and a room just for me. I had a proper bedroom, with a flyscreen on the window.

Chapter 5

'Hey, we're nearly there.'

Private school girl looks newly groomed. Hair brushed into a ponytail, fresh pink lipstick. She reminds me of a girl from school, Shelley Turner. Always perfect, though her face was often a little sad.

'Nice top.' It's a colourful open-necked blouse. I admire women like her, always smart, fresh, clothes coordinated.

I pull off my headphones and enter the engine hum with the rest of the cabin. The air smells of lipstick and farts. I roll my neck side to side and flip open the shuttered window. Sunset has left a lemon afterglow.

'You did well to sleep,' says private school. One of her knees jigs up and down. 'Are you going to York tonight?'

'I'm getting collected. If he's got the message.'

'Boyfriend?' She grins.

This trip has twenty minutes left, way too short to explain. 'School friend. I left York two years ago. It was just temporary. I've had a lot of homes.' I drag myself upright and tweak my knickers out from where they've ridden up my bum.

'I think home is more about the people you love, not a fancy house or sexy suburb.'

I stare at her in genuine bewilderment. 'I've never heard anyone say "sexy suburb" before.'

She laughs gently and touches my arm so naturally she must think we're friends.

Dots of light lead down the dark hills of Greenmount. Perth CBD glitters ahead. Sitting up, I feel something tender for the lights and the velvet black where the ocean meets the land. It's a dangerous feeling, a soft one. The lights rush to meet us. The wheels bite against tarmac. We skid, and taxi, and eventually bump to a stop.

'Hey, I'm Jenny.' She holds out her hand and we shake. 'All the best with everything.'

'Lola. Thanks. You too.'

She gets up, makes her way through the throng of people getting bags out of overhead lockers, and is gone.

I stare through the window. I'm shocked by the familiarity of the airport, and the butterflies start up again.

Last time I was here, my goal was to get as far away from York as I could without leaving the country.

We're shuffling down the aisle like a human caterpillar when I feel something against my backside. I twist to discover bald guy behind me, his bag against my bum.

'Mind giving me some space?'

His mouth smirks up at one corner. 'Sure, love.'

The pressure goes. I face the front. The pressure returns. When I turn, his face is the picture of innocent amusement. He gives his bag a shove. 'Sorry.' He winks.

I glare at him. 'You bloody will be, if you don't stop it.'

Around us, there's the sound of throat clearing. 'Give her some space,' says a guy in a suit.

'Yeah, she's just a kid,' chimes in a stout American lady.

Bald man huffs. His eyes swivel to the rest of the staring passengers.

'Everything okay up there?' A blonde steward with a sliver stripe through his long fringe, cranes his neck to see me between the full-sized adults.

I close my eyes for three seconds. It doesn't work. 'No. Baldy, here, is fascinated by my arse.'

The plane is suddenly silent for a few long seconds before it descends into sniggers and throat clearing.

'Steady on,' says bald guy. He backs up and treads on a lady's toe. 'Sorry. Sorry, love.' He has one hand up, signalling 'I come in peace'.

Everyone wriggles and sorts themselves out.

Silver stripe gives me a coded look of understanding as we start to shuffle towards the front of the plane. I lift my eyebrow and smile.

We're released up the off-ramp like a plane's innards. As I traipse beneath the domed tube, Perth's heat is a warm hug after the refrigerated aircon. I veer to the side, drop my bag and pull off my jumper, letting other passengers stride past.

The airport is a lounge room compared to Melbourne's. Family can wait right outside the door at the top of the exit ramp.

Trailing my bag behind me, I like the smallness. Then, just as fast, I hate it.

I brace for familiar faces instead of a sea of strangers. I glance through the window at a Qantas plane. The Flying Kangaroo.

One week.

'Jane?' No one has called me that for two years.

He's through the double open doors. Curly hair, shining green eyes, wide face. Walshy. *Bam,* that punch in the chest. Quick in-breath. *Oh Lord. How am I going to survive a week?*

He's wearing black, flat-front work pants and a pale T-shirt with a rip on one shoulder. I can see where his collarbone meets the shoulder joint, his brown skin—the most beautiful thing I've seen for years. That glimpse stirs me somewhere inside.

Walshy stands there, arms hanging by his sides, his head on a slight angle as he watches me walk up. His cheeks dimple with a smile.

'C'mere.' He pulls me against his chest. I breathe him in, the sweat and cologne smell of him. He rocks me a bit, muttering 'Jane' softly a few times and each time it settles some internal yearning. He kisses my head, strokes his hands up and down my arms.

I look upwards. His eyes are bloodshot.

'How are you?' I ask.

'Alright.'

'Mary said you work all the time since you got back from Carnarvon.'

'Yeah.' He runs his fingertips over my scalp down to the nape of my neck.

My scalp starts to buzz. I feel like I've had spirits to drink, a few shots, straight down. The muscles in my legs shiver, and I want to wrap them around his waist like a monkey.

21

Passengers hug and talk and walk off. Bald guy stomps past, eyes fixed ahead like he's justifiably annoyed. I'd flick him a rude signal, but Walshy's warm body distracts me.

Jenny passes. She raises her eyebrows and winks, and then strides briskly towards the bag carousel.

'Your hair's longer,' Walshy says. He pushes it off one shoulder and traces a finger along my collarbone.

'So's yours.' I look him over. His chest is wider, and he's thicker and healthier. 'Station life suits you, huh?'

His eyes meet mine. 'Yeah, it did.'

'But you came back?'

Walshy nods and turns to face the bag carousel. 'Felt like it was time.'

'I only have a carry-on.'

'Okay.' He takes my hand and my bag handle and tows us along like he's a dolphin and we're in his wake.

'Ah, it's so warm here.'

'Cold in Melbourne?'

I can see the edge of his jaw and I feel lighter. Outside, lights line the path, and moths flutter around the globes. Speckled geckos hug the poles, waiting. High up, a lone Pacific gull circles a spotlight, orbiting it like a false sun. It's a long way from the sandy coastline, where it should be sleeping in footsteps left by walkers.

'Freezing.'

My Melbourne market sandals slap along the concrete as we walk to Walshy's white Ford Falcon ute. Its lower third is tan-coloured from dust. He bought it from a neighbouring farmer when he turned seventeen. He fishes around in his pocket for the keys. I go around to the passenger side and get in.

Inside the cab, his white work shirt is thrown on the driver's seat. He climbs in, moves the shirt and folds it carefully on the middle seat. I give him a long look as he starts the car.

Walshy gazes back like a mirror. 'You know Blossom died at the Women's Retreat?'

I shake my head. 'I didn't realise it would be so sudden. Is that why you came back?'

'Partly. She told me about the aneurism. Didn't say much. Then she

22

was gone.'

I gaze ahead. 'I'm glad she didn't die in the Flower House.'

The road darkens as soon as we leave the industrial area. The car hugs the single white centre line. Walshy is steady on the speed at first, but then accelerates up to the limit, which feels fast after city driving.

'In Victoria, the road lines are yellow.'

Walshy's arms are straight, hands gripping the steering wheel, a slight frown on his face.

'Talk to me.'

He clears his throat. 'What do you want to know?'

'Are you dating? Is your old man still buggering up the farm? Are you working at the pub waiting for a miracle, like him dying?'

He snorts, shakes his head. 'You know me. How about you?'

'You're deflecting.'

Looking ahead, he smiles.

'Are you angry with me?'

His smile fades. 'No. I love you. You know that.'

I twist my face and look out the window.

'Sorry.' He sighs. 'Tell me about Melbourne.'

After a pause, I tell him about all the houses I've house-sat, the cafe I worked in, the course I was doing at TAFE. The dogs and cats that came with the houses, how I missed them each time I moved. Safe, predictable waves of words.

Walshy picks my hand up off the seat between us and kisses the back. 'I'm glad you're here.'

My heart jumps, but then pauses—an uncomfortable sensation like it might not start up again.

I take my hand back. 'Someone on the plane said York was on the news. Serial rapist.'

'Yeah. They found another doll.' Walshy frowns again. 'Makes everything feel different. Like that first time.'

A shiver slides over my skin.

'Lisa still around?'

'Yeah. In Northam.'

'She'd be what, twenty?'

'Same age as you.' We share a look, and my heart thing happens again.

After an hour, we arrive, and Walshy pulls into the space beside the Flower House. It hunkers inside its wild gardens like a wombat in a ditch. The tallest sprouts and flowers are black bouquets against the sky, the undergrowth lost in the dark, solid shadows of mystery until sunrise.

We get out, the familiar *scritch* of shoes on gravel as Walshy walks around the back of the ute and grabs my bag. He holds out his hand and leads me around the back of the house, beneath the wisteria-covered pergola, a honey-scented cave leading all the way to the kitchen. It envelops me like a warm sheet.

'Welcome home.' Walshy opens the old screen door, and, after a moment, I enter. He holds out his hand and then draws me down the hallway into my old room. He drops my bag on the floor beside the bed. A pile of his clothes sprawls in the corner of the room. His rolled-up swag leans against the wall.

'You moved in?'

'I just keep my clothes in here.'

It smells fresh, like he's changed the linen. I want to ask questions, but everything is fragile and uncertain.

Walshy wraps me in himself. We kiss and kiss and kiss. It's more and better than I could have imagined or hoped. His hand goes up the front of my cami, and he moans a little. I kiss his moving neck, his shoulder, whatever I can reach. My blood flows, melting like it has been frozen in my veins for two years. I surrender everything, relaxing, my whole body letting go.

Walshy chuckles when he sees my Donald Duck knickers.

'Very cute.'

'You can get anything in Melbourne.'

Walshy lowers me back, and his mouth finds where I ache for him. A wave surges through me. I'm molten. I can't think.

There can't be anything but this.

He completes me.

As soon as we finish, he speaks. Still breathing heavily, he mutters, 'I'm dating Shelley Turner.'

Chapter 6

'You're the foster kid at the old backpackers.' He turned around and looked me up and down.

I was nine, and he was twelve. I'd been living with Blossom a few weeks.

We were standing in the free lunch line at York primary school. If you had a special card, you got free lunch. The kids with packed lunches sat on bench seats in the undercover area near the canteen.

I stared right back. One of his eyes had a bruise along the brow ridge. He had a cut on his chin, and dark fuzz lined his upper lip. Muscles threaded his arms beneath the checked shirt he wore instead of the school uniform.

'Who's askin'?'

'Walshy.' He stuck out his hand.

I didn't take it. His eyebrows went up at that, and he put his hands beneath his armpits, offer retracted. 'What's your name?'

'Why have you got a black eye?'

Walshy shrugged. 'I'll call you Jane then, because of your hair. You know? From Tarzan.'

I didn't react. He turned his back, and I studied the stitching on the back pocket of his blue denim jeans.

'Another free luncher.' A scrawny red-haired kid from a group of four on the bench to my left smirked. They all had sandwiches or a lunchbox or a muesli bar in a colourful packet. I knew I was in for my first fight.

'Close ya gob, Michael Slattery, or I'll close it for ya.' Walshy stepped out of the line.

The boys' eyes shifted, their expressions morphing. The redhead's face was on fire. He swallowed, the bump in his long neck bobbing up and down. 'Sorry, Walsh man. Didn't see you there.'

Walshy stared a moment longer, but then he smiled suddenly. 'Have yourself a nice lunch, sandwich boy.' He resumed his position in line.

My whole body flooded warm. Someone had stood up for me. That had literally never happened.

I got my lunch and watched Walshy from beside a tree. Up on the oval, he was playing cricket. The other boys jostled for his attention. Along the wall beside the oval, four girls cupped their mouths to each other's ears and stared in his direction. I walked over.

A blonde one saw me. 'The lower grades eat on the grass area next to the canteen,' she said.

'I'm nine.' I crossed my arms.

They ignored me. 'Hey? So, who's Walshy?'

They turned to look me up and down. 'Why's your dress so long? Makes you look funny.'

I shrugged. 'Who is he? Walshy? You lot treat him like he's somethin' special.'

A skinny girl with mousy hair smiled. 'He's awesome.' Her eyes checked the other girls, like she was afraid she'd said something stupid. A tall blonde girl elbowed her, and I directed my next question at her.

'How come he's got a black eye?'

'Who's askin'?' She looked annoyed that I was still there. As if I cared; I was used to cold welcomes.

'I'm a foster. Live in the Flower House. He stood up for me.' It was more than I usually said to girls like this.

They loosened up, softened. 'That's Walshy. He's tough.'

'But fair,' said the first girl. She looked back and sighed. 'And cute as.' The others agreed with little sighs, no longer talking to me but to each other.

'His dad pushes him around,' said a brunette with tightly crossed arms. She had a direct look and eyebrows that would scare a younger kid. 'His mum left when he was three.'

'We're gonna be his first girlfriends.' The girls giggled and resumed cupping their mouths against each other's ears

'What—all at once?' But they'd forgotten me.

Each day, I kept up my vigil, watching Walshy.

He did weird stuff for a tough kid. He adjudicated fights between other kids, although he rarely had to use his fists. He dropped into Mrs. Burt's house, the old lady that lived next to the school, on his way home. He always had bruises.

Chapter 7

I wake to the sound of screeching. A flock of excited New Holland honeyeaters flashes past the window.

The room's almost empty. Walshy's swag and most of his clothes are gone. After he'd told me about Shelley, my mind went blank. I bundled my thoughts into a corner and told him to stop talking. That we'd talk about it in the morning. Walshy had curled around me and I made myself forget what he'd said, so I could sleep. I should've known he'd run.

I groan and flop back on the bed, one hand over my eyes.

Through the window, the chirps come loud and shrill, and my chest lifts.

My bum is stuck to the sheet, and I'm immediately pissed off. He didn't even ask if I was still taking the contraceptive pill. I clean myself with the top sheet, get up, and dress.

I pad back through the house and out the side door at the edge of the kitchen, onto the front veranda. The sun is already warm, the air humming with flying insects. It feels airy and relaxed, like nothing bad could happen here. There must have been rain because the garden looks good: the roses flowering, waxes covered in pink-purple flowers, grevilleas and banksias stretching scruffily in all directions. I reach out and pull a cherry-coloured rose petal off, stroking the velvet side with my thumb. The air smells fresh, the sky is open and blue with no traffic noise.

A slight breeze stirs the papery grey wings left from flying ants into a cluster by the wall. Walshy's outdoor bed is still there with a grey military blanket and uncovered pillow.

I sit on his bed and lift the pillow to my face. The bed creaks loudly, but it won't collapse. I used to crawl on behind Walshy when he'd come in after dark, sore and exhausted. I'd curl around his back, put my arm over him, let him know he wasn't alone.

'Hey, Lola!'

My heart sinks. *Perry. Awake not two minutes and he turns up.*

Perry has lived in the house across the road ever since I first arrived in York.

I straighten my legs and push my skirt down over my knees, exhaling with control. 'Hi, Perry.' I give the right amount of smile.

He's wearing bone-coloured shorts, lace-ups and a white tennis shirt. His blond hair shines pale gold until he enters the shade. He stops in front of me, hands on hips, and looks me over. 'When did you get in?'

'Last night. How are you?' I wonder if I smell of sex.

He shrugs. 'Same. I guess.' He jerks his head to the side. 'I know Walshy's gone. Saw him drive off with the swag in the back of his ute at about five. He's hopeless with this stuff.'

'What stuff?'

'The funeral. And you coming back.' He grabs one of the poles that holds up the roof and swings himself up onto the veranda. 'Hear about the doll rapist?'

'Yeah. Horrible.' A weird shiver runs over me.

The veranda vibrates as he strides across and opens the screen door into the kitchen. The burner cracks, and I hear the hollow metal sound of the kettle being filled. Perry makes me feel invaded, but I summon some patience. It is nice here. If Walshy would hang around long enough for us to sort some stuff out, I could stretch my stay another week. Blossom's will and the house need sorting.

'Had coffee?' Perry calls.

'No.'

'He's smart. The rapist. Never leaves evidence.'

'Evil people shouldn't be called smart.'

'What if he's not evil?'

'Why are you standing up for him?'

'Not!'

29

'Ugh.' I look around. The road and paths are empty. Tall eucalypts stretch into the powder blue. A grey fantail lands on the veranda lace, its fanned feathertail swinging back and forth.

When we first met, Perry was wearing orange terry towelling shorts. His mother had dragged him across the road and, smiling hard, introduced us. 'This is Perry. He's your age and adopted too.'

'I'm not adopted. I'm a foster,' I said.

At ten, he was skinny, had hair cut chunky like wheat stalks, and stared at me. In state care, you'd get smacked in the mouth for staring like that. I poked out my tongue because I didn't want to hit him and get returned to care. Nothing bad had happened in the Flower House, and I wanted to stay. I probably should have smacked him, though, because then he kept turning up.

He watched Blossom and me every time we worked in the garden, spying on us. We didn't talk, we just worked. Sometimes, she turned on a mini transistor radio that sat on the edge of the veranda. She always turned it up if a Beatles song came on.

There was so much to do in the garden, which had been left to go wild. Perry had asked Blossom if she'd just moved in. I shushed him, but she said yes. She didn't say anything else. Perry became interested in the intricacies of the plant growth, fertilisation and propagation. He took cuttings and disappeared into his greenhouse at the back of their property.

Then, one day, he did this awful thing. A tiny grey and tan silvereye crashed into a window and twitched on the veranda, stunned. We didn't have curtains, and birds often mistook the window for the reflected sky. Normally, they shook themselves off and flew away, but before it could, Perry climbed up and grabbed it.

'Just leave it. It'll fly off.'

'But I don't want it to.'

I looked at Blossom, who kept on gardening.

'Perry. Leave it alone!' He ran. I chased him but he disappeared into his back garden with it. I hated him so much. Probably had it stuffed so he could stare at it.

When he came over next, I went straight up and shoved his chest. 'Stop coming over here, bird-killer!'

He huffed over to Blossom. 'Blossom can I still come over, please?

Please?'

She straightened slowly, pulling her head away like he might bite, her hands resting on the shovel handle. She looked over to where I was fuming, my arms crossed hard to stop myself whacking him. The corner of her mouth twitched. 'Lola doesn't like boys,' she said.

'One day a week? Just one?'

Blossom shrugged and started shovelling bulbs again, big bunches that needed breaking up and replanting.

'Thank you! Thank you!' He jumped around like a stupid pogo stick.

From then on, he came for a whole day once a week. I ignored him. As the years passed, Perry liked matching his clothes and wearing a jumper around his neck with the sleeves tied, like the male models in junk mail catalogues.

'Here you go, white and one.' Perry hands me a cup. With a disgusted grimace at Walshy's bed, he sits on the edge of the veranda instead, legs hanging down.

I blow the top of the coffee. Perry never adds enough milk.

He takes a big sip of his murky coffee and glances back over his shoulder at me.

'Nice of you to finally turn up, by the way. Didn't you get my messages?'

'I got a new number. I only came back for the funeral.'

I stare at a bee on a yellow rose. It's joined by two others, which burrow in, nuzzling its centre.

'What have you been doing for the past two years?'

'I'm almost through a hospitality certificate. One paper to go.'

He glances at me in his weird, offended way, and then shrugs and picks a paint chip off the veranda post with his nail. 'Well, not much is different here. New shop down on main street. Basketball courts got done up. Few extra lights. That's about it.'

We retreat to our own mental places for a few moments.

'Bet you answered Walshy's messages.'

'Didn't get any.'

He tilts his head like he doesn't believe me. 'Hmm? Interesting. Thought at first you'd run away together, but then he'd grace us with his bushy faced presence every few months, and I was told you were living it up in Melbourne.'

I scoff at that.

'Anyway. You look great.' He smiles wide. He has nice teeth—I'll give him that.

I make a non-committal sound.

'What are you thinking?'

'I hate when you ask that.'

'Well?'

'All right. Walshy. How long has he been with Shelley? Didn't he just get back?' I can't stop the tight feeling around my heart.

'Buhp-baaah.' Perry makes his annoying, wrong answer horn sound and rolls his eyes.

The sound gives me the sensation of stomping on a huge thorn, a piercing of flesh. 'Fine. Tell me who you're dating then?'

Perry flutters his eyelashes. 'No one. But I did have a couple of offers.'

I try to sound interested. 'That's good.'

I wait. He finishes his coffee and puts the cup down beside him.

'Fine then, Oh Predictable One. Walshy has been with Shelley Turner—prima ballerina—ever since he got back. Joined at the hip.'

My stomach drops. 'What do you mean? He's never that serious about girls.' I try to stay calm, waiting for Perry to agree with me.

Perry bugs his eyes, and then grins. 'It's like *Lady and the Tramp*.'

'Walshy's not a tramp!' I fight to speak over the horrible lump in my throat, my jugular pulsing. Why didn't Walshy tell me before he slept with me? Would it have stopped us?

He always had a girlfriend when we were younger, but now he's twenty-three. It's not the same as primary school when girlfriends and boyfriends were almost a game. It's definitely not the same if it's Shelley.

'Compared to her he is. Seen her house lately?' He makes an impressed sound. 'Bloody palace out there on the hill. Mr. Daddy Pilot has just bought a new Porsche.' He flapped his hand. 'The Jaguar was *so old*.'

'Shelley's nice.' My throat thickens, deepening my voice, and I have to keep my mouth open to breathe.

Perry notices. He reaches out and touches the back of my hand. I move it away.

'It's a *good* thing, Lola. He can finally stop being the Pope. The whole "no jiggy till the wedding" thing is a joke. A man needs what a man needs if you know what I mean.'

'God Perry! No details please!' I breathe through the urge to cry. *Shit, shit, shit.* 'So, who did you get offers from then?' I turn my face so I can wipe a tear off my cheek.

Perry clears his throat and squints like he does when he's thinking. 'Hmm? My secret. What about you?'

I just want you to fuck off. 'You came over here to gloat about Walshy and Shelley, didn't you?'

He gives me a smart-arse look. 'You're pissed Walshy did something other than dote on you the last two years? Friends are happy for each other. You *are* friends?'

'Stop being a smart-arse, Perry, or I'll put a bag over your head. I'm happy for them, all right? By the way, you still make shit coffee.'

He scoffs. 'You're still the rudest person I know.'

'Good.'

'You and Walshy almost deserve each other.'

Chapter 8

When I was twelve, the headmaster punished me with humiliating 'scab duty'—picking up rubbish from the school grounds in plain sight of the other students.

I had been at high school for three weeks, but I was still wearing the primary school uniform because I didn't have a high school one. That was not the reason I got punished.

The netballers, dancing The Nutbush badly, had dared me to flash my bum at a group of boys to earn the chance to join in. Not baulking at a challenge, I did as they dared. I'd forgotten we were right next to the headmaster's office. He saw everything and shouted my punishment through the window.

'Scab duty. Athletics Carnival. All day tomorrow!'

I went into shock. I'd had my share of hits, shoves, scraps and punishments, but never something so public. From that moment, I couldn't sleep or eat. That night, I counted my few coins and checked a road map for escape routes and good places to camp—for the rest of my life.

I really put some research into it, but the Flower House had grown on me. Blossom never asked anything of me. She went away to her women's retreat from Friday to Monday. She left me what cash she had, gave me the department allowance, and let me do the shopping. I was happy and free.

I turned up at the headmaster's office before school. The headmaster was the biggest man I'd ever seen. With his black suit on, he reminded me of a gladiator. My courage was balled up so small inside me I could

34

have pooped it out like a currant.

'Oh, Lola. Yes.' He nodded like he knew me well. 'You're to pick up every scrap of rubbish throughout the carnival. I hope it inspires you to act with decency in the future.'

Words crammed in my throat, an appeal to get it done before or after school, but his face was set.

I lifted my scrawny chest and saluted. 'Sure, sir. I'll start right away.'

As I walked around, collecting rubbish, I tried not to look at people, but I could still hear them.

'She's still wearing the primary uniform.'

'Tiny enough.'

'Looks anorexic.'

'Scab! Scab!'

'Shut up, dickheads.' I knew that voice. The noise level dropped.

Walshy stood right in the middle of the crowd. Students were wearing their faction colours: red, green, yellow or blue, but Walshy wore his own uniform. At fifteen, he still got away with his version: blue jeans and a checked flannel shirt rolled at the elbows.

I had seen him earlier in the playground, his neck under the possessive arm of a pretty girl with blue ribbons in her hair.

Walshy didn't look away, smirk, or whisper. He held my gaze and gave a nod. A message from one survivor to another. It stirred the strength I'd built over years of state care.

To the hecklers, I lifted my fist and showed my middle finger. Sniggers.

I curtsied to red faction. 'Thank you, idiots. If you don't mind, I have a very important job to do.'

I made the punishment a task to excel at; completely absorbed, I was constantly moving, my focus on getting every scrap of litter off the ground. I zigzagged back and forth as runners whizzed by and high jumpers leapt, and long jumpers flew and skidded.

As the day heated to 29°C, I rarely stopped. The streaming sweat was my armour, proof of my dedication. Spotless grass was my victory. I drank little, ate nothing, and soon began to feel like the top of my head was lifting off. Still, I scanned the grass, bending, grabbing, making a run for the bins, like the task was an Olympic sport and I was earning a gold medal.

Near the end of lunchtime, a teacher excused me from my job precisely as the beating sun overwhelmed me. Suddenly, I was on the ground, staring upwards.

'Oh dear!' said the teacher. 'Are you all right?' Her saucer-shaped eyes stared through thick lenses.

My head pounding, I realised I must have fainted. Before a scene started, I sat up, waited for the spots of light in front of my eyes to stop dancing, and then got to my feet. 'Tripped,' I lied. 'I'm going now. Thanks.'

Unsteadily, I walked off towards the library, where there was a quiet girls' toilets. Checking I was alone, I leaned on the basin. My cheeks were flushed, and my neck and hair wet with sweat.

I splashed my face to cool the heat squeezing my brain. I gulped water, feeling my stomach stretch. Then I entered a cubicle, put down the ceramic lid, sat down and leaned against the wall. It was cool, private and quiet.

The door creaked open.

'You all right, Lola?' A girl's voice.

'Who's that?' I closed one eye and squinted through the gap between the door and the wall.

'Gerri. Walshy's girl. He arksed me ta check on ya.' Her chewing gum snapped.

The pretty brunette girl I'd seen with Walshy earlier stood in front of the mirror, playing with her ponytail and chewing gum with her mouth open. The buttons on the neck of her blue faction shirt were undone, revealing a hint of a black-lace bra. Her tight skirt ended high on taut thighs.

'I'm fine.' A terrible soft surge went through me. My stomach clenched.

'Righto.' The girl opened the door and was gone. It bumped closed behind her.

I turned, lifted the toilet lid and vomited. After a few minutes, I came out of the cubicle and stood before the mirror.

My eyes were bloodshot, so I washed my face and rinsed my mouth. I tugged my zip down as far as Gerri's, until I could see ribs jutting from my sternum, each bone joined with a little bump and a dip.

I zipped back up and wound my finger in my hair, stretching out my chest to look taller. My finger got tangled in my hair. I retrieved it, sighed, rubbed my eyes.

My dress, past my knees and baggy, had been designed to fit better as I grew. But I hadn't grown.

I went and sat in the library, pretending to read as the words swam before my eyes. My stomach burned. It hadn't eaten a proper meal in two days.

* * *

After school, I was late leaving, and it was quiet.

'Jane?'

I looked over. 'That's not actually my name.'

'Suits you, though.'

Walshy stood with his back against a brick wall, like a drug dealer. He was lean, muscular, with the tiny bum and bowed legs of a cowboy.

I wished I had chewing gum and hair I could twiddle. He idled towards me, something bunched up in his hand.

'I got you a uniform from the second-hand.' He let it drop out, so I could see it was a school dress, a white and blue thing with pleats.

I checked his eyes for mirth, but he was staring straight at me. I tried to tuck my hair behind my ears but there was too much of it.

'I didn't shit myself.'

He smirked. 'I know.'

After a moment's hesitation, I took the dress. 'Thanks.'

'Didn't think you were old enough for high school. Bloody bastard, picking on a little girl.'

'I'm not a little girl. Why are you still here?'

He shrugged. 'Stuff to do.'

My stomach ached. 'I'm going home.' I shoved the dress into my bag and began trudging towards the school gate when my legs buckled. On hands and knees, I drew my feet underneath me and wobbled, stars going off like fireworks in front of my eyes. Blood dribbled from one of my knees.

'Hey, I gotcha.' Walshy was suddenly there, hoisting me into his arms like a child. Surprisingly, I wasn't angry. I just lay there.

'Geez, you're light.' He glanced around, as if he was seeing whether there was somewhere to put me. 'Do you think you can sit on my handlebars?'

I focused on his face. He'd shaved his cheeks and top lip. He smelled like shaving cream, like the older boys at the home. Thick lashes swept his green eyes, and his lips sat out in a semi-pout.

My head throbbed with heatstroke. 'Yeah.'

He carried me to his bike parked just outside the school fence, his full backpack dangling from the handlebars. The bag was stretched taught with bottles and cans. He must have picked them out of the bins.

He set me down on the curb and went to get his bike. I wiped the trickle of blood off my leg with a gum leaf before dropping it into the gutter with the ants and gum blossoms.

'C'mon.' Walshy steadied the bike between his legs as I climbed on. Balanced there, legs akimbo above the front wheel, I gripped the bars. We began to move. Walshy's fringe flapped by my right shoulder. It was like it wasn't real. Me this close to the school's tough guy.

'Fall backward if you're gonna fall,' he said. I imagined tumbling back against his chest, and all my hunger and pain vanished for a few seconds. What would it feel like to rest my cheek on his shoulder?

We headed straight down the road instead of turning at the Flower House, his bag clinking all the way.

'Where are we going?'

'Bakery. You look hungry.'

'Oh yeah?' My socks concertinaed around my skinny ankles. I remembered my bumpy ribs and scowled.

'Saw you eating the other kids' leftovers at recess. Done it myself once.'

Shame surged through me. 'Shouldn't have watched me.'

'You watch me.' His wavy hair flickered out of the corner of my right eye. I could hear him breathing.

'Do you like donuts?' he said.

I started laughing, and it got louder and louder. My head rolled back and all I could see was sky.

'Hang on! Jeez, your hair is in my face.' Walshy chuckled sort of warily, like I was nuts. But it didn't matter. Nothing mattered. Walshy had seen me scavenge food. Walshy had got me a uniform. Walshy had no reason to help me. Yet here we were, pedalling to the bakery for donuts.

The bakery windows were heaven. Rows of glistening, flaky, buttery, iced, crispy delights. I stood outside swallowing my saliva while Walshy entered the deli next door. I heard him talking to the owner, cashing in the recyclables. Five cents for a can, ten for a bottle. The shop owner handed him a paper bag and patted him on the shoulder. Walshy came out staring into his hand, sorting coins with his thumb.

'What's that?' I indicated the paper bag, as he slid it into his empty backpack.

'Mrs. Burt. The old lady near the school.'

Walshy handed me the backpack. 'Wait here a minute.' He opened the bakery door and the bell jangled.

When he came back out, he handed me a paper bag with a jam donut inside. We ate right there on the path, sugar all around our mouths, grinning at each other as we chewed. A lady walking along the footpath with a little boy grabbed her kid's arm and yanked him away when he walked too close.

Afterwards, Walshy dinked me to the Flower House, and we both got off and walked around to the back patio. We flung our bags down.

'I have to cut your hair.' A bead of sweat trickled down the side of his face. He flicked his head, and his fringe flew back and then slowly slipped forwards.

'Fuck off.' I turned away, so he couldn't see my crimson face.

'Do you want friends or not? Looks like a fucken bird's nest. Trust me.'

I stared at him. He didn't blink. 'Trust you?'

He nodded. 'You've been here ages, and you still don't have friends. You swear a bit, but there's no real reason.'

'You're a fuckin' expert?' I laughed.

Walshy's eyes flickered. 'I know you're here on your own.'

'How? You gonna dob me in?'

'To who? I ride around on my bike. I see stuff.'

'Department—there's rules for foster kids.'

'You're all right, aren't ya?'

'I can look after myself.' I scuffed the ground with my foot.

Walshy pushed his hand through his hair. 'I reckon if you stop acting so angry, and tidy up a bit, you'll be fine.'

'Why do you care what I do?'

'We could be mates.'

We stared at each other. After a while all I could see was his eyes, not his face.

'You've got plenty of mates,' I said warily.

Walshy smiled wryly, shook his head like I wasn't getting it.

'You have! Girlfriends too.'

'They just think the bruises are cool.'

Walshy's girlfriends did gloat about how tough he was. Warned everyone not to mess with them or Walshy would pay them back. Even the boys, scared or admiring, vied for his approval. They didn't treat him like they treated each other. Was it possible Walshy didn't have any real friends? Friends he didn't have to act tough around. Friends that knew he scabbed out of bins for the refund.

'I just need a better brush,' I said, looking out between my shaggy curtains of hair.

'You need a haircut.'

He was right.

'I'll get some scissors.' I went and got a towel and Blossom's flower scissors and sat on a chair in the garden. 'I'm letting you because of the donut. Don't stuff it up.' I wiped a smear of jam from the inside of the paper bag.

Walshy sucked a side tooth and regarded me. 'Jane. This is my first, okay?'

Sucking the last of the jam off my finger, I considered him for a moment, appreciating his honesty. 'Coral said curly hair is very forgiving.'

'Who's that?'

'Hairdresser.' I liked the way he didn't put any guard up between us. Maybe I'd tell him about it one day.

Walshy did his best, but it was pretty rough. After he had ridden off, I ripped a piece of the paper bag with the bakery name on it and took it into my bedroom. I removed a matchbox from a hole in the wall, hidden by a picture, and slid the tiny inner box out. Coral's creamy pearls nestled near Heartbreak's last match, with its blackened end. I added the folded bakery paper, closed the matchbox, and stowed it back inside the hole in the wall.

* * *

The day after Walshy cut my hair, I wore the proper uniform to school, and I got a friend. Not just any friend—Shelley Turner. Gorgeous, bright, talented Shelley Turner. Two days later, I also had a boyfriend.

Walshy came over every day after school. He taught me how to steal. Nothing big or valuable. Eggs and vegetables from people's henhouses and gardens, never too much, never the same place two consecutive nights, and never from a house with a dog.

He showed me his secret fishing and yabbying spots at the river. We would fish and then start a small fire to cook our catch, eating it hot, burning our tongues.

Before I started working at the inn, I had a paper round for a while, and Walshy and I collected recyclables. On the weekend, we stayed behind after footy games, searching beneath the audience stands for coins. If we found enough, we'd buy meat pies and soft drinks and have burping contests.

We cleared the garden out the back and planted vegetable seeds. Walshy repaired the coop, and we got two chickens to replace the ones taken by a fox.

'Come to Broome with me,' he said one day. 'We'll save up and stay in a hotel with palm trees outside.' I listened to his stories and his dreams as we worked together, and knew I never wanted to leave.

Chapter 9

Perry jumps up to his feet and smooths the crinkles in his shorts with both hands, like he's ironing.

'What about you? Broken any more hearts?'

I shake my head. 'Not my modus operandi.'

Perry gives a fake shocked look, hand over heart. 'Moi?'

I smile sarcastically. 'You're too fashionable for me, Pesky.'

'Do not call me that.'

I smirk.

'You just can't see what's right here waiting for you.' Perry starts walking away, voice fading as he rounds the corner of the house. Suddenly, he reappears, head tilted on the side.

Fucking jack-in-the-box. Always trying to catch me out. I put down the hand I was giving a rude signal with.

'I'll come over day after tomorrow, okay? We'll catch up.' He waits.

'Maybe.' I make sure he's gone before I give the one-fingered salute again.

Inside the kitchen, one bread crust is left in an open bread bag. I drop it into the toaster and watch the element turn red.

There's no butter in the fridge. The bench is lively with ants. A honey jar sits at the centre of marching black lines, like sheep tracks heading to water. They dot round the rim and inside of the jar, some moving, some drowned. I put the jar in the sink and eat the toast dry, not because I'm hungry, but because I don't want to faint.

I'm wiping the bench when I hear footsteps clomp along the side of the house.

'Only me!' It's Mary's voice. She yanks open the back door and pulls me into a quick hug. She's wearing the usual inn uniform of black pants and white blouse, and her greying hair is tied in a low ponytail.

'Welcome back, prodigal daughter! Sorry about Blossom, love.'

'Yeah.'

'What's new? Apart from … you know.' She rubs her face with one hand. 'You alright?'

'Yeah. Bit weird being back.'

'Yeah, but it'll grow on you again. Where's Walshy?' She looks around, hands on hips.

I swallow hard. 'Looks like he went camping early this morning.'

Mary examines my face. 'You two all right? He's been okay since he got back from the station. Did him a world of good out there with the cattle and a million hectares to spread out.'

'S'pose it was me turning up.'

'Hmm. Oh crap, he's supposed to work. Wouldn't happen to be available tonight?'

I nod. 'Sure. Yeah, be good to see Freda. She still there?'

Mary grinned. 'Course! Nothing changes, Lola.' Her expression changed. She pulled something out of her back pocket, a white envelope marked 'Lola.'

'Blossom left this with me to give to you. She said there was no will.'

'Really?' I open it by tearing along the top with my finger and pull out a card with a picture of a lady on it. I turn it over. A key is sticky taped to the back.

'What's this to?'

'She didn't say. Told me you'd know where to look.' She shrugs.

I turn the picture back over. It's like a postcard with a blank back. The picture is a painting of a glamorous lady with long, red curly hair, wearing a crimson, off-the-shoulder dress and black heels.

I give Mary a questioning look. 'I have no idea what I'm supposed to do with this.'

'That's Lorrelai,' says Mary, pointing. 'She was jailed for the murder of her lover's wife. Blossom had a real interest in her.'

'Oh. The one whose room you made a tourist attraction. Blossom sent me a clipping about it.'

Mary lifted and dropped both hands. 'Planned to, but it never happened. Whole bunch of stuff got in the way, including Blossom. She begged me not to do it. Said she knew heaps about the case and was sure Lorrelai was innocent and so it was wrong and disrespectful etcetera. Nevermind. I've got a painting of her somewhere at the inn, though, if you want to see it.'

I shrug.

I turn the card over and carefully remove the key before holding it up. 'Looks like a padlock key. Any hints?'

'Sorry, love. No idea.' Mary makes an apologetic face. 'Um, we need to talk about the house too.' Awkwardly, she scratches the back of her neck. 'Blossom said the real estate agent would call once she died.' She watches my expression carefully. 'You probably don't know; it's a rental.'

I feel like the breath has been knocked out of me. 'But we didn't pay rent. I know because Walshy and I paid the bills.'

'She said it was on loan.'

'That doesn't make sense! On loan? What? For ten years?' I glance around. 'It was always ours. I'm sure it was.'

'I'm sorry.'

I get a shaky feeling. *The shabby old Flower House is not ours?* Without it, a huge chunk of my life disappears. The thought sends me spinning off like a dry dandelion seed. The Flower House and garden were my forest, my own private world. Even when I was away, I dreamed about them and woke with a split-second's shock that I wasn't there.

'Okay, okay, hang on.' I hold up one finger, like I can reason with this. 'Someone must have let us stay, right? Maybe because it's so run-down. Surely, I can rent it. Maybe they'd sell it to me. Can't be too expensive.'

I see the idea forming. *But why would I want it? I don't plan on living here, do I?* Yet, suddenly, I'm fond as hell of it, like it's family. Walshy still lives here too.

Mary shrugs. 'I don't know, sorry. Talk to the real estate about it.' She tightens her lips in sympathy. 'If you're staying, I'm sure there's other rentals you could look at.'

'Not like this.' My voice drops. 'This was the one place that felt …

you know … like a home.' I look around me, as if it's something different now. Walls and ceilings, building materials. A shell with a huge garden no one tends anymore. A lump forms in my throat.

'I thought it would always be here.'

Mary squeezes my shoulder. 'You can stay with us if you like, Lola. Better than being alone here.' She gives an uncomfortable shrug and clears her throat. 'Not after what's happened.'

'The rapes.' I shiver. 'Was it someone we know?'

Mary shakes her head. 'Not really. It's a small town, though. Such a shock. I think we all hoped he was gone. Better still—dead. It's shaken us all up.'

'It's been years.'

'Yep. Bloody creep, leaving a doll again! Few people'd like to get hold of him around here, I can tell you.' She shakes her head. 'Sick bastard.'

'You think he's still around?'

'Who knows? Either he comes here to hunt or he's bloody good at hiding among us.'

'I'll lock up. Promise.'

Mary sighs and nods. 'Let's talk about the funeral after work. Sorry. I know it's a lot.' She gives the room a quick glance over. 'You going to stay, or go back to Victoria after the funeral?'

'Ah, I don't know.'

'Righto. I better scoot.' She turns for the door and lets herself through. 'See you in a few hours!'

'Bye.'

I feel the key in my hand. Despite everything, a little thrill runs through me. Blossom has left me something. I turn a whole circle, wondering where to start. It's good to have something to distract me from thinking about a rapist who leaves a doll, or about Walshy being with Shelley.

Chapter 10

My first boyfriend, Gary, was the younger brother of Shelley's boyfriend, Bart Rickley. These associations meant the netballers started talking to me—not deep conversations, just hello when they saw me, and goodbye after class. They let me sit beside them and lent me erasers and the occasional bit of chewy. I had gone from invisible to visible. It felt good.

Walshy told me I had to bring food to school and stop swearing at people. Anyone else, and I'd have told them to fuck off.

He'd begun coming around after school, hanging around before his shift at the Lion Inn. I got into the habit of making bread; got pretty good at it too. Walshy watched, elbows on the bench, chin on his fists.

'Can you bring my lunch too?'

I kneaded the dough, delighted in the warm, thick feel of it. 'Anything else, sir?' I smiled and he smiled back.

'Don't put Vegemite on it. Fucken road tar.' He flicked his fringe, his punctuation for everything.

'Want me to cut that off?' I pointed at his fringe.

He glanced about, like he had no idea what I was talking about. Then he got it. 'Nah. Girlfriend's an apprentice hairdresser.'

'Kylie?'

He shook his head. 'Tanya.'

'Jesus. Another one?'

I saw Walshy every day before school and handed him a homemade sandwich, casting a look around like we were dealing in stolen goods.

He said I was a legend. Something fluttered in me every time, like a drug.

I finally began to put on weight, probably all the bread and Walshy's regular gifts of food. My uniform filled out at the front. I got boobs. Gary got all hot and sweaty about them.

One lunchtime, about three weeks after we became girlfriend and boyfriend, Gary started groping me against a tree at the far side of the oval.

'Jesus! Get off!' I shoved him away.

Walshy appeared out of nowhere and grabbed the back of his shirt. Gary swung his arm. Walshy caught it and punched Gary in the stomach with his other hand.

'You're dropped,' Gary said to me when he could finally breathe.

Walshy grabbed my bag and stalked off, and I followed him. He walked like he was annoyed, but when he turned, he just gave me my bag and said, 'See you later.' He pointed to a female teacher walking towards us. 'I'm about to get a couple days holiday.'

Walshy got a three-day suspension. The very next day, the netballers turned on me.

In the change rooms after sport class, they teased that Gary had got me pregnant. Shelley walked in and pulled me outside by the arm.

'Have you got your period yet?'

'No.'

'Go get a test from the chemist, and tell me tomorrow if it's'—she cupped her mouth and whispered—'positive.'

I closed my fingers around the twenty-dollar note she pressed into my hand. She hung onto my hand for a bit longer, staring right into my eyes. Then she sighed and let go, like a bit of energy had seeped out of her and left her deflated.

'Jesus.' She twisted her pretty bangles around her wrist and sucked her lower lip. It made me feel worse.

I didn't tell Shelley, but I couldn't go to the chemist. Everyone would know.

At home, I paced while I waited for Walshy, the money still sweating in my clenched hand. He arrived on his bike with a torn shirt, a swollen cheek, and a cut above one eyebrow.

'Shit, not again. Come inside.' I walked ahead, put the money on the bench, and set up the first aid things on the kitchen table.

'My good shirt too,' Walshy grumbled.

'Shouldn't the police take him to jail?' My heart beat too hard. I hated seeing him like this, knowing a grown man had fought him, and Walshy hadn't been able to stop it, not like at school.

'I'm almost sixteen,' said Walshy. He made a soft hiss sound as I wiped his eyebrow with a cotton swab. Sweat dampened his forehead and top lip. 'I'm not old enough yet. I just gotta stay out of his way for a bit longer.'

I didn't tell him that knowing what his father did to him stopped me sleeping sometimes. Then I had an idea.

'Hey, Walshy. You know that bedframe on the veranda? Why don't you sleep there if you need to?'

I held another cotton ball to the top of the antiseptic bottle and soaked it, squeezed it out and dabbed the cut. I tried not to show how badly I wanted him to stay.

'Huh?' He hissed and winced. 'Um yeah, okay. Thanks.' He examined his hand. 'I think my finger is broken.' He showed me his left hand.

His ring finger was swollen. 'Yeah, looks like it.' I straddled his leg, my back towards him, his arm trapped beneath mine. 'Stay still. I'm splinting it.' I used a popsicle stick and tape. 'They taught us first aid when I was in care.' I wrapped a soft bandage around the finger first and taped on the splint.

Walshy leaned his forehead between my shoulder blades. 'Thanks, Jane.'

I felt suddenly hot and strange sitting on his leg like that, when before it'd been nothing.

I remembered what I'd been bottling up all afternoon. 'You know Gary?'

'Yeah?'

'He might have made me pregnant.'

'What?' He shoved me to stand up.

When I turned around, his face had a dark look. 'Did you go around to his place? Jazes, Jane!'

Walshy always mispronounced his blasphemy because he was scared of God.

'I didn't! I didn't!' Adrenaline raced down my arms and legs like poison. I shook my hands, as if I could shake it off.

Walshy looked strangled, the artery bulging at the side of his neck. 'Well, where then? When? Fuck!'

I tried not to get choked up. I couldn't look at him. I scuffed a weed with my toe. 'At the tree,' I said in the smallest voice. 'You saw him. Shelley said I should get my period, but I haven't.'

Walshy went quiet. After a moment, he changed his position, one elbow propped on his leg, his splinted finger up like he was making the rude sign. He looked up; his gaze steady.

'Have you ever had a period?'

I shook my head, heat and colour flooding my face. 'I should definitely get it. All the other girls have.' My breath stuttered out. The seriousness of it sat in my chest like a bowling ball.

'Didn't you learn about that stuff before you came here?'

'No! I usually hung round by myself. Or with the little kids.' I didn't want to tell him why. I still wet the bed when I was there. The staff made me sleep in the younger children's section.

Walshy bit his lips together, and the tension eased from his face. 'Sometimes I really like you, Jane.'

When I saw him relax, I did too.

'Come with me.' He got up, all angular and wincing, like an old man. He grabbed my hand and walked stiffly outside to his bike, indicating the handlebars. My hand sweated in his, and I got that tight feeling again.

I jumped up and got my balance, the bars radiating warmth against the backs of my legs. 'Where are we going?'

'The farm. I'm gonna show you something important.' Walshy took a moment to get on, extending his popsicle finger out straight while his other fingers grasped the brake lever.

With Walshy standing on the pedals to see over my shoulder, the bike wobbled, straightened, and then smoothed out on the bitumen.

It was a twenty-minute ride along the road, and it was beautiful. The wind was in my hair and against my skin, and Walshy was right there by my shoulder. Partly cleared sections of forest gave way to fences and sheep and dust-coloured kangaroos that only materialised when they lifted their heads at our passing.

Blue-tongue lizards basked on the bitumen, and ravens dismembered a rabbit carcass, a brown falcon hovering above, waiting. Walshy and I held our breath simultaneously as we passed. The ravens flew over to the verge and then hopped two-legged back to their ragged feast.

At Walshy's gate, I jumped off, rubbing the outside of my thighs. I shaded my eyes and squinted at the house.

'Are we going in?'

'Don't worry. Dad's gone.' Walshy swiped the back of his hand across his top lip and leaned forward from the seat to undo the gate. The sun beat hot on my head and back.

'I wasn't thinkin' about that bastard.'

'Liar.'

I got back up on the handlebars, and we rode right past Walshy's farmhouse. I took a good look as we passed. It wasn't like the house in my nightmares. It was a white, modest old thing with a water tank squatting at the side, an old bathtub, and some stalky rosebushes with white and red flowers. But you can't tell horrors from outside. A white picket fence doesn't mean a happy family and scones on Saturday.

I jumped off the bike in front of a three-sided shed full of rectangular hay bales, and Walshy leaned the bike against the bales.

I followed him towards the closest fence line, running every few steps to keep up, despite his limping. He pointed at the mob of sheep. Most had their heads down, noses to the grass until one lifted its head, then all of them did.

Walshy leaned on the wire fence. 'The ewes are the smaller ones, right? Then there are the rams, the big fellas, with huge ball bags.'

'Fuck, Walshy, I've seen sheep before.'

Walshy exhaled in an impatient way. 'Just shut up, will ya? Watch them.'

I rolled my eyes and leaned into the fence, my arms draped over like Walshy's, although I had to wriggle down to avoid cutting my boobs in half. Not the slightest breeze cut through the sun.

After twenty minutes, swinging on the fence like wet clothes, I was ready to burst.

'We've been here bloody ages,' I whined. 'I'm thirsty. And hungry.

Got any food?'

He shook his head. I turned my back on the sheep, closed my eyes and dropped my head back so the sun burned my face. 'Walshy, why do you change girlfriends so much?'

'Huh? I dunno. You watching?'

'Hmm.' I turned back and noted the way Walshy had his ankles crossed, the jut of his shoulder blade beneath his T-shirt, the skin between his hair and collar at the back of his neck. I pushed my hands into his back pockets and leaned my cheek against his back.

'What are you doing?' He moved a bit, so I took my hands from his pockets and wrapped them round his waist.

'Don't.' He undid my hands.

'Why? You do it with all the other girls.'

'You're not all the other girls.'

Grumbling, I came to stand beside him, my arms crossed. 'Why? Why can't I be?'

'You're Jane. Hey, look!'

A few sheep began moving in a circle. One mounted another. Washy jolted upright and said really quickly, 'There! See? The ram is mounting up. Next, he'll mate her.'

I didn't want to look at Walshy. I could hear my guts rumbling. Walshy knew way more than me, I knew that. But I didn't want him telling me about that sex stuff because I wanted him to marry me one day, and for that to happen, he had to stop seeing me as a kid.

'Near the ewe's bum, the ram is putting his, you know, cock ... ah, *penis* inside, and squirting seed into her. The seed swims up to her womb and a lamb will start to grow if the ewe's egg is there.'

My belly shrank right up like a deflated balloon. I squinted, chewing an oat seed my tongue had found in a back tooth.

'So, do you get it?' Walshy persisted. 'You can't get pregnant unless a boy —'

'Fuck off! I'm not a goddamn sheep.' I marched back to the bike and leaned on the shed, my face turned away, tears secretly dribbling down. I wiped surreptitiously and waited, arms crossed, my heart bumping behind my ribs.

We didn't speak of it again. He was right. Gary hadn't done that to me, so I wasn't pregnant. I spent Shelley's money a few months later on a chocolate cake for Walshy's sixteenth birthday. And when I turned thirteen, I got my period.

On someone's front porch, Walshy found a rocking seat with a cushion long enough to be a mattress. We put it on the old metal bed frame on Blossom's veranda, which faced the garden and the neighbour's fence, making it private.

I couldn't believe Walshy was the sleeping man who stretched out on our veranda. The first night, I crept to the screen door between kitchen and veranda and watched him until my legs itched. He stayed a night here and there at first. After a while, he never left. It was a good place to chat late into the night, an audience with the garden by moonlight.

At sixteen, Walshy constantly had a new girlfriend. He brought food home for me when he was invited for dinner at their houses. We'd sit outside on his bed, staring at the stars while he relayed their family rituals. I wasn't bothered too much about his girlfriends, until one day, at around fourteen, I couldn't stand it. It made me feel tight and short-tempered. I snapped at him when what I really wanted to do was feel his arms around me.

I prayed he wasn't putting his cock-a-penis into them. That made me feel truly sick.

Chapter 11

In Blossom's room, the bed is stripped. Her favourite knitted rug is folded on the end of the mattress. I imagine the church ladies had a hand in that. They have a knack of turning up when help is needed, as if God whistles them in like sheepdogs.

The window is closed, the curtain drawn. I open both. The bare mattress has a yellowish circular stain. Hard to tell if it is new or not. My stomach churns, although I try not to feel anything about any of it.

Inside the wardrobe, a handful of old clothes hangs on the rail. Underneath is an assortment of ugly shoes. I'm surprised to see a pair of Jesus sandals and a high-heeled shoe. Blossom only ever wore sandshoes or work boots.

I stick my hand in all the pockets of the jackets and tops, check the overhead shelf. Nothing but a couple of old bus tickets and books on gardening. Relieved, I leave the room.

There's nothing to unlock in my room, but I strip the bed and take the sheets out to the laundry. I shove them into the washing machine, add washing powder and switch it on. On the floor beside the machine, there's a dank-smelling pile of Walshy's clothes.

My search through the house is short. There is nothing lockable and very little furniture. When I began house-sitting, the rooms felt cluttered with books, pictures, statues of things because I wasn't used to it.

In the kitchen, I heap instant coffee into a cup, emptying the last of a packet of powdered milk and then adding hot water. Outside, a splendid fairywren and his grey-green female partner hop from bush to bush. The metal spoon clinks inside the porcelain. Both birds take flight, and I'm staring at a twanging empty branch.

I notice that the main garden is taller, wilder than when I left. The square vegetable garden Walshy and I once created hosts only dead tomatoes, an onion gone to seed, and a lone papery bloom rocking in the breeze.

The garden shed has a concrete floor and hooks on a board three feet up, with tools hanging from them. A wheelbarrow is parked in the middle, and my old bike is leaned up against the wall. Everything has a light coating of spiderwebs.

The unoccupied chicken coop looks sad and empty.

I stand in the middle of the garden, which hems me with its friendly community of leaves, insects, birds and flowers.

This key thing seems weird for Blossom. She was never cryptic or into games. I try to determine her thought process. She knew she was going to die. She didn't even have enough stuff to bother leaving a will, but there was something she wanted me to have. She leaves me a key to open it. It must be of some value.

My heart lifts. A small possibility, but maybe she secretly tucked away some money so I can buy the Flower House.

Something flaps at the edge of my consciousness, and I head for the laundry. It's separate from the house, with a wisteria-covered pergola between the two. Wisteria and pink Bougainvillea flowers ramble across the laundry roof. Pollen-drunk bees fall off to stagger across the painted concrete beneath. I watch so I don't step on one.

About eight years ago, a new fence was built along the back of the property because the old one fell down. Trouble was that the council checked the property boundary and discovered our back fence was supposed to be closer in. The new fence had to be built slam up against the laundry, making it impossible to open the door more than two inches.

Blossom made me help her put an old bookcase in front of the door to store laundry and garden paraphernalia. 'Pity about the door,' she said. 'Good hiding place, though.' For her, it was an odd thing to say.

From the bookcase, I remove the washing powder, snail pellets, sard soap, gloves, and empty glass jars, placing them along the opposite wall.

I walk the bookcase out towards me, corner to corner, until there's room to get behind it. I slide the key into the lock that secures the old door, and the metal arch springs up. My pulse quickens. Removing the padlock, I then shove the door open a couple of inches. My eye to the opening, I spy a mattress of dead leaves jammed in the three-inch gap between wall and fence. That's all, just rotting leaves.

Outside, footsteps come from near the house. I hurry from the laundry.

'Hey.' Perry appears beneath the wisteria arch. 'What are you doing?' His eyes make their customary travel down my body and back up.

'Just some laundry.' I brush dust off my butt, battling disappointment that he's not Walshy.

'What do you want to do? We can go to a café.'

'Ah, I'm looking for something. Blossom left me a key.'

'I'll help. Just like old times.' He shows his teeth.

'No, it's okay. I have some stuff to do before I go to work.' I return to the laundry and put the sheets into the washing basket. Perry follows me over to the clothesline. I peg up a sheet. Perry tries to help. I wave him away.

'Aw c'mon Lola. I've waited two years. Least you can do is have a coffee with me.' He gives me his customary hurt look and then studies my hair and reaches his hand out. I duck.

'Don't.'

Perry used to like touching my hair. He wanted to pet it, but it felt creepy, like a lizard on my head. I got fast at slapping his arm away. Perry used to huff and pout.

'Meanie. You can touch mine.'

One day I got fed up with it. 'Why would I touch your damn hair? Weirdo!'

'Don't call me that!'

'Stop *touching* me then. It's creepy!'

'But it feels nice.' He went quiet and hugged himself around the ribs, sniffing and looking everywhere but at me, but then he smiled. 'If you fight me, it means you like me.' He cupped his mouth and whispered, 'I like you too!'

If his mother hadn't interrupted right then, I would have used my vast vocabulary on him.

* * *

'Surely, you've got half an hour. Let's go to the café.'

'Sorry, Perry. It sounds too much like a date.'

Perry's jaw twitches. 'Wouldn't want that, would we?'

'Perry,' I say in a tired voice. I reach deep inside for patience. I remember that, if I stay, he'll be my neighbour again. 'Thanks, but I'm not in the mood.'

He glowers at me, shakes his head and walks off. 'Fine, I'm going.' He strides back over the road to his house, back stiff. The gate slams behind him.

Something drops on the ground by my foot. My Donald Duck knickers. Relieved they waited for Perry's departure before they put in an appearance, I peg them up and return the basket to the laundry.

Rather than risk Perry returning when I resume my search, I take a quick, cold shower.

Beneath the stream of cool water, my thoughts return to Shelley.

* * *

How my belly had fluttered when I'd walked into the drama room that first time for a dance concert rehearsal. It was cool and dark, and I was just able to make out Shelley in the middle row of seats, sitting by herself.

'Lola!' She stood up and scooped the air to draw me over.

My face coloured with pride. Not only was Shelley Turner the prettiest, richest girl in the school, she was talented and nice. A ballet dancer, she competed regionally and had won a couple of titles. It was weird that she wasn't the queen of a big group, like the netballers. Everyone said hello and stopped and stared when Shelley approached, but she sat alone unless she had a boyfriend, or she went to the drama room or library. Everyone knew she had sex with her boyfriends. It gave her an edge that made all the boys turn and watch when she walked by. I thought she looked lonely. Like a tragic princess. *Was it possible to be too beautiful?*

I found out she liked Walshy, like all the other girls, but they never went out. They were too equal in a way; able to pick and choose anyone but each other.

'You made it!' She had checked my hair and re-secured the clip she'd given me a few weeks earlier, following the Walshy haircut. A soft, floral fragrance emanated from her.

'I dumped Bart after Gary broke up with you.' She gave me a quick hug.

Who dumped who was important, I'd discovered. The one who did it first was the winner.

A handful of other students, all girls, talked in low voices while they waited for the dance teacher, Ralph Higgins. He was a ballet dancer who'd won some sort of national dance award and was coming to help us with our Christmas concert this year. The headmaster said it was going to be *phenomenal*.

When Mr Higgins finally walked in, Shelley sat upright, uncrossed her legs, and stared. The talking stopped.

Mr Higgins didn't look like a teacher. He was dad age, with longish dark hair, a narrow face and a curved Roman nose. His skin was a deep gold, his body all bounce and muscle. He wore black stretch leggings and a loose shirt, open a long way down, so you could see his ribs and chest, which looked weird and girly.

I wanted to laugh, but Shelley went bright pink and was hardly breathing, so I didn't.

Mr Higgins stopped in the middle of the room, his heels together, toes out, arms loose at his sides. His quick, dark eyes scanned us all like he was disappointed. Then he saw Shelley. He stared at her for a few seconds. 'You must be Shelley Turner?'

Shelley nodded hard, her face going even pinker. She got prettier when she blushed.

'Excellent. I've seen you compete.'

Everyone stared at Mr Higgins like he was God. I didn't get it. To me, he was just a funny-looking man in leggings.

He stopped staring at Shelley, and she started to breathe again.

'Hello, everyone. Call me Ralph.' His voice had a superior drawl.

Ralph instructed everyone to introduce themselves, and then he stood up the front, facing away. Each arm curved in a C shape, like he had no elbows, and he began dancing. The introductions faded as everyone stopped to watch. Ralph leaped this way and that, his taut buttocks moving like conjoined oranges inside his stretchy pants.

We all clapped.

Ralph bowed at the applause. His legs were even lumpier than before he'd started dancing. They looked like the pictures from the anatomy book in the library.

'That is the routine for our dance chorus,' he said, his chest going up and down. 'Nice simple steps repeated. With pretty costumes, it will come alive.' He swept both arms up, like he was praising us. 'You are the ones that will warm up the crowd before our real stars take centre stage with the school band.' He flashed a glance at Shelley. She sat very straight with her chest lifted. 'Be here for rehearsal at lunchtime. We've got six weeks.'

We talked about costumes and routines, and Ralph taught us some basic steps before he clapped us back to the stands so he could show off again until the bell rang.

On concert night, Ralph was Shelley's partner, gliding around her, catching her leg and twirling her body like she was a beautiful mannequin in a pink gauzy skirt. I was spellbound by Shelley's skirt flowing and cascading over Ralph's head as he held her up with one hand. We weren't jealous, but proud, hoping our stars would dazzle. I'd done my job in an itchy pastel blue dress in the chorus with nine other girls.

When I got home after the show, I realised I'd forgotten the dance shoes Shelley had given me. Holidays were about to start. Chances were I'd never see the shoes again if I didn't go back.

It was dark, but the door to the auditorium was still open. Only two cars were still in the carpark. Still in my dress, I tiptoed in. The lights were off, so I had to feel along the entry passageway to the main room. Coloured fairy lights lining the stage cast the only light.

I told no one what I saw —not even Walshy. Shelley, luminous in pale pink, facing forwards. Ralph, all in black, pressed close against her back, one hand on her stomach. Shelley's head was thrown back, her pale throat stretched out, and Ralph's was bent around hers. They were kissing, their cheeks moving like they were sucking the same ice cream.

Chapter 12

I'm starving. I delay my search again so I can run to the corner shop for bread, cheese, milk, and fruit. I consume an apple while I fry a cheese toastie.

When I go back to the laundry, it's already afternoon. I listen carefully. Nothing except my own heartbeat.

I move the shelves further forwards and push open the door. *Clunk.* Just two inches of opening. A metallic sensation tingles through my muscles. Dim light filters through the Bougainvillea foliage.

I lie on my stomach and push my arm through the gap. I feel along the edge of the house, eyes closed, and hope nothing moves. The marbled scorpion is native around here, so are huntsman spiders and venomous centipedes.

My arm is fully extended, but I can feel only leaves. I start digging down into the wet mulch, rationalising that there is lots of antivenom in Australia. Then I feel something. It's pliable and crunchy—a plastic bag. There's something solid inside.

I grip the bag between finger and thumb, but it slips. Swearing, I try again, pinching so hard my nail shears through the plastic. I shuffle back into the laundry, dragging what looks like a ball of wet leaves towards me. Finally, it's at the gap. One more tug gets it through.

Under the muck is a red-and-white postal bag with nothing written on it. I stand up and wipe it at the sink, washing my hands before cutting off the top with the scissors Blossom kept on the windowsill.

Blossom made a flower arrangement for church every week. It was a highlight to watch her create something beautiful out of our garden, her concentrated frown blocking out everything else. It was like her hands could make something she never expressed. We delivered them to the church, but we never stayed for the service. The church ladies often had a bag ready just for me. Inside it, I would find lollies, second-hand clothes, shoes, paper and pencils. The priest, Father Bickley, resplendent in his long robes, would nod to Blossom. I always hid when he looked at me. After Blossom got into the habit of going away weekends, I didn't visit anymore.

I open the bag. There's a book inside. The pink fabric cover contains no title, just her name, Blossom Brenton, like a diary. A diary? Would Blossom really leave me her secrets?

My hands shake as I flip open the front cover. There's a portrait in lead pencil. Straightaway, it's familiar, and after a second, I know why.

It's the lady from the postcard Blossom left in the envelope Mary gave me. *Lovely Lorrelai.* Blossom's signature is scrawled down the bottom.

Chapter 13

She's wearing a long, dark, sleeveless dress that is cinched in at the waist to hug her hourglass figure. She stands in front of a big tree. Dark curls cascade over her pale shoulders. It's definitely Blossom's work. I'd seen her doodle sketches down the side of the newspaper or on the telephone pad. I know she was good.

I turn the page and find a two-page scene, then another and another. All rural-themed: dogs, kids, a garden, someone working. It's a woman, but not Blossom, fine-boned and petite. Each sketch has Blossom's signature underneath it, more angular and childish than I remember.

I think about the newspaper clipping Blossom sent. I thought she'd sent it because it was about the Lion Inn. But now, after Mary's account, and yet another picture of Lorrelai, I realise her interest in this lady runs deep.

I flick forwards a few more pages, but the places and the theme are the same. Pictures of strangers. I sigh hard, tipping my head back, eyes closed. It's all she's left me. Unsure if I want to cry or growl, I check inside the front and back covers before holding the book by the spine and shaking it hard. Nothing falls out. I check inside the postal bag. Empty.

I slam down the sketchbook and storm out the back door. Pacing the length of the back patio, I silently reason. Blossom was different to other parents. She never came to school events or cooked for the school canteen or helped me dress for assemblies, or even bought me a school uniform. The church ladies did that, while Blossom watched on, there but not there. She was a token parent, an adult who could sign things and do legal stuff. She got on with her life, and she let me get on with mine.

After a while, the garden, scent of wisteria nectar and the gentle noises of York soothe me.

The phone rings, and I jump up and run, knowing suddenly what I'm supposed to be doing. 'I'm sorry, Mary! On my way!'

Con and Mary have owned the Lion Inn for years. Walshy started doing stores and dishes for them when he was fifteen. I started a couple of years after he did.

'Mary? Con?' I stand my bike against the wall and then jump up a single concrete step through the back entrance. It has a long bar, two pool tables, poker machines and small round tables with high stools. The bar is stunning—deeply lacquered slices of a huge local jarrah tree that was damaged in a burn-off. There's a story about it on the wall.

Tonight, the bar is freshly laid with long red-and-white towels and bowls of unshelled peanuts. By the end of the night, shells will litter the carpet like autumn leaves. Three or four men sit at the far end of the bar, their voices rumbling about weather and football. I don't know how they revisit this conversation every week of every year without dying of boredom.

'Hey!' Con is in the doorway, his chin shadowed with stubble. He looks me over, and then pulls me into a quick, hard hug.

'You look good. Like you're fifteen, but good.' He stands back and makes a show of looking past me.

'Walshy's gone camping.'

'Again?'

'Yup. Where's Freda?'

'Kitchen.' Con runs a hand through his hair and narrows his eyes. 'You got a boyfriend from Victoria now?'

I shake my head.

'You one of them chicks that likes chicks?'

I roll my eyes. 'I had two dates back in Melbourne. *With men.* Nothing serious.'

'You ain't hangin' out fer Walshy are ya?'

'Course not!' Then I see her. Aunt Marilyn. Walshy's mum's sister. The shock is immediate after two years not knowing anyone anywhere when I was in Melbourne.

She's wearing high heels and a tight purple dress. I swerve so that Con is between us. He looks over his shoulder, and then questions me with his eyes. Behind him, she trots unevenly out through the door, a cigarette clamped between two fingers.

'She's Walshy's auntie, ain't she?'

I nod. 'She's always hated me. No idea what I did to her except be friends with Walshy.'

I remember the first time I saw Marilyn. I was about twelve. I didn't know who she was, but I noted the wide-eyed stare she'd given me, like I was some kind of monster. I assumed it was my appearance—I was used to that. Then Walshy pointed out that she was his aunt. He also told me she was married to the dancer Ralph Higgins, and that he steered clear of both of them. That suited me fine. Marilyn didn't want her nephew too close to me, and I didn't want to get too close to her either, especially not after I'd seen Shelley with Ralph that night.

'Bit of a royal fuck-up, that family.' Con clicks his tongue. 'They never speak y'know. No love lost, eh?'

I shrug and back away. 'True. I'll get started. Sorry I'm late.'

Con's considerable eyebrows shoot upwards. 'An apology! Geez, Lola. You getting all civilised?'

'Shit no!'

I go through the side door into the kitchen, and Freda sees me instantly.

'Hey, Lola!' She is short, round, pink-faced and wears an apron and gloves 24/7. She tries to hug me, but her hands have pink meat on them, so we chest bump instead. 'Walshy said you were coming!'

'Hey, Freda.'

I wonder if Marilyn is staying, whether I'll have to serve her table. She'll recognise me, give me her best cold stare. With luck, she won't bother to talk to me. I'll just have to pick my nose and pull my knickers out of my bum to put her off.

'I'm up to the armpits in pork mince.' Freda indicates a steel bowl piled high with meat. 'Con got a bargain. It's pork sixteen ways tonight!' She puffs her cheeks.

I laugh. 'I'm looking forward to getting my hands dirty.'

'That's the way, girl!'

I wash my hands at the sink, looking around for my old apron. It is hanging on a hook behind the door, where it's always been. Nothing here changes. I sling it over my head and tie it up at the back.

'Freda?'

'Yes, love?'

I check over my shoulder and lower my voice. 'Walshy's with Shelley Turner now?'

Freda shrugs unconvincingly. 'Can't keep up.'

'God sakes!' Something rises inside me and shakes me all over. It's been building all day. How could he do that— take me to bed the minute I landed when he was with Shelley? How could he be so blind? Couldn't he see what he did to me?

Freda's voice draws me back. 'Maybe you should sit down for a sec, huh. Honey?' She nods at a chair, goes to the sink. She comes back, wiping her hands on a tea towel. 'You've been gone a long time.'

'If I did what Walshy does, I'd be called a slut!'

'He was away a long while. He took a break from everything. Everything.'

'You think he's changed?' Then it occurs to me he's just cheated on his new girlfriend—with me. That fact sucks the heat out of my anger. 'You know what he's like.'

'He's kind, though,' says Freda gently. She stands beside me, her hand on my back, rubbing up and down. 'Remember that old lady by the school? The one who couldn't walk as far as the shop? No family. Who checked her every week? Walshy did. He's had a rough life.'

'I know, I know. Argh.' I put my face in my hands.

'You should ask that boy out, from across the road.'

'Perry? Ew! I'm not that desperate.'

'No one really knows 'less they try.' She gives me her best motherly look. 'I love Walshy. I do. That young man has some issues to sort out. But he'll make a good husband one day.'

'Do you think he wants to be with Shelley? Really be with her?'

Freda shakes her head. 'It's new, love. Who knows?'

I glare through the door, where I can see the edges of dining tables. One has trousered legs underneath.

Freda sighs. 'He's always been great with you. You never let him down. Like two orphans, you are. Feels like we all had a hand in bringing that boy up. But you ...' She smiles softly and shakes her head. 'You hit him in the heart, you did. Wouldn't let anyone touch you. But you've got to have fun at your age.'

I can hardly breathe. The walls, the familiarity, the same damn battles are closing in on me. I can barely stand being here. An urge to call a cab and head straight for the airport almost sends me out the door.

The sound of cutlery rattling comes from the dining room. 'Anyone going to feed us 'round here?'

Freda's gaze flickers. She takes a deep breath, moves back. 'Wipe your face, love. We got work to do. Things'll sort themselves out. You'll see.'

I wipe my face and slide my pad and pencil out of the apron pocket. *My God. Exactly where I left them.*

'Tell me about Melbourne! Does everyone eat out every night? Walk the streets till two am?'

'That's only in Richmond and Carlton. The restaurants are good. People are sociable.'

Freda smiles, her face glowing like I've opened the door to a room of wonder. Then her expression changes.

'I'm fine,' I jump in. 'Blossom was sick. She didn't say much. You know how she was. Feel like I never really knew her.'

'Yeah.' Freda clicks her tongue. 'Still, you two seemed to match. You being a fierce, independent little thing, and Blossom just getting on. You feel any different after your travels?'

'Nah, same bad temper, Freda. Dumped a whole glass of iced coffee on a guy's lap at the café for being a rude prick. Nearly lost my job. Had to lie and say it was an accident.'

Freda chortles.

'Hey, sorry to bust in, but we've been waiting an age.' A skinny guy with a moustache, wearing shirt and jeans, hugs the doorframe. He looks me over, eyes stopping at my chest.

I stare at him, picking the location on his face I'd like to jab a fork. *Sit down and shut the fuck up.* The words are right there on the edge of my tongue.

'Be right with you, sir.' Despite my exaggerated tone, I'm rewarded with a smile.

I turn and see Freda's shocked expression. 'What?' She barely hides a smirk.

'*Be right with you, sir,*' she mimes.

I put on a smile and walk towards the man, who steps back to let me pass, his hands up. I scan the room. Aunt Marilyn is not there. I've never seen her eat anyway, just smoke—like she lives on fumes.

Chapter 14

On my break, I walk down to the laundry and wash my face. I think about Shelley with Walshy, although I try not to. I don't want to visualise the first kiss or them holding hands. It twists me up. He's always dated other girls like he's working his way around the links in a chain. But this feels different. Shelley is different. She's the diamond on the chain.

Shelley introduced me to dancing, hairstyles and treated me like a little sister. And she told me secrets.

I was sixteen the night of my year ten social dance. Two days earlier, I'd almost collided with Shelley outside the bakery. She was nineteen by then, and I'd never confessed I'd seen her with Mr. Higgins. It became one of many mysterious things about Shelley that stayed within her aura of quiet glamour. I'd never dream of asking her about it.

'I missed my social. I'd love to help you get ready,' she said.

Fashion wise, Shelley had followed Madonna's lead. She wore her hair teased and was wearing a lace top and heaps of bangles, which jangled when she moved her arms.

'Would you? I have no idea about that stuff. Can you make me look like the other girls?'

She smiled. 'I can make you look better than the other girls.'

Shelley sourced a straight sapphire-blue dress with thin straps and a sweetheart neckline. It had a kick-split up one side, so I could walk. She arrived that night with borrowed black heels and the confident poise of someone used to attracting glamour, like metal filings to a magnet.

She started by dabbing foundation all over my face. She lined my eyes and daubed my eyelids with green and grey shadow, then dusted a line of sunset pink along my cheekbones, her movements making the bangles clink. She dabbed along my cheekbone with her ring finger. 'Best finger for delicate work,' she said.

How amazing. You had a finger for makeup! I immediately forgot which one it was.

When she was finished with my face, I looked like a girl from one of the magazines at the hairdressers. I could barely speak; when I did, it was someone else's mouth moving and my voice coming out. 'Thanks, Shelley.' I made faces at the mirror.

She stood behind me, parted my hair at the side, brushed it down hard, and applied gel and spray, twice. My brown curls transformed into waves that floated just above my bare shoulders. I'd worn it that length ever since Walshy had cut it four years back. Gelled down, it looked sleek and grown-up, like Ingrid Bergman's from *Casablanca*, one of Coral's favourite movies.

Shelley sniffed and wiped her cheek, and her bangles slid towards her elbow. I realised how thin she'd become. Then I saw the white lines across her wrist. It took a moment to realise what they were. Scars. Sliced straight across her wrist, like she'd leaned hard on guitar strings.

I'd seen a girl with similar in state care. It was commonly known the girl had tried to take her own life. My heart did a big beat and paused before it restarted.

'Shelley?'

She saw my eyes and quickly dropped her arm to her side.

'What happened?'

Shelley wet her lips and swallowed. 'I get emotional sometimes.' She smiled weakly. 'I'm fine.'

I waited, my heart beating fast. I was confused. She had everything. She was so lovely.

'But, how could you … hurt yourself?' I touched her hand, and she seemed too real, as if her glamour had been a mirage and inside, she'd limped along, injured and delicate.

'I—I … made a mistake,' she said in a wobbly voice. 'And I felt sad.

Really sad. Like there was nothing to look forward to.'

Shelley put her hand low on her belly.

I froze. 'Oh no.' My heartbeat pounded in my temples.

'Not now. But I was … when I was fifteen.' She shook her head and closed her eyes for a moment. 'You can't tell anyone.'

'I won't. Shelley?'

Her eyes opened and took on a flat look I'd never seen in her. It scared me. 'I …' Her chin quivered. Shelley frowned and shook her head like she had trouble believing something. I'd never seen her face so sad. 'I had an abortion.'

The words weren't right. They didn't belong to Shelley, but equally they did. She was the glowing princess who did adult things before anyone else, who moved through us but didn't touch us.

'Oh, Shelley.' A big lump sat in my throat.

'It was why I missed my social. Don't say anything. Now or ever. Only Mum knows.' Shelley took a staggered breath in. 'Promise me.'

'I promise.' Even her mother knowing such an intimate thing was Shelley all over. She owned her parents, like she was an adult too, only more important. They did whatever such a perfect beauty required.

Shelley wiped her face on the patterned scarf she wore around her neck.

'Shelley? Please don't do it. Don't hurt yourself again.' A big tear dribbled down my cheek. The thought of it, of her bleeding all over her porcelain skin, was grotesque.

She shook her head. 'I'm all right now.' Her nose looked red and swollen, which skewed her smile a bit. She stroked my cheek with the back of one finger. 'Now don't you start.'

I swallowed hard, trying to think of something bland. Dog poo. Lawn beetles. I had to be strong for Shelley. She was the one who needed to cry. I grabbed a tissue.

'Should I re-do that black stuff?' I carefully wiped smudged eyeliner from under my left eye.

Shelley frowned and shook her head. 'It looks fine. You look beautiful. Just have a great night. For me, okay?'

'Okay.'

She moved around, stood in front of me and held up the red-red lipstick. 'I don't want you to think about it. Please? And don't ever say anything to Walshy.'

I couldn't speak for a moment. 'Are you going away again?'

Shelley paused, and then realisation came. 'I didn't leave,' she whispered. 'I just didn't go out much. Anyway ...' She shook herself. 'Tell me about Perry. He's handsome, isn't he?' She shrugged and smiled like a little girl.

'I guess.'

She waited till my mouth was still and then applied the lipstick and held a tissue there for me to dab it with. Standing back, she appraised my face, tipping her head one way and then the other, like I was a picture she'd drawn. Her gaze met mine.

'You don't sound sure.'

I sighed. 'I'm not good at this stuff.'

Shelley sat beside me. 'Don't you want a boyfriend?'

'No.'

She smiled, which was a relief to see. 'Okay, let's get your dress on.' She slid it off the hanger and undid the zip. Looking at me, she stopped, her lips pressed together. 'No other bras?'

I looked down, panicked. 'This is the only one that fits me.' It had come in a bag from the church.

'Ah well, no one's going to see it. Let's go shopping soon, okay? You're big busted. You need special lingerie, so you don't get a crone's neck.'

'Okay.'

She zipped me up, checked my cleavage, and flattened the seams of the dress over my bust. 'Wow, girl! He won't be able to take his eyes off you!'

I made a face. 'Shit.'

Shelley smiled and kissed me on the cheek.

'Go have fun. You look like a movie star.'

Chapter 15

The night air is fresh and still. Inside, the inn hums with voices, laughter and music. On the way up the path, there's a flash of light to my right, along the back wall of the cider rooms behind the golden wattle. In summer, the plant bursts into sun-yellow fluffy flowers, magnetising bees, which fill pollen panniers on their hind legs. Con trims it when it gets out of control. Sawn-off branches and cut grass indicate a recent prune.

I walk off into the stubby grass and hold the branches apart. A tiny window about a foot wide is stained dirty orange from bore water. I check the wall back and forth. The cellars have no windows. This must be the room from the newspaper clipping.

'Lola!' Mary is framed by the kitchen door.

'I'm coming!'

I meet her halfway. She wears an apron over her work clothes.

'How was it tonight?'

'Like I never left.' I turn towards the hidden window. 'Hey, is that the murderer's room down there?'

Mary nods. 'Yeah. I was going to show you that. The Lovely Lorrelai. Has a ring to it doesn't it?' She points to the far-left end of the main building. 'She used to dance out back, where that old stage is. You know where we keep the dry goods at the other end of the restaurant? There's still a bit of old red curtain there. You want to come down and have a look at the room?' She searches her pants pocket with her hand and grabs a torch.

I follow Mary down the path past the laundry and cellars. She pushes back a curtain of honeysuckle near the fence. Behind it is a door I've never seen. I help by holding up the vine. It smells overly sweet. Petals fall on my hair, neck and arms, along with a dead bee.

Mary turns toward the laundry for light. The metal shaft is stiff, and an insect crawls along my neck just as the lock clunks open with an odd, sucking *pop*, like the room is airtight. Mary pushes the door inwards, and I follow on her heels.

It's like a limestone cave. In the middle, a bed is covered by a faded bedspread. The floor sticks with grainy insect poo, decaying leaves and dead spiders. Beside the bed is an empty cupboard, both doors wide open. Overhead, a long black cord hangs down, its end padded with grey spider webs.

'Who'd Lorrelai kill?' I like the name, the way it forms on my tongue and rolls out of my mouth.

Mary's face lights up. 'Her lover's wife. At *nineteen*! Got a life sentence.' The words echo in the room.

'Really? How?'

'Strangled her and shoved her off a bridge into the Avon during a storm.'

'Geez.'

'You know how the river gets.'

I did. When we were younger, Walshy and I had watched water levels rise up the measuring stick after heavy rain. As the river swelled, it breached low areas and created temporary pools where frogs would spawn. Soon after, tadpoles would dart around the puddles and kids would catch them in ice-cream containers. We weren't allowed near the river during storms.

'Apparently, she kept the victim's wedding rings. I did a quick search about the case before we proposed the tourist thing.'

I don't know what I was expecting, but the room gives me nothing. Lorrelai seems like a whisper in the dark, pencil on paper, glamour and legend. Blossom wanted me to know about her, but it's like trying to catch rain. I can't concentrate enough to latch onto any meaning besides a gnawing jealously about Blossom's interest in Lorrelai. She was far more concerned with a criminal than she had ever been in me. I'm suddenly so tired, I long for bed.

'I know. Bit underwhelming, isn't it? Poor woman died shortly after she got out of prison. Blossom told me that.' Mary locks the door, and I yawn as I follow her back up the path.

'I found what Blossom left. It's a book full of her sketches. Just … pictures. Nothing I recognise. Oh, and one of Lorrelai. You're right—she was totally obsessed with her.'

Mary looks over her shoulder. 'Really? Well, I guess it's nice to have something she made.'

I can tell she's surprised that it's nothing else too.

'Mary, will Blossom be cremated?'

'Yes. She left me a letter that lists her preferences. Didn't want family contacted. Hadn't seen them since she was a girl apparently.'

'Where are they? She told me nothing.'

'Same. Just gave me instructions when she knew she was sick.'

'What am I supposed to do for the funeral?'

'Don't worry. I hope you don't mind but I've pretty much organised it. Everyone's agreed to pitch in. Church will do a service. The canteen ladies from your old primary school are happy to do finger food for the wake. We're putting on a spit roast back here, which will bring in the punters, so we'll foot the bill for the coffin.' She touches my shoulder. 'It's the basic model, but you can't look a gift horse in the mouth.'

This means I'm supposed to take free stuff without question. 'She wouldn't care. Thanks,' I say with a hitch in my chest. 'Just don't pay me for this week. Sorry I don't have any other savings.'

After I finish stacking the big dishwasher and press start, I cycle home, hoping to see Walshy's ute parked beside the house. The driveway is empty.

* * *

Walshy and I developed a birthday tradition. Yabbying down the river, followed by cake. But for my fifteenth, it was raining heavily. He strutted out in his best clothes, smelling of aftershave, and my stomach clenched.

'Are you going out?'

He looked down at his clothes and then up to me. Something glinted in his eyes. 'No, it's your birthday.'

'Oh. Right. I didn't know we were getting dressed up.'

I made some mashed potato to accompany the roast lamb I'd

bought with our birthday fund, all the while aware of him in the way I would be of a fire burning in the corner. The roast had emptied the money jar. I'd whipped our eggs into a meringue topped with passionfruit from the vines beside the school gate that everyone helped themselves to. Apart from the roast, cream had been the only other expense.

Walshy was quiet when we ate.

'Everything okay?'

He had looked up and nodded, but his smile came a second too late. 'Thinkin' about, you know, the future. Where I should go and stuff.'

I got a jolt. 'Thought you were staying for the farm?'

'Dad won't let me do anything but work my guts out. Got to get something of my own.'

'You got the ute.'

'Yeah, can go wherever I want, I guess.'

I put my fork down and crossed my arms so he wouldn't see my hands shake. 'What's up? You broke up with what's-her-name?'

'Don't say it like that.'

'Why? Why do you have to date like you're gonna die tomorrow and you can't miss any girls in a 100-k radius?'

Walshy sat back and frowned. 'They're just girls.'

I rolled my eyes. 'I know, but you like them.'

He shrugged. 'Course.'

I scoffed. 'Well, they sure do like you!' I picked up my fork and shovelled mash into my mouth. There is only one way to eat some things, and that's with your mouth completely full of it. Like mash.

And donuts.

Walshy shrugged. 'I'm not serious about any of them.'

I frowned at him then. He never opened up about anything like this. It was a bad sign. 'You never want to get married?'

He shook his head to agree.

'So why go dating anything with legs? You know what they call you?'

He closed his eyes and nodded. 'Yeah, the Pope.'

'I didn't know you were religious.'

He smiled as he forked up some mash but didn't eat it. 'I'm not religious.' He filled his mouth.

'Why don't you date me? I'm a girl.'

He stopped suddenly, as though his brain had run into something. 'You're different to the others.' He began chewing slowly.

A familiar lump rose in my throat. 'You know, I used to want to marry you one day? I thought I just had to get older and you'd want to go out with me. But I realised you just wanted a kid sister. I must be the only girl you haven't tongued.'

Walshy went crimson and swallowed hard. 'Don't fucken say that, Jane.'

'What? The truth? Ugh.' I leaped up and started tidying, my hands trembling, not knowing what I wanted to say or what I was feeling. I just knew something was changing and that Walshy might leave. 'Pavlova can wait. I'm going to Monopoly group.'

'What group?'

'The girls from the hairdressers meet up every month. It's not as boring as it sounds. We wrestle for Mayfair and Pall Mall. Plus, there's ice cream and beer—sometimes mixed together. Right up your street.'

Lies, just lies.

His face fell. 'I haven't given you a present.'

I stare at him and sigh. 'Save it. Give your girlfriends a present.' I kissed him on the top of the head and scooted out the back door. 'Then, for fuck's sake, screw someone. You're not a eunuch.'

I went and sat in the garden shed until I heard him leave. I cried so hard my sides hurt, and then I got the vodka Blossom kept in the bottom of the pantry and drank it all, wincing and alternating with water until I passed out.

Later, I woke up in my bed to Walshy taking my shoes off.

'I'm sorry,' I slurred. 'Please don't fug anyone. I lerve you.' Then I vomited.

'I didn't. Shh. It's fine,' he muttered as he cleaned up. He sounded sad and tired.

After that he wouldn't meet my eyes the same way, and I felt like I'd broken something between us. I didn't say it, but I was sorry. So sorry. To me, he was the most important thing in the world.

Chapter 16

The Flower House is lit by a half moon. Silver coats every surface. Only the shadows slink black, like an old photo. The garden cushions the house, as though the building has sunk down inside it. I can't see the rust and holes and damage. Or the fading artwork. The rose perfume wafts into the air. I never could smell it unless I'd been away.

I know all the scents, the tastes. I could live here with my eyes shut. It's my space ... and Walshy's. Our sanctuary. The gum that bonded everything—and maybe the last thing holding Walshy and me together. It could be gone soon. It was never ours. Another temporary part of my life.

With a heavy heart, I let myself in via the side gate and walk beneath the arch of purple wisteria beside the outdoor laundry. The screen door slaps behind me as I go to the sketchbook on the kitchen table. I open the front, cover a yawn with my hand and admire the first picture. Lorrelai. This is all Blossom has left me.

At the sink I have a long glass of water then sink into a chair at the table.

I begin at the start. The old paper crackles when I lift the page. The first two-page scene looks like a camp. Empty chairs and sprawling logs semicircle a fire surrounded by caravans, tents, dirty-faced kids, and dogs. The pictures are all in lead pencil. There's the odd dirty fingerprint.

Over the page is a sketch of the inside of a shed with corrugated walls. In the middle, a woman is milking a goat on a stand. In the upper corner, a smaller goat sits with its legs folded underneath its body. The lady wears a plait down her back, and her head is tipped forwards, her hands beneath the goat.

Maybe Blossom had been to this place. Maybe I'll find out something about her through her sketches.

Next page is a lady drawn side on, a plait dangling over one shoulder, an apron covering her dress. She is kneading dough with both arms straight, a bread loaf pan resting beside her on a bench. I look closer, examining her features before I realise who it is. Lorrelai. Again.

I flip back and forwards, checking the women in each picture. Lorrelai. Contrasting the classy portrait, she's dressed plainly in apron and work boots, her hair a thick rope down her back, but it's definitely her.

Blossom was obsessed. Maybe she had met her. Idolised her, even loved her.

In primary school, we were supposed to ask our parents about their youth, compare the fashion, economy and culture to our own. Apart from saying she grew up around the local district, and then got involved in the women's movement, Blossom dodged my questions.

I remembered talking to Mary. Blossom had begged her not to do the tourist thing, insisted Lorrelai was innocent.

I'd never seen Blossom passionate about anything.

With that in mind, I take it slowly. A mystery is a mystery, and my curiosity flickers brighter than my annoyance, like a flame on kerosene.

I examine the next scene. Lorrelai is grating apples, a barrel and bottles around her like she's making juice.

Over the page, she's crouched in a leafy vegetable patch, dangling a bunch of carrots in one hand, dirt clinging to the pale hairs at the carrots' tips. She's looking up, smiling.

Over the page, Lorrelai is in profile breastfeeding a baby. Her head tilted down, her blouse open, her gaze tender.

I pause. Mary didn't mention that Lorrelai had a baby. She was only nineteen when she went to jail.

I chew my lip, remembering walking down the street with Blossom, getting groceries. She always avoided a pram, walked around it on the footpath, looked away. Whenever a small child stared at her, Blossom pocketed her hands, twisted her head away, and cleared her throat.

Why would she draw Lorrelai with a baby if there wasn't one?

Next scene, Lorrelai is milking a goat again, like one of the earlier sketches, but this time there is a baby in a sling on her back. The next few pictures show her gardening, picking apples, washing bowls in a river, all with a baby.

Mary said the murder was in 1971. Thirty-five years ago. Blossom would have been a teenager of similar age to Lorrelai. She's not the baby, and neither am I.

When I turn the next page, I'm surprised by a different woman. She fills the page, her dark hair parted down the centre, her arms up over her head, her pointed ballerina feet bare and dirty. She's wearing a loose white dress, and her cheeks are hollowed, her saucer eyes blank but haunted. Pencil shading outlines collarbones, ribs, pelvis, wrists, tendons and veins. It's like a skeleton dancing. It's macabre and a bit tragic.

I turn the page. The next sketch is similar to the others. Two people dining at a small table in a cramped room off a kitchen. Plates of meat, potatoes and peas. A man sits across from Lorrelai, a sturdy, dark-coiffed man with a beard. A jewellery box sits open on the table, one of those ones that starts a tune when the lid opens, a little porcelain ballerina pirouetting. But this box is different. Where the dancing ballerina normally twirls is the ghostly dancer instead. I wriggle in my seat, letting a shiver pass over me. Then I stand up and go to the window, my eyes on the garden.

A sinister feeling sinks inside me. I draw the kitchen curtain and close the door. I don't know what I'm hiding from. I listen hard. Warm wind rattles the dry seed pods of a carob tree.

Blossom is trying to tell me something. I think about it. A murderess who once danced and stayed at the Lion Inn, where I've worked for years, was important to Blossom. She kept this sketchbook hidden for a long time and ensured I received it only after her death. So why would she leave it to me? No explanation, just a bunch of pictures? What's within these pages she especially wanted me to know?

I walk around the table where the sketchbook lies open at a page where Lorrelai stands in a garden with a sling on her back.

What if Lorrelai gave birth to her lover's child? Where is that child now? What if there was something bad about the wife? Or her lover. What if he had a hand in his wife's murder? Surely that pretty lady from the pictures would've needed some help strangling someone and throwing them into the river.

I lift my eyes, and there's static on everything like an untuned television set. What if Blossom is right and it wasn't Lorrelai who committed murder. She spent ages drawing her theory, constructing the story. Then she hid it away. Or perhaps she knew her obsession was a bit strange, or her theories farfetched, so she left it for me because she didn't know what else to do with it.

My head swoons. If I was still in Melbourne, I'd be waking to an alarm for a morning shift, but here it's only two am, and I haven't slept for twenty hours. If I could keep my eyes open, I would.

I get into the shower, turn on the water and gasp at the cold. I know every crack in the walls, every missing tile. This place is like a second body. It has kept my secrets. Kept Walshy's. We are safe here, the two of us. Our life exists in these rooms. It's the closest thing I've ever had to permanence.

How much is an old place like this worth? I wonder if there's a chance the bank would loan me enough money. Or Walshy, if he wanted to buy it.

The only people I know with money are Shelley Turner's family. The thought of the Turners makes me remember Walshy is with Shelley, and the world descends on my shoulders. Does he expect me to leave again? Was what happened when I arrived merely a one-off? A sweet reminder? Maybe he's changed after being away. Maybe I'm no longer his only lover.

Before I go to bed, I head to the veranda and close the door carefully behind me. The air warms my shower-cool skin. I sit on the outside bed, searching out each plant with my eyes, listening to the odd rustle of leaves indicating the night movements of small things.

A clunk draws me to the edge of the veranda, where I can see the road. Perry's outside light into the garden has flicked on behind the high wall. I've never been in there, despite him boasting about all his plants, half of them propagated from our garden. I listen, but there's nothing else.

The light goes off. It's a sensor; a rat or a cat has probably set it off.

Yawning, I turn back, but something catches my eye. A shadow moves along Perry's fence, a figure bent over. I freeze against the pole and watch. The figure straightens and looks around, and I realise it's Perry. Quietly, I move back inside and lock the screen door. Then I go through the kitchen and lock the back door too. A shiver ripples down my spine.

I climb into bed in knickers and a clean T-shirt. I've folded Walshy's clothes in the corner of the room, put on new sheets, and taken the T-shirt he wore to the airport, to bed with me. Holding it near my face so I can smell it, I close my eyes and drift to sleep.

Chapter 17

When I wake, it's late. In the garden, a wattlebird squarks angrily. Wearing shorts and a singlet, I wander into the kitchen and the phone rings. The real estate agent introduces himself. 'Mary told me to call.'

Head full of sleep fug, I struggle to get my thoughts in order.

'Oh, right. I'm Lola and I've lived in this house most of my life. It's really important that I stay here. I'm happy to rent.'

'Look, I'll be straight with you, Lola. Two things might happen to the property. Least likely, rental. Most likely, demolish for redevelopment. York has grown popular over the last decade.'

'What? Knock it down? What about all the history and the garden? Could it be heritage-listed or something?'

He laughs for longer than is polite. 'Blossom had a private arrangement with the owner, which was void when she died. The owner wants to make a move. Sorry.'

I rub my eyes and remember that swearing could earn me a hang up and lose me the house. 'Okay. Who are they?'

'Not at liberty to say.'

'Tell them I'll buy it, please.' My bank account contains barely enough to fly me back to Melbourne. I shove my hands into my back pockets and find a twenty-dollar note. I pull it out and stare in shock.

'You can ring the office when we've sorted the listing. But it's already had interest.'

I must have worn these shorts when I went out last. I always kept a little for a taxi in Melbourne.

'You still there?'

I'm still staring at the money. 'Yeah. Hey, how much would a down payment be? I've got a twenty here. You take bribes?'

* * *

'Mary?'

She's behind the bar and ducks her head through the back door with an impatient expression.

'Remember Lorrelai?' I run the back of my hand across my forehead to remove the sweat.

She nods quickly, squinting into the bar. The noise level indicates more patrons than usual for Friday lunchtime.

'Did she have a baby? And do you know anything about the woman she killed?'

Mary shakes her head, and her mouth pulls down. 'Baby? Not sure. Wife was nuts, though. Really cuckoo. Sorry, Lola. Getting hammered in here.'

I can see she's going to ask me whether I can stay.

'Okay, gotta go.' I hurry out.

Back at the house, I pace so I can think.

The wife was nuts? Back then, mental institutions were hellholes. I'd seen a black-and-white film about Ararat Lunatic Asylum, near Melbourne, which was supposedly haunted and offered ghost tours. The film showed patients shuffling around barefoot in sleepwear or underwear. Some were tied to beds wearing straitjackets they couldn't get out of. Electroconvulsive therapies tried to zap their brains back to normal by attaching horrifying cables to their heads, stuffing something in their mouths while they twitched.

Did that happen to the wife? Was she the dead-looking dancer wearing a nightie like she'd escaped from an institution?

Lorrelai was important to Blossom. Blossom wanted to reveal something about her or perhaps about what happened, decades after the fact. She chose me. I look over at the book and my heart starts skittering. Is there something in those pages about the murder Blossom kept secret?

Chapter 18

Fifteen years ago, I'd been standing behind a door when my five-year-old gut told me there was something bad on the other side.

Pearls shone all over the wooden floor, some still rolling a little because they were too identical to be real, machine-manufactured, perfectly spherical with one tiny hole to hang by.

Coral's necklace used to break all the time. I had seen her thread it back together over and over again. The thread was meant to be nylon, like fishing line, but she only had cotton. I liked watching her repair it, handing her a single pearl at a time in my tiny fingers. But after she died, I couldn't find all the pearls. I was relocated to the Children's Home with a handful of pearls inside a matchbox I kept in my pocket. I never got to put it back together.

Now, my gut is telling me something else. I turn the pages of the book until I get two pages of black. A thrill of dread runs down my back. Only three things are drawn here: a bridge, a woman running, and a man running behind her. Overhead, white veins of lightning split the sky.

Wait ... there is something else. A date. 1971.

* * *

I leaf to the end of the book and the last picture is of a church with closed doors followed by blank pages.

I pull on my sandals and cycle back down to the inn.

The bar is half full, the patrons relaxed, the occasional laugh cuts through the music.

I find Mary in the cold-room behind the bar, clutching a carton of beer bottles. She smiles over the top.

'Hey, Lola!' She puts the carton down and wipes her forehead with the back of her arm. She sits on the edge of an empty shelf, and the whole structure squeaks. I rub my goose bumped arms against the cold smoke pouring through the vents.

'Walshy back yet?'

'Nope. I've been looking through the sketches. It's all about Lorrelai and the murder case. Do you know if Lorrelai's lover, the husband, got questioned? Also, did he have a beard?'

Mary holds up both hands. 'Lola, it was ages ago. I have no idea. I'm starving. Come have something to eat.' She rocks forwards onto her feet.

'Are you sure Lorrelai didn't have a baby?'

Mary frowns. 'I don't recall her having a baby. I know the husband was her lover. Voila—her reason for getting rid of the wife.' She spreads her hands like it's all the explanation needed.

'What else do you know about it? Was Lorrelai still living in that room outside?'

Mary shakes her head. 'No, it happened in Northam. She got fired or something, moved to a caravan park there. I read about some of it so I could get some tourists to spend a few bucks here. Go to the Northam Library. That's where I went.'

I take a deep breath. 'Okay.'

'You're all stirred up.' She puts a hand on my shoulder. 'But we're here for you, okay? You got a job here if you need it, a bed to sleep in. A meal. Now c'mon, eat.'

I nod and follow Mary like a lamb. She brings out two plates of stew with herb-speckled dumplings and salad. My mouth waters. Dumplings are another food you should jam in your mouth; the doughy bulk fills right up to the roof.

'Whoa, girl. You'll get hiccups.' Mary sits opposite and eats her way through her own serving. 'Better?'

I chew a bit and swallow before I talk. 'Thanks for this, Mary. You know, I think Blossom knew something. Something she never told anyone. She believed Lorrelai was innocent, and if that was the case, someone else got away with murder.' We finish, and Mary waves me away from collecting the plates.

'Go sort out your mystery. And keep me posted. It's getting interesting.'

* * *

I hurry home in the humid afternoon. Heat streams off the bitumen. Inside the Flower House, I go into each room, check it, and then lock the back door. I don't know why I'm so creeped out. All this was ages ago. But it feels like the sketchbook has clawed open a crack into the past.

Blossom hid it in a crazy spot for me when she died. It's the only connection I have left. And it feels like a message. She's trying to tell me something in true Blossom style. Let me work it out for myself.

I take a deep breath and let it out slowly. There's something I have to do. I leave the sketchbook, head for the phone and flick through the phonebook to find the number for Births, Deaths and Marriages. Alternately fearful and impatient, I'm redirected through several points of contact until I finally introduce myself to the right officer.

'My name is Lola Harris. I need a copy of my original birth certificate. Not an extract—I have that—but the original. I was named after a relative and brought up in the state system. I don't know my parents' names.' The officer confirms my caseworker's name and runs me through the relevant requirements and documents I'll need.

I replace the receiver. It is done.

I stand still for a moment. Then I go grab the sketchbook.

In the bathroom, I flick the light on and close the door. The window is that rippled glass which is too warped to see through. I sit on the edge of the bath, balance the book on my knees and thumb forwards to the stormy, running scene.

The river is all lines and swirls, flowing fast. Lightning forks overhead. I can imagine how fierce the rain, how loud the thunder, how immense the currents. The river changes so much. It can be fierce or calm, deeper than it appears.

The Avon Descent, a two-day race between Northam and Perth, where people paddle kayaks and canoes over a hundred kilometres of rocks, pinches and rapids, is known for its challenges. About ten years ago, in 1995, someone died during the race.

In the sketch, the woman is well ahead of the man. If it's the wife, why is she running towards the river in the thick of a storm? What made her run? What is so urgent that they're both out in the dead of night?

Willing the picture to give me more, I focus on the man. He carries a torch and stares at the beam on the ground. His eyes are wide, searching. He doesn't look murderous. He looks scared. Unlike the woman, he's dressed for the weather: a warm jacket, trousers and boots.

The woman's face is expressionless, like someone in shock. She doesn't look scared; she looks blind or mad. Her high heels are incongruous with the shapeless dress, which is stuck to her bony body, her breasts and ribs visible through the fabric.

The one picture left in the sketchbook after the storm, the church, seems to signify a natural end. A death. Then, between the storm scene and the church, the sketchbook falls wide open. I notice something near the spine. A ripped edge. I run a finger along it. Someone's ripped a few pages out. Right where a murder could have happened. Did Blossom know about the missing pages? Did she remove them herself? The postal bag was sealed when I found it. Why would she leave me a story with the crucial part gone?

Carefully, I close the book. What happened next? Did the man reach the woman? Strangle her and push her into the river? Or was someone else on the bridge, waiting?

I go outside for some fresh air. It's late afternoon, long shadows painting the ground. The air is still very warm, and in the sky, the small white shape of a plane slides across the blue.

* * *

Back inside, I turn on the lights and put the sketchbook in the pantry, placing my copy of the *Country Women's Association Cookery Book and Handy Hints* on top and closing the doors.

The cookbook was Coral's. I took it when the ambulance came, before I was taken away. I knew I'd never go back to that house. I'd never get anything that belonged to Coral, not even a photograph. That's the thing with not belonging. Nothing is really yours. Not family photos. Not even your bedroom. You get used to nothing being your own. To walking away.

I shower in cold water. It makes me gasp, but it's fresh and clean and good. I cup my hands, slurping handfuls until my head feels better.

Days like this suck you dry. It was something Blossom always said on hot days. The real stinkers, forty degrees and over, when the garden wilted, the grass frizzled, and the ravens hissed in the shade with their beaks open, watching panting dogs dig to keep cool.

Blossom knew about the outdoors. She had a farmer's tan, leathery skin, scabby ears, and a weathered red V below her neck. She was strong and capable, far more comfortable with plants and vegetables than with people.

I wonder what it will be like at Blossom's funeral. I can't do a speech, because I didn't really know her. I still don't. What would I say? *I was grateful. She provided me with a house, somewhere Walshy and I could live.* Did she know the house would be taken off us when she died?

I towel off and pull on the shirt I use to sleep in. I imagine some of Blossom's sketches. Something hovers around my thoughts like a bee round a bloom, almost ready to land. I go out and get the sketchbook. Cross-legged on my bed, underneath the light, I open it on my lap. The pictures are so lifelike, yet so mundane. Lorrelai going about her life while Blossom sketched her in a caravan park in 1971.

I go to one picture that's stayed in my mind. Lorrelai with her hands in the dough, flour up one arm, some on the bench, a smear on her forehead. A spoon and bowl and a box of yeast, a fabric bag labelled SALT. I turn the page. Lorrelai in the vegetable garden, a pea pod in her hand, dirt under her nails, a dark curl stuck to her temple. A grinning Lorrelai grating an apple, hand gripping the fruit, eyebrows up like she's talking to someone. The person behind the camera. *Click.*

I leave the book, walk to the kitchen, and turn on the pantry light. There's flour and salt and two sachets of yeast. I check the best before date. After heating water in the kettle, I add some to a cereal bowl and drop in some sugar, picking out two ants. Tap water makes it tepid and then a sprinkle of yeast goes over. Beige blooms rise to the surface. I measure three cups of flour and two pinches of salt into another big bowl.

I can see Lorrelai working. She is sweating a little, stringy muscles standing out in her arms. She talks as she works. She smiles. She falls silent, wiping her hands on a cloth, reacting to the baby, hurrying to the crib. I see her eating with the big, bearded man, peas falling off her fork. Or swatting a fly as she milks, her hands pumping rhythmically.

I see her waist thinning as she reaches overhead for an apple, as she bends down and places it in a wicker basket.

Blossom didn't make bread; she didn't cook.

I add the yeast mix to the flour, combine wet and dry, knead it, and then flop it out onto the floured bench. The dough is warm, dense, tacky as belly fat. Using both hands, I knead again, then I lower it into the bowl and cover it with a tea towel. It will double in size before morning.

The clock ticks. The fridge hums. There's a dusting of flour on the back of my hand. I slap the dough through the tea towel like it's a mate I'm sharing something with.

'You were there,' I say to the empty kitchen, and I laugh, feeling elated that Blossom has finally told me something. A secret. A big secret.

She didn't just draw pictures about a famous murder story. She knew Lorrelai. She watched her and sketched her. Maybe they were friends who spent time together and shared secrets. Secrets about Lorrelai's affair with a married man, and later, secrets about the murder of his wife.

Chapter 19

'That's where we keep it.' The young receptionist taps into a keyboard and nods towards a Microfilm machine and photocopier in the back corner.

I've taken a bus to the library in Northam. If I stay, I'll need a driver's licence, because the bus system here is so patchy. I'll have to wait for Mary to pick me up afterwards.

It is cool and quiet. The air conditioner hums, and someone clicks a pen.

'The newspaper articles are in order of date.' The receptionist's eyes scan the screen. 'I can see here that Lorrelai McAllister was charged with a crime committed on 3rd September 1971.' She makes eye contact. Her irises look ridiculously huge through the thick glass.

'Maybe start with articles in September 1971,' she suggests. 'Sorry. It can take time to find what you want. Get the film from those filing cabinets over there and pop it into the machine. The entire newspapers are in there.'

'Thanks,' I say quickly and walk down the back of the library.

* * *

After Shelley finished my makeup and left that night of the social dance, I had some time before Walshy was due. He was working, but he insisted he pick me up and drop me home, despite Perry's parents offering, because the social was over in Northam.

I tried not to think about Shelley. It hurt that she had been in so much pain. I hoped she had had someone to look after her, someone who loved and cared about her. It was strange worrying about a girl who had everything. Maybe it was possible that Shelley could be as sad and lonely as anyone, even with parents, expensive things, talent, beauty and loads of money.

Keeping her secret felt odd and lonely. I'd never kept anything from Walshy.

He made a shocked noise when I opened the ute's passenger door.

'Jazes! Shouldn't you cover yourself up a bit?' He had gazed at my cleavage, and then closed his eyes and turned away.

'Does it look that bad?'

Walshy looked back and seemed a bit lost. '*Jane*.' Then he sighed. 'Nah. I'm just not used to it.'

Conscious of every smooth, combed hair on my head, the thick feel of makeup on my eyes and cheeks, the rustle of the skirt, I reversed into the seat. I had to back in, then plop down because I couldn't separate my legs.

'I don't have anything else.'

'It's not that. You look great. It's just ...' He shrugged and looked away again.

A lump welled in my throat. 'Should I wash my face? Wear a cardigan?'

Walshy shook his head and inhaled until his chest rose all the way up. 'Sorry. I'm just not used to you looking like that.' He started the car and looked over and smiled a bit.

I put my seatbelt on. 'Don't worry. My legs are jammed together. No one's gonna get in without serious injury.'

'Jane!' He shook his head, suggesting I'd missed the point.

'What? All right. Let's just go to the creek. It's going to be a full moon. Yabbies.' I held up both hands, snapping fingers to thumbs like claws.

Walshy blinked a couple of times, long enough to show he was considering it. I latched on like a yabby to a chunk of meat. 'C'mon. I don't really want to go anyway.'

'I can't take you to the creek like that.' He frowned. 'Besides, I gotta go back to work.'

I slumped back and pulled the low V-neck edges of the dress neckline together, but it just opened again. Walshy was right. I felt naked. My boobs were jumping out. I rounded my shoulders to make it better.

We pulled on to the road and Walshy leaned his arm on the windowsill. Paddocks zipped by on both sides, and then the car darkened as the road cut through forest.

'So, are you into Perry?'

I shrugged. 'He's okay. He has two arms and two legs.'

'Why are you going with him then?'

'It's not a big deal. I had to have a partner. No one goes alone. Most of the girls choose a guy that will look good in the photos. I just want to see everyone trying to walk in high heels. Carnage. Definite carnage.'

'So, Perry will look good in your photos?'

'What? Nah, I'm talking about the others. I don't care.'

Walshy checked the side mirror for a long time, his face creased in a frown. Warm air buffeted around us. It had been 35 degrees and heat still rose up from the road. 'You gonna kiss him?'

'Huh? No!'

He gave me an unfamiliar look.

'What?'

Walshy lifted a shoulder. 'Just gives me a funny feeling.'

'Just take me yabbying!'

He didn't say anything, but he smiled faintly as he looked across. 'Despite all the goo on your face, you're still my Jane.'

'Goo?' I grinned.

'You wouldn't know how to kiss anyway.'

I looked out front. The car ahead switched on its headlights. Walshy didn't switch ours on. Silence roared between us.

'Sometimes you make me really cranky, Ben Walsh.'

He grinned. 'Am I wrong?'

A blush spread over my neck and face. I wondered if it was visible. 'No. But you don't have to be an arse just because you've tongued every girl at school.'

His eyebrows bounced up. 'Steady on, Jane. I'm not that bad.'

I stared at him with my mouth open. 'You seriously are.'

He pulled the car over and tugged the handbrake on. A car whizzed by, buffeting the ute. Then he stared at me for a long time. 'Do you think I'm a bad person?'

I had my arms folded, staring out the windscreen, feeling the rumble of the idling engine. I shook my head.

'What do you think of me, Jane? Say it.'

My mouth twitched. I had no idea which of the things in my heart I wanted to say out loud. The thing that bubbled up first definitely wasn't coming out. Love. I wanted to say, *I love you, dickhead!* I didn't say anything.

He sighed and put the car into gear. Ducking his head to check the traffic, he pulled onto the road. In Northam, we drove into the carpark with all the other cars. God it was busy. Nerves darted all over me. Even with the stiffness between Walshy and me, it was easier in here than out there.

'Go on. Have a good night,' he said quietly.

Carefully I got out and then put my head back inside the door. 'Nine-thirty?'

Walshy nodded, his eyes a bit sad or sorry or something. He watched me walk up the stairs, backed out, and drove off.

'Hey.'

Perry was smiling. He looked me up and down. 'You look *amazing*.' He was wearing a cream suit. Everyone else wore black.

'Thanks. Great suit,' I said.

'Want a drink?' He crooked his elbow out, like I was supposed to take it.

At the drinks table, teachers smiled hard, scanning surreptitiously for pashing couples or smuggled alcohol.

It started easier than expected. Perry smiled like the corners of his lips were stapled up. Everyone was focused on themselves, adjusting their clothes, testing the feel of walking in heels, wearing bow ties, slicking lipstick. The music thumped. Silver and black balloons and streamers decorated the basketball courts. Bags of confetti and glitter were rigged up either side of the stage. On the dance floor, students were all trying move naturally, which made them look like Thunderbirds puppets.

To prepare for the social, we'd done six weeks of biweekly ballroom lessons. Ralph Higgins had returned to town for the job. But no one could really dance, not like Shelley. We just stepped when we were told and shuffled or rocked.

I kept trying not to think about Shelley. I kept thinking about her.

'Let's dance.' Perry waved his hand in front of my face. 'Your lessons will be wasted.'

I became aware of the music and people, and of Perry. Despite being annoying, he looked and smelled nice. I tried to lighten up. But without Walshy there, it felt empty. I had such a strong yearning for him that it sucked the air out of me.

The night dragged, despite me dancing most of the time. Other girls looked at Perry, but he only saw me. Boys looked at me too, their eyes travelling from the floor to my boobs and back down, like they didn't recognise me. It was strange and powerful. I understood then why girls wore all this stuff. You could be someone new, and people admired you.

Eventually, my skin warm and tacky, we went outside with glasses of cola. Then, as I had dreaded he might, Perry made his move. He stood behind me, encircled me with his arms and pulled me back against his chest.

I could feel his thigh on my butt. He spoke against my ear. 'At my school, they keep us locked away from girls like you. You're so cute.'

Hackles rose down my back. I pushed his hands off me and twisted around. 'Walshy got suspended for punching my boyfriend.' It happened before I knew what was going to come out, and then it sat between us like a dropped knife.

Perry drew his neck back in like a surprised chicken. 'Why'd you say that?'

I shrugged and got hot. 'C'mon. Let's go to the dance floor.'

He grabbed my wrist. 'Tell me!' He was holding me back. His hand tightened. 'What were you thinking?'

'Stop it! I hate when you say that!'

He released me, glaring like he hated me. 'Can't you just relax? Bloody Ben Walsh all the fucking time!' He pushed his fingers through his hair like he was trying to push something off his scalp.

I walked back to the dance floor, found a group of three shy girls I knew from biology class and together, we did the chicken dance.

The night was ruined.

Finally, nine-thirty came, and I was one of the first outside, brushing glitter from my arms.

Walshy was chatting to a farmer who'd parked alongside his ute; each leaned an elbow on the windowsill.

I carefully wobbled downstairs, one at a time, and then walked briskly in tight, short steps across the car park to Walshy's ute.

'Hey. Can we go?' I looked back where I'd been. Perry was nowhere to be seen.

Walshy gave the farmer a wave and turned to me. He put the ute into reverse and twisted around, arm along the back of the seats. 'Good night?'

'I guess. Nice decorations. God, I'm hungry.' I closed my eyes and rested my head back.

'You okay? Perry try anything?'

'Nah. I just want to go home.' The car accelerated, and the breeze on my face eased the tension from my bones.

We pulled up beside the Flower House. I was halfway out of my seat when I realised Walshy wasn't getting out.

'Aren't you coming?' I sagged back in. 'Oh right, you have to go back to work.'

'No. I've finished.'

'I thought you weren't seeing anyone at the moment. Can't I just have you for one fucking night?' I fought the urge to cry.

He raised his eyebrows and sucked a tooth. 'I saw him with his arms around you.'

'Huh?' I stared at the side of his face, the way his jaw muscle twitched.

'I can't believe you, Walshy! You're mean about my outfit, then you act like I get around because I have one date! But it's not me who gets around!'

The Flower House was silent and dark. Blossom was away. Some tall hydrangea blooms moved with the breeze. We listened to the *tick, tick* of the cooling engine.

'I'm going out,' said Walshy flatly. 'See ya tomorrow.'

I glared at him. Surprisingly, he didn't look angry, just defeated. I gave up and got out. 'Go then. I don't care.'

I stomped inside and listened to the Ford ute back out, and then I covered my face and made a real mess of my makeup.

Chapter 20

In Northam Library, microfilm loaded up, I find what I'm looking for.

'WOMAN FOUND DEAD IN AVON RIVER AFTER STORM'

'Bingo.' A prickle electrifies my skin.

'A woman's body has been found in the Avon River in Western Australia's Wheatbelt Region near Northam. The body has been identified as Dora Del Saur, 36 of Northam Caravan Park. She was last seen leaving the caravan she shared with her husband Edward Del Saur, about five pm on September 2ⁿᵈ. Mr. Del Saur reported her missing the next morning.

I read the next line twice. *'Mrs. Del Saur is survived by her husband, Edward Del Saur, and six-month-old baby, Joseph.'*

There *was* a baby. It belonged to the victim, Dora. This makes me feel jumpy. Blossom had made Lorrelai look like the baby's mother. In the sketches, she looks so natural with him. Yet she murdered the baby's mother.

The next is a short article which states that a nineteen-year-old woman from Northam has been taken in for questioning. This is followed by a longer article.

'NINETEEN-YEAR-OLD WOMAN ACCUSED OF MURDERING DORA DEL SAUR'

'Lorrelai McAllister 19, of Northam Caravan Park, stands accused of the murder of Dora Del Saur 36, whose body was found in the Avon River September 3ʳᵈ this year. The victim, also of Northam Caravan Park, was reported missing by her husband, Edward Del Saur after leaving the caravan where she lived, at five pm the previous day.

Miss McAllister is accused of strangling and then drowning the victim off the caravan park's bridge around midnight, September 2nd during a storm. Miss McAllister is a previous employee of the Del Saur family.'

A date is set for the hearing.

'WOMAN CHARGED WITH DROWNING MURDER'

'PERTH - The Crown would allege that Dora Margaret Del Saur drowned after being strangled and thrown into the Avon River during a storm at Northam Caravan Park, the Western Australian Supreme Court was told yesterday. The prosecutor, Mr. Liam Harper, QC, said the Crown would allege during the murder trial that Lorrelai Anne McAllister 19, followed the victim to the bridge on September 2nd with the intention of murdering the victim after her position as Del Saur family help was terminated and her relationship with Mr. Del Saur ended. The Crown prosecutor, Mr. Liam Harper, QC, said the case presented by the Crown would be based on eyewitness accounts and compelling circumstantial evidence.

Mr. Harper then detailed eyewitness accounts from four long-term Northam Caravan Park residents. The jury heard that Miss McAllister had been seen kissing Mr. Del Saur and had moved into the Del Saur's caravan with the victim. Miss McAllister had also assumed full time care of the victim's infant, Joseph, and the running of the Del Saur household.

Mr. Harper then presented a witness who heard an altercation between the accused, Miss McAllister and Mr. Del Saur shortly after he returned from hospital where he was supporting his wife, Dora. The victim Mrs. Del Saur had suffered ongoing health issues but was physically well the night she died.

Mr. Harper said on the night of the murder, Miss McAllister was seen leaving the caravan she shared with Pierre Dupont after the breakdown of relations with the Del Saur family, and then running towards the bridge where the victim was murdered. Miss McAllister previously denied leaving the caravan that night. An eyewitness confirms a scream was heard from the direction of the bridge about midnight.

Mr. Harper presented an autopsy report of the victim which proved she died by drowning and that there was also bruising around her neck consistent with strangulation. The bruising indicated an attacker with small hands, such as a woman. A map of the park was presented, indicating the short distance between Miss McAllister's place of residence, and the bridge where the victim was murdered, and the site where the victim's last known attire, a white night dress was discovered.

Mr. Harper also presented the victims' wedding rings which the accused was found wearing on her left hand the morning after the murder.

There's a few more details and then:

Miss Lorrelai Anne McAllister was then charged with having murdered Dora Margaret Del Saur at the Northam Caravan Park Bridge at Northam, Western Australia on September 2nd 1971. She replied in a small voice: "Not guilty, your honour."

The accused lived with a local postman in a riverside caravan after losing her job of three years at the Lion Inn, York. She was raised in the Saint Gertrude Orphanage. She was sentenced to twenty years for the murder of Dora Del Saur with a non-parole period of fifteen years.'

There's a sketch of a woman with eyes downcast, her hair scraped into a low ponytail. Dark smudges are visible beneath her eyes, and she's wearing a round-neck T-shirt that makes her look like an inmate.

I try to picture Lorrelai: nineteen, jobless, living in a caravan park. It's not a place you choose to live. You're either born in one or you're down and out. Then she had an affair with a married man. Maybe she already knew him. But there's a problem: the wife. Then there's a storm. The wife is eliminated.

A little gooseflesh prickles the backs of my arms.

A picture below the article shows a man with a child and a woman in a hospital bed. The woman has long black hair and stares blankly at the camera. The man has dark hair and a beard and is gazing at the child. It stops my breath for a second because it's him, the man from the sketches. If he was in his mid-thirties in the picture, he'd be seventy now.

They might have planned it, Lorrelai and Ned del Saur. The wife was in the way, after all.

My heart is drumming like crazy. Is that why Blossom did that second last sketch of the big man running after his wife? Where was Lorrelai then?

Perhaps Blossom witnessed something that wasn't in the reports. She just wasn't the sort of person to go to all that trouble to hide sketches if they were fantasy. But why leave them to me? She could have taken her concerns to authorities years ago. When she was alive. When something could be done about it.

Unless she was scared.

I glance around. Did someone else know about the sketches? Know what they'd lead the observer to believe? A sensation creeps over my skin, like somebody has whispered near me.

I look over my shoulder. Two female staff are putting books away and another is on the computer. A man wearing glasses is examining books with his head tilted back, the fluorescent lighting making his eyes two small pinpricks.

What if Blossom was right? What if someone else caused Dora's death? What if Ned Del Saur killed her?

On the computer beside me, so I don't lose the articles, I type in the name Ned Del Saur.

The first articles that come up are about the murder. I keep scrolling. Nathan Del Saur shows a professional profile and headshot. I type Joseph Del Saur. Then I try Jo Del Saur, and Edward Del Saur and Ned Del Saur. Then I type Jo and Ned.

There's a picture of a group of people on a football field. The children, mostly boys, wear solemn expressions and matching uniforms. Central in the picture is a dark-haired man holding a football in one hand and a framed photograph in the other.

'DWELLINGUP TIGERS TRIBUTE MATCH FOR JO AND NED'

'Jo Berry loved his weekend footy and his mates. When he developed a limp, he and his teammates joked about it. "We didn't think anything of it at first," said Jo's father, Ned. "The boys were always getting knocks during the game, and Jo was pretty stoic." After the limp worsened, doctors confirmed the worst. Joseph had bone cancer. "Jo fought this bloody disease for two years," said Ned, breaking down. "It was cruel, but he was brave, my boy." The Northam Tigers organised a tribute game in Jo's honour after he passed away earlier this year, aged just fourteen. The team wore a black band on their arms and held a sausage sizzle after the game. "All funds will go to bone cancer research," insisted the Tigers coach. Rest in Peace, Jo.'

'Hello?' An older woman with a friendly smile cuddles books to her chest like teddy bears. 'Sorry, love, the library is closing in five minutes,' she whispers.

'But it's not two o'clock yet.'

'Yes, dear, but it's Friday. Early close. Sorry. You'll have to come back on Monday.' Her name badge says Lynn Lee. Lisa Lee's mother. The breath catches in my throat. How must she feel after another sex attack like the one on Lisa?

She waits calmly, as if she knows what I'm thinking, her wavy grey hair in a neat ponytail. I wonder if she was once blonde like Lisa. A clock ticks.

'Do you want to print anything before you leave?'

I nod, reading quickly. 'Yes, this page please.' Then I look at the football one. It's a long shot, but not impossible. I indicate the second computer. 'And this one.'

Mrs. Lee presses buttons, and the photocopier whirrs. A page sails out and she hands it to me and then several more come out. I slide them all into my backpack. She touches a switch, and the screen goes blank.

'Thanks very much, Mrs. Lee. Sorry.'

She smiles, a kind, weary smile that makes me feel guilty. Her family must have been through hell. I should say something meaningful, but the enormity of it leaves me speechless.

* * *

Lisa didn't go to her school social dance. No one saw her for ages, and we weren't surprised. It was an uncomfortable thing we eventually got used to. Then, four years later, the attacker struck again, and another young woman's life changed forever. A doll was found at the scene. Chloe left town with her family. With her leaving, it seemed like some of that night left too.

Now, eight years after the original attack, the one that stopped us thinking we lived in a safe place, it had happened again. *Why has he come back? Why does he leave dolls?*

There's a bit of a wait for Mary to pick me up, so when I get back to York, I'll have just enough time for a quick shower before work.

Outside, I breathe in the wattle-scented air and glance across at the Northam Community Hall, remembering the night my dance was held there, the night things changed between Walshy and me forever.

* * *

Walshy woke me when he walked across the veranda. I had lain awake for a while, going over the events of the social dance and our argument and wondering where he'd gone and torturing myself about him being with another girl.

A *thump*. A few quick footsteps. A pause. *He's drunk*, I thought. I couldn't see the time, but I knew it was late. I heard him creak onto his bed.

I padded barefoot through the kitchen and out through the screen door to the veranda. There was just enough moon to see, that's all. I climbed on behind him, and he flinched. He was shirtless, just wearing jeans.

'You okay?'

'Sore ribs. Bit of an accident.'

I got up on my elbow. 'What? Car accident?'

'Yeah. Kangaroo jumped out. Can still drive the ute, but the front's busted up.'

'Shit. Are you badly hurt?'

'Nah. Sore chest. Hit the steering wheel.'

I sniffed. 'Are you drunk?'

'Few beers.' He turned over, sighed sadly. 'I'm sorry about before.'

I put my hand on his shoulder. 'Me too.' Something patted down on the bed between us, and I craned my neck and felt around until I found a sharp-cornered square packet. I held it up and squinted. Walshy snatched at my hand, pulling it away. Then I realised what it was, and my heart fell.

'You've got condoms?'

'One,' he said, sighing as he lifted his hips and shoved it back down into his pocket. 'It was your idea.'

I jack-knifed up and swung off the bed. 'Excuse me?'

'I got them because of your suggestion. You seem embarrassed that I'm not doing what everyone else is doing.'

I leant over him, poking the air with my finger. 'Don't you bloody blame me! You want to get drunk and screw around, take responsibility for it!'

'Jane!' Walshy grabbed my hand. 'I don't do that!' His green eyes looked dark and glassy, as if he wanted to cry. 'You must think I'm a shit person.'

I shook my head.

'So, what do you think of me, Jane? You can't even look at me, see? Why does it matter what I do? Girls round here want to go out with me. Stuffed if I know why.' He put one hand over his eyes and his voiced lowered. 'But I'm no good for anyone. That's why I keep moving.'

'You're good for me. I miss you when you go off all the time. Those girls don't even know you, but I do. I know how great you are.'

He looked up from beneath his hand. 'Do you think you know me?'

He bit his lip and shook his head. 'I don't know me, Jane. I don't know if I'm a good person.'

'You are. You always have been. It's your dad who's the bastard. You're nothing like him.'

'So why did Mum leave me with him?'

I swallowed hard, realising Walshy had carried that question with him everywhere. 'Maybe she was forced to because she was scared of him.'

'He's angry because it was me that made her leave. She had that depression thing after I was born.'

I got onto my knees beside him. 'No way, Walshy. No way! A three-year-old is basically a baby. No baby can make a man be the bastard your father is. Did he say it was your fault? You can't believe that. What an absolute shithead!'

I put my head on his chest, felt how fast he was breathing.

'Then why did she leave me?'

I looked up. 'She left *him*, Walshy. No one could live with that man. He doesn't even have friends. Workers can't even stay out there on the farm. Only you stay.'

He stared up at the sky, his face soft, a small frown wrinkling his forehead. 'I'm glad we met, Jane,' he murmured.

'Me too.' I shuffled forwards to kiss his prickly cheek.

Walshy smiled gently and pushed my hair back off my face. 'I've wanted to ask you out, but I know you deserve better. I can't stand the thought of you going out with anyone else. I'm sorry. I must seem really crazy.'

My heart thuds right through my torso. 'You do? I thought you didn't like me like that. I … I only want to be with you.'

'You don't think I'm a Tom Cat?'

'Not a bad one. I'm only jealous because it's not me.'

We kiss then, and it's a relief, like someone's switched off the pain tap that's been running for a year. The kiss changes, deepening into this lovely, longing thing that melds us closer and closer.

I don't remember the exact point it changed, grew more serious. I was drinking in the smell of him, running my hands up and down his back. He was beautiful, muscular. We began touching, exploring, peeling off clothes, feeling each other's skin. Gradually, he rolled over, so I was underneath him. A pressure started and I tensed.

'Go soft,' Walshy said gently. 'Shh.' He kissed the side of my neck. I started to release my muscles, fibre by fibre. The rose perfume was delicate in the night, the scent of waxes spicy as Walshy and I made love.

Next morning, when I woke, Walshy slept beside me. I touched his hair lightly, and he sighed in his sleep.

I thought about Shelley while I waited for him to wake up. I hoped she was okay.

* * *

When he woke, Walshy ran to the deli for milk and heard the news. Another girl had been raped in Northam. Fifteen-year-old Chloe, a local, grabbed on her way home from cheerleading at the football. At the scene, another doll had been left.

That weekend was surreal. I was floating on a tide of sleep deprivation, love, disbelief, and horror. A hush fell over the town, and we all thought of Lisa without saying her name. Everyone who'd been at the game where Chloe had been, was questioned.

Even Walshy was questioned, but he'd filled his ute with fuel at The Lakes service station where he met up with a mate, so they had him on CCTV.

Months later, there wasn't a single suspect.

Chapter 21

I start my shift at the inn about an hour after my return from the library. It's suddenly busy. A cricket team, still in grass-stained whites, falls through the bar door, chuckling and backslapping. Behind them, Shelley Turner walks in. I measure my next breath and attempt to behave normally by folding serviettes, but my hands have become flippers, my arms, jelly.

Around me, the inn has a life of its own, a drone of voices, laughter, clinking of glasses and cutlery. The jukebox competes with the spurted mocking jingles of poker machines.

'Hel-lo.' She comes right over.

'Shelley, hi.' My heart goes *whump*.

Shelley looks like her mother: blonde hair in a dignified bob and her clothes soft and expensive-looking. Minimal makeup in soft pink tones accentuates her fairness. I remember what Perry said about *The Lady and the Tramp*. I imagine Walshy loping through the door with his swag on his back, his battered hat and dirty clothes and dust in his stubble.

They don't match. They never have. I'm his sidekick. His Jane. His partner in crime. *So why is he with her?*

Shelley walks right up to me, arms outheld. We hug. She's cool and smells of perfume. 'Lola! I heard you were coming back! I'm sorry about Blossom.' There's a posh lilt to her voice.

I'm glad she didn't say Walshy told her I was coming back, like they were a couple and I'm the third wheel. We stand back and look at each other. It's hard to meet her eyes.

'Thanks. You look well.' I get stuck right away.

'Are you okay? About Blossom? Everything?'

'Yeah, I'm fine.'

She clucks her tongue and shakes her head. 'Shame. I was so shocked when I heard. You must be sad.' She tightens her lips, and then smiles. She's still so pretty. 'But it is great you're back. Are you staying? We must catch up. You're working?' She looks around.

'Yes. Working, I mean. Not sure how long I'll be here.' I get a nasty tug of guilt. Shelley is genuinely sweet. Persistently innocent, as though she's incapable of being tarnished, no matter what. 'But I have time for a quick chat. How are you?'

A pretty crinkle happens between her eyebrows. 'Oh, you know I'm seeing Walshy. Which is great. I mean, he's a lovely guy.'

I swallow and nod. 'I heard. Have you seen him today?'

'Farmer out Railway Road said he saw Walshy packing up his campsite, so I guess we'll see him soon.' She sighs and looks around. 'Probably yabbying again.' She looks at me, her head tilted. 'You know, on your birthday, he insisted on going yabbying, said he had to. It was pouring with rain!'

My cheeks warm and a light switches on inside me. I get a shock that Walshy's been camping so close these last few days. Whenever he left for these trips, I knew he was somewhere out in there the dark, but I didn't usually know where until he'd returned.

On my birthday he'd remembered me. He kept our tradition.

'He went to the airport to collect you, and then he didn't make it for dinner the night after. I knew he'd be camping.' Shelley shrugged. 'He can't handle anything too emotional.'

'So, how long have you two been going out?'

Shelley frowns. I thought she'd be all gush and giggle, but her face is serious. 'Three weeks, but it's been a bit of a disaster. I mean we get along well,' she says quickly. She fidgets with her hands and chews her bottom lip.

She is waiting for me to say something. Me. I'm lost for words for a moment, then I incline my head towards the back door. 'Do you want to go outside?'

She nods and follows me out. The sun is low, sending a deep yellow glow over the trees. Overhead, there's the noisy scrabble of roosting galahs, wattlebirds and cockatoos.

Shelley takes a deep breath and levels her gaze with mine. I feel like she knows everything. My face warms.

'I need to ask you something.'

'Yes?'

She sucks her lower lip. 'This is embarrassing.' Shelley closes her eyes and inhales. 'Did you tell Walshy ... anything about me?'

'I kept my promise, Shelley.' I wonder if my previous loyalty will make up for what happened with Walshy when I arrived. It was forgivable, wasn't it? Because I didn't know.

Shelley exhales slowly. 'Thanks. But this is not about what I asked you to promise. It happened before that, after the Christmas Concert we did together.'

Her meaning hits me, and I blush harder.

Shelley looks around before she speaks in a low tone. 'I know you came back to the hall when everyone had left. I saw the silhouette of someone walking out. Your hair gave you away.'

'Oh.'

'You saw us, didn't you? Me and Ralph.'

I nod.

She exhales. 'Did you tell Walshy?'

'No. I told no one.'

Shelley sinks a little, the relief clearly loosening her muscles. 'That's good.'

'Are you going to tell him?'

Shelley's eyes widen, and she shakes her head rapidly. 'No. No. I never want to think about it.' She gives her body a hug.

'I saw Marilyn here yesterday.' I see the flicker in her gaze, but I want to hear her explain how she was with Ralph Higgins, Walshy's uncle, when she was fifteen. How could she find him attractive? He was a teacher. It would be like kissing your father.

'I know. Still has friends here, unfortunately. But she and Ralph don't live here anymore. He works for his father down south.'

I reach for the honeysuckle and pinch off a flower. 'So, why has it been a disaster, you and Walshy?'

She drops her head back, as if to examine the sky. 'Timing. Just bad timing.' She lifts her head back up to look at me. 'I mean, our first date, in Northam three weeks ago, was ruined. Then Blossom died.' She crosses her arms, shakes her head disbelievingly. She still wears bangles on her wrists, wide resin bangles that don't move or jangle.

'What ruined the first date?'

'I got called to the hospital.' She sees my confusion. 'The serial rapist who leaves the doll. It was that night. My best friend, Allie.'

* * *

My heart is still pounding when I almost run into Freda in the kitchen doorway. She backs into the room as I enter, a cheerful look on her face.

'You alright, Lola?' She looks past me. 'Oh. You've been talking to Shelley.'

I nod, but my throat is dry. 'Yeah.' I hold out my hand to check if it's shaking. It's still, but that's not how it feels.

'What's wrong?'

'I didn't know that girl who was attacked was Shelley's friend.'

Freda takes a big breath. 'Yes, terrible. Older than the other girls, too.'

'What happened?'

'Allie's a vet nurse in Northam. Another vet nurse dropped her near home, and she was walking to her house.' Freda clicked her tongue.

Something gnaws at me, like a mosquito. 'Do the police think the attacks are connected?'

'Oh, I'm sure they've tried every which way to get to the bottom of this. I heard a detective from the city is getting involved now that there's been three.'

'I don't remember an 'Allie' from school.'

'She didn't go here. She came from over Geraldton way. Shelley met her at a dance competition.'

'Oh yeah. I remember. Shelley sprained her ankle, hobbled around for her eighteenth birthday.'

It had been a big deal at the time, a huge party at the hall, with entertainers and everything. I remembered Shelley's face, her forced smile, the sadness underneath.

'Hmm,' said Freda. 'Some people thought it was bad taste, the party. Straight after Chloe.'

I squinted, remembering the tight, uncomfortable atmosphere, how many of the girls' fathers had stayed outside the hall where the party had been held to ensure the girls all made it home safe. I was younger than the other girls but scored an invite because I was friends with Shelley.

'Is Shelley all right?'

'Ah, yeah. Weird how Shelley keeps coming up.'

'What do you mean?'

The phone rings in the dining room, and Freda's attention flickers. I hear Mary answer it.

'Lola? Phone!' calls Mary. I back into the dining room and reach for the handset. 'Real Estate guy,' Mary hisses. She puts her hands on her hips and stays close, as if ready to back me up in a fight.

'Yes? This is Lola.'

'Oh, hi, thanks. Sorry for interrupting you at work. I just wanted to get back to you on that bribe.' He chuckles.

I frown and tap my foot. 'Yes?'

A few people walk into the dining room and start pulling out chairs to sit on.

'Ah, yes, well I mentioned to the owner that you wanted to stay in the house, rent, or put in an offer. I have some good news!'

I cup the phone to my ear and glare at a woman who's laughing too loudly.

'Yes, what did he say?'

'Oh, he's happy to meet with you. He was shocked that someone else, a dependent of Miss Brenton, was still living there. Anyway, I have his number here for you to get in touch.'

'Hang on, I'll grab —'

Mary immediately hands me a writing pad and pen.

'Go ahead.' I write down the phone number as he speaks and read it back. Then he continues. 'His name's Ned Berry. Owns Berry's Produce.'

I stare at the pen in my hand and the name I've half written. Ned B —

The newspaper article. Jo Berry. Ned Berry.

'Lola? Hello? Did you get that?'

I swallow. 'Yes.' My voice has a weird, thin quality. 'I got that.'

He hangs up.

Mary takes the phone off me and returns it to the wall. 'Okay, Lola?'

I stare at her a moment. 'Not sure. What do you know about Ned Berry? Berry's Produce?'

'Just that. The company delivers fresh fruit and vegetables.' She shakes her head in question.

I bite my lip. I feel like I've drunk ten coffees. 'He owns the Flower House.'

Mary shrugs. 'Blossom worked in the market gardens. Might be how they met.'

My mind spins. Ned Berry let Blossom stay in his house free of rent. Blossom drew a picture implicating Ned Del Saur in the murder of his wife. Ned Del Saur had a son called Joseph. Jo and Ned Berry. Could Ned Del Saur have changed his name following the murder of his wife?

Mary makes a face. 'Sorry to hurry you, but we got a crowd out there.'

I draw in a quick breath and try to focus. Grabbing my apron, I tie it behind my waist. 'Yep. Got it.'

Chapter 22

Walshy and I didn't last long. A few weeks after we became lovers, he went quiet, his gaze shifted away. He frowned more. He came home less. He went out for beers more and more, leaving me home alone, worried. One night, he didn't come home.

Next day, about mid-morning, I heard his ute. I ran outside. Walshy climbed slowly from the driver's side.

I waited on the back veranda while he rounded the front of the vehicle.

'Oh my God.' I held my hand over my mouth. He was covered in mud and blood. Cuts stippled his face, and his shirt was torn. He looked worse than I'd ever seen him, even after a fight with his dad.

I stepped towards him, but Walshy lurched back and held up a hand to stop me.

'What happened?'

'A fight,' he said. 'Dad.'

'At the pub?'

Walshy inched past me towards the back door. 'I need to shower. Don't touch me.'

'Are you alright?' I reached for his elbow. He flinched away.

'Don't touch me.'

I swallowed hard and stayed where I was. 'I'll put the kettle on.'

The bathroom door stayed closed a long time. I could hear the water running. His tea was half cold by the time he walked slowly out.

Without the mud, his face was pale and he had a split in his lip and a purple bruise shadowing his jaw.

Hands clasped tightly, I waited at the table. Walshy winced as he sat, one leg sticking out stiffly. He crossed his arms and glanced up briefly, then he frowned at his extended leg instead of making eye contact.

'It started at the pub. Him calling me the usual—waste of time, bag of shit, good-for-nothing. I'd had a gutful. Gave him a good slug to the jaw. Thought that'd be it.' He scoffed. 'Shoulda known better. Kinda knocked the wind out of each other in front of everyone. I could heard them, the blokes around us, saying chip off the old block, like father like son.' He ran a hand down his face. 'I knew it was true.'

'No, it's not, Walshy.' I reached over, but he moved his hand out of reach.

'We took it outside, down the street, all the way to the river where he'd parked. Maybe he'd planned it. I don't know. By then, no one was left but us. Then he went and got his gun from the ute. I couldn't fucken believe it. He really wanted me dead. Absolutely hates me.' He swallowed, and a second passed. 'I wrestled it off him. Threw it in the river. He finally left. Said I wasn't worth the piss on his boots. I stayed down by the water with a bottle of rum. Slept in the mud and duck shit.'

'He's mad and dangerous, Walshy. Get a restraining order against him.'

'I'm a Walsh,' he said. 'Nothing you can do about it.'

'We can get past this. We can move away if you like.'

His eyes lifted to mine. 'This has got to stop.' He indicated from me to him.

'You and me? What happened doesn't change anything. We're great.'

He shook his head. 'It's over. It should never have begun.'

'Don't say that.' My voice went high. 'I've always loved you. We've always had something special. I've never wanted anyone but you.'

'Course not. I was kind to you. I fed you. You hardly had a choice.'

'I'm not a fucking stray!'

Walshy shrugged and looked out the window. 'I know. You've got guts, Lola. You're going to be the one of us who works, who can hold a family together, do the normal stuff.'

He never used my real name, and it chilled me. 'I just want to be with you.'

He didn't move, just his lips. 'I can't do it. I'm broken, Lola. I was probably born this way.' He sighed. 'I'll stay till you're eighteen, then I'm going to go work on the stations up north.'

'You're talking shit.' I got up and went to him. He held up one hand and gently pushed me back.

'I should never have started anything with you.' He left his hand on my belly. 'You're the only one I care about losing, and believe me, if we stay together, we'll break up. It's how I am.'

Words jammed up my throat.

His hand dropped away, and I covered my face with my hands. Sobs worked their way from my body up into my throat.

Walshy did not hold me. He didn't even touch me. I felt more alone than I had when Coral died. After a few minutes, I sat down on the floor with my back against the fridge.

I stayed there and cried. Walshy limped out onto the veranda and stared at the garden.

When I finally got up, still wiping my face and nose on my shirt, the world wasn't the same. It was cold and empty. Colourless.

I had to move, do something familiar, something normal and comforting. I put things out on the kitchen bench. *Flour, sugar, butter, eggs.* I listed ingredients in my head, so I had something to focus on. Otherwise, everything spun round and round.

Flour, sugar, butter, eggs. I began to mix things together.

After a while, Walshy came inside. He still looked pale and strange. He said nothing, just stared at me and the ingredients.

'Don't look at me like that.'

He went back outside and stared at the garden.

I made dough, cooked other recipes from the CWA Cookbook while it rose, punched it down harder than was necessary, and plopped it in the loaf pan. I turned on the oven. Then I showered for a long time, made the bed, put washing on and fed the chooks.

Things I'd suppressed for a long time flashed before me like film clips, all gritty, sweaty, real. I saw Coral's bare feet, and then the same feet with heeled sandals on, walking out the door to the car. I saw Heartbreak's car drive away, saw Walshy's ute and saw how similar they looked.

I pounded pastry and mixed sultanas into stiff dough. I chopped apples to make the thoughts go away, to stop the pain.

I had eaten some lunch and was in the kitchen when Walshy dumped his bag on the veranda. The screen door screeched. He gave a shake. He peered about like he was a stranger in our kitchen. After a time, he slumped down on a chair. 'I was going to camp out. But I might stay. What do you think?'

'I have to cook.' I paused a moment. 'Stay.'

It was a small comfort, Walshy being around. Eating toast. Making coffee. I cried on and off as Walshy went in and out, slowly moving around my determined industry, pale and quiet like I was a burning planet, him the moon.

It went on all day. I baked until we needed more flour, eggs and milk. Walshy went out and got some so I could keep going. Around eight o'clock, I was done. The pain, the real sting, was gone. I was exhausted.

'I'm going to bed,' I said.

Walshy looked up from where he sat just outside the back door on the patio. 'Okay.' He got up slowly.

I felt him standing there, the other side of the flyscreen. 'It's okay. I'm okay now.'

'Yeah?' He came in cautiously, holding the door so it didn't bang. He slid his hands into his back pockets. He looked at everything on the kitchen bench. 'What are you going to do with all that?'

It was like ten cooks had visited and attempted to bake everything in the CWA Cookery Book. Scones, loaves, cakes, slice, biscuits and pies, and an apple pie with the lattice top still steaming.

'Church,' I said. 'It's Sunday tomorrow.'

Chapter 23

My eighteenth birthday was the day before I left for Melbourne.

We'd had a small party that night at the inn, Walshy and I, my usual hairdresser, two girls from the bakery, and Freda. Walshy was quiet, made it through dinner, and then said he was going home. He'd given me a look before he left. The plan had been to go wild on Con and Mary's free drinks. But I couldn't shake that look. He wanted to be alone with me.

I lasted half an hour out with the gang before I had to go home. The others moaned, but they were tipsy enough to forgive without question.

When I got to the house, he was sitting on the edge of the veranda, legs dangling over the edge. The end of his cigarette glowed in the dark. His exhaled smoke drifted, swirling Milky Ways in the dark. He didn't smoke much, just a couple with a beer on Friday nights. When he went camping alone, he didn't take anything but water, a swag and something to trap game with. It was like a detox. He always came back clean and calm.

He held out his hand. I sat beside him, keeping my hand in his, and he held it against his leg.

'You okay?' I asked. He squeezed my hand and nodded. We looked at the garden and up at the stars.

'I'm going up north,' he said. His face looked lovely in the evening light, tanned skin, a light stubble that made him look like Tom Cruise.

'When?' I asked.

'Soon.' He turned, face half lost in the dark.

I swallowed hard. A black bubble of panic started to rise beneath my diaphragm. 'What do you expect me to do?'

'Be the one of us that works.'

'We're okay, aren't we?'

'I don't know. We're different now. We're stuck. We need to move on.'

'I don't want to move on.'

He turned to face me. 'But we need to. There's a big world out there. I'm going to find a place so big I can't even see the edges. Work hard. Make something of myself.'

'Will I see you again?' Tears were dribbling down my face. His hand came up slowly and he wiped a tear with his thumb.

'Yeah. Yeah.'

'You don't sound sure.'

'I love you, Jane. I always will. But I need to know who I am. Then maybe I'll know how to love you.'

* * *

In the morning, there was a note on my side table, and Walshy's swag was gone.

'*I'm sorry.*'

I didn't cry when I booked the Qantas flight to Melbourne that day. I knew I had to get away as quickly as possible.

Blossom had been at the Women's Retreat, so I'd left a note. I called her once I had a new number, told her the PO box I'd set up for mail.

The house-sitting idea came from a lady who sat beside me on the bus en route to Perth airport. While I waited for my flight, I registered with a housesitting agency.

My first job was in a beautiful two-storey house with a pool and a white poodle. It felt like I was in a resort. The café job and TAFE course came shortly after. For a while, I felt like I'd found a solution to the pain and confusion. But I was in a holding pattern.

Walshy, York, and what had happened, were like sounds on the other side of a wall. As one year became two, the noise grew louder, more insistent.

Then Blossom died.

Chapter 24

In my break, I pace and wring my hands. Energy rushes through my body like the rapids that dot the twisting lengths of the river after rain.

I walk outside near the honeysuckle that has hidden Lorrelai's door for years. I need time to think. I lean back onto the wall, and the stored sun eases into my back and reminds me to breathe. I look sideways at the locked door—the former home of a woman accused of murder at nineteen—a door closed until recently. It reminds me how long the sketchbook has stayed hidden before I unlocked it, before Blossom tried to tell me something.

Ned and Jo Del Saur.

Ned and Jo Berry. Ned Berry, the owner of the house Blossom and I lived in.

Blossom appeared to care about next to nothing. But she cared about Lorrelai. And she cared enough about a child like me that she went to a state care facility and gave me a life and a house—a house owned by someone who could be linked to the murder of Dora Del Saur. Linked to Lorrelai. A woman Blossom was fascinated by, and probably friends with. A woman she wanted me to know about.

When did Lorrelai get out of jail? How much time elapsed before she died?

I feel a bit sick and swallow acid down into my stomach. I take a deep, deep breath.

My ears catch the sound of footsteps on the footpath. It's a normal sound, innocent, but nothing is innocent. People lie. Someone attacks girls in the dark.

I remember how I felt when the first rape happened. The shock shared by the community. When bad things happened we all drew closer to one another. A bushfire. The death of a local in a car accident. Even now, Blossom's death was bonding us. People were providing for her funeral. She had been one of them, one of us. Our community, my home.

Still, I feel like we're missing something, something that could prevent another attack or even catch the rapist. Surely, if there's so long between attacks, something triggers him to do it.

I mentally list them.

School social – Lisa, 1998. Football game – Chloe, 2002. Vet nurse – Allie, 2006. What else happened around that time?

My break over, I return to the kitchen and keep running meals out to diners. When some finally begin to leave, my mind wanders back to the owner of the Flower House.

If Ned Berry really is Ned Del Saur, and he owns the Flower House, I need to know. According to Blossom, he could have been pivotal in his wife's murder, but Lorrelai got the blame. Blossom had insisted to Mary that Lorrelai was innocent.

I rush through the clean-up and call goodnight to Freda.

'Lola?' Mary walks in, making me jump. She's holding out something familiar. 'You left it in my car,' she says, dangling my backpack.

'Thanks!' I take it and sling it over my shoulder. At home I can compare the pictures in the articles with the sketchbook.

'Gotta go. I think Walshy's getting back soon.' I rush out, desperate to exit before someone else wants something.

Out near the road I walk along beside my bike, steady it, and then push off. Gravel covers the verge like ball bearings. I wobble along the shoulder on the bitumen. A moment's inattention could skin my knees and elbows. Every muscle fibre twitches, like I'm plugged into an electrical socket. It weakens my legs, runs down my back, chest, and arms, making my hands shake.

I could be living in a murderer's house.

Pedalling along the edge of the road, the night is black as pitch. *Where is the moon?* There are no streetlights after the primary school.

The gravel beneath the tyres crunch like pearls. *Be careful. Be careful.*

I look up and see the smoke and diamonds of the Milky Way.

I lean the bike against the side of the house and walk up to the back door. The house is still and silent, but the door handle is hanging broken, and the door has a dent in it.

I halt. 'Walshy?' Slowly I go inside and slide the roasting fork from the box of utensils. I hold it front of me, tines glinting in the moonlight. Carefully, I walk through every room, turning on lights. At first, it seems like everything is in place. But in Blossom's room, I find it looks disturbed. The cupboard doors are open, and her belongings have been rifled through. I certainly did not leave it like this. It makes me feel sick.

In my room, my sunglasses and wallet are still on the side table. It's only when I return to the kitchen that I notice the table is bare. The sketchbook had been right there in the middle, probably still open.

My heart is pounding, and there's a void where the pictures had been. I close and lock the back door, the solid one that we rarely use unless it's really cold. I lean against it, trying to think clearly.

Someone has taken the sketchbook. That means there is something inside it that is real, precious, even dangerous.

I shuck off my backpack and stare at it like it's alive. All my photocopies are inside. I can still compare the pictures.

My hands shake as I squat down on the floor and open the bag. I lay the pages side by side on the floor. I look first at the one of the threesome featuring Ned and his family from the court case, and then the football one. I grab a pencil and draw a beard on clean-shaven Ned Berry. Then I focus on the eyes. I compare the two. A shiver ripples down my back. It's not just the eyes, but the gaze, face shape and nose: Ned Del Saur and Ned Berry are identical.

* * *

Quickly, I unlock the door and rush outside. *The man who might have killed his wife owns the house. He knows I'm here. Blossom's sketchbook, implicating him, has been stolen!*

Perry's light is on. I grab my bike and pedal across the road, jump off, dump the bike against his fence and open the gate, peering around it. The garden is a shock: thick, green, full of ferns, natives, palms and roses.

'Perry?' Light shines around the door of a little shed at the back of the yard. I head in that direction, knock and listen. 'Perry?' I try the handle. It opens. Shielding my face against the glare of the fluorescent bulb, I let my eyes adjust. When they do, I see string hanging around the wall with things attached by pegs. Knickers, panties, G-strings. Women's underwear? Then I see something familiar: my Donald Duck knickers. My stomach drops like a rock.

'Who's there?' Perry's voice calls from outside.

I run out, half-blind from the bright light, turn, and race for the gate. He stands backlit by the porch light, arms a little out from his sides like a wrestler.

'Lola? Oh, fuck. Lola, wait!' He lurches towards me.

I make it to my bike; shoes slipping in the gravel, I swing my leg over.

'Lola! Lola!' Running footsteps.

Panicking, I pedal blindly. My wheels slide sideways on gravel, and then the world is upside down. I'm weightless … until the split second my face collides with the ground. There are brief fireworks, pain and then blackness.

Fabric brushes my cheek. My eyes won't open. Blood floods my mouth and nose. I'm lying on my back. Pain and throbbing in my face and leg. My thoughts swim.

I'm younger, much younger. It's a car, a sedan like many of the others in the full carpark, sun shining off the paintwork. In the back seat, something nests among boxes and costumes, layers of tulle. Its face is frozen. Cheerful. A dead face, unseeing eyes, a painted-on smile. A mannequin? No, smaller.

A doll.

PART TWO

Chapter 25

Lorrelai bowed deep, straightened, flicked her red hair, kissed her gloved fingertips and blew them to the crowd. Jazz music gave way to Aretha Franklin's 'I Wish I Didn't Love You So', her smooth voice crooning out from two dusty speakers on either side of the stage.

Claps and whistles surged from the fifty or so farmers, veterans, and John Lennon lookalikes and bounced off the old sandstone walls, shaking the framed black-and-white photographs of York's colonial harvesting history. Feet tapped and stamped, the rhythm rising up from dark jarrah floorboards scored like braille from decades of boots and heels.

'Thank you, my darlings!' She waved and skipped around before slipping through the gap between the burgundy curtains.

In the dark, Lorrelai removed her gloves, her pale, slender arms sprouting like tulip stems. She wiped a drop of sweat from her nose tip and strode down the side of the room towards the kitchen, grabbing her wrap from a hook on the wall as she passed. She pulled the edge of her panties down to cover her bottom and slung the wrap around her body as her spike heels clicked along the wooden floor.

'Whoa!' The barman's wide body and the box he held blocked her entrance to the kitchen.

'Move aside, Dez! I don't have time for this.'

His lips formed a pout. 'Oh, Lovely Lorrelai, *my sweetheart*,' he sang.

'Hush. I'll be waiting tables in five minutes and I'm starving. Get out with you!'

'Just checkin' out the fine filly!' He clicked his tongue, his gaze running down her legs before he stepped aside. 'Come grab some beer nuts. Pierre stuffed up the deliveries, so we got Northam's batch. Silly old blighter.'

In the sweating kitchen, with its central metal bench surrounded by food, food, food and one dumpling of a cook, Lorrelai snatched a spring roll from a huge pile and jammed it into her mouth.

'Hey!' said Chella, the dumpling. 'Get dressed and come help. Big crowd tonight!'

Lorrelai grinned. 'Because of me. Hmm,' she murmured, her mouth full of spring roll. 'Almost as good as mine.'

Chella rolled her eyes, her face pink and sweaty. 'Had to do it all meself with you wagging your pretty tail around!'

Lorrelai laughed. She grabbed another spring roll. 'Give me a sec. I'll be right with you!'

Outside, cold air kissed her tacky skin and coaxed steam from her décolletage, neck and face. The kitchen and bar lights spread a glow on the untended grass and concrete path between. A wooden sign with faded paint reading 'Toilets' was nailed to a wonky post.

'Ah, the come down,' Lorrelai lamented, tightening her wrap. 'Lovely Lorrelai one second, dogsbody the next.' She hummed as she tottered down the narrow path between the inn and the laundry and cider rooms, a combination of sandstone and concrete that made up the unseen side of the grand Lion Inn 1943.

Aretha still played inside her head. She'd chosen it specially, but chances were Harry was too busy to notice. Maybe, after all this, she'd go see whether her homegrown talents had a place in a dance troupe in the city. She and Harry could find a nice place in Perth, by the ocean at Scarborough or Cottesloe. White picket fence. Tidy kitchen with lace curtains and colourful wallpaper.

In the laundry, Lorrelai checked over her shoulder. She touched her belly down low and bit her lower lip. Lipstick, waxy and artificial. She tasted and smelled everything these past few weeks. Rather than feel sick or fat, as she'd heard pregnant ladies complain, she was aware of her skin, her heartbeat, her warm heavy breasts, her hair falling over her bare shoulders. Beneath the yellow stage light, jazz blaring like a horn, she was sensual, ethereal, in love.

Lorrelai washed and dried her face and examined her blue eyes and rouged cheeks in the cracked mirror above the trough. Her red hair was out, curling almost in spirals, and dark where it was wet against her temples. She moved one way, and then the other, shimmied slightly and laughed. Then she hugged herself against York's autumn chill.

Lifting her arms, she gathered her hair and twisted it into a bun high on her head, securing it with four pins from off the sink. She eased a tendril out from each side, turned to the side and examined her flat belly and cream thighs beneath elasticated straps. It was three months since her last period. When would she start to show?

Bootsteps sounded on concrete. Lorrelai held the wrap tight at her throat. 'Who is it?'

'It's me.' That deep, dark, silky voice.

Lorrelai looked sideways, smiled slow. Harry. He looked good and he knew it. Black shirt and pants, eyes and hair dark like the night. She wound a tendril of her hair around her finger.

'Hey, baby.'

'Hey.'

Lorrelai shook her head when he held out his hand. 'I haven't showered, handsome.' She shivered a bit in the cold. Harry's eyes went downwards.

'I always liked you dirty.'

Lorrelai giggled. 'Harry! Did you see the crowd? Was it a record?'

Harry nodded, grinned, crossed his arms and leaned back against the doorframe. 'You look sexy.' His gaze rolled over her, his eyes flickering as if jagged on a thought.

From the open back door to the bar came The Rolling Stones—'(I Can't Get No) Satisfaction.'

'Yeah. I feel great. Better than usual.' She smiled, one shoulder lifted coyly to her cheek in that way he liked.

Harry cleared his throat and pulled up his chest. 'Hey, we gotta talk.'

Lorrelai shimmied over and took one edge of his collar in each hand. She pulled herself into his body warmth. 'Sure, baby. Why don't you take me to the flicks? *Dirty Harry* is showing in the city.' She giggled, leaning her cheek against his chest.

'No, it's about work.'

Lorrelai was aware that Harry's warm hands had stayed by his sides. 'Oh, work!' She smoothed his collar and kissed the edge of his jaw, leaving a pink lip stamp that she smudged away with her thumb. 'What you got in mind?'

Harry put his hands on her waist and gently pushed her back a step. 'Don't do that. I can't think.'

Lorrelai stepped back, felt the change. 'What?' She wrapped her arms around herself and jigged on the spot, her legs covered in gooseflesh.

Harry frowned, looked at the ground, and cleared his throat. 'The thing is …' His eyes flickered up and darted away. 'You'll have to leave.'

'Huh? I gotta go help with the meals. Must be fifty, sixty people in there.' She jerked her shoulder and sniffed.

'No, I mean leave here. We can't have you walking around here *pregnant*.' He shuffled his feet, stretched his neck, loosened his collar like it choked.

'I wasn't planning to leave.' Lorrelai got tight in the throat. 'I can stop dancing when I start to show, work behind the bar again. You need good barmaids.' She couldn't stop her teeth chattering.

'Not pregnant ones. You can come back after, though. If you don't get too mouthy with it.'

Lorrelai's throat got cluttered up, and she took a shaky breath before she spoke. '*Jesus*! I'm only *just* pregnant. Hardly had time to think. Didn't plan on giving it up.' She brushed her nose with the back of one hand, and then rubbed her palms together. 'God, Harry. You sure know how to send a girl into a spin.' She crossed her arms, hugging herself against the cold. 'Well, where will you put me? Will I move into the big house with you? What about Victoria?'

'Lorri …' said Harry.

'Yes?' She managed between clicking teeth.

Harry shook his head slightly. 'Don't be silly. You didn't think I was going to take you in?' He glanced over his shoulder. When he turned back, his black eyes were resolute. 'Victoria and I … we don't always agree, but we can't have a dancer, a pregnant one at that, living under our roof. We're known. We're businesspeople. We go to church, host weddings.' He threw his hands up and then slapped them down against his legs.

Lorrelai pointed a shaking finger at him. 'You said you loved me.'

'Course I love you, doll. But wives don't just disappear. I'm a married man.'

Lorrelai pulled close and clasped her arms around Harry's waist. 'I understand. It'll take time. We can tell Victoria together. Just don't rush it. We'll move away later.'

Harry unclasped her arms and gave them back. He tilted his head, both serious and sad at the same time. 'Babe, it's over. You gotta go. I'm sorry.'

'Over? What? You and me?' She clutched her hands against her chest, the fingertips going numb.

He nodded.

'Straight after I told you I was expecting? Go? Go where? I've been here three years! Orphanage hardly going to take me back. There is nowhere else!'

'Just away. Away from here.'

'How could you? It's yours, Harry!'

Harry lifted a shoulder. 'Who knows?' he said.

'You *know* it's yours!' Lorrelai's voice broke. 'Haven't seen anyone since that church boy ages ago. He was my first, you know that, and now you—only you!' Her voice wavered. Electricity coursed through her body, and it felt dangerous. 'I love you, Harry! You know I do. You said you loved me more than her!' Tears trickled down her face.

'Shhhhh.' Harry grabbed her arms and walked her backwards, behind the laundry to the grassed rubbish area. Near a blackened lump of a hundred burned things, he pulled her into his chest. Lorrelai trembled against him, tears burning her eyelids. 'C'mon. You knew how it was.'

'*No*,' Lorri whimpered.

Harry waited until her crying slowed. Above them, gum tree leaves swished, caught by the night breeze. An owl hooted not far off, interrupted by the tired drone of a late-night truck passing on the road.

'Lorri,' Harry said quietly. 'I made some enquiries.'

Lorrelai pulled back, wiping her face with both hands. She felt the softness return to him. 'Yes?'

Harry frowned and stared at the stone block that housed the men's toilets. 'Job going with Pierre. You know, the postman? He lives in Northam, near the river. His wife died. He's getting real old, needs a hand. He has a bed spare in his caravan, at the park there.'

Lorrelai blinked several times in pure shock. 'A *caravan* park?'

Harry shrugged. 'It's an opportunity.'

Lorrelai breathed slow and deep. Being this upset couldn't be good for the baby. She had to stay calm, under control. After a moment, she hissed through her teeth. 'You'd have me stay in a caravan with an old man? A single man? Harry, look at me!'

Harry frowned and worked his jaw. 'Lorri, there ain't a lot of options for a girl like you.'

'A girl like me?' She pushed Harry in the chest. But he didn't budge. 'I work harder than anyone here! The kitchen, dining room, bar, out back checking cider, then dancing, Harry. I bring in the crowds! A girl like me!' Lorrelai's hands shook, and her knees wobbled. She turned away unsteadily, hugging herself.

'Honey, don't be unreasonable. I'm trying to help. You can't stay here.'

Lorrelai swallowed a few times before she could speak again. 'In the pink room?' She waited while her heart beat loud in her ears. 'It's mine, isn't it? Rent paid from work done? I can use it to sleep in if I can't sleep inside anymore, not just as a changeroom. Get some work nearby.'

Harry sighed loud and heavy. 'It's freezing,' he said quietly. 'But Victoria found a new girl, and she'll need it as her changeroom. Cutie. Vicki says she's like Goldie Hawn.'

Lorrelai swung around, her mouth open, face blazing. 'Victoria *knows?*'

'Course she does. I told her.'

'We were going tell her together!' Tears gushed down her face, dripped off her jaw and chin. How quickly man and wife had banded together, decided her fate. As if they had the right. As if their being married and running a business made them gods.

'That was *your* idea. I knew it was fantasy. Victoria *knows* me.' He stood there, arms at his sides. 'New girl comes tomorrow. Blokes could use a change from a redhead.'

Lorrelai concentrated on breathing. 'Tomorrow?' Spots of light danced before her eyes. Life had fallen away. She stood atop a cliff, a huge icy void around her feet.

Lorrelai closed her eyes and drew in a long breath before letting it out slowly. 'You're ... I can't ...' It was like she'd had it all. She was higher than the clouds, but her lover was ripping everything away. She latched onto something concrete. 'It's *my* room. You said it was.'

'Sorry, babe.' Harry didn't blink. He looked like he was made of stone.

'You're ditching me ... with your own child in my belly? Really? You'd do that?'

Harry lifted his big hands and dropped them. He twisted away. 'I knew you wouldn't be easy about this,' he sighed. Then he turned back and paused. 'Go with old Pierre. He comes by at eight in the morning. Why don't you get him to stop in Northam on the way?' He looked over his shoulder, leaned in like he was sharing a secret. 'You know that place that gets rid of little problems like yours?'

'Ours! You bastard!' Lorrelai slapped his cheek.

He jerked backwards. 'Crazy bitch!' he growled. 'Least I made some enquiries!'

'Enquiries? To get rid of your own baby, you piece of shit!'

Harry glanced around. No one was there. His mouth was tight, his eyes dangerous. He opened and closed his fists a few times.

'I want you out,' he growled. Hands and jaw clenched, Harry turned on his heel and strode away.

Lorrelai's whole body shook as she watched him until he disappeared into the Lion Inn, the jukebox streaming out Simon and Garfunkel's mellow 'Bridge Over Troubled Water'.

Chapter 26

At just past eight, Pierre pulled up in a green Bedford PC Van. New in 1950, it was now a loud, rigid unit that rumbled beside the curb like a grumpy beetle with a small cab for a head.

Pierre, older than Lorrelai remembered, slid out, clutching the door. When he looked up, his forehead was wreathed in wrinkles. His hunched back meant he had to stretch his chin up to stop looking at his feet.

'Hello there.' Hand to car bonnet, his eyes travelled over her outfit.

Lorrelai wore her best full-length tartan ankle-sweeper, a long-sleeved purple top with a wide white collar, white knee-high boots, a red coat and lipstick to match. A yellow scarf was tied around her hair, its ends trailing down her back. 'It's the fashion in Perth,' she said with a sniff.

'Course it is, love.' Pierre tipped his hat. 'Just thinking you won't need to dress up where we're going.' He replaced his hat and hooked his thumbs inside brown braces that held up voluminous tan trousers, frayed at the cuffs. His equally oversized shirt was rolled up to the elbow, suggesting he'd shrunk.

'I'm Lorrelai, by the way. Thanks for this.'

Pierre gave her time to say more. When she didn't, he gestured to the rear of the van. She followed with her bag. 'I keep me parcels back here.' He grunted as he opened the double rear doors, his hands misshapen, knuckles chunky. He bent, took up her bag and lifted it into the back.

The van was half full of stacked cardboard boxes and paper-wrapped parcels. Pierre closed the doors, but one stayed ajar. He shoved it with his shoulder, with minimal impact. Lorrelai pushed with one hand until they both heard the *click*.

'Thanks, love. Needed a boy to take over about five years back.' He led the way to the passenger side of the cab and opened the stiff little door. 'Watch your head.'

Lorrelai smiled tightly as she compressed and contorted herself into the seat. Her temples pounded as soon as the door closed. Otis Redding's '(Sittin on) the Dock of the Bay' droned from the speakers. Lorrelai quickly wound the dial down. She wound down the window too, to breathe in the freshness of the morning, but got a mouthful of exhaust fumes.

Pierre hauled himself up by the door frame and pulled the door closed. 'I was happy Harry mentioned you was lookin' for work yesterday morn. I don't need help with the driving, mind, just the parcels. And some cookin' wouldn't go astray.' He put his hat on the seat between them, released the brake, and the van slowly rolled forwards.

'Yesterday morning?' Engine noise engulfed her question as Pierre accelerated. Lorrelai closed her eyes a moment, anger hard and tight inside her muscles. She had intended to turn for a last look, but now she stared firmly ahead.

Lorrelai had taken a few naps during the night, wrapped in every warm thing she owned, alert to any sounds at her open door. Her nose running, eyes watery she had imagined Harry coming to her, his words of apology, his warm hands. But her only visitor had been a mangy fox that had paused outside her door, sniffing the doorframe, its breath small grey puffs in the moonlight.

It was like being sixteen again—just a nameless, hard-working girl from the Saint Gertrude Orphanage before she'd caught the bus to the Lion Inn to work in the kitchen. She thought she'd be at the inn for a long time. A persistent lump sat in her throat like an unchewed walnut.

Chapter 27

After delivering parcels to several lonely mailboxes, they followed the road to Northam and crossed the Avon River. On the other side, Pierre pulled the wheel right, and they veered off onto a dirt track. He steered quickly left and right to avoid potholes, the van rocking them side to side like sailors in rough seas.

Northam Caravan Park was a large rectangle. The main road and train tracks formed the top border, and an old orchard and river formed the bottom. A footbridge over the river led to native forest. The side boundaries were the fenced sheep paddocks of adjacent farms.

'This was Crown Land, but people came and stayed until a whole bunch of us made it permanent. Council put in some showers and toilets.' Pierre pointed at a rectangular brick building. 'Been here over ten years.' He gave a proud little nod.

Two massive Moreton Bay figs both anchored and halved the park. The top half was taken up by tents and caravans, colourful patchwork of tarpaulins spreading outward, two green Land Cruisers and a boxy, sky-blue Crosley station wagon. Below the trees was an open area before the old orchard, and nestled in the bottom right corner, beneath a kurrajong tree, was a caravan with a shed and water tank behind it.

Pierre leaned forwards and turned the radio volume up. Elvis Presley's 'In the Ghetto' was in its death throes. Lorrelai closed her eyes.

When she opened them, she tried to see the settlement as more than a bunch of haphazard shelters for the homeless. People had lived their lives here. Children had grown up. How was she different to them? Here she was—pregnant, single, jobless—like she'd fallen right into this life.

They motored slowly down the side of the park and stopped next to the lone caravan. Children ran alongside and swirled around the car as Pierre pulled on the handbrake and Lorrelai swayed forwards. Suddenly, voices and barking dogs assaulted Lorrelai's eardrums, and she gasped.

Six or more skinny kids stared at her through the window. One little girl grabbed onto the windowsill with grubby hands. A dog bounced as high as the window, snapping pointed teeth. Lorrelai jerked back with a squeak.

'Are you on the telly?' said the girl, panting. Her eyes were a startling blue, her mouth ringed with dirt and missing both top teeth. She pulled herself up, peering inside the cab, muddy feet drumming the door. Other kids clamoured for space.

'Lemme look! Lemme look!'

'Yeah, me too!'

'Lucy!' the girl yelled suddenly. She dropped back down and waved the others in like she'd found gold in the mud.

'Git away!' someone squawked. The dog ducked a slap and ran off, barking.

'I Love Lucy! I Love Lucy!'

Lorrelai sank down with a whimper.

I Love Lucy, an American sitcom featuring Lucille Ball, was played on TV screens in every home as well as at the Lion Inn. When the actress had dyed her hair red, patrons at the inn assured Lorrelai that, with her wide blue eyes, Lorrelai was her twin. Lorrelai had even given in to pressure and been Lucy as part of her routine a few times.

'Please leave me alone,' said Lorrelai, hand to forehead. Nausea rose like sour milk from her belly.

'Go play in the tree!' called a deep male voice.

Lorrelai shaded her eyes. A tall, dark-bearded man stood next to a chopping block, split wood littering the ground around him. Next to him was a corrugated iron dome half full of neatly stacked logs. 'Quiet, you lot! Leave the lady alone!'

'Awww,' they whinged in unison. The little girl blinked a few times and then jerked forwards as a taller boy bumped into her. A scuffle started as the clamouring group ran towards a swing beneath the tree. Several began climbing up, shouting for challengers while two children fought over the swing.

The man wiped his forehead with the back of his arm and turned his back. He put a round of wood on top of the chopping block and lifted the axe two-handed. Muscles moved beneath his sweat-damp shirt. *Whack!* The wood split into two raw-edged, deep-red logs with the tangy smell of vinegar. Lorrelai detected other smells too: possums, decaying fruit, straw, campfire smoke.

'I need someone to check the parcels to the map and separate them in lots ready for me to deliver. Got bad eyes y'see,' said Pierre.

In front of the car, the old orchard swelled with fruit. Apples and pears hung from every branch like tiny uteruses. Flying gnats hovered over a mulch of mottled leaves and rotting fruit on the ground.

'This is me.' Pierre pointed at the lone caravan held up by bricks and bits of wood. It was a classic soft-cornered Dee-Jay, white and red once but now faded to a rust colour. Three windows lined the front, with long narrow ones either end. Mildew speckled the cracks and creases, and paint flaked off like dandruff. Long grass made a skirt around its flat tyres, interrupted halfway by stairs leading to the door.

Lorrelai put one hand over her eyes and leaned her elbow on her knees. Her teeth hurt from being clenched. Her ears rang.

Pierre talked quietly as he unpacked, chuckling occasionally as if having a conversation with himself. Then he lifted his voice to include her. 'Got me own private space down here.' He slammed the van's rear doors, knocking the air out of the vehicle. 'We use bottled gas. I'm hitched up to a water tank, see?'

Lorrelai looked up as Pierre carried her bag slowly up the caravan steps and disappeared inside.

'Need a hand?' said a voice so close she jumped. 'Don't worry about the dogs. They only bark at strangers. You'll get used to each other.'

It was the woodcutter. He smiled. His teeth were very white against the black beard, his eyes deepest blue with creases branching from their outer corners. Working in the sun had lent his skin a tawny shade. He held out a large, square hand. 'Can be a bit overwhelming at first. I'm Ned.'

Lorrelai shook hands through the window. He stepped back and raised his eyebrows. She nodded for him to open the door. Ned crossed his arms. She opened the door and swung her legs out.

'That's it,' he encouraged, a small smirk twisting his mouth. 'Nice boots.'

'Thanks.' Lorrelai said dryly as she slid out and got her balance. 'I'm not feeling well.'

'Really? That's no good. The aromas are so fresh here.' He grinned sympathetically.

Lorrelai forced a smile, tightened her coat around her, breathed in the organic smells and gagged. She bent at the waist, hands to her knees, breathing and breathing. She felt a hand patting her back.

'There you go,' he said quietly. 'Take your time.'

Lorrelai took a few more deep breaths. Holding one end of her scarf over her mouth and nose, she slowly straightened. 'Thanks for calling off the kids.'

'If you want to blend in, you might consider a change of outfit.'

Despite the lumberjack clothes, the holes in his shirt, the patches on his knees and elbows, Ned's face was appealing. His shoulders were wide, and no salt and pepper greyed his temples like Harry's. He was older than her church boy had been, she guessed, more rugged. Lorrelai felt suddenly annoyed that she'd silently compared him to her lovers. All they'd given her was heartache.

'I don't want to blend in.'

Ned looked around, hands on hips. 'Fair enough,' he said. 'You staying long?'

She shook her head. He gave her a moment to add something. Then he turned and walked back to the chopping block, a brief wave over his shoulder. 'See you round.'

Chapter 28

Inside the caravan was slightly better than outside. Double bench seats ran either side of a table, and the kitchen had a fridge, stovetop, benches and cupboards. A double bed took up the far end. One of the bench seats had a pillow on it, and a thin line of wire was tied from one side of the van to the other with a cotton curtain hanging from it. She looked around, but there were no other beds.

Pierre stepped forwards. 'Scuse me.' He reached for the curtain and pulled. The cotton drop divided one bench seat from the rest of the van. Dread descended over Lorrelai.

'This is yours.' Pierre indicated the bench seat with the pillow. 'Make it your own.'

Lorrelai turned around, grabbed her bag, and walked out through the door. She stopped on the top step. Uphill, beneath the tree, the dirty, gap-toothed girl turned towards Lorrelai, who stood there like a passenger awaiting a plane. Her little face lit up.

A girl on a bicycle careened down the hill whooping, legs out either side, pedals spinning.

Lorrelai stepped back inside the van and closed the door, still holding onto the handle.

'Right then.' Pierre blinked in the sudden gloom. 'Make yourself at home. Kettle's on the stove. I'll be back before dark.'

'Thank you,' Lorrelai said numbly, putting down her bag. Slowly she sat on the end of the bench seat. 'It all happened so fast.'

'Ah, never mind. Oh, share Maria's clothes if you like. Lord knows she has no need for them now. All in there, on her side.' He jerked his thumb over his shoulder at the double bed.

'I'm sure I won't need them. Sorry for your loss.'

After Pierre drove away, Lorrelai made a cup of tea from the old, blackened kettle on the tiny stovetop. She sat down at the table and stared through the back window overlooking the shed and the kurrajong tree. She sipped slowly.

From her case, she pulled out a cardigan. She looked around for somewhere to put the case, but there was nowhere except under the table, so she put it there. She didn't mind that it looked so temporary. She hoped it meant something.

When packing the previous night, she'd been startled by the scant belongings she owned. What would they all think when she didn't turn up? She should have said goodbye. She should have told them what a bastard Harry was. Instead, she'd gathered everything she wasn't using from the room, threw it on top of the pile behind the laundry and lit it. It was supposed to have been cathartic, but the pile burned like it was on holiday.

In the morning, a slim thread of smoke rose into a fresh sky. Only then had she realised her temper had got the better of her. She should have sold, not burned, everything.

* * *

From inside the caravan, Lorrelai heard the morning age to afternoon. The window that opened into the park revealed a thoroughfare to the fruit trees and the river, where kids tumbled and climbed, ate and fished and chased each other, casting eyes at Pierre's caravan until their necks couldn't twist further.

Peering through the curtain, she watched the last of the children trail uphill. She waited. Finally judging the toilets to be empty, she dashed over and back before anyone saw her.

As afternoon stretched on, Lorrelai went through the kitchen cupboards, mindful of Pierre's expectation of being fed.

The camphor-scented cupboard housed plenty of flour, yeast, oats, salt and sugar. On the floor, in a basket, fresh produce was confined to rubbery root vegetables and potatoes. Empty glass bottles gathered dust beneath the sink, and the small fridge revealed only eggs and a bottle of milk. Lorrelai thought of Pierre's baggy clothes, the belt and braces strapping them to his skinny, bent-up frame.

Pierre arrived after sunset, washed up, and set the table for three.

She gave him a questioning glance. 'I've only cooked enough for two.'

'It's fine, dear. Maria's a small eater.' He inclined his head to the empty seat beside him. 'Yes, love. I got some help.' He dipped his head, as though listening to a reply. 'Lorrelai, this is my wife—Maria.'

Lorrelai stared from the empty seat back to Pierre. 'H-hello, Maria.'

Pierre accepted her egg-and-root-vegetable hash with thanks, and then brushed his hands off. 'Back of the Bedford is full of Monday's parcels.' He passed her a folded piece of paper and wiped grease off his lip with the back of his index finger. Bristles stuck up in front of his nostrils like grass near a cave and his cheeks were patchy with bristles like he'd shaved without a mirror.

'I've numbered the zones on the map. All you need to do is put a number on the parcels to match the zones with their addresses. Numbered boxes are kept in the back.' His cheeks and neck trembled as he spoke, like the muscles were twitching.

Lorrelai opened the paper and discovered a dozen zones. 'I'll do it after dinner,' she promised.

'Sundays are my relaxation days. Catch up with friends and so on.'

A torch swung from a hook inside the postal van. Lorrelai climbed in and switched it on. Two bulky bags sat down one side of the van and stacked numbered boxes down the other. Lorrelai checked a few parcels, looking for the addresses. She unstacked the plastic containers and matched addresses to the numbered boxes in the right zone. She then stacked the higher numbered boxes towards the front of the cab, leaving the ones with the lowest numbers just behind the double doors to be delivered first. The whole time, she could hear women and children in the shower block, their voices shrill and echoing inside the concrete block walls.

Lorrelai closed the van's doors and leaned back against them. She looked up at the bright pinprick stars dotting the sky. She peered around the other side of the van. A stocky woman emerged from the showers and marched uphill. No sound came from the block.

Lorrelai got her soap, towel and underwear. The toilet block was as charming as a giant brick, but a light stayed on over the door and a sign promised hot water. Crickets chirped beneath the ground as Lorrelai picked her way across to the entrance. Above, possums scrabbled along branches, over roofs. Through the ventilation holes, she could hear them munching as she showered.

Back in Pierre's caravan, she climbed onto her bench-seat bed and shuffled around until she was covered with rugs.

From down the end of the van came the regular drag and whistle of the old man's snore. A silvery sound wound up from the river, and overhead were the loud, irregular bumps and hisses of possums.

Exhausted, rugs pulled tight beneath her chin, Lorrelai softened into the rigid bench seat and went to sleep.

Chapter 29

The next morning, after Pierre left, Lorrelai peered out of the window. Sunshine lifted her heavy heart. She put on her makeup, brushed her hair, and dressed in her green dress, cardigan and knee-high white boots. When she swung open the caravan door, she could see her breath swirling in the air. On the top step sat a basket with bread, jam and half a dozen eggs. Tears gathered in her eyes and dribbled down her face.

She leaned out. No one was walking away. She grabbed the handle.

'There she is!' came a yell.

Lorrelai saw a grubby girl on a swing beneath the big tree. The girl waved her friends over, and they started running downhill. Lorrelai backed inside, locked the door, and waited. When the children's voices came closer, she sank onto her knees. After a while, they got bored and ran off to climb fruit trees, pick fruit and fill buckets.

Lorrelai made Pierre eggs on toast for dinner. He said nice things about her dress and her cooking, and her spirits lifted.

'Y'need some sunshine, love,' he said.

'I like working at night. I'm used to it.'

'Yes, dear.'

She needn't have worried about the old man being single or interested in her. With his ghost wife to chat to, he was as married as ever.

As far as work went, Lorrelai's tasks were simple. Her days took on a rhythm. In the evening, after dinner, when the park retired into tents and caravans, she ventured out and sorted parcels. When the shower block emptied of women and children, she took a late but solitary shower.

During dinner on her third night, Lorrelai pointed at the shed through the window. 'Is that the cider shed?'

'Yep, but it's pretty empty. My back's no good for pickin'.'

'You mind if I take a look?'

'Go for your life.'

Next morning, Lorrelai pulled a few dresses out from Maria's wardrobe. They were all plain; light blue, yellow, bone, ankle-length, the previous decade's fashion. She held one up against her body. It was a size or two larger than she was. As she touched her lower belly, she felt a little lift. There was still no bump, but she'd be needing larger dresses before long.

She selected a yellow cotton dress, her favourite colour, and wrapped a stained apron over the top. Then she braided her hair down her back and left her face makeup free. She found a straw hat above the kitchen sink and pushed it onto her head, pulling on her worn lace-up work shoes to complete the look. Outside, two children playing on a swing uphill took no notice. Being a Monday, there were fewer children in the park, the older kids having piled into the vehicles with the men early that morning for school.

Beneath the kurrajong tree with its drooping black clusters of pods was the small corrugated-iron cider shed. Lorrelai opened it, stepped inside, and closed the door behind her. Shards of light poked through the many gaps and nail holes.

Tension eased from her body, as the yeasty, sweet–rotten smell of cider reminded her of home. Apart from two barrels, there was a grater, tray and press, still dirty from use, and a container of prover on the single shelf that ran around the walls of the shed. She remembered the cider room at the Lion Inn, between the laundry and her pink room, the fresh, bubbly brews, the giggly groping with Harry after a glass or two.

She opened the door and emptied the debris from the barrels before washing them out using a bucket and rags. She carried the grater, tray and press outside and checked there was prover left. The least she could do was offer Pierre a cider with his dinner to ease the creaks in his old bones.

Downhill fifty feet, the river slid past. She'd liked its sound immediately: a background burble that blended into the fabric of everything. Apart from some ducks and geese, the riverbanks were empty.

Checking uphill first, Lorrelai carried the grater and press down to the water and scrubbed them. She soon had her boots off, her sleeves rolled up, her dress tucked into her knickers. She liked this plain, hard, physical labour. She'd always been strong. She imagined returning home to York stronger and healthier. Her sensitive breasts tingled, as if reminding her that nothing was ever going to be the same.

* * *

On her return from the water, Lorrelai noticed a quince tree. She found a stack of buckets and quickly harvested the fruit before the children noticed, leaving them inside Pierre's caravan. Then she went back out and filled four buckets with pears and apples.

Sweating, she checked uphill. A little boy rode a bike over a mound of dirt. A woman hung out washing, two dogs asleep at her feet.

In the shed, Lorrelai grated the apples and pears until her buckets were empty and left the flesh to brown on a wide tray.

On the tiny stove inside the caravan, she filled a saucepan with chopped quinces, adding enough sugar to almost empty the bag. She lit the flame and brought the mix to a gentle boil. Watching the bubbling surface reminded her of the kitchen at the orphanage, the huge stove and pots brimful of quinces, oranges, and apricots the girls had collected, depending on the season. It was a job she enjoyed, the sweet smells and sticky fingers, the mesmerising cutting and chopping.

Lorrelai returned to the shed, squeezed the fruit gratings into the barrel and closed the lid. It felt nice to have made something from nothing. It felt like a small step in the right direction.

* * *

After lunch, a deep ache started in her belly and radiated down her thighs. Lorrelai turned off the thickened, sweet-smelling jam and went to bed.

She rose only to cook eggs for dinner and to go to the toilet block, and it was there that she discovered she was bleeding. When she used the toilet, and felt the warm, wet gush, she knew it was over.

She showered for a long time.

Chapter 30

By the time Pierre left the next morning, the pain had eased, but Lorrelai felt heavy and dull. She stayed in bed late, and when she finally rose, the sun was high and bright in the sky.

She dressed in her ankle-sweeper and spooned the marmalade into four empty jars from beneath the sink. She lined up the jars and cooked a nice dinner of eggs and potatoes. Then she packed her almost untouched bag and sat it by the door.

Lorrelai walked down to the river, crossed the bridge, and headed along the other side, breathing in the fresh air and the honey scent of gum blossoms. In the bush to her left, marri, red gum, zamia palms and banksia made a green-grey collage. Sunlight pierced the canopy in holy, radiant shafts.

As she reached the track that followed the river and turned for the bridge to the park, she saw a bent old woman with long raven hair wearing a voluminous white dress. The woman wheeled suddenly into the forest and disappeared.

Perhaps she needed the toilet, Lorrelai thought, but when she drew close to the spot, the woman still hadn't come back out.

Lorrelai peered into the trees and down at the ground. A narrow track of tramped dirt and crushed leaves led straight inwards. Lorrelai listened. A magpie called. Several ravens argued as a truck dropped into a lower gear on the main road.

'Hello?' called Lorrelai. She waited, glancing around. The place was deserted, the night falling. Tracks rambled all over the place. Deciding that the old lady had probably emerged at another end, she wandered back to Pierre's caravan.

On her temporary bed, she opened her bag and counted her money. She rubbed her forehead. It would be nice to earn a weekly wage again, not just work for a bed that wasn't even a bed.

As she slid her purse down the side of her bag, she felt a small round-cornered box. She pulled it out and opened the hinged lid, admiring the silver cross on its fine chain. It had been a gift from her first boyfriend, Tom. He had told her it would help protect and guide her, but she'd been too broken-hearted to wear it. She gently lifted it out of the box and fastened it around her throat, the metal cool beneath her fingers.

* * *

Over dinner, Lorrelai regarded Pierre fondly. 'Thanks for taking me in. Can you drop me back to York tomorrow?'

Pierre frowned deeply. 'Already, dear? Thought you was here to stay?'

'Time for me to go back to the Lion Inn,' said Lorrelai, as she finished her dinner. She looked around. Now that she was about to leave, she felt a strange warmth for everything. But the thought of the inn was much cosier. A toilet she didn't have to share with dirty children. A bedroom with a door. Roast dinner in the kitchen with the staff every Sunday.

'Right, I see,' said Pierre. 'Probably be glad of the help. Poor Harry broke his foot, so Victoria has to shout the commands. Must say, she's a bit of a natural.' He chortled and shook his head.

Lorrelai swallowed hard. Victoria would not reemploy her, not after so short a time. Until Harry was back in charge, she had a snowflake's chance in hell.

Lorrelai pushed her plate away. 'How long does a broken foot take to heal?'

Pierre cleared his throat loudly. 'A month or more.'

'I see.' She cleared her throat. 'Tomorrow might be a bit soon, Pierre.'

'You'll stay? Goodo.'

Lorrelai heard the possums gallop on the roof of the caravan that night as though they were horses. She balled her fists beneath the covers and wished they'd shut the hell up.

Chapter 31

The next day felt like a false start. Lorrelai had picked apples and tried to make pie but there was no butter. She'd unpacked her bag and dressed in her own clothes, only to change again to go outside, wiping off her lipstick so as not to be noticed. Her body felt heavy and sore, her breasts tender and leaking. In the end, she had wallowed in bed, rousing herself just before Pierre drove in at the end of the working day.

Over a dinner of soup made with undesirable vegetables and powdered stock, Lorrelai rested her chin on her fist and watched Pierre eat hungrily.

'Good day?' she asked lifelessly, hoping for some distraction or the news that Harry had healed miraculously.

'Yes, dear. Busy as always.' Pierre wiped his mouth with a hanky from his top pocket. 'Want me to sell the marmalade on me run?'

Lorrelai looked over at her half dozen jars on the sink. The orange-brown jam glistened sweetly. She straightened. 'Yes, thank you.'

'What about the cider? Want me to sell that too?' Pierre tapped the side of his nose. 'Couple customers been askin'.'

Lorrelai straightened. 'You think if I made enough jam and cider, I could make some cash before I leave?'

'For sure.'

Lorrelai took up her spoon and tried the soup. It was salty, but not too bad. Maybe, instead of waiting for the days to pass, she could use the next month to get ahead. 'Can you do some shopping? We're almost out of everything. I tried to make pie, but there was no butter.'

'Sorry, no time. People here at the park should have everything you need. Butter from up at Ned and Dora's. Big caravan with the veggie gardens and goats.'

'Ned? Dark hair and beard?'

'That's the one.'

'He's married?'

'Baby too.'

Lorrelai tried not to feel disappointed. She tucked her hair back and sucked in a deep lungful of air. Okay,' she murmured. 'How much money should I take?'

'Take that.' Pierre twisted and pointed to half a bottle of sherry sitting beside the stove. 'There's no cider left out there unless yours is ready. Dora loves a drop. Makes her dance.' He winked.

The men all arrived home about the same time each day, their tired, deep voices drawing the evening inwards. Every day, she looked uphill for the dark-haired woodcutter. Every day, she was disappointed.

* * *

A few more days idled by. Lorrelai's breasts grew, rather than deflated, and leaked at odd times. She folded a cloth lengthways and slipped it beneath her blouse.

During another long shower, Lorrelai tried to raise her mood. She could make a little money while Harry and Victoria cooled off. It would give Harry a chance to miss her.

The sound of a man singing issued from the adjacent block. She turned off the water. It was unusual that anyone was in here so late. Hand to the wall, she listened as the heat seeped out of her skin. Someone was making a good attempt at Elvis Presley's deep, throaty 'Can't Help Falling in Love.' She smiled and then hummed along.

The song ended. A long pause followed.

Lorrelai heard the shower turn off. She shivered and quickly hurried through drying and dressing. She rushed outside, shading her eyes. Beyond the single light globe, the evening was three-quarters dark. Smoke from campfires and farmers' paddock burns hung in the air like a heavy mist. No one was in sight.

That night, behind her curtain, Lorrelai felt the ache of loneliness. She closed her eyes and thought not of Harry but of Tom.

At eighteen, she'd just started dancing at the inn, making a little money. Quite a few of York's young men had left to try their hand at being a soldier in Vietnam or had been conscripted.

She'd found him sitting on her bed in the pink room after a performance one night, a straight-backed young man with wispy blonde hair and his hat in his hands.

'Jesus! You scared the hell—!'

The young man jumped up and held out one hand. 'I'm sorry, so sorry, miss! Please don't shout. I won't hurt you. I promise on God's name.' His voice was naturally soft. He put his hand over his heart.

'You can't come in here.' Lorrelai stood just inside the door, so she could retreat if necessary. 'I dance,' she said carefully. 'It's called burlesque. It's a bit of fun.'

He wore black suit pants and a light blue shirt with the sleeves buttoned at the wrist and all the way up to his Adam's apple. He was tall and slim, yet to fill out properly, and looked just old enough to drive. His shoes were black and shiny, like a banker or lawyer.

He stared at her like she'd spoken a foreign language.

'You're here to save me, aren't you?' Her heart pounded anew.

Nancy, her mentor, a travelling dancer who'd stayed a few months, had warned her about this—people confusing the dancing for stripping and prostitution. Even with the hippies swishing around and talking about women's rights and abortion and the contraceptive pill, attitudes out here in the country changed notoriously slowly. Sometimes, it seemed like the scenes on the television with protesters against the war, half-naked hippies at concerts, wasn't real.

The young man blinked. 'No.'

'Then why are you here, Mr. ...?'

He swallowed and shook his head. 'Please don't ask my name,' he said, looking out through the door. 'Just call me Tom. Do we have privacy?'

'If I call out someone will come,' said Lorrelai.

'Please don't be afraid. I would never hurt you.'

Lorrelai took a deep breath and took a step into the room. She dumped her feather boa and sat down on the bed, crossing her legs, still in her scant dancewear. Tom moved away from the bed and stood with his back to the far wall, turning his hat around and around in his hands like it was a steering wheel.

'Tell me your business,' said Lorrelai.

He went pink and then darker. It made his white-blonde hair and eyebrows look like they were glued to a red ball. He glanced at the open door as though he might either leave or close it. Then his eyes dropped. 'Please forgive me.'

'For what?'

'May I sit down?'

Lorrelai pointed at her chair, which had about four outfits slung over the back of it. He carefully threaded his arm beneath the clothes and held them out in front of him. 'Where would you like these?'

He put them on the end of her bed without looking at her, and she caught the strong scent of aftershave. Tom sat on the chair, put his hat on the floor, and clasped his hands. 'I would like to make love to you.'

Lorrelai laughed and clasped her hands around one knee. 'We have a misunderstanding. I don't do that.' She turned her foot in a circle.

The young man blinked fast, licked his lips, and took a deep breath. 'I'm not making any assumptions,' he said.

'Yes, you are!' Lorrelai snorted. She stood up and approached him, and his eyes stayed on her eyes until his neck was stretched up and she was almost standing on his toes. 'Like I said, I dance. You won't believe this, but I am still a virgin.'

His face reddened more. A spark of delight went through her.

'What I meant was, I don't expect anything, but I hope you'll consider. I've seen you dance, you see. I've also seen you walk around in a dirty apron, serving meals. And the thing is, I rather think I love you.'

She huffed and turned away, picking up her waitressing outfit and her soap and towel. But she was rattled.

'Your sweet words don't make a difference. Go on. Off you go.' She waited, but there were no footsteps to the door. She turned around, surprised. 'City is your best bet.'

His eyes widened. He held up his hands, palms pressed together. 'Please don't go, Lorrelai. I need your help. You see, I'm from the rectory. I'm studying to be a priest.'

Lorrelai gave him a look all over. She imagined his lanky frame in priest robes. Her memories of the orphanage where she was raised, and the gentle look about him, caused her to pause.

She was about to say that a professional lady could accommodate his needs, but a feeling she wasn't accustomed to came over her. Possessiveness. She sat down, her legs crossed at the thigh.

Tom's whole body breathed out. 'Thank you.'

'I'm confused. Don't you go into the church because you've decided God is more important than sex and marriage? Aren't you above the needs of the flesh?'

Tom was nodding. 'Yes, that's right. I am devoted to a life serving God, but I'm distracted by a serious curiosity about ... well ... being with a woman.'

'I see.'

'I feel I can better serve God and the church the rest of my life if I lay this feeling to rest.'

'What if it doesn't work?'

His face settled. 'It will. I'm certain of my calling.'

Lorrelai sighed. 'Priests can marry. I've heard of it. You don't need to butter me up.'

'Not if they want to be in the clergy. I mean everything I say. I'm a dreadful liar, I promise.'

They shared a private smile. 'How long do you have?'

Tom looked at a plain silver watch on his right wrist.

'Until you enter the rectory?' Lorrelai clarified.

'Oh, three months,' he said.

In the end, it was easy. They used those three months like oxygen, Tom sneaking down to the pink room where Lorrelai waited, sneaking back out before dawn. They fell in love. Then Tom, as he had promised from the start, left to serve God.

Chapter 32

The sun was out early, although cold air stayed in pockets. Lorrelai rose and collected two buckets of apples. Most, she left in the shed to make cider with later, but she took several to the caravan and sliced them up, placing them in a pot with water and the remaining sugar to make pie filling. She'd had to turn the corners of the sugar bag inside out to get enough.

Clothed in work shoes and Maria's dress and apron, her own bright scarf knotted over her hair, she headed uphill. Young, scrawny park children spilled from caravans, all tangled hair and dirty clothes.

Head down, as if walking into strong wind, she approached the largest caravan, a blue and silver Roadmaster about one-third bigger than Pierre's and in better condition. Fenced gardens sprang off the back and sides, the first dominated by tall weeds and tomato plants heavy with rotten fruit, sinking their branches right to the ground. Wooden stakes were laid in an impotent pile inside the fence. She could hear chickens, and a goat bleated. From somewhere inside, a baby whined.

Lorrelai knocked. Near the biggest fig tree, a kelpie barked at nothing, stretched, yawned and sat in the sun. The dogs hadn't barked at her since she'd started wearing Maria's clothes. It was like she was in disguise. For now, it suited her.

Lorrelai knocked again. 'Hello?'

The door opened a crack. A pale woman peeked out, dark eyes squinting hard, lank black hair draping her shoulders. She shaded her eyes with fingers tipped with long, untended nails. 'Yes?' she whispered.

'Hello, I'm Lorrelai. I'm staying with Pierre.' She pointed down the hill.

The woman opened the door and looked. An animal smell wafted out. In the light, her small body was a skeleton inside a dirty, long-sleeved white nightie that fell from neck to knee. She had old lady hands: blue-veined, tendons showing. Lorrelai remembered the old woman in the forest.

'Dora,' said the woman.

Lorrelai tried not to stare. There had to be another Ned aside from the woodcutter—an older one, bent in the back, married to this poor woman.

'Oh, yes. I think I saw you walk in the forest the other day.'

Dora's eyes narrowed. 'Who are you?'

'Um, just a relative of Pierre's. Not staying long. He said you have butter, and to bring you some of this.' Lorrelai held up the sherry.

Dora's eyes cleared and she lost ten years. She turned away, into the dark, and then emerged a few seconds later with a small paper-wrapped cube and a cardboard egg carton.

Lorrelai took the two and handed up the liquor. 'Oh, thank you,' she said. 'I'm trying to make pie. There's so much fruit.'

Dora took the bottle to her bosom like a precious gift. 'You can have more eggs. And bottled tomatoes.' She glanced at Lorrelai's head. 'Lovely scarf.'

'Thank you.' Lorrelai dropped her voice to a whisper. 'You have a baby?'

Dora's face sank, and she gained ten years back. Below her right eye, the skin twitched.

'It never sleeps.'

Lorrelai was unsettled by the change in the old woman, but she had heard this about babies. 'Okay then, I'll leave you to rest,' she whispered. 'Thanks again.'

Dora nodded but stayed outside the door.

Lorrelai felt eyes on her back all the way to the fig trees. A small movement beneath the trees caught her eye. By the closest tree trunk was a scuffed brown boot.

'Hello?' she called.

The boot disappeared. Lorrelai shook her head.

* * *

Once in the caravan, Lorrelai rubbed a chunk of butter into some flour and added oats and cinnamon. She spread the lot over the soft heaps of steamed apple.

Later, in the shed, she processed the rest of the apples from the morning pick. An urgency crept into her work. She'd had a bad feeling ever since seeing Dora.

She put the grated pile of fruit flesh into a bowl and left it to brown and develop the sugars that would become alcohol. A short time later, she returned with three clean bottles from beneath Pierre's sink, squeezed the macerated fruit in some cloth, and poured the dark juice into the bottles. She added the last of the prover, wrapped the bottlenecks with cloth and secured each with string.

The bottle she'd given Dora was the last. Nothing else was left on the shelf that lined the shed walls above the barrels. The first batch of cider was a few days from being ready. It was May. Autumn was almost gone. She needed some more space and more prover if she was going to brew enough cider for profit. There was room enough for barrels on the floor, but nowhere for more bottles. If bottles were on the floor, rats would knock them over to get to the sweetness.

Plenty of wood lay around the park. Off-cuts from the old mill made up clotheslines, seats and shed doors. She could find enough for half a dozen shelves in ten minutes. She just needed someone to build them. Pierre offered, but Lorrelai shook her head.

'Have a break, Pierre. You work too hard.'

Pierre nodded. 'How about Ned? Dora's husband.'

Chapter 33

The next morning, pale sunrise eased through the curtained caravan windows. Outside, Pierre's van, loaded up with Saturday morning deliveries, growled and clunked on its exit from the park. Lorrelai changed out of her nightie, noting the folded cloth across her breasts was damp again. She replaced the cloth with a dry one and hoped it would end soon.

At the tiny bench, she mixed flour, yeast, salt and water, kneaded the dough and left it to rise. She doffed her apron, pulled on a warm cardigan and retraced her steps of the previous day.

At Lorrelai's knock, the door opened fast. Lorrelai stepped back. Dora's eyes softened with recognition, but the skin by her right eye still twitched. Dora's skin looked yellow and Lorrelai could smell the rotten-sweet breath of a drinker. A cold, sinking feeling soaked right down to her feet.

'Do you have time for tea?' Dora's bony hands found each other, interlaced and trembling, like someone confessing. 'I have a little time before I go out.' She lifted her arm to shade her eyes. Long wiry hair darkened her armpit and the smell of sweat and urea wafted out of the caravan.

'Sure. How about over there?' Lorrelai pointed beneath the tree.

Beneath the fig, Lorrelai found two mismatched seats in front of a cold stone fireplace. After brushing the leaves off them, she dragged them into the sunshine and sat.

Around her were the shrill of birds, a radio, a distant train. A rustle of leaves came from near the tree. Lorrelai twisted around.

'Hello, tree person.'

A young woman of about fifteen or sixteen ducked her head out, and then an open book and a busily drawing hand emerged.

'What are you drawing?'

'You,' said the girl.

Lorrelai sat back, hand to her chest. 'A portrait?' Out here, the idea seemed both ridiculous and delicious. How she'd love to forget where she was, to dress up, put on her red lipstick and pose for a portrait.

Lorrelai sighed. 'Are you going to ask my permission?'

The girl stepped into the open, eyes wide. 'Shit.' She closed the book, tucking it beneath her arm. She was stocky with brown hair and eyes. Her thick brown corduroy dress was dotted with tiny red and green flowers.

Lorrelai smirked and adjusted herself into a more portrait-like pose with one leg extended. 'That better?' The girl grinned.

'Did you get the basket we left?'

'Oh, it was you? Thank you!'

'Here's tea.' Dora wobbled down the steps with a cup in each hand. 'Unfortunately, the help hasn't arrived today.'

Lorrelai flushed and sat forwards to receive her cup. 'Sorry, I should have given you a hand.' The faint feeling of glamour mocked her and was gone.

Dora sat down, smoothing her nightie before picking imaginary specks off it. Her wrists were bony hillocks of gooseflesh.

'We need a maid. I've tried to tell him.' Dora shook her head. 'Can't expect me to take care of it endlessly.' Delicately, she pinched the cup handle and tilted the rim against her lips.

Lorrelai frowned. 'The baby isn't yours?'

Dora's face broke open, a sudden, ugly transformation that revealed horse-like teeth. She set down her cup, threw back her head and brayed, hands on her stomach. 'Oh no! No!' She wiped her eyes and opened her stick-arms wide. 'I'm a performer! I couldn't possibly have a child! It would end my career.' She fluttered her eyes and then pressed her palms between her knees and stared off at the trees.

A snort issued from behind the tree.

Lorrelai ignored it.

'Dora,' she said gently. 'Are you alright?'

Dora turned and smiled. 'Of course, dear.' She patted the back of Lorrelai's free hand with an icy palm. 'I'm preparing for a huge show. We'll move from city to city.' She closed her eyes and inhaled indulgently. When she opened them again, she wriggled her brow. 'I'm the lead female dancer. My name'—she gestured with a royal wave—'is on top of the list. I'm literally on top of the list.'

A cold ball sat in the centre of Lorrelai's chest as she watched Dora talk. Animated. Non-sensical. Stringy hair. Sallow skin. Dull eyes. Curved upper back. Lorrelai had seen healthier corpses.

At the orphanage, the older children had sometimes helped lay out the bodies of elderly nuns who died there, covering them with a sheet so they were ready for the undertaker. It upset Lorrelai the first time, but the nuns said death was natural and heaven glorious. What was there to cry about?

A baby started wailing, the noise jolting Lorrelai back to the present.

'Is that the baby, Dora?' The sound reached right under her skin. Dora sank down, drew in her neck like a threatened turtle, and stared ahead. Lorrelai touched Dora's arm, and the woman flinched.

'Dora? Is that the baby?' The crying grew louder. It hurt Lorrelai to hear it. Dora's eyes closed.

'God in heaven,' she whispered, as a shiver went through her.

Lorrelai twisted towards the noise, waiting for Dora to get up. 'Are you waiting for it to go back to sleep?' She could feel sweat, warm beneath her armpits.

Dora blinked once. 'No. Never goes back to sleep. Not on its own.' She exhaled as she leaned on the chair arms and slowly got to her feet. She wore big old boots—men's boots—the thick laces trailing in the leaves.

'Dora, is your husband back today?'

Dora squinted hard, clearly confused. 'Husband?'

'Um. Sorry, I mean I just wanted help with some shelving. In exchange I could work, maybe around the garden?'

Dora stared at the caravan like it was a mountain she had to climb. 'Every night, Ned comes.' She frowned for a long moment. 'Take the baby. Take him away!' She started walking slowly, as if the boots weighed a tonne.

Her hand to her chest, Lorrelai leapt to her feet and started forward.

'No!' Someone grabbed the back of her skirt. The girl. She clutched Lorrelai's skirt in one hand, her sketchbook in the other.

'She has to look after him. She's his mother.' She let go of the skirt.

'But will they be okay? Dora is … is …' ahead of them Dora opened the caravan door, and the wailing crescendoed, and then quieted as she disappeared inside and closed the door.

'Totally mad.' The young woman sighed. She leaned back against the tree; her arms crossed.

'Is something wrong with the baby? Why does it keep crying?'

'Why are you crying?'

Lorrelai wiped a stray tear off her cheek. 'I don't know. It just sounds wretched.'

The girl sighed. 'Nah, baby's fine.' The girl shook her head, then she blushed and twisted her heel into the ground. 'You're beautiful.'

'Hmm?' Lorrelai swivelled back and forth from the caravan to the girl. 'I should go and see if they need help.'

'No. Tried that. She just gives up, leaves you to do the lot. Ned paid me for a bit, but then couldn't pay me. I don't even like babies and I'm not working for free.' She shrugged. 'Got to get out of here one day.'

'Is Ned a good man?'

'S'pose. It's not his fault, if that's what you're asking. Dora's been mad from the start.'

'I'm confused. Pierre said they were married.'

'Yeah. He married her cos she was pregnant. And she was okay at first. But, I dunno, she got weird.' She shrugged. 'You can't believe anything she says.'

Lorrelai peered up at the caravan again. 'I'm worried.' She could hear the baby whinging. 'It stinks inside.'

'I know,' said the girl. She exhaled loudly, like she was sick of the subject. 'She does the laundry *eventually*. Just don't give her booze. She's worse with booze.'

Lorrelai went crimson.

The girl's eyes widened. 'Oh shit! You didn't?'

'I didn't know!'

The girl glanced all around and then turned back at Lorrelai. She dropped her voice. 'Don't tell Ned. I won't tell. Want me to go steal it back? How much was there?'

'It was only half a bottle of sherry yesterday morning,' said Lorrelai, her throat scratchy. 'Smelled like she'd been drinking just now.'

'It'll be gone,' the girl said with certainty.

Lorrelai swallowed. 'Is Ned the angry type?'

The girl frowned and then shrugged. 'He's all right.'

Dora's caravan had gone quiet.

Lorrelai turned back to the girl. 'What's your name?'

'Blossom.' The girl pointed uphill. 'Peggy is my ma. I'm one of eight —only girl.' Blossom rolled her eyes. 'Expects me to mother them instead of school, but I'm gonna run away and be a feminist and artist.' She threw a guilty look over her shoulder and then gave Lorrelai a challenging stare. 'Don't tell her.'

Lorrelai raised her eyebrows. 'Okay. Are you any good?'

Blossom blinked a couple of times and wriggled. 'Won a prize at school before Ma gone an' withdrew me.' She crossed her arms and looked into the distance. 'Why you livin' with old Pierre?'

'Needed a place to stay. Got fired. I was a waitress and dancer at the Lion Inn in York.'

'Really?' Blossom said breathlessly. Her eyes shone.

'I'm going back soon as I can.'

The girl nodded, her lower lip jutting. 'Can you pose for me before you go?'

'Sure.'

A door clicked and a child laughed. From over the paddock, sheep bleated.

Blossom touched Lorrelai's arm. 'Tomorrow?'

Chapter 34

Later that evening, Lorrelai ate omelette and apple pie with Pierre. She rifled through Maria's clothes again and changed into a pale blue skirt and white blouse. She left her hair out and tied a necklace of coloured beads and stones around her neck on top of the cross. After a moment's indecision, she tied an apron around her waist.

The caravan park was dark. The trees rustled with busy possums. Bits of fruit, leaves and debris rained down from the canopy. Lorrelai skirted the edge. The scent of campfire, frying onions, and lamb fat wafted through the evening air. Songs and voices were split by bursts of laughter, a cranky shout, a clanging pan. The Beatles hit 'She Loves You' belted out from one of the vans, and someone was singing along with enthusiasm.

Holding a fresh-baked loaf of bread, Lorrelai watched the ground carefully so she wouldn't trip on exposed tree roots or the old bicycle the children shared.

Loud cries and terse voices issued from Dora and Ned's caravan. Lorrelai stopped and listened. After a minute, the sounds decreased, the voices like they were underwater.

Lorrelai knocked with her free hand. Heavy footfalls rocked the unit, and Lorrelai backed down the steps and stood at the bottom. She licked her lips, lifted her chin.

The door opened outwards, and Ned's head popped out—the same Ned she'd met on day one, his thick black hair and beard speckled with sawdust.

'Yes? Oh. Hello.' His voice was deep and calm, and his eyes tracked all the way to Lorrelai's feet and then back up to the top of her head. 'Took my advice, I see.'

He came out properly, straightened up, and rolled his shoulders. Turning, he shut the door behind him before taking a seat on the top step. He brushed the dust from his beard and ran his hand back through his hair three times.

'Hello, Ned.' Lorrelai changed her stance. 'I came by yesterday.'

'Yes?'

Lorrelai swallowed. 'I, ah … made some bread for you both.' She handed it over, and Ned took it and looked at it from end to end. 'Did Dora mention me?'

Ned shook his head. 'No, but that's not unusual.' He held the bread close and inhaled, his eyes shut. Then he pulled off a chunk and put it in his mouth. After swallowing, he said, 'Hmm. You're a good baker. Now, let's see, we have plenty of bottled tomatoes, beans, but the root vegetables aren't quite ready. Grubs got into them with me working and Dora with the baby.' He scratched the back of his head but kept his eyes on her. 'Eggs are already collected for the day.'

When he paused, the sounds of the night peeped in like a shy audience—a lamb calling, a far-off dog, someone banging dishes, several radios competing and someone singing Louis Armstrong's 'What a Wonderful World'—badly.

'How long have you lived here?' she asked.

Ned took another pinch of bread and spoke out one side of his mouth. 'Year and a half. You've been here a fortnight, and I still don't know your name.'

'Lorrelai.' She held out her hand, and he shook it gently. 'Actually, I was hoping you could help me with some shelving in Pierre's shed,' she said. 'I need more space to make cider and brandy. I was going to offer to work in the garden in exchange.'

The shy audience grew bolder. Owls called and kids and dogs squabbled. Lorrelai breathed in the cool of the air, the darkness that faded out the dirt and poverty.

Ned watched her, his gaze flickering along her arms and over her chest. 'Don't look like the manual labour sort.'

'I'm stronger than I look.'

Ned held out his hand. 'Give me your hand.' Slowly, she offered it, and he turned it palm up and swept his thumb across it. 'Really?'

Lorrelai felt a little shiver. She could smell the wood-dust scent of him and something heavier. She took back her hand. 'Waiting tables, baking, and cleaning doesn't make callouses. But if you don't want—'

'Steady on.' Ned held up one hand. 'I didn't mean …' Behind him, the crying started again. He sighed and twisted around.

Lorrelai felt her chest tighten like her ribcage had constricted. The cry stuttered, its origin a place of deep hurt and sorrow. A lump filled her throat.

'Are you all right?' Ned was giving her a curious look. 'Sorry, I don't have a hanky. Lucky to have a shirt on my back.' He gestured to his clothes: thin beige shirt, heavy work trousers, shiny with wear, socks half off, long toes sticking out.

Lorrelai wiped her eyes and her nose with the back of her hand. All she could think of was the poor baby crying its tiny heart out.

'It's just cold,' said Lorrelai, a stream of emotions washing through her. She stared at his black beard, trimmed to the shape of his face like a mask. 'Why is the baby crying?'

'He's hungry, don't worry.' Ned cleared his throat and frowned, as though placing a layer of caution between them. 'Ah, I'm going to get the little chap a drink. Don't mention the brandy to my Dora.' He winked, stood, and pulled up his belt. 'Have you ever milked a goat?'

Lorrelai shook her head.

Ned smiled. 'I'll show you, if you're keen. We could *definitely* use your help. Wait right there.' He walked inside.

Soon he was back, offering a bucket. 'Chicken scraps,' he said. Then he turned and went back inside. He emerged with two buckets and a sling, like a cocoon, tied to his back. The baby was inside. 'This way.' He strode along a hard dirt path between the fenced garden and a thick thatch of bamboo.

'We grow potatoes, tomatoes, beans, zucchini and radish in there.' Ned indicated the first yard. 'Beets, cabbage, broccoli, carrots, pumpkins in there.' Vines from the zucchini and pumpkins jumped the fence on all side, tendrils reaching out and brushing dew on them as they passed. Lorrelai's eyes were on the bundle in the sling instead of the ground. She tripped, catching herself up after a few steps, just before she ran into Ned. She drew a deep breath, steadied herself.

They stopped at an open gate in front of a shed. Two white goats emitted a volley of bleats and stood on their hind legs inside, but only one pushed through. The smaller one was on the other side of the wire. Ned held the buckets high.

'Chickens in that one,' he said over the noise, pointing to an enclosed wire yard with a half shed at one end. 'Throw the scraps through the door.'

A dozen or so chickens clucked in the process of roosting, bobbing their heads and fluttering up to settle on wooden perches like an audience in a stadium.

'They'll eat whatever the rats leave, in the morning.' Ned sighed. 'It's better to feed them earlier than this.' He pointed to beneath where they were roosting. 'That's where they lay, see? Nests have covers that open from the outside. Go on around the side. If there're any eggs, you take them.'

Lorrelai walked around and lifted a lid. A chicken fluttered off the nest with a loud gurgle. Peering in, Lorrelai saw two pale shapes. 'Oh,' she whispered with delight. One at a time, she lifted the eggs out and nestled them in her apron pocket. They were still warm, like skin. She held one onside her pocket for a few moments. Ned tilted his head, watching with a small, curious smile. Then he led the way into the goat's yard and closed the gate behind them.

'They could jump out if they wanted,' said Ned, as the goats bleated in unison. 'Goats can climb trees, you know. But they got it good here —let out to graze in the day, feed and shelter at night.'

'How often do you milk?' The fragrance of straw and dirt, animals and vegetables wafted around her, alive and warm rather than rotten or dirty. Things rose from the earth anyway, from the dirt and animals, and people were sustained by what grew —eggs, meat, milk and vegetables. 'You've got a great set-up here.'

'Yeah. Bit of work to maintain, though. Milking morning and night. Bottling tomatoes when it's the season.'

The goats bleated again. 'Steady on, you two. I know it's late. Butter churn there.' He pointed to a section of the shed, where a wooden keg sat on a stand with a handle. Lorrelai sniffed, smelling something sweetly sour.

Ned disappeared into the gloom at the back of the shed, shuffling around, shaking out grain to half fill a bucket. The goats clamoured to get their noses inside, the smaller one bleating so loudly that Lorrelai wondered if it had got stuck or something.

Ned held the feed up high and strode over to a wooden stand to shake it into a bucket at the end. The doe jumped her two front, then her back feet, up onto the platform and stuck her head through the V-shaped bail to reach the grain. Ned closed the bail and patted her neck. Next, he got the kid goat's bowl, decanted some of the mix into it and left it in the second half of the shed. The kid snorted into the bowl and began to chew.

'What's that you feed them?'

Ned lifted a small stool from beside the wall and placed it behind the doe. He sat down. 'Concentrates. Grain and a little molasses. Goats won't eat off the ground. Posh buggers. Yet wild ones will live on the side of a cliff.' He faced the doe's flank, his knees wide. 'Here Maisy. Warm hands—promise.'

Lorrelai smiled. Ned leaned forwards. A sharp *zip-zip* started. She moved closer, looked over his shoulder. As Ned squeezed, a white stream erupted from the end of the teat and hit the base of the empty bucket. His hands pumped alternately until the bottom of the bucket was white. A few minutes passed, and the milk sloshed up the side of the bucket, topped with foam. Lorrelai crouched next to Ned, her cheek almost touching his elbow.

The baby grunted a couple of times, and Ned hushed him gently. 'We get Maisy into kid, and she makes milk for us all when it's born.' He looked over his arm at her. 'For Bub, too.'

'Dora said he doesn't sleep.' Lorrelai put her hand on the bundle and ran it back and forth, like she was comforting it. She'd never seen the baby's face, only heard it crying, a sound that tuned into her brain, switched on her tears.

Lorrelai moved out of the way as Ned removed the bucket and pressed a lid on top.

'Dora hasn't been right since she got pregnant. Worse since the little one came along. Won't even name him.' He busied himself with releasing both goats. The kid immediately rushed beneath the doe and butted her udder, latching on. After a minute, the doe lifted her back foot and kicked. The kid shook its ears, stunned, and then followed her outside.

'I do what I can, but I've got to go earn money or we'd all starve.

Okay, let me get Bub a bottle and we can walk and talk about some exchange of work.'

Lorrelai followed Ned towards the light of the van, feeling a pull like glue adhering her to the place.

* * *

She waited outside the caravan for Ned to come back out, the baby slung across the front of him. He tipped a bottle down to its tiny face.

'Gosh,' breathed Lorrelai. Pulling the edge of the sling, she peeked in at him. A thatch of dark hair above two bright eyes. 'He's lovely.'

Ned winked. 'Only three months.' He straightened. 'Walking calms him.'

They wandered past the tree where Lorrelai and Dora had shared tea. Ned's free arm cradled the sling, and Lorrelai felt an emptiness settle in her arms, like she needed something in hers. She folded them across her chest and cleared her throat.

'How long have you been married?'

Ned lifted an eyebrow. 'You ask a lot of questions.'

'Sorry.'

He exhaled. 'Dora turned up after I'd moved here. I was already part of the logging team working in the forests. She made those gardens in a week, worked night and day. And then just ... stopped. Wouldn't get out of bed. Found out she was expecting a few weeks later.'

They headed up towards the road, past the caravans. Tarpaulins stretching between the homes made them appear joined, and light shone through the openings.

Lorrelai was happy not to speak. She liked wandering beside Ned's solid form, listening to the grunts of the suckling infant. It seemed different in the park with Ned and the baby, all the edges seemed smoothed.

'How many shelves do you need?'

'About two shelves on each side. Six in total.'

'You able to take care of Bub? The garden?'

'The garden, yes. I've never looked after a baby.'

'Dora neither.' Ned glanced back over his shoulder. 'Sent her to the doctor, but he just said to get some rest. Jesus.'

He heaved a great sigh and checked the bottle. Removing it, he tucked it into his waist and patted the sling. 'I can't do any more. I only stop to sleep.'

'I thought Dora looked poorly.' Lorrelai hesitated before she said the thing that had been on her mind. 'She talked about performing. And then she told me to take the baby.'

Ned shook his head, kept walking. Lorrelai ran a few steps to catch up. 'Can I hold him?'

Ned turned, already tucking his hands into the sling. He lifted out a bundle of white blanket, the infant's ruddy face poking out the end, and handed him towards her. 'Here,' he said, angling the child along Lorrelai's front until she circled her arms beneath him.

'Head goes inside your elbow. Other arm here.' The baby's weight rested into Lorrelai's arms as Ned's hands slid away.

Lorrelai held the warm bundle against her, gazing at the baby's pale, smooth, sleeping face. His eyes fluttered, and she could see the eye rolling beneath the fine, blue-veined eyelid as though deep asleep.

'He doesn't usually get this much attention.' He smiled at her, and she smiled back. 'C'mon, let's wander.'

With Ned's hand on the middle of her back, they walked along the train tracks, up one edge and then back downhill towards the cluster of dwellings. Lorrelai kept her eyes on the baby, relying on Ned's guiding hand.

'Dora was a performer. She was amazing. I set up the stage, you know, did the heavy lifting. Stood in for the chorus if someone was sick. But even then, she'd go funny.' He sighed. 'I've been married a year, bachelor just as long.'

Lorrelai hitched the baby up a bit, amazed at how heavy he'd begun to feel. 'You can sing.'

Ned turned to face her and nodded. 'It was you in the shower, wasn't it? Couldn't have been anyone else.'

A feeling inside Lorrelai swelled bigger, warmer. She smiled. 'And you ... Elvis?'

They were almost back at the caravan. They stopped, and Ned gently took the baby and held him along one arm, like a football. 'Can you start tomorrow? I can't do the shelves till the weekend, mind. Logging all day, all this when I get home. The garden is way behind.'

'Yes, I can.'

'Take what milk and veggies you need as pay. We don't have much else right now.'

'Okay. I'll start in the morning.'

'Good, good.' He nodded, and then frowned, as if ticking off a list in his head. 'Beans need harvest, many of them probably too old now but keep some pods for seeds. Spinach seedlings lined up by the fence are ready to go in.' As he spoke and his body moved a little, so did the baby, but he didn't stir.

'Don't worry. I'll get it done. I'd start now if it wasn't so dark.'

Ned grinned. 'I like your spirit. You came at just the right time, Lorrelai.' He held out his free hand and they shook on the deal. Then his face sobered. 'Unusual to see someone like you here. You in some kind of trouble?'

Lorrelai removed her hand and tightened her cardigan around her body. 'Just finished my job unexpectedly. But I'm going back soon.'

'Ah.' Ned took a long breath and turned. His gaze went right up to the top of the Moreton Bay fig, its foliage so wide and so thick that from here, it blanketed half the sky. The trunk was so convoluted that the children hid there during hide and seek. 'Magnificent trees, aren't they?' After a few moments, he turned back to face her. 'I start milking at first light, feed Bub, and then head out for work. He sleeps until the sun cracks the hill.'

'I'll come at sunrise.'

Ned gave her a warm smile before he turned for his caravan. 'Tomorrow, then.'

Later, in bed, Lorrelai lay on her side with one hand under her cheek. The moon was bright, its shadows stencilling the flower pattern from the curtain to the quilt. A yeasty smell rose from the dough proving on the bench. Tonight, no possums thumped, no dogs barked. After the turmoil of the last few weeks, something felt right about the world.

Chapter 35

Lorrelai woke early from a deep, heavy sleep. Yawning, she got up on one elbow and swung her legs out. The damp towel slid down from her breasts, and she put it aside and tugged on a fitted skivvy, slipping another cloth up the front, pulling her plait from where it was trapped beneath the top. She smelled bread, and her mouth watered.

'Thanks, Pierre,' she said, slipping a dress of Maria's over the top before she opened the curtain.

Bent over in front of the stove, Pierre straightened. 'Two loaves, dear?'

'One for us, the other for Ned and Dora. I'm helping them.' She yawned and searched around for an apron, pulling one off the door rail before tying it behind her. 'We'll get fresh veggies, milk and eggs in return.'

'Lovely!' Pierre rubbed his hands together, a twinkle in his eye. 'Mind if I eat one of those eggs for brekkie? Got a big day ahead. Butcher pays me with a roast leg o' lamb today!'

'Of course.'

Once Pierre left, Lorrelai made more soup. She could imagine fresh vegetables snapping under the knife, and her soul lifted.

Lorrelai put on her straw hat and headed uphill. The baby was crying already. She knocked once, twice, and then opened the door.

'Hello? Hello? Just me, Lorrelai.' She peered inside. The strong smell and loud wailing slapped her senses. In front of the drawn curtains sat Dora. She was wearing her old nightie, her hair knotted at the back of her head.

'Dora? Are you all right?' Lorrelai put the soup and bread on the table and bent closer. Dora's head turned, but she stared at the floor.

Lorrelai touched her arm and spoke over the noise. 'I've made bread and soup.'

Dora looked at the food, but then away, wincing.

Lorrelai ripped back the curtain and went to the cot. 'Okay now, little fellow. What's wrong, huh?'

The tiny boy's face gleamed wet and red. He had kicked his covers off and his stick-thin legs pedalled the air, tiny pink grub toes splayed. Lorrelai took off her hat and placed it down on the table.

'Should I pick him up?' Lorrelai watched as his tiny fists clenched and shook, his lips quivering as he gulped air.

Dora's eyes snapped over to her as Lorrelai reached in, slid her hands under the baby, and gently clutched him to her shoulder. His back was wet. At first rigid, his body softened.

'Oh, sweetheart.' Lorrelai turned. 'Dora, do you have a dry nappy for him?'

Dora swallowed. Corrugations moved beneath the skin of her throat. Then she pointed at a small pile of folded squares.

'Nappies?' Lorrelai leaned back, so the child's weight rested into her chest, and then went over and, with her free hand, picked one up. It unfolded out to a square.

Lorrelai supported the baby's head as she lowered him down. 'I haven't changed a nappy, Dora.'

'I have.' The caravan bumped as Blossom bounced in. She dumped a grey wide-brimmed hat on top of Lorrelai's hat and took the baby's legs.

Lorrelai moved over to give her room. Blossom removed the pin from the wet nappy and dropped it into a nearby bucket. The baby's bare bottom was scarlet and sore.

'Oh my God, what's wrong with him?'

Blossom threw Dora a dark, telling look. 'Doesn't change him often enough, hey Dora?' With her free hand, she folded the fresh square corner to corner, forming a triangle.

'Now,' said Blossom. 'We clean off the piss and cover his butt in cream. Should be some here.' She patted around. 'Where's the cream for the baby's bum, Dora?'

Dora shrugged.

Blossom shook her head and rolled her eyes. 'For God's sake. Okay. Lorrelai, can you get some dripping from the pot on the sink?' Blossom pointed to the kitchen, flapping the rag in her hand like she was in a hurry. 'Wet this, too. We wash the piss off and it stops burning.'

'You mean *this* is why he's crying? I thought ...' Something flared inside Lorrelai. She wished she'd ignored Blossom and gone to the baby the first time she'd heard him screaming.

Blossom gave her a gentle push. In the kitchen, Lorrelai found the jar of dripping and took it to Blossom, who efficiently washed, dried, and creamed the baby's bottom, then fastened the dry nappy.

'Are babies always this skinny?'

Blossom gave her a withering look and shook her head, a heavy message in her eyes.

'Ned ... milked,' Dora said softly.

They both turned and stared at her. A wave of anger crested in Lorrelai, but it had nowhere to crash on Dora's slumped shoulders and deathly pale face.

'What's the time?'

Blossom scoffed. 'Time for first drinks, eh Dora?'

Sternly, Lorrelai cleared her throat.

'Sorry,' Blossom mumbled, and her face fell.

Lorrelai passed her hand over her eyes. She remembered Ned's instructions for the gardening. She already had her work boots on. In her mind, a neat circle of sizzling root vegetables surrounded a crisp lamb roast, but the need oozing from Dora and the baby gripped her whole being.

'Dora, how about I feed the baby so you can do some washing? Have you eaten?'

Slowly, Dora shook her head.

'Go on, then, have some bread while it's still warm.' Lorrelai gave Blossom a look, and the girl nodded intuitively. 'I'll stay, but I'm bringing my drawing pad. We had a deal.'

With Blossom's help, Lorrelai tied the baby in the sling across her torso. Outside, Blossom handed her the bottle, and Lorrelai fed the baby.

'Why are you crying?'

'Poor little thing.' Lorrelai turned away, moving side to side, like Ned had. 'Dora's really sick.'

'In the head,' muttered Blossom sulkily, kicking at the ground.

'I was hoping to start in the garden, Blossom. But I'll need some help.'

Blossom glared, and then sighed hard. 'Fine,' she said. 'As long as I can draw, and I don't have to look after the baby.'

'Deal.'

They made their way to the fenced gardens. The first was bigger than Lorrelai realised, stretching past the back of the goat shed and all the way up to the edge of the caravan.

'Jesus,' said Blossom. 'What a bloody mess.'

There had been rows at some point. Now, rotten tomatoes dragged down branches, beans fought for space along the wire, and weeds thickened the mess. Over the top, winged insects floated.

'This way!' Blossom strode off towards a wire gate. 'Can't let them goats in here.'

The goats lifted their heads, their lower jaws swinging a circular chew, and bleated questioningly.

Lorrelai closed the gate. She checked the baby. Tiny hands were fisted against his cheeks, his lips pink and swollen from sucking, but his eyes were closed. A soft feeling swept through her. She took a moment staring at the flushed cheeks, the chin like a thumb tip, the lower eyelashes soft as the fringe of an orchid petal.

'How long are you staying, Lorrelai?'

'A few weeks more.'

'Ma reckons she's gonna marry me off to some bloke in town.' Blossom made a face. 'I'll run away before that happens. Maybe go with you.'

The intensity of Blossom's face communicated something. 'I see.' Lorrelai reminded herself she was here temporarily. She didn't know enough to comment. She twisted around to the buckets stacked by the fence. 'Let's get started on the beans. Keep some of the old ones for seeds. We'll pull out the old tomato bushes and dig up some potatoes, too, if they're ready.'

Lorrelai and Blossom moved along the fence, picking beans. Most went into a bucket for the chickens. Then they started pulling out tomato bushes. Lorrelai could hear them both breathing, feel the sweat trickle through her hair, down her face, sense the heat trapped beneath the straps of the sling.

Blossom stayed close, shuffling along with her butt almost on her heels, her hands moving much faster than Lorrelai's. 'So, where did you come from? I was born right here in an old caravan.'

'I grew up in an orphanage in Kalamunda. My parents were killed in a car crash.'

'Really? Shit. Did the nuns whip you and feed you porridge and cold water?'

Lorrelai snorted. 'That was the dark ages. The nuns were nice. Strict, but nice. We had jobs, but plenty of food, time to read, time to play.'

They went to the chicken enclosure and emptied two buckets of ruined vegetables. The chickens flapped over, made curious noises, and then pecked and scratched.

'So, how'd you start dancing for men?' asked Blossom as they started near where they'd left off, this time digging for potatoes.

'Women too,' said Lorrelai. 'A travelling dancer stayed a few nights once, taught me some steps and left me with a feather boa. It's called Burlesque. Funny, sexy, but not stripping.' She looked around, but they were alone.

Blossom handed potatoes to Lorrelai, who wiped each one on the grass before dropping them into a bucket.

'I'd watch a stripper.' Blossom grinned. 'Naked women are something holy.'

Lorrelai laughed. 'Dancing is wonderful.' She stopped for a moment, letting her head drop back so the sun warmed her face. She massaged the back of her neck. When she opened her eyes, Blossom wasn't there. She was sitting cross-legged by the fence, her sketchbook open on her lap, pencil in hand.

'Keep going,' said Blossom. She bent over the paper, glancing up every now and then.

The gardening seemed endless. Eventually, they finished emptying buckets of ruined vegetables and lining all the good vegetables up along the fence.

When the baby woke, Blossom ran to the caravan to fetch another bottle, and they carried all the buckets to Ned and Dora's caravan. Lorrelai's muscles ached down one side of her back, and she was hungry, thirsty and tired.

Blossom set her bucket down with a huff and pushed her plait back. 'Right. I've got to go.' She strode off, flicking dirt off her skirt.

Lorrelai stuck her head inside the caravan. It was dim again, the curtains closed. The bread and soup sat exactly where she'd left them.

'Dora?' She waited. All was quiet. A foot stuck out from the bottom of the curtain that screened the spare bed. The sole was dark with dirt, like the barefoot children.

Lorrelai left her boots on the step and changed the baby's nappy. He made soft gurgles and chirps like a happy baby bird. She picked him up, swayed with him, inhaled the sweet scent of his skin. As she lowered him into the crib, his eyes fluttered and closed.

* * *

In Pierre's caravan, Lorrelai sliced off a wedge of bread and heated vegetable soup in the saucepan. After eating, she lay down and closed her eyes. When she awoke, it was with a start, her head full of fog.

Outside the small window, the kurrajong tree cast shadows across the shed—long shadows. She sat, annoyed she'd slept too long. She ran her fingers through her hair, plaited it and tied the end.

Even before she began walking uphill, Lorrelai could hear the baby wailing. Beneath the trees, white caught her eye, and she realised it was Dora. Cup in hand, she was slumped halfway down the chair, still wearing her nightgown.

'Dora?' Lorrelai walked faster.

Dora's head turned slowly. Her eyes were heavy lidded and blank, her lips slack. From one of the tents, Tom Jones crooned out the soothing tones of 'Green, Green Grass of Home.' Lorrelai felt a sudden longing for the orphanage, where grass draped the hill below the buildings and the girls used to run through it during free play.

'Does Bub need feeding?'

Dora looked away and took a gulp from her cup, her throat moving in several deep swallows.

'Dora, he's crying. When did he eat?'

Dora sighed but did not move to get up. Her lips closed in a long line, like a satisfied frog.

'Ugh!' Lorrelai strode to the caravan and went inside. She picked the baby up and jiggled him up and down as she checked the fridge. It was empty. The baby was sweating and hiccupping, suggesting he'd cried for a long time. His nappy was soaked.

'Okay, Baby Ned, shhh,' Lorrelai whispered. She laid him down and changed his nappy. Then she placed him on the table, on top of the sling, and softly sang the chorus of 'Green, Green Grass of Home' to him. His wails dropped in volume and then fell to exhaled hums, and then his eyes closed. It felt like the morning again, with absolutely no progress made.

Lorrelai tied him to her body, using the sling, left the van, and stomped over to Dora. A half-empty bottle of straw-coloured liquid glinted from beneath Dora's chair.

'Dora, where's the milk?' Lorrelai rocked the baby, patting his back. 'There were two bottles this morning.'

'Sold them.' Dora flapped her hand.

'What about the baby?'

Dora yawned. 'The baby, the baby,' she said, closing her eyes. Her mouth yawned open. After a second, she sucked in a long snore.

'Dora!' Lorrelai squatted, grabbed the bottle from under the chair, sniffed the top and scowled. 'Where'd you get this?'

Dora winced and opened one eye. 'An admirer.' She fluttered her fingers, reaching for the bottle.

'No!' Lorrelai stood and upended it, both of them watching as the liquid puddled at Dora's feet. Dora looked up and held out her hand. Lorrelai tossed her the empty bottle.

'You can't do this when you have a baby!'

Dora yawned, tipped her head back, and closed her eyes again, her arms folded around the empty bottle at her breast.

'Ugh!' Lorrelai stamped her foot, and the baby whined thinly. 'Shh. Shh.' Lorrelai rubbed big circles on his back through the sling. 'Good boy,' she said soothingly. 'Go to sleep.'

It was late afternoon. Kids were leaving their play and disappearing into caravans to help with animals and dinner, throwing glances over their shoulders at Lorrelai, Dora, and the baby. Dogs ambled after them and sat waiting on the doorsteps. Corellas were a screech of white across the dark blue sky.

Inside the sling, Bub's eyes were shut, but his breathing was fluttering rapidly.

Lorrelai strode up the steps of the caravan, grabbed a milk bucket and went to the goat shed.

'C'mon, Maisy,' she called. 'Here's your feed. Be a good girl.' She repeated what Ned had done the previous day, but when it got to milking, she struggled.

She curled first one hand around the nearest teat and then the other. Nothing. She took a deep breath and squeezed from the top down, grasping from index to pinkie like Ned had. A few drops squirted out and dripped off her little finger.

Lorrelai concentrated. She managed to go slightly quicker—left hand, right hand, left, right. Some white shot out, spraying in all directions like an over-pressurised hose. The goat flicked her tail, did a little tap dance, and kicked over the bucket.

'Damn!' Lorrelai rinsed the bucket at the tap by the fence. The kid bleated pure anguish from the other side.

The next time, Lorrelai tried to aim the teat inside the bucket. A few bendy streams hissed against the inside. The goat twitched her tail and stomped.

Against Lorrelai's back, the baby stiffened, wriggled, and began to wail, soft at first and then louder and stronger.

Lorrelai began to sweat. Her fingers ached. She murmured comforting things, and then she began to sing.

'Maisy, Baby and Lorrelai,
hit by an apple that made them cry,
please, oh please don't let me die,
Maisy, baby and Lorrelai.'

Progress was slow. Maisy twisted her neck around, bleated loudly and stomped her foot. Lorrelai grabbed the bucket out just in time. 'No, you don't!'

Lorrelai moved the stool closer and waited. Maisy burped sullenly and chewed her cud.

Lorrelai kept trying. After an age, there was enough milk for a baby's bottle, but still a fraction of what Ned had milked. 'That'll have to do.' Lorrelai sat back. She heard a giggle.

Blossom was crouched by the gate, her pencil moving over the sketchbook on her lap.

'*Maisy, Baby and Lorrelai,*
got some milk so the baby didn't cry.
Maisy was good because she didn't want to die,
Maisy, Baby and Lorrelai!'
'How long have you been there?'
Blossom shrugged. 'Five minutes or so. Made a great sketch of you.'
'What!'
'*Blossom!*' called a voice from way off.

The girl slipped the pencil behind her ear and jumped up. 'Got to go.' She swung away, her plait flying out from the back of her head.

As Lorrelai neared the caravan, she saw Dora walking towards the showers, arms swinging, her towel over her shoulder. A black feeling gripped her; she made herself breathe it away.

When Lorrelai finally got the bottle to the baby, she almost cried again. She could hear her stomach growling, and her desperation for the toilet sent an ache through her lower back.

She heard car doors open and men's voices. Ned couldn't see her like this. She put the baby in the crib, the bottle propped on his chest.

* * *

Back in Pierre's caravan, Lorrelai busied herself slicing beetroot, potato and carrots from the garden. She sprinkled a little dry spice over them and slid them into the oven. It was too late now to cook a roast, but eggs would be fine.

After dinner, she showered late, crying warm tears under the tepid water. She didn't have the energy to wash her hair. Was this motherhood? Able to strip every ounce of patience and energy from you? Able to turn women into wrecks of themselves?

Chapter 36

After Pierre left in the morning, Lorrelai ate toast with tea and then cleaned up. From the top step, she threw a handful of breadcrumbs to the fairy martins and welcome swallows, tiny darting movements that fluttered and pecked between leaves. For a moment, she wished she were one of them so she could zip around above the park and over the river.

Ned and Dora's caravan was quiet. Lorrelai checked in and found the baby and Dora asleep. She pulled the door closed behind her and went to the garden. The spinach seedlings sat along the fence where the tomato stakes lay, and the tall weeds were wet with dew.

Planting seedlings and completing the weeding took three hours. When she was finished, she passed by the quiet caravan and ate lunch down at Pierre's.

Lorrelai treated herself to a sleep and afterwards to a walk along the river. The coolness of dusk crept up from the river like a mist, as Lorrelai lit kindling inside a ring of blackened rocks, letting it burn down beneath a heavy metal plate. She put Pierre's lamb roast into the camp oven with the vegetables and set it over the coals. Then she shuffled close enough to the dark orange coals to absorb the warmth.

* * *

Pierre whistled as morning light prised Lorrelai's eyelids open. Despite a good meal and a glass of cider, Lorrelai's night was restless and dream filled. In one dream, golden hair spread across her pillow in her room at the Lion Inn. Then the hair turned black, and a baby started crying. She woke in a sweat.

She got up, shivering in the morning air. Her nightie was damp, and when she showered, opaque fluid seeped from both breasts. She stared at her leaking nipples, the drops weaving down her bare torso like sticky tears.

'For goodness sake,' she said and pressed her forearm against them.

Uphill, she again found Dora in the spare bed. The sleeping woman's arm hung down through the opening, the slim fingers limp. Lorrelai stared at the wedding and engagement rings which had slid to Dora's first knuckle.

In the crib, the baby jerked, and when Lorrelai looked in, his eyes fixed on her. Then his fists waved, and he cooed.

'Morning, Baby Ned.'

Lorrelai left a new loaf of bread on the table, tied the baby in the sling around her body, and went outside.

She found a box and tucked baby Ned inside, his feet free so he could kick his legs. Looking down at him, she thought about baby Moses from the Bible.

She weeded, raked, and tidied until the garden looked new. Soaked with sweat, she stood back and surveyed her work. Seedlings formed neat green lines, dirt was raked clean between rows, order was restored. Overhead, sheets of damp cloud hung so heavy she could feel their moisture as she breathed.

Around her, the bees were busy. They arrived each morning, one or two at first, and then a few dozen, crawling all over the flowering plants with a low droning hum. Nearby, the goats and chickens milled around, making contented sounds as they ate. Insects lifted, landed, lifted again. Everything was alive. Everything was real—as real as this tiny child beside her.

Lorrelai felt a rush of heat as her breasts leaked. She peered around quickly, and then pressed her forearm across them. When she removed her arm, two damp circles stained her chest.

Once the gardening was done, Lorrelai gulped water from the tap and returned to Ned and Dora's caravan. All was quiet. She soothed the sleeping baby in the crib, watched the rise and fall of his tiny chest for a moment and covered him with a light blanket.

Quietly, she made coffee and buttered a slice of bread.

Outside, small birds twittered, and children called to each other.

'Ma made scones.' Blossom waved. 'Already put jam on for you.'

Lorrelai sat upright. 'Blossom! Just what I needed. Stay with me. You can just sketch.' She patted the chair beside her.

Blossom dumped herself down. 'Nah, can't. Ma is determined to make a good wife of me.' She crossed her arms. 'He's got three goddamn kids. Three! Needs me to look after the little wretches.'

'Where's his wife?'

'Died.' Blossom leaned forwards, her jaw set. 'Haven't even been out of this town yet!' Her chest rose and fell with a sigh. 'I want to go places, see things, drink and smoke!' She got up and paced to the tree and back twice.

'She can't force you surely. You're too young.'

'She can,' said Blossom, her fists clenched, leaning forwards. 'We got nothing, see? Boys are handy for the mill, but me?' She lifted her hands and then dropped them back against her thighs. 'He's promised her a house! *Me* for a *house*.' She made a disgusted noise and looked off down the hill. 'Made me try on her horrible ol' wedding dress for size. I'm the only miserable bloody girl. Wish I wasn't.'

'Anything I can do?'

Blossom shrugged. She spoke after a moment, her voice quiet. 'I'm not joking about running away. I'll burn her bloody wedding dress before I go too, just see if I don't.'

* * *

That evening, Lorrelai walked uphill through the thickening carpet of figs and leaves to the sounds of the settling birds and families. Inside the dim stillness of Ned and Dora's caravan, Dora and the baby slept on. Lorrelai sniffed. The warm medicinal smell of alcohol lingered in the air.

'There you are.' Ned, grim-faced, appeared on the steps behind her.

Lorrelai blushed. 'What's wrong?'

'Why'd you bring liquor?' he whispered angrily. 'Thought I made it clear!'

Lorrelai broke out in a sweat. 'I did bring some on the first day, but —'

'So, it's you I can thank!' He threw up one arm and twisted away.

Heart pounding, she followed. Ned sat beneath the tree, his expression stony.

'I'm sorry,' Lorrelai muttered. 'I did bring some on my first visit, but not since. Promise.'

Ned's chest rose and fell—the only sign he was alive. He finally looked sideways. 'Who then? Everyone should know by now.'

'I don't know.'

Ned made a curious, throaty noise. 'She's worse on it. Like a child. I can't watch her all the time.'

Downhill, a couple of the older children ambled across the bridge and stopped in the middle to peer into the wide river, rounding their bodies over the rail. The surface was calm and dark.

'Did you see the garden?'

Ned took a deep breath, exhaled, and rubbed his eyes. 'Yeah. It looks great. Sorry, I'm stuffed. Maisy and the kid were together when I got home the night before, so there was no milk. Baby cried for hours.' He brushed the side of his head with his hand, and sawdust sprinkled his lap.

'Oh God! I'm so sorry!' Lorrelai crouched down by the edge of the chair. 'I didn't know. I tried so hard. Baby Ned was screaming. It was a nightmare.'

Ned tilted his head. 'Baby Ned?'

Lorrelai swallowed. 'That's what I call him.'

Ned nodded slowly. 'I'm sorry.' He leaned forwards, elbows to his lap, and sighed heavily. 'I'm not at my best. Please forgive me.'

'Of course.'

He smiled, and some tension seemed to ease from him. 'All right then, I'll shower quickly and, if you have time, I can show you how to milk.'

Baby Ned's cry floated out from the caravan, making them both look that way.

Ned's brow arched up. 'Milking it is, or we'll all go deaf!'

In the milking shed, with Ned coaching from over her shoulder and one of his hands on top of hers on Maisy's teat, Lorrelai learned to milk faster.

'That's it! Trap the milk towards the tip, and then domino your fingers down towards it.'

Lorrelai giggled as the white liquid squirted out. 'That's so much better than last night.'

'We'll make a milkmaid of you yet!'

The warmth of his big hand over hers lit her like a street lamp. She could barely concentrate on the task.

'Ned, what did you mean about being married *and* a bachelor?'

Ned cleared his throat. 'Is that a question you should be asking?'

Lorrelai relaxed at his teasing tone. 'You're the one who said it.'

He patted her shoulder and stood. Lorrelai felt the sudden loss.

'We don't sleep in the same bed. Apparently, we've only had a couple of dates. But it doesn't look promising.' His deep voice filled the small shed.

'I heard you arguing the other night.'

Zip, zip, zip, the milk level rose up the side of the bucket.

'Makes no sense anymore.'

Lorrelai kept going until she couldn't squeeze any more milk out. She removed the milk bucket and twisted around to find Ned standing in the middle of the shed, gazing into the middle distance, tuned to some faraway channel. 'What is it, Ned?'

He frowned. 'Something's wrong.' Suddenly, his face dropped, and he ran for the gate, swung round the gate post and propelled himself towards the van.

When Lorrelai got to the caravan, all the lights were on. She leapt up the steps. Ned stood in the middle, the baby to his shoulder, his head brushing the ceiling. Everything inside seemed large and strange, orbiting around Ned at its epicentre. Tendons stood out in his neck.

'Wake up!' Ned patted the baby's back, his eyes wide.

Lorrelai closed the gap between them. 'Show me.'

Ned held out the baby and his little head lolled back. 'Oh, Jesus! Dora! Dora! What have you done?' cried Ned.

Lorrelai clutched her throat, a sensation in her midsection like a kick.

Dora tumbled out through the curtained opening in her nightie, one hand shading her eyes. 'Huh?' She shrugged. 'Oh, he had a little drink. Makes him sleep.' She nodded at an empty glass bottle on the table.

'What? Liquor! Oh my God! Oh my God!' Ned shouted.

Lorrelai blew on the baby's face. He moved slightly. 'Give him some air! In his mouth, quick!'

Ned focused on Lorrelai and then on the lifeless baby in his arms.

He lifted the baby and puffed into his mouth, like he was kissing the crook of his arm. The baby straightened slightly. He was so still, his lips mauve.

'Do it again!' Lorrelai's voice came out strong, but beneath her, the ground fell away. She grabbed Ned's trouser pockets. 'Hurry!'

Ned bent his head and puffed again. One of the baby's legs jerked.

'He moved!' Lorrelai bounced on her toes. 'Again. That's it!'

Ned puffed again. An airless cry came from his arms. Ned choked, a sound of pain like a wounded animal. The sound tore right through her, and Lorrelai began to cry too.

Baby Ned's cries grew stronger.

'Oh God! Oh God, thank you!' Ned held the baby to his shoulder, tears streaming down his cheeks. Behind him, Dora just stared.

'He's okay,' Lorrelai said to Ned. She held a handful of his shirt, and he kept his eyes on hers, like he was drawing strength from her. For a minute, they were the only two people in the world.

Dora stumbled back through the curtains, lay on the bed and tucked her feet up inside her nightie.

'Can you get a bottle ready?' Ned said quietly. He wiped his face with one hand, then walked out and down the stairs.

In the sudden emptiness, Lorrelai prepared a bottle, her hands shaking so much she spilled some. She noticed Dora's wedding rings, shining silver, on the edge of the sink.

Outside, she found Ned near the tree, handed him the bottle, and pulled her cardigan tight. Ned tipped the bottle to the baby's lips and rocked gently from side to side.

'You cold?' Ned lifted the elbow of his feeding arm and jerked his head to indicate she come in. After a moment, she ducked under, so close she could feel his warmth. He pulled her in. 'There you go.' He kissed her forehead. 'Thanks, honey. Thank you so much.'

Lorrelai shivered into Ned's warm body, her head against his chest and her other arm around his waist. She watched the baby feed, his eyes closing peacefully, cheeks moving rhythmically.

'He's beautiful,' she murmured. The three of them rocked in the cool quiet of the evening. Beatles music from one of the vans uphill and light flooding between the tarp structures like an odd, comforting jigsaw suggested that nothing had changed. Yet everything had.

A sound came from the caravan. Ned turned and went still, his arm tightening around Lorrelai. She looked back over her shoulder.

Wearing a nightie and high heels, Dora wobbled down the steps and set off downhill, humming.

Lorrelai tilted her head and watched Ned give Dora's back a look she hoped he never gave hers.

Chapter 37

As agreed, Lorrelai hurried to Ned and Dora's at sunrise. Ned was waiting in the doorway with the baby tucked into his side. His black hair and beard were newly combed, and his face was soft with fatigue.

'Baby Ned is fine,' he said in a low voice. 'I'm a bit knocked around, though. I'll be starting late, so it'll be dark when I return.'

'I won't leave Baby Ned, even when he's asleep.' She glanced inside. 'How is Dora?'

Ned pursed his lips and looked away. 'Slept like the innocent. Went out again this morning. Honestly? I don't care.'

'Does she know I'll be here?'

Ned looked back at her, his face frowning over mingling emotions. 'She doesn't seem to know. Or care.'

'Does she need to see someone? I'm really worried.'

Ned shook his head. 'I've tried that. Hopefully, she just needs some rest and no alcohol. This morning, I told Peg that Dora could've killed the baby. She said she'd keep an eye out.' He touched Lorrelai's shoulder and looked into her eyes. 'Now, don't you worry about anything except the baby. Go to Peggy if you need anything.'

After Ned left, Lorrelai put her basket of ingredients on the table. She put Baby Ned down to sleep, made a pie and slid it into the oven. After cleaning a little, she folded laundry and put the night's nappies outside to soak in a bucket. She wondered how Ned and Dora could exist like this: Dora in her own world up one end of the caravan, Ned shouldering everything else up the other end.

As Lorrelai sat sipping tea, Dora came up the steps and sat on the top, facing out. She took off her shoes, wet and muddy, and dropped them there. She got up, went to the spare bed and climbed up.

'How are you, Dora?' Lorrelai waited. She heard Dora yawn behind the curtain.

'Big show,' Dora said with a sigh. 'Record audiences. Don't disturb me. Tonight it's the Sydney high society.' Another yawn.

Lorrelai stared at the curtain, listening as Dora's breathing became deep and even. Then she sighed and prepared a baby bottle in the kitchen.

Her hand protectively beneath the baby in the sling, she walked outside and along the path to the garden. She stood there a moment, staring at the fresh cleared earth. Then she went to the second garden. She let herself in and turned a bucket upside down and sat on it.

Ned made a few jerky half-hearted cries. 'It's coming, honey.' Lorrelai unfastened the sling and pulled out the bottle. Baby Ned snuffled against the front of her blouse.

'Hey, it's coming, Baby Ned.' Lorrelai offered the bottle's teat, but the baby kept nuzzling her blouse. She went still. She glanced over at the caravan. Where she sat, towards the van's back corner, she couldn't see in any window. She looked all around. Behind her was the line of bamboo stalks, and to her right, the goat and chicken sheds. Ahead of her were tall weeds, and beyond, big trees lining the main road.

Lorrelai set the bottle down on the ground and unbuttoned her blouse. She slid her arm under Baby Ned's head and pulled him close as he latched on to her nipple. Pain pinched from nipple to breast, and then, slowly, it eased.

Oh, beautiful boy. Sweet, sweet boy. Lorrelai's chest fluttered, and she sniffled gently, a lump constricting her throat. But there were no tears.

After a few minutes, looking swiftly around, Lorrelai gently pulled away from the baby and turned him around. He snuffled, his tiny fists opening and closing impatiently, and then he fed from the other side.

* * *

Ned arrived an hour after sunset. Lorrelai had just finished milking the goats and had swapped a bucket of vegetables for some of Peggy's chicken meat.

181

'Hello?' His head appeared at the door. His gaze flew to the curtains in front of the bed.

'Dora went for a walk.'

They exchanged a look, and a tremble went through her at knowing that a secret lay unspoken between them.

'She slept this morning. She's been out for hours.'

Ned exhaled and gave a heavy head shake.

Lorrelai poured the milk into sterilised bottles and put them in the cold box, her hands shaking.

She had fed the baby again after lunch. All day, a persistent lightness, as if she was walking just above the earth, had buoyed her. But now, it felt different, all shaky and uncertain, like she'd stolen something.

In the kitchen, Lorrelai checked on dinner. The potatoes were frothy and boiling. In a deep pan beside them, half a chicken Peg had exchanged for butter and vegetables simmered in milky water with thyme and oregano.

'Something smells good.' Ned smiled and caught her eye. 'I'll get washed up so you can go. You got time to feed Bub again?'

Something jumped inside her. She examined Ned's eyes, but they were blameless.

'Yes.' Lorrelai wiped her hands and went to the crib. She lifted the baby to her shoulder. The floor rocked with Ned's departure.

When Lorrelai heard the door click, she quickly opened her blouse and rested the baby on her lap. He latched on as if they'd been practicing for weeks. He finished both sides, and then whimpered and shook his fists. 'I haven't got much left now, Baby Ned.'

She carefully separated herself from the baby and buttoned her blouse. Then she grabbed the bottle of goat's milk and completed the feed.

Once Baby Ned was asleep in his basket, Lorrelai whirled into action. She grabbed the bottle of milk and poured the remainder down the sink. Heart beating hard, she washed the bottle, teat and screw top, dried her hands on a tea towel, and then sat down at the table.

Ned ducked his head as he entered. He had showered and combed back his hair. 'Hey,' he said when he saw her. He smiled softly and bent over the crib. 'Ah, he's asleep.'

He took a seat on the other side of the table. 'All okay?'

Lorrelai rubbed her palms together as she rose. She was almost too guilty to speak, the secret wedged in her throat. 'Yes, fine. Dinner's almost ready. Fresh veggies in that bucket there.' She interlaced her fingers, examined his face.

Ned gave her a steady look. 'I mean, how are you?'

'What do you mean?'

Ned rose, filling the room, changing its light. She caught her breath.

'You're amazing. I can't believe my luck that you're related to Pierre. I didn't know he had relatives.'

Lorrelai swallowed. 'It's late. I'd better go.' She picked up her basket and turned for the door.

'Can you come back tomorrow? I'll have money then. It's payday. Is that okay?'

The look on his face melted her. They shared a long glance. 'Sure.'

'Lorrelai, there's a market in town this Sunday,' Ned went on. 'You can buy almost anything, barter. Take some cider. One of your pies, maybe? We can have a day out.'

'Oh.' Lorrelai smiled. 'That would be nice.'

'Great.' His gentle smile became a yawn, and he shook his head at himself and massaged the back of his neck with one hand.

The truth of what she'd done sat in the air like a beautiful deep secret. She moved for the door, keen to be alone. 'Goodnight, Ned. Bye, Baby Ned.'

Ned caught her hand. Lorrelai froze. 'Take tomorrow off, honey. You've earned it. I'll stay with the baby.' His thumb swept across her palm.

'Okay.' She nodded quickly and withdrew her hand. 'Night, Ned.'

Lorrelai rushed down the hill. Pierre was reading. He gave her a nod and then kept reading.

Behind her curtain, Lorrelai lay on her back, staring at the curved ceiling. She had fed like a mother. It had been so natural. The baby needed her milk, and it had come.

When she'd arrived in this awful park, she felt like she'd been banished, away from the home she knew, her lover, her work. She'd felt so alone. Now, none of that mattered. She knew exactly why she was here.

Chapter 38

Lorrelai woke with electricity licking through her veins. She patted her chest. Her breasts were heavier, fuller. She could barely believe the miracle. She swung her legs over the side of the bed, dressed quickly, and hurried to Ned's caravan.

A rooster crowed, and the sheep from the neighbouring farms bleated as the sun glowed behind the trees on the far side of the train tracks.

'Knock, knock.'

'Hel-lo!' Ned smiled, a full bottle of milk in his hand. 'Pay will be here about midday. I'll run it down to you.'

'Okay. I won't stay long. How about I feed the baby first?' An urgency bubbled up inside her.

Ned shrugged and handed her the bottle. 'Sure, thanks. Just pop him down for a nap when you're finished.'

Baby Ned's thin whinge became more insistent. Lorrelai picked him up, and her breasts started to leak. She wanted to push Ned right out the door.

'You go ahead. I've got him.' She sat at the table, jiggling her knee impatiently.

Ned headed out the door, buckets in hand. 'Righto, boss.' He winked and closed the door behind him.

Lorrelai listened until she made out Dora's long, deep breaths over the sound of her own pounding heart.

She breastfed, checking over her shoulder several times. She was finished by the time Ned returned with a bucket of milk.

Ned and Lorrelai had coffee together and chatted about everyday things.

On her way back down the hill, Lorrelai felt like the sun was shining from her chest.

* * *

Later, Ned came with tools for the shelving. As she watched him work, Lorrelai realised two things. Ned was a good father, and an honest man, and she needed to tell him what she'd done.

'Can I bring dinner up for you?' she offered.

'You sure? That would be great.'

For the next hour, Lorrelai was quiet. She provided tea when Ned took a break, and then busied herself in Pierre's caravan.

'All done!' Ned called.

Lorrelai joined him outside the little shed door. The fresh smell of wood came from six new shelves. 'You've done a great job.'

He was right behind her when she turned. He took a step back, regarding her for a moment. 'Lorrelai, why haven't you got a man?'

She swallowed and dropped her gaze. 'I did. At the inn.'

He cocked his head. 'You got a bad temper? Bad habits? Deformities? Two wooden legs?'

Lorrelai chuckled. 'No. Two good legs.'

Ned smirked. 'Damn fool should've married you. I would have.'

Lorrelai looked down, her cheeks heating. 'He's married.'

'Ah.'

'He said he wasn't in love with her, but it didn't matter anyway, in the end.'

Ned took her hand.

'Sorry to hear that,' he murmured. His eyes lingered. 'You're a good woman.' He squeezed her hand, let go, and set off up the hill.

* * *

Lorrelai took a walk in the forest. She repeated Ned's words in her head many times. *Should've married you. I would have.* Every time, she felt like she was expanding. She imagined his mouth moving over the words, the intensity in his eyes.

Would he still say that when he found out she was secretly breastfeeding his baby?

Lorrelai headed back across the bridge and up to Pierre's. At the steps, she paused, staring uphill at Ned's caravan. She saw movement at the door. Dora swept out like an oversized moth, a flowing black cardigan over the nightie, her feet bare.

Lorrelai went inside Pierre's caravan and pulled the door half closed. Ear to the opening, she waited. Dora grew closer, and then passed. Lorrelai could hear her muttering.

Once Dora had crossed the bridge and disappeared, Lorrelai quickly gathered the dinner and set off uphill.

Ned's caravan door, wide open, shuddered in the breeze. Under the kitchen light, Ned stood at the sink, pouring milk.

'Hello. Am I too early?' Lorrelai walked in and put her basket on the table.

Ned smiled sideways at her. 'Never. What have you got there?'

Lorrelai unloaded the contents, listing what was for dinner: 'A leek and chicken pie made with Pegs' chicken and your vegetables, a fresh loaf of bread, and a bottle of quince jam.'

Ned came over and kissed her cheek. He gestured to the spread on his table. 'What've I done to deserve this?'

'We both work hard,' said Lorrelai. 'Time for a rest and a decent meal.' Inside the cot, the baby made a small sound of exclamation, then it drew out, as if he was making a statement. Lorrelai went and looked in the crib. 'Hey, gorgeous. How are you?' The baby flinched, then stuck his hand in his mouth.

'He's been great,' said Ned. He finished washing up and dried his hands. He joined her at the crib, baby gazing. 'It's like he's got rid of the grumbles or something.' He touched the edge of her hand, and then held it. 'Lorrelai, I think—'

Lorrelai removed her hand and turned to face him. 'Let's eat,' she said.

Ned searched her eyes for a moment but nodded. 'Sure.'

They sat down opposite each other. Lorrelai was pulsing with nerves as she served the pie. Ned frowned, cleared his throat.

The baby began to whinge. Ned put down his cutlery. 'Every time,' he said, with a look of relief, like the task absolved him of something.

Lorrelai was quick to her feet. 'I'll get him.'

'Oh.' Ned sat back down. 'Bottle is on the sink.'

Lorrelai brought the baby to the table and set him up across her lap. She undid her buttons and cradled the baby's head until he'd latched on. She was aware that Ned had gone completely still, cutlery still clutched in his hands.

'You're breastfeeding him?'

'Yes.'

More silence. Lorrelai looked up.

Ned's face was expressionless. His eyes snapped, and he swallowed hard. 'How?'

'My milk came in. I miscarried, shortly after I arrived.'

Ned was silent. But then he cleared his throat and muttered, 'What's going on?'

'I was pregnant. That's why I was kicked out. But I miscarried.'

The baby continued to suckle. Lorrelai felt like a thief, the stolen item in her lap. 'He latched on yesterday. It ... it was so natural.'

Ned's expression tightened. A muscle in his jaw twitched.

Lorrelai pulled back from the baby and did up her buttons. Baby Ned began to kick and fuss. 'Ned?'

'Get out.'

'But, Ned, I—'

Ned hit the table with the side of his fist and cutlery jumped. 'Get out!'

Lorrelai got to her feet, carried the baby to the crib, and laid him down. His tiny face screwed up, and he started to cry.

'I'm sorry.' She left without looking back, her heart in her throat.

* * *

Lorrelai curled up on her bed, fully dressed, her heart racing and every muscle tense. Her heart pounded for a long time.

Ned wasn't just angry; he was livid.

She couldn't think. Where so much had been before there was now a void. Eventually, she heard the silvery sounds of the river, an owl hooting, and the bump and scratch of possums. She tuned into the rustlings, her mood set by the water, and closed her eyes.

Just as she drifted close to sleep, there came a knock at the door. Lorrelai jumped, her eyes popping open, every muscle tensed. She waited. Another loud knocking.

Pierre shuffled out from the back of the van. He opened the door.

'Hello, Ned?'

'Hi, Pierre. Sorry, it's late. Is Lorrelai in?' His deep voice sounded so close.

'Ah, in bed, I believe.'

She heard a pause.

'I'm awake.' Lorrelai got up reluctantly. She pulled her cardigan tight and tugged back the curtain.

'I'll leave you to it. Goodnight.' Pierre ambled back into the caravan, whistling.

Lorrelai took her time shuffling to the end of the seat and finding her shoes.

Ned stood looking up from the bottom step, hands on his hips. 'Can we talk?'

Nodding, she walked out into the cool and closed the door behind her. Ned indicated they should walk over near the shed. Lorrelai walked ahead between the caravan and the shed, where it was dark but for the light shining from Pierre's kitchen. Gently, Ned took her by the shoulders.

'Lorrelai, I shouldn't have spoken to you like that. I got a shock. I thought … I don't know what I thought, but it scared me.'

'I didn't mean anything bad by it. He just nuzzled and … it happened naturally. But I understand if—'

'No.' Ned interrupted. He had his eyes closed and was shaking his head. When he opened them again, he stared directly into her eyes. 'I got a shock. I'm sorry.'

'I really care about him, Ned. And you. None of this was planned.'

'I know.' Ned drew her in against his chest, hugging her firmly. Slowly, Lorrelai put her arms around him. It felt good to be close again. As his warmth eased from him into her, she felt everything settle back into place. Relief coursed through her.

'Please come to market with me. They do delicious garlicky skewers at the Chinese food truck.' He brushed his fingers down her hair and kissed her forehead.

'Sounds terrible, but I'll come.'

He looked down, loosening his arms but still keeping them around her. 'You scare the hell out of me.' He leaned down, and his mouth came to hers, his tongue opening her lips.

Lorrelai was too stunned to return any kind of kiss. Ned's tongue was a demand, his lips a question, and his urgency forced her back until she found herself up against the side of Pierre's caravan. By then, Lorrelai realised her hands had found his hair, and her tongue found his too.

Chapter 39

Lorrelai wore her green dress, white boots, a white jacket and red lipstick. She walked uphill and smiled at the two women banging dusty rugs against a tree.

'Jeesuz! It's Brigette Bardot,' said one. The other chuckled.

'Wish I had a waist like yours! Four babies made a room for themselves, and it's still for rent!'

They both laughed, leaning on each other. Lorrelai laughed too and gave them a wave.

She walked up Ned's caravan steps and poked her head inside the door. 'Morning.'

Ned was smartly dressed and was packing a bag on the table, for the baby. His proud-shouldered posture sent a jolt of intense joy through Lorrelai. She had imagined his posture, his walk, his smile, and the smell of his clothes. Truth was, she couldn't think of anything else.

His brow shot up when he saw what she was wearing, and even that tiny movement made something jump in her skin.

The markets yielded a good selection of ingredients that Lorrelai salivated over. Ned bought the supplies that Lorrelai suggested. Then she got some for Pierre's as well.

Moving around the stalls, food tents and displays, she and Ned were never more than a few feet apart, attuned to the slight sounds and movements of each other's bodies and the carousel of human noise and animals wanting to be back in their paddocks instead of in tiny yards for petting and display.

When the light fell and the stalls were packed away, Ned and Lorrelai were among the last to leave the refuge of the showground. In the vehicle Ned shielded her by sitting in the front seat as she breastfed the baby in the back.

Eventually Ned turned the key and sat back. She saw him watching her in the rear-view mirror. Without a word, he looked away, and then pulled out of the car park.

'I had a great day, Ned.'

His cheeks pulled up and his eye corners creased.

Back at the caravan park, Lorrelai washed the baby while Ned tended the chickens and goats. She put her groceries in the basket she'd left the previous day and waited for Ned to return. When he got to the top step, he glanced around before he entered. He pulled the door closed behind him.

'Last night, after you left, I went walking with the baby. I felt so alone. Today, it felt as if I had a family.'

Lorrelai's heart quickened. Ned approached and took both of her hands.

'Lorrelai, will you marry me when I get a divorce from Dora?'

She coughed a little. 'My gosh. You're getting divorced?'

'My wife is long gone. I have to be honest with myself.'

Lorrelai looked at the curtains that screened the spare bed.

'Out again,' said Ned, not taking his eyes off Lorrelai.

Lorrelai swallowed. 'Is this because I take care of Baby Ned?' Blossom's earlier conversation surfaced in her thoughts.

Ned shrugged. 'I want you.'

Lorrelai felt flushed. She looked down at their feet, both in socks, which touched at the toes.

'When you're divorced, I'd love to talk about this again.'

Ned made a sound of relief, took her by the shoulders, and kissed her hard. When he let her go, Lorrelai was a little breathless.

* * *

Lorrelai didn't want to leave Pierre's caravan when she woke the next day. She couldn't determine whether it was the overwhelming feeling of happiness, untarnished by anything that might yet happen, or whether the previous nights' events were so huge that she needed time to think.

She knew the feeling between her and Ned was different to anything that had come before. The urgency of his kisses left her in no doubt where they were headed. *And that,* she thought from her precarious perch behind the thin privacy of the curtain, *is the problem.*

Lorrelai's days started early and ended late. She arrived for the baby's early feed, and then fed him late before she returned to Pierre's.

Dora slept so much that it was like she had ceased to exist in the real world. But Lorrelai never forgot she was there. Frequently, Dora woke squinting and cranky, shoving things out of her way, before leaving the caravan.

Dora never asked about the baby. She didn't even look at his cot. Even so, Lorrelai never let Dora catch her breastfeeding.

Ned moved with a boy's exuberance, but he touched her with the gentle hands of a man. His smile gave her a golden feeling, his hungry kisses kept her warm, and the danger in his gaze kept her on edge and more alive than she'd ever been.

Using the sling, Lorrelai carted Baby Ned everywhere. She found a square bucket on wheels, to which Pierre attached a handle, so she could collect apples or vegetables and take the baby with her. Baby Ned was settled and entertained by the movement, Lorrelai talking to him like he understood, the leaves and birds moving above them.

Weeks passed in industrious bliss. Blossom turned up at odd times, sketchpad in hand, and sketched while she watched Lorrelai work. Lorrelai was aware of her and careful not to reveal her double life, but she enjoyed Blossom hanging around, chatting and sketching, even though the girl would fall silent sometimes and stare off into the distance.

Each morning, Lorrelai woke in a thrill of excitement. She loved sharing coffee with Ned and the twinge of sadness she got when he left for work. Their end of day kiss was worth waiting all day for—every bit as urgent, if not more, than the first, forcing her against the side of the van or back against the creaking table, not built for such things as a grown woman and an eager man. When they had to stop suddenly, he laughed like it was a fantastic game, helping her to her feet, shaking his head, adjusting the front of his pants.

Each night, Lorrelai found it increasingly difficult to leave after the baby's last feed. Until, one night, Ned took her hand and led her to his bed.

The baby was asleep in his cot in the main section of the van, and Dora had left before dinner. Ned closed the curtains and turned to her, his fingers to his lips. Lorrelai nodded.

He started by taking off all her clothes. She stood there, compliant, as her apron, dress, and bra were carefully removed, as if he was trying not to touch her skin at all. He turned her slowly, admiring her slim waist, round bottom, the taut muscles in her thighs, her breasts, softer after feeding. Turning her to face him, with one finger he tugged down the front of her panties, like he was taking a peek, before letting the elastic slide back up. 'Pretty,' he said. He turned her around again, and pressed his body tight against her back, wrapping his arms around her like he might squeeze the air from her lungs.

'Oh, Lorrelai.'

She felt his breath quicken on her shoulder as he held her there, his hardness growing and pressing against the cleft of her buttocks before he released her. Then he turned her around again, kissed her, and then pushed her gently back onto the bed on her back. He slid her panties all the way off and spread her legs as he leaned over her.

'You're still dressed,' she whispered. She found the edge of the coverlet and pulled it across her top half, nipples hard with cold and eagerness.

Ned held his finger to his lips and pulled the blanket back off. He set her arms back down on the bed and kissed her chin. Grinning, he wriggled downwards, kissing between her breasts, and then down her stomach, past the hair and between her legs, until he was invisible.

Lorrelai stared at the ceiling, lost in the sensation of her skin swelling and moistening beneath his tongue. She watched as he stood up again, unzipped his trousers, and leaned forwards. He hooked his hands behind her knees, and then, on his knees, he thrust himself inside her, lowered himself down, and exhaled. Lorrelai watched a vein stand out and throb on Ned's flushed forehead, until all the tension inside her welled and opened, and she felt her body rise to meet his and closed her eyes.

Later, they heard Dora clamber into the spare bed. Ned tightened his arms around Lorrelai and kissed her shoulder. 'It's okay. She never sleeps in here.' He sounded sleepy, and Lorrelai had almost been asleep too, but now she was restless. She squeezed Ned's hand where it rested on her hip.

'Should I go?' she whispered.

'No. No.' He kissed her shoulder again.

His breathing grew slow and regular, but Lorrelai's skin jumped. She fought to stay still. Reaching back, she found a soft handful of him and moved in a way that made him grunt in surprise and wake suddenly. As he woke, he hardened, and he grasped her by the hips, pulling her backwards until he had pushed all the way inside her and they made love a second time. She fell asleep with him curled around her buttocks, shaped like lovers in a Roman painting.

* * *

Over the next few days, Lorrelai moved a few things up to Ned's caravan.

Dora barely existed. She spoke incomprehensibly, she wandered in and out all night, she slept during the day. Temperatures dropped steeply at night, so when Lorrelai insisted, Dora wore a shawl over her nightie. She danced a lot under the tree, or on the bridge with her arms out, humming to herself. Sometimes she tottered in heels or barefoot, and clearly drunk, down the hill. Lorrelai remembered her walking off into the trees all those weeks ago.

One day, Lorrelai saw Dora picking apples. She was placing them in a basket left by the children.

Glancing around furtively, Dora hurried down to the river and across the bridge, walking along the edge of the forest until she was obscured by the pepper and willow trees that grew along the river. Lorrelai slowly went back inside. If she followed now, Dora would hear her. But she would follow the path later when Dora had returned to the caravan.

In Pierre's caravan, Lorrelai took out bread ingredients. She jumped when Blossom plonked down on the top step with her sketchbook. 'Don't stop,' said Blossom. 'I'm sketching.'

Lorrelai looked at her, Dora's furtiveness fresh in her mind.

Blossom frowned at the page, her wrist curving as she drew an outline, looked up briefly, and kept drawing.

Slowly, Lorrelai added water to yeast and sugar. She mixed the flour, salt and yeast and kneaded the dough.

On Sunday, Ned and Lorrelai left for market. Dora was dancing beneath the fig tree, flapping the hem of her nightie like a flamenco skirt. She laughed suddenly without preamble.

From the car, Ned and Lorrelai stared at her until Ned switched on the engine and drove out of the park. When they arrived home at sunset, Baby Ned asleep in Lorrelai's arms, Dora was nowhere in sight.

That night, as Ned and Lorrelai lay side by side in the double bed, they heard Dora come up the stairs. Both froze. Inside the caravan, her footsteps hesitated several times, and then Dora's head appeared between the curtains. Ned and Lorrelai lay straight as corpses, apart and alert. Dora gazed around the small room. Ned lifted his head.

'Dora?'

Dora's eyes were small and round, her face childlike, her mouth moving without sound. She turned away.

Lorrelai looked over at Ned, but he held up one finger. Sounds of shuffling came from the other end of the caravan.

Lorrelai waited a minute before she got up and peeked through the curtain. Dora was on the spare bed, drawing in an address book that had no names. She hummed and scribbled. The baby made a sound in his sleep. Dora went still. Her hand tightened around the pen.

A cold sensation chilled Lorrelai. After a moment, Dora continued scribbling.

On the bed, Ned's hands were clasped beneath his head, his eyes wide. 'My God,' he whispered. Lorrelai got in beside him and took his hand. 'Let's bring the baby in here with us.'

Ned and Lorrelai ate together. They set a place for Dora, but she never joined them. Lorrelai wondered what Dora ate. She would see Dora chewing sometimes as she moved around. Fruit grew wild everywhere, like the dark, juicy blackberries on the wiry bushes along the river. She watched Dora carefully for signs of recognition. But Dora lived her strange, ghostly life alongside them.

Ned didn't talk about Dora, and Lorrelai didn't mention seeing her take apples into the forest. It could be innocent. What would be the point? But she didn't trust Dora with the baby at all. She kept seeing Dora's hand tightening around the pen.

Chapter 40

One cold dawn, a few weeks later, Lorrelai rushed uphill for Baby Ned's feed. She'd stayed the night with Pierre because he needed help with everything after he'd crushed his finger beneath a box. Outside Ned's caravan, the car was running.

Ned jumped out of the driver's side, ran over, and took both her hands in his. He was shaking.

'I'm taking Dora to hospital. She's really sick. This morning she came back covered in mud and blood. I had to carry her to the car. It's bad, really bad.'

'Oh my God.' Lorrelai stared at the vehicle. 'Are you taking the baby? Leave him with me. I'll feed him.'

Ned turned and walked away. 'I'll take him. I fed him already. Can you keep an eye on everything until we're back? The caravan key is with Peg.' He didn't wait for her to answer. He climbed into the driver's side of the Landcruiser, slammed the door, and drove away.

Lorrelai shook from head to toe. Mud and blood? What had Dora done?

Lorrelai's breasts began to leak. She walked downhill and got her shower things. Under the water, she pushed her fingers from the outside of her breast towards the nipple and washed her milk away. A magpie carolled through the window. Lorrelai focused on it to tame the panic in her chest. It carolled on and on, like it would never end, as she shivered beneath the warm water.

Ned and Dora's caravan stayed quiet and dark past sundown. Lorrelai fed the chickens, collected the eggs, milked the goat, and took it all to Peg. She couldn't eat. In the shower, she washed her milk away again.

Three days passed. A solid brick of dread buried itself inside her. She worried about Ned and the baby. She dreamt of them in the hospital, the blood and the mud, and Dora. Dora disappearing into the trees. Dora's hand going still at the sound of the baby.

Pierre started complaining about shortness of breath and stayed in bed. When it got really bad, one of the men drove him into town and he returned with a bottle of penicillin from the doctor.

One afternoon, Lorrelai walked and walked in the trees along the little track she'd seen Dora take. After a time, and starting to doubt there was anything to see, she came to a small shed made of grey wood.

The door wasn't locked. Inside, the air was warm and sour, smelling of dead rats and off milk. Lorrelai covered her mouth and nose with her hand. It was a spirit-making set-up with a big glass bottle, tubing, and a vessel full of rotten fruit. Also inside the tiny space were a chair, clothes, a feathered hat, and a pair of gloves. A large glass bottle lay on its side, and a dark splash on the wall looked like blood.

Lorrelai imagined Dora drinking from the bottle and then her abused stomach erupting, blood hurtling from her mouth. Imagined her stumbling back through the dark, falling into the muddy edges of the river. Lorrelai hurried out, leaving the door swinging behind her.

* * *

Lorrelai gardened and worked. She made herself food and forced herself to swallow. She had nightmares and woke saturated with sweat and milk.

Five days, Ned and Dora's caravan stayed abandoned. Lorrelai let herself into Ned's van and made coffee. On the sink were Dora's rings. Lorrelai looked at them for a long time before she slid them both down her ring finger on her left hand. She held her hand to the light, saw the sparkle of the little diamond. Why hadn't Ned returned? She could do nothing except wait and wait.

She tried to slip the rings off, but they were a tight fit. She looked around for soap. There was none. She'd have to take them off in the shower and bring them back later.

Ned returned with the baby the next day. It was midday when he climbed from the green Landcruiser and went to the child seat in the back. His face was lined, his eyelids droopy with fatigue. When he saw Lorrelai waiting, he handed the baby to her.

'I'm going for a shower.'

Lorrelai nodded and took Baby Ned into the caravan. He felt heavier, and he smelled different. When she offered her breast, he twisted, pushed against her and whinged. Lorrelai prepared a bottle of goat's milk, but he arched his back and turned his face away. She tried to comfort and kiss him, but he pulled and whined until Lorrelai put him in the crib, where he fell asleep. She waited for Ned to return from his shower.

He walked up the stairs and draped his towel over a hook on the side of the cupboard.

'Ned? Are you alright?'

He folded his arms, his gaze on the floor beside him. 'Dora bled from the stomach. Doctor said she had ulcers from drinking.'

Lorrelai waited, but he seemed to have drifted away. 'What are you going to do?'

Ned shook his head, and then he dropped his arms. He gave her a quick look, but there was no softness in it. 'I need to walk.'

Ned was gone for over an hour. His expression was broody when he returned. Lorrelai had washed the baby, but he'd been sleepy, so she returned him to bed without offering another feed and then sat wringing her hands at the table.

Finally, Ned clomped up the stairs.

'Better?'

Ned had an unblinking, haunted look. 'I found something in the forest.' He came in and clutched the side of the table. 'She had her own distillery!' He shook his head and sucked his lower lip into his mouth. 'Her own supply. This whole time.'

'I saw her disappear into the forest once,' Lorrelai admitted. 'I didn't know what it was until you took her to hospital.'

Ned stared at her suddenly with bloodshot eyes. 'Why didn't you say something?' Lorrelai flushed as she remembered the apples.

'She could have just been walking.'

'Oh my God!' Ned closed his eyes and rubbed one hand from his forehead down to his beard. He spread his arms and shook his head. 'I could have prevented this from happening, Lorrelai. You've been here every day. Why, in God's name, didn't you say something?'

'I don't know.'

'You weren't suspicious?'

She chewed her inner lip. 'I didn't want to know, Ned. She scares me.'

'Well, I did want to know!' Ned shouted, hands to hips. 'For God's sake! The doctor probably thought I was a monster. Don't you see? I could have helped her!'

Lorrelai's face blazed as she stood up. 'This is not my fault!' she said. 'Dora is sick. I told you we should do something!'

'But you knew all along!' He turned away, chest rising and falling.

The baby gave a tired whine. Ned dropped his voice. 'Maybe both of us did this to her. I think you'd better move out.'

A heaviness settled over Lorrelai. 'What good would that do?'

'You weren't at the hospital. It was horrible. I felt so guilty.'

'No, Dora's done this to herself, Ned.'

'She's not rational!' He turned and banged the table with the side of his fist. Lorrelai jumped backwards. 'God! She's like a child. I should have looked after her!' Ned straightened, running his hands through his hair. He was shaking. 'I need you to go,' he said carefully.

Lorrelai grabbed her cardigan. Ned half-turned, his eyes narrowed. 'Are those ...' His voice was a strange whisper. 'Are those her *rings*?'

Lorrelai cringed. How could she have forgotten to take them off?

'Oh no, I'm so sorry!' She pulled them hard enough to make her finger hurt. 'I saw them on the sink. They just got stuck. I forgot!'

Ned shook his head, and his whole body trembled. His face was pale, but his words came out eerily calm. 'No,' he said. 'Keep them. I'm sure I owe you about what they're worth.'

Lorrelai kept tugging at them, the skin around her knuckle bunching frustratingly.

'Take them!' he said louder.

'I don't want them!' she said, tears snaking down her cheeks. 'I don't want to be paid. That's not why I'm here.'

Ned faced her squarely. 'It is,' he said calmly. 'I employed you to help, and you helped.'

She stared, unable to believe what Ned had said. 'You wanted to marry me.'

'I'm married,' Ned said.

Lorrelai's heart drummed, and for a moment she couldn't see clearly. A strange waver in the air made her feel like she was about to faint. When her vision settled, she headed for the steps, and then ran down and down, and kept going all the way to the river.

She stood on the edge, breathing fast, tears streaking her face. A Pacific duck and its mate glided along the water's edge, the iridescent emerald fleck in the span of its wing catching the light. They shovelled the reeds with their bills, turning on the water to face each other, webbed feet busy beneath the water's surface.

Swallows zipped in and out of the tea-tree and weeping willows and reeds that lined the riverbank. The stalky trees were cluttered with peewee nests, old clusters of straw, mud and sticks.

Halfway along the bridge above, two young men were heaving a branch off the bridge. It had fallen from one of the big gums lining the river, smashing a hole in the railing. The water swallowed the branch as the boys shuffled back to avoid tumbling through the gap after it.

Lorrelai turned, staring back into the park. How different it looked. It had been a home, but now? She'd let herself believe she was connected to something, part of a family. But, again, she was obsolete. A wisp of smoke. She didn't belong here. She didn't belong back at the inn. Even her bed was a seat, borrowed and temporary.

Chapter 41

Lorrelai stayed downhill of the Moreton Bay fig trees. Her milk dried up. She had to force even toast and jam down. She could feel her hip bones against the inside of Maria's dress as wintry winds tore through the park.

Pierre coughed and coughed. The doctor came, leaving more penicillin and instructions with Lorrelai as if she was his nurse.

Dora returned a couple of weeks after Ned had asked Lorrelai to leave. Lorrelai watched from behind a tree as Dora got out of the vehicle. She wore a skirt, blouse and coat, her hair in a plait down her back. Fig leaves shook in the wind and obscured any sound.

While Lorrelai watched, Blossom emerged from the crowd of tents and strode downhill. She knocked on Pierre's door and looked around until she found Lorrelai beneath the tree.

'You two no good anymore?' Blossom nodded uphill, but Dora had disappeared inside the caravan and the door was shut.

Lorrelai leaned back against the tree, shook her head.

Blossom didn't look too worried. 'Men,' she said, like it explained everything. She lifted a red book. 'Here's your portrait. Want to see? I had to improvise a bit because you never posed for me.' She opened the book's cover to reveal a picture. 'Come out where it's light.' She walked out from under the canopy and gave the grey clouds a wary look.

Lorrelai followed and looked over Blossom's shoulder. 'Blossom, it's gorgeous!' It could have been a black-and-white photograph. Lorrelai, posing in front of one of the fig trees, long curly hair blown over one shoulder, smiling slightly like she knew a secret. She wore an off-the-shoulder evening dress, hugging her body all the way to her ankles and high heels.

'When I get paint, the dress will be red.'

'Blossom, you're really talented. You could easily sell that.'

The girl blushed, dropped her head. She quickly flipped to the middle of the book and lifted it for Lorrelai to see.

It was Lorrelai with the baby at her breast, her head tilted down, a dreamy look on her face.

'You knew?'

'Ma saw you at the markets. Look at the others. They're all of you.'

Lorrelai took the book and slowly turned the pages. Page after page carefully captured scenes of Lorrelai gardening, baking, milking.

She closed the book and handed it back to Blossom. 'I can't stay here anymore.'

Blossom took the book and slid it up beneath her arm. She reached for Lorrelai's hand. 'It's okay,' she whispered. 'Let's run away together.'

Lorrelai gave the girl a long look. 'Yes,' she said, and something jumped inside her, the first spark of life she'd felt for days.

Blossom's face lit up. 'Really? When?'

Lorrelai looked around, saw the sludge of cloud darkening the forest. 'After the storm.'

The roar of Pierre's car came down the lane between the fence and trees, with one of the older boys at the wheel. He had taken over while Pierre was unwell. Pierre had a cough that rattled through the caravan every night.

Blossom put her arm around Lorrelai's waist, grabbed a handful of her dress, and squealed.

'Blossom!' Peggy's voice came from uphill.

The girl's smile dissolved, but a determined look replaced it. 'Neither of us belong here,' she muttered. 'I'll pack tonight.'

'Honey, are you sure?'

'I like women.' Blossom turned. 'I can't get married. I can't. Don't hate me. I know I'm different.' Lorrelai reached over and took Blossom's hand.

'Oh Blossom, you poor thing.' Lorrelai shook her head. 'I won't hate you, no matter what.'

'After the storm,' said Blossom quietly and moved away. Book beneath her arm, she strode up the hill.

Chapter 42

There would be no sunset; there was too much cloud. Thunder rumbled like a sore belly all afternoon. Uphill was a feast of movement: tightening ropes, nailing bits of tin, young men calling to each other. As the thunder grew louder, so did their efforts.

Lorrelai showered early and grabbed some apples so she wouldn't need to leave the caravan. Movement uphill caught her eye. Dora in her old white nightie again, dancing beneath the tree in high heels. She swirled, took three leaps towards the tree, landed, and bowed. Around her, the breeze lifted her skirts and floated her wild, wild black hair around her shoulders like a dark veil. Dead leaves tangled around her skirt and heels.

Lorrelai tightened her cardigan as a gust of wind threw leaves swirling, swirling up to knee height, chilling her skin. Over the forest across the river, the sky was dark. The wind whistled through eddies of leaves. Suddenly, a searing light cut the sky in shards. She hoped it had hit Dora's secret shed and burned it to the ground. Even from a distance, she wanted the baby to be happy and healthy, and for that to happen, Dora had to get well.

Lorrelai reached Pierre's caravan just as the first mist of rain wet the steps, gusts swishing in behind. The Moreton Bay fig shook small, round fruit onto the ground. She looked uphill and saw Ned poke his head outside, gesturing to Dora to come in. Dora continued to leap and bow. It was as if her hospital stay had reinvigorated her.

Lorrelai secured the door and checked on Pierre, refilling his water glass and placing it beside his bed with a dose of penicillin. His cheeks were flushed, and his crackly chest rose high and low with each breath.

She stood listening to the rattle of Pierre's expirations. With the back of her hand, she touched his cheek. His skin was warm, not hot. Lorrelai closed his curtain, made herself some dinner, and ate eggs on toast alone by the glow of a single candle.

Inside herself, past the sadness, Lorrelai felt a settling, a resolution. She would not trust her life to a man, would not leave herself so vulnerable again. After leaving, she and Blossom could forge a new life somewhere else. The women's movement was gathering momentum. Women could take the pill and live without a man. She would live for herself. Do what she wanted.

The caravan lurched, and she grabbed for the candle and sat holding it, watching the flickering flame. Then she snuffed the candle, cleaned up, and put things away.

Mid-evening, it was dark as oil. Lorrelai gave Pierre his medicine. With it, he drank a full glass of water, ate half a piece of buttered bread, and then pushed the remainder away.

'No more, my love,' he whispered with his eyes closed. He coughed, his bony body jerking with the effort. Outside, the wind howled.

Lorrelai closed all curtains and blinds tight. Caravans, sheds, and tents rattled. The floor shuddered, the curtains shivered, the loose things moved restlessly on shelves and inside drawers. Lorrelai packed her bag, leaving only a warm outfit, and sat on her seat bed.

Storms came and went. She willed it in so it would be over sooner.

As if responding to her desire, a clap of thunder was followed by the roar of rain. Water and leaves hissed against the windows like snakes. Lorrelai slipped on another cardigan.

Pierre coughed and coughed, as if a demon was clawing its way out through his throat. She went down and made him sit forwards and pressed two pillows behind him. She spread eucalyptus and camphor ointment on his chest and gave him senega and ammonia to drink. He winced at the bitter taste, but he quickly fell back to sleep.

The wind kept up—an urgent conversation of nature and sky over the tiny, hunkering park. Pitch night closed in. The caravan rattled and shook like an old lady. Pierre's cough abated, replaced by the regular sound of his snores.

Lorrelai went to bed in her clothes, pulling the covers up close to her neck. She could hear the river, could imagine the roil of the water, its speed as it pushed along and outwards, expanding, surging down the riverbed. Tonight, the Avon frightened her.

Thunder cracked and boomed, and something metallic clattered to the floor, making Lorrelai jump. But it was just a fork left from dinner. Maria's fork. The ghosts were not even safe.

Lorrelai pulled the blanket over her head and closed her eyes. 'Oh Lord,' she whispered. 'Please make it stop.'

* * *

Lorrelai woke with a start. Lightning flashed so bright, everything glowed. She wasn't sure how long she'd been asleep.

A great boom of thunder pounded the sky, rumbled down the tree trunks into the ground and quivered up through the tyres of the caravan. Lorrelai felt the power inside her chest through the chambers of her heart. For a moment, all was silent, except for the muted swish of rain. And then she heard it—a thin scream.

Getting up, she drew the curtain aside. She listened hard as she stared through the black square of window, her hand on the cold glass. Lightning flashed again, and the park, trees, bridge and river lit up. And then she saw someone illuminated on the bridge.

Lorrelai opened the door, but the handle was ripped from her hand and the door crashed against the body of the van. She shaded her eyes, but the lightning made her blind. The caravan hiccupped as gusts swirled inside, wetting the floor, flapping the curtains. The old frame creaked. Thunder clapped overhead, and Lorrelai clamped her hands over her ears. She crawled forwards on her knees and grabbed the door handle. Lightning flashed over the bridge, and again she heard a scream.

Chapter 43

Next morning, everything gleamed and dripped. The storm had retreated, a monster afraid of the light. A weak sun rose behind a wet sheen of cloud.

Lorrelai opened the door and shoved a pile of wet clothes along the wall behind it. She shaded her eyes to look uphill. Her body was stiff, her elbow, knees and head sore. She leaned down and rubbed her knee, where a red-mauve bruise was blossoming.

People filled the park—so many people. Strangers. They moved like stunned ants, bending to pick up debris, staring at it, either pocketing or dropping it, walking on, bending down again.

Dogs, big strong Alsatians sniffed about, pulling people in dark uniform along by their leashes. *Police dogs*, she realised. The Park mongrels barked at the ends of their string and electrical cord leashes like devils.

A search. A missing person. Lorrelai closed her door and sat trembling on the edge of her bed.

Someone pounded on the caravan door. Lorrelai jumped.

'It's me, Ned.'

She swallowed, limped over and opened the door, and then sat at the table. Ned looked over his shoulder and then pulled the door closed behind him. His forearm was looped around the baby's belly. He straightened, put his hand under the baby's bum, and held him facing outwards, the infant's tiny legs pedalling the air. 'Dora is missing.'

Lorrelai nodded, her lips numb. 'Baby Ned's, okay?' she whispered.

'Of course.' Ned looked at her bare feet and back up to her face. 'Get dressed,' he said. His eyes flickered down to Pierre's end of the caravan. 'We mustn't tell anyone,' he said in a hoarse whisper. 'About us.'

Lorrelai whispered, 'Okay.'

Ned looked at her bag and frowned. 'Are you leaving?'

Lorrelai nodded.

Ned's face smoothed, and he closed his eyes and rubbed one large hand down from his eyes to his beard tip. 'I can't be taken from Joseph.' He looked at the baby, who was waving his arms around. 'We named him when we were at the hospital.'

'That's a good name.' Lorrelai held out her finger, and the baby wrapped his hand around it and tried to pull it to his mouth. 'Dora's always out walking,' she said. She placed her hands in her lap.

He gave her a curious look. 'Didn't you hear the storm? Trees have had branches ripped off. The river is in flood. If she was out in it …' He shook his head.

Lorrelai pulled her cardigan tight, conscious of her thin nightdress. Her teeth chattered as she peered through the window. 'There are so many people.'

A group of searchers surged toward the river like a tide.

Ned caught sight of the pile of wet clothes, blinked a couple of times then looked back at Lorrelai. 'If something bad has happened, they'll say it was me,' he said.

Lorrelai swallowed. 'Please don't say that.'

'Did you see anything last night?'

'No.' The silence stretched for several moments.

'Just be careful.' Ned gave her a heavy look.

Lorrelai's lips quivered. She nodded.

Ned opened the door and left.

*　*　*

In the afternoon, a local found Dora's body. Naked. Bruises around her neck. A long way down the river. People winced at how broken it had been. Lorrelai vomited.

Everyone had to talk about it, as though it would mess up their insides if they didn't get it out. Whispers grew into suspicions, theories, accusations. Fear rose like the muddy, stick-heavy water until it jabbed conversations from all angles.

All evening, things washed up along the river. A white wedding dress, which caused a stir when searchers thought they'd found a second body. When they reached it, there was nothing inside. Debris washed up, stranded on the banks or swirled in eddies: leaves and sticks and rubbish, but also a doll, a bicycle, a dead possum, a drowned puppy.

Children stood barefoot beside the river, one with its head in a woman's skirt as a man reached out to the puppy with a stick so the children could have a funeral. The idea seemed to settle people.

The adults were either curious or in blank-faced shock about Dora. Everyone shook their heads. But there were no tears; not like there were for the puppy.

Police said no one was to leave. During the day, they interviewed Ned. They interviewed the park people from uphill first.

From the door of Pierre's caravan, Lorrelai saw Peg's children lined up, with Blossom at the end in a posture of reprimand, her eyes down. She tried to see past Blossom's bowed head, her white part and neat brown hair in two plaits, but Blossom did not look up. Lorrelai wondered if the girl had packed.

Finally, the police came to see Lorrelai. She was dressed and waiting for them, wearing Maria's blue cotton dress, thick stockings, work boots and a long white apron. Her hair was secured in a plait, all tendrils tamed with pins.

'Hello,' said a young policeman with cropped black hair, bulgy eyes and a red nose. He pulled a handkerchief out, wiped his nose, and shoved it back into his breast pocket.

'Lorrelai?'

She nodded. 'Yes, sir.'

'I'm Constable Pickles.' He cleared his throat. 'Did you see Dora Del Saur last night?'

'No,' she said. 'I was here all night with Pierre. He's got pneumonia.'

'Did you leave the van at all during the night?'

'No.'

The man and his buddy looked her over, then over the caravan, then over the cider shed. 'What's in the shed there?' said the older one. Atop his head, his comb-over flipped back in a breeze. He finger-combed it back into place.

'A little cider.'

The cop wrote something on a small notepad. 'Apparently, you are the Del Saur family's help?'

'Yes,' said Lorrelai. 'I was.'

'Notice any problems? Fighting, that kind of thing?'

Suddenly, Lorrelai seemed sticky in the mouth. 'Dora has not been well. You know —' She broke off and tapped her temple. 'But she's been a bit better. Ned has been very patient with her.'

'Is that why you moved in?' said the older cop. Neither moved, all eyes on her.

Lorrelai coloured. She and Ned had been subtle, but some would have noticed her not leaving at night. 'Yes. The baby needed night feeds. And it was more comfortable there.' She glanced over her shoulder. 'Pierre is an old man,' she whispered. 'He talks to Maria, his dead wife. Sometimes it's hard to sleep.' On cue, a racking cough issued from deep inside the caravan.

Both cops winced. They waited until it stopped. The young cop wrote again in his notepad. He looked up. 'Were you having an affair with Mr. Del Saur?'

Lorrelai felt her face heat up. She bit her inner lip. 'No. I was just there to take care of the baby.'

The cop didn't write anything down, just gazed at her. 'Can I ask how you got those scratches on your arms?'

Lorrelai looked at her arms and saw what he meant. 'Oh,' she said quickly. 'I picked apples to make pie the night before last. The branches must have scratched me.'

'I love pie,' said the older officer. The younger one murmured in agreement. 'My missus doesn't cook desserts.' He patted his portly stomach. 'Probably best.'

'Hmm,' said the younger, and then looked back at her with a smile. 'I'd love to try some Mrs. ...?'

'Oh, Miss McAllister. I go by Lorrelai.' She made herself smile.

The young cop's smile faded. The older one cleared his throat and pulled his chin in, so the wreath of skin below formed a soft pink pillow of flesh. They shared a look and then stared at her, their eyes narrowing.

'But *Miss* McAllister,' said the young cop, emphasising the title. 'You're wearing wedding rings.'

Lorrelai's heart stopped for a moment. She looked at her hand, and there they were. Why hadn't she taken them off? Why didn't she think to do it?

She would be honest: Ned had paid her with them because his wife had discarded them. But, by God, it sounded ridiculous. Could they be anyone else's? Her grandmother's? An heirloom? Lies bubbled up and popped, leaving nothing.

A yell came from the river.

'Got something!' All faces turned that way. Activity buzzed from around the edge of the river which had risen up the bank overnight. Lorrelai shaded her eyes. The two cops took a few steps back so they could see.

Lorrelai was shaking, trying to pull off the rings. Why hadn't she remembered the damn rings? She gave up and clutched the door frame, peering out.

A cop was on his knees, another had a stick in both hands and was grimacing with effort. A sopping wet white sheet on the end of the stick had leaves stuck to it. He held it up, his face surprised at first, and then his expression changed. His eyes widened and he grinned. 'Well, look at that will you!'

'What did Mr. Del Saur say his wife was wearing when she disappeared?' asked one of the cops standing in front of her. Two policemen jogged over; one towing a dog on a leash, white drool hanging from its jowls.

Another cop checked a notepad. 'White nightie. Wore it everywhere.' He looked from Pierre's caravan to the river's edge as if judging the distance from one to the other.

Lorrelai stared at the fabric on the end of the stick.

One of the policemen banged on Pierre's caravan wall with the flat of his hand. Lorrelai moved so he could ascend the steps. The caravan twitched with the movement inside.

Men's voices came from the end of the caravan and then the policeman appeared at the door. 'Miss McAllister, we need you to come in with us.' He glanced at his partner, whose eyebrows went up. The first policeman continued. 'You said you did not see Dora and did not leave the caravan? That's not Pierre's recollection. He said he woke when the door slammed and called out. When there was no reply, he glanced out the window. Pierre said he saw you running towards the bridge.'

PART THREE

Chapter 44

I'm on my back, head cushioned in a pillow. A silvery fluorescent light gleams from the ceiling. From somewhere above, I hear soft, regular *beeps*. The bitterness of smoke and blood sits in my throat like I've been licking hot bitumen. Pain lurks behind my eyelids, inside my skull, in my nose, below my eyes, and in one of my knees.

I try to focus.

Disinfectant. The squeak of rubber-soled shoes. Hushed voices. Metallic sounds. *Hospital?*

My eyes are tight and swollen, and I'm only able to open the left one. I rapidly blink back tears. A constant *throb-throb* in my temples makes it feel like I have twin hearts.

'Jane? Are you awake?'

I turn towards Walshy's voice. He's unclear, as if we're separated by frosted glass. But it's him: wide cheekbones, darkness of stubble, green eyes. A warm hand takes mine.

'Lmlmlm,' I manage. I meant to say, 'You're back?'

I try to lift my hand, but it's tied to something. I attempt to moisten my lips, but my tongue has turned to leather. Freeing my other hand, I then point to a glass on a wheeled tray table.

'Dink.' God it's hard to do anything. Forming the word, then making it come out of my mouth. 'Thirsty.' A sharp pain shoots through my skull. I wince and breathe through it.

'I'll get the nurse.'

People talk, and a bell goes off somewhere. Footsteps, faster, faster, the rattle of something on wheels. 'Code Blue!' The noise recedes. I imagine never-ending corridors with rooms branching off, beds with white sheets.

Then there's a cup and a straw and, hallelujah, water in my mouth. It tastes bad. I cough and splutter. Stuff runs from my nose. Someone dabs my nostrils. There's blood on a tissue. Another tissue is pushed into my hand. There is a tube is taped to the back of my wrist.

'There now, take it slowly,' says a calm female voice. I track across. A young, pretty nurse with a ponytail and pink lipstick. She wears a navy blouse with about six pens in her breast pocket and waves at me like I'm a kid.

'Something for the pain?'

I nod slightly.

'I'm Renee, your nurse. Are you allergic to anything?'

I go to shake my head but think better of it. 'No.'

A tiny cup is held against my lower lip and pills are tipped into my mouth. 'Thanks.' I manage to swallow without choking.

'Do you know where you are?'

I move my eyes, scared to turn my head. The lime green walls and curtains confirm my initial guess. 'Hospital.'

'Can you tell me what day it is?'

Sunlight shines through the window. Something comes back. Friday night. I'd worked, and then I saw Shelley. Then I had to get home urgently.

I want to get the questions right, so lipstick girl doesn't do the stupid wave. 'I worked Friday night. It's Saturday?'

She nods. 'Good. Do you know why you're here?'

'Um.' I hope they'll think I'm just working through stuff. My face is tight, one of my eyes a mere slit. I'm getting a whole lot of black. Then my bike. A small shock happens, like I've hit something. 'I crashed?'

She nods. 'Good, okay. I'm going to unstick that eye. You ready?'

I nod.

She holds the closed eye open with her fingers. There are pale blue gloves on her hands. Walshy takes my hand. I pull my head back into the pillow as far as possible, but she keeps coming. She's relentless. She seems to grow in size as liquid falls on my eyeball, and I hiss inwardly. It's like hot mercury. I blink and blink, but I'm so swollen it is more of a twitch, twitch.

'Okay now, just look straight ahead.' She has one of her pens.

'Argh, no!'

'It's okay. I'm just looking into your eyes, Lola.'

The pen has a little light at the end, which she shines into one eye and then the other.

I get my breathing under control. 'Am I alright?'

'You've broken your nose and knocked yourself out,' she says. She looks over my head to Walshy. 'It's important we orientate her and keep her calm.' Her gaze returns to me. 'You came into Northam District Hospital at ten o'clock last night. It's almost lunchtime Saturday. Welcome back.' She smiles. 'Now, let me get some ice on all that swelling.' She turns and leaves.

Broken nose? Shit! I could end up looking like a rugby player or a pug. I turn and see Walshy, who takes my hand and smiles. His expression is tight, complexion paler than normal.

'You're back,' I say. It sounds more like, *yo bock.*

An expression flickers across his face. 'Yeah. Got back early this morning. Perry told me where you were.'

'Perry?'

'He found you by the road last night. He and his mum brought you in.'

I frown, look over at the window, close my eyes. I hear the nurse return.

'Here's the ice,' she says.

Walshy's other hand presses something soft and cold lightly over my eyes.

'Don't go,' I say, fingering the callouses at the base of his fingers. 'I love you.'

* * *

I smell honeysuckle, flowers so sweet they're sickly. I'm outside Lorrelai's room at the inn. The door opens inwards and there she is—Lorrelai, long, curly hair, glamourous dress, smiling. Her mouth moves, but there's no sound.

'Where's the baby?'

She frowns, shakes her head. 'There's no baby.' She backs into the room. I push open the door, but it's Shelley Turner wearing Lorrelai's red dress. Her mascara has

217

run, like she's been crying.

'Please don't tell anyone.'

* * *

I wake with the dream fresh in my head. Lorrelai. Shelley. Then I remember what I found out at the inn, about the third victim being Shelley's friend. Information comes at me like slaps to the cheeks. Blossom's sketches. The house I grew up in belongs to Ned Del Saur, husband of a murdered woman.

The ice has fallen off my face, and my eyes can open a bit more, so I can see better.

Walshy has gone. A knot tightens beneath my ribs. The past and the present inch closer, like hungry dingoes sniffing the edge of my consciousness.

Using the hand control, I sit the bed up. My head is swimming, but I need to see and breathe and wake. I'm starting to think more clearly.

I have things I need to do—urgent things. I need to get to the Flower House and make some calls. Then I remember: the door was broken, the sketchbook missing, things sifted through.

I have to tell Walshy about everything. I'm dizzy just thinking about it.

It all seems too big, too overwhelming, like a wave has risen above me and will wash down and engulf everything.

I'm suddenly busting to pee. I press the call bell. A solemn *dong-dong* starts up, and above my door, a small light flicks on.

An efficient older nurse helps me to the bathroom. My knee throbs when I put weight on my right foot. 'I'll wait outside,' she says.

I gather the voluminous blue gown and sit on the toilet. My head swims as I get up and wash my hands at the sink.

'Jesus!' In the mirror, my face is a mess. I cough up something nasty into the sink and my throat feels clearer.

I look like one of those old people on the news who's been assaulted in a 'cowardly attack'. Both eyes are purple and red, one worse than the other. A deep graze shears along my cheek to my nose, which is covered with white plaster. I have a fat upper lip and a graze below one nostril. I gently lift my top lip to check my teeth. They're all there.

Dizzy again, I'm grateful for the nurse's solid body to lean on as we hobble back to the bed.

Even in bed, my head weighs a tonne. I feel like I've slept beneath a hundred layers of earth, and sleepy bees circle my eardrums.

'You're awake.' Walshy's in the doorway, hands thrust in his pockets. He's clean-shaven, wearing a white shirt and black denim jeans. He looks like heaven. I hold out my hand, and he walks over, takes it, and kneads gently.

'You okay? Your eyes are both open.'

'Hmm, yeah. Ice works wonders. Bit stiff and sore.' With my fat nose, everything sounds nasal.

Walshy's mouth tightens in sympathy. He lets go of me to find a chair and pull it up close. Then he takes my hand and holds it against the mattress. He leans in. 'I'm sorry I wasn't here last night.'

'Walshy. I need to tell you something.'

'Jane. The back door is broken.'

I get up on one elbow. My head swoons like my brains have moved side to side. I feel a bit sick. 'I know. They stole the sketchbook.'

'Sketchbook?'

I sigh hard. 'Geez, Walshy. Your timing really sucks. You've missed everything!'

'Seriously, I had to sort out my head, and I couldn't with you there. Having you back is like being caught up in a hurricane.'

I can't help smiling a bit. 'Is that a good thing?'

'Hurricane Jane?' Walshy chuckles. 'Always.' Then his expression sobers. 'Going out with Shelley wasn't my idea, but at the time, there seemed no reason to say no. I'll let her know it's off.'

'I thought that you might have been keen on her for years.'

He shook his head and sat back, a puzzled look on his face. 'She *is* lovely.'

'Okay, shut up!'

Walshy chuckles and takes my hand. 'I was going to say, she's a nice person. It just wasn't a *thing*. She's delicate. Someone you've gotta really commit to. And you can tell she's holding back. She's never really relaxed or … natural.'

I swallow, unsurprised that Walshy has picked up on something. 'Good. Now that's sorted, Tom Cat, I've gotta tell you about this sketchbook!'

Walshy shakes his head good-naturedly. He looks relieved and he listens without moving as I fill him in.

'Lorrelai was nineteen when she was jailed in 1971 for strangling the crazy wife of her boyfriend. Then she's supposed to have thrown her off a bridge into the river.' I cough and must spit into a tissue. It comes away crimson.

I take a long drink of water. My heart is beating faster. 'I went to the library because this woman, Lorrelai, just kept coming up. Blossom was determined for me to know about her. I believe I know why.' I catch my breath. 'I think Blossom was there when the murder happened.'

I check there's no one hanging around the door and lower my voice. 'Blossom's sketches are so good, Walshy. She's drawn Lorrelai a dozen times, doing everyday stuff, and then the pictures get darker, more serious. One, right near the end, shows the husband chasing his wife towards the river in a storm. The murder happened during a storm.'

Walshy frowns.

'Don't you see?' I implore. 'Blossom implicates the husband in the murder.'

Walshy takes a deep breath, less impressed than I hoped he'd look. 'They're sketches?' He shrugs. 'Maybe she wanted to give you something other than her death to think about when she died. Anyway, who knows how she felt about this woman. Murderers have admirers too.'

'Sure, I know that. But ...' I close my eyes, a throb starting in my temples. 'The pictures are so freaking detailed, almost like photographs. And listen, after that picture, there's pages missing.' I take another deep breath. 'I looked up the husband, Ned Del Saur. But I couldn't find him. Then I find a football article about a Ned whose son died, and the son has the same name as the baby from the Del Saur family. This Ned, though, is called Ned Berry. I compare the photos from 1971 with the football article, and he looks the same. Walshy, I'm ninety-nine percent sure that Ned Berry *is* Ned Del Saur.'

Walshy sits back and crosses his arms. 'It's a long shot, Lola. It's possible for two different Neds to have sons of the same name. Neither name's uncommon.'

'You're right, but apart from them looking identical, there's something else. Did you know the Flower House was only on loan to Blossom? That we didn't pay rent, but didn't own it either?'

Walshy frowns and shakes his head. 'Definitely no rent. I'd remember that.' I glance at the doorway before I speak.

'I found out who the owner is. Walshy, *Ned Berry* owns the Flower House.'

Chapter 45

The doctor is happy with my recovery, but he won't let me leave. Frankly, I'm relieved. My head spins when I try to stand or walk.

All the talking, or maybe all the time between pain meds, has gone on too long. A new, vicious headache with bonus face pain comes on.

I am given soup and a soft biscuit; more pain meds and water, and the blinds are closed. Walshy shuffles deep into the chair beside my bed, his arms crossed like a security guard.

I drift off to sleep, waking only briefly to refuse dinner before sinking under again.

* * *

I see the sketchbook buried under leaves down the side of the laundry, wedged between wall and fence. The plant material is getting rained on, composting. The plastic bag is fading, but inside it's protected and dry. The sketches are caught in limbo, waiting. Forgotten until I opened the cover and let in the light. But someone was waiting for these sketches to surface. Someone knew about this sketchbook. Someone waited for the day they could steal it.

* * *

Next morning, I manage to finish a whole piece of toast, a pasty-coloured boiled egg, and a cup of coffee. My face still feels tight and sore across the bridge of the nose.

Renee disconnects my drip but leaves the plastic port in my arm. When I get up to take a shower, she makes me sit on the edge of the bed until the room stays still.

The bathroom is pristinely white and shiny. I use the soap from the dispenser on the wall. The nurse said it is both body wash and shampoo. It smells okay, not like hospital.

It's nice to put on my own clothes—a skirt and T-shirt Walshy brought in, along with a plain pair of knickers. A little flash happens in my brain. A row of women's underwear along a wall, my knickers among them. Perry's shed! That's why I ran and crashed!

Heart pounding, I get back into the room. The doorway fills.

'Hello, Lola.'

I turn so quickly I get dizzy and have to sit on the edge of the bed. Perry stands in the doorway, wearing a small smile, navy chino pants, and a white, buttoned shirt.

'Oh. Hi, Perry!' My pulse screams through my veins as I try to stay calm and work out what to do. My skin creeps over my belly when I see his perfect manicured nails—hands that secretly steal women's underwear in the dark.

'You looked miles away. Mind if I visit?' He enters before I can answer. 'Your eyes look bad.'

'Yeah—yeah, I know.' My breath comes faster. I can feel my face colour. Do I want him to go, or should I just ask him outright what he was doing with my underwear? *But he may not know that I know.*

Perry's black boots squeak. They're new and shiny. He sits carefully on the visitor chair, pinching the pants above his knees to bend his long legs. 'How are you?' He sits unnaturally still, unblinking. His pupils expand into the irises.

I make a quick decision. 'It's weird not remembering. I heard you found me on the road?'

Perry takes a breath and slowly sits back, legs crossed. 'What's the last thing you remember?'

'Hitting the ground.' I don't blink in case I miss something.

'Before that?'

Neither of us blink. 'It's vague.'

He blinks and then makes himself smile. 'I heard you come into my yard. Trespassing, but I'll forgive you.' He clears his throat. 'You were sprawled face down when I followed you outside. Did you hear me call out?'

I shake my head. It feels like a tactical game. Ask questions, reveal nothing.

'You were bleeding. Cut right across your cheek and nose. One of your shoes was broken. I carried you into the garden. Mum drove you here.'

I imagine him carrying me, my arms drooping down like a rag doll. I almost remember something … then it's gone.

'Why into the garden?'

'Gate was open and there's a couch out there.' He sighs, making a sympathetic face that looks completely fake, and then runs his free hand through his hair. The silky blond strands slip through his fingers and immediately return to the same position. 'I'm just glad you're okay.'

'Perry, weird thing. I woke up with a nasty taste in my throat, like I'd smoked marijuana.'

He shrugs. 'I was smoking before I found you.'

'But I could taste it.'

Perry takes a deep breath. 'Smoked the rest before we took you to hospital. I put you on the couch I have in the garden. Thought you might wake up.' He flicks something invisible off his arm. 'I was stressed.'

A bodily reaction happens; I'm suddenly covered in a thin sheen of sweat. I can imagine him, casually smoking while I'm passed out cold on his couch like an injured bird. Did he look at my underwear? Did he touch me when I was unconscious?

I keep my voice calm. 'Perry, did you tell the police you sat there smoking instead of taking me straight to hospital?' My hands are trembling, sweat dampening my armpits.

'What, tell the cops I grow my own weed? What do you think? *Buhp-baaah.*' He makes his stupid horn noise, stands up and rolls his eyes.

'No, tell them about the underwear, Perry! My underwear!' A wave of anger snaps through me like electricity, and I suck in more air. 'Stop making that fucking noise! Get out! Get out now!' I'm half out of the bed, ready to poke his fucking eyeballs out.

Perry pulls in his chin, eyes wide.

I grab the nurse call bell and press the button, and then press again as the slow *dong-dong* happens. There's another button on the wall that says Code Blue. I press it.

Perry's eyes grow wider as they follow my every move. 'No-no-no!

Don't! They'll think it was me!' Perry loses his composure, his arms out, his face flushed and petrified.

Beeping starts, growing gets louder and louder. For a moment, everything is silent, but then there are fast footsteps, rattling, calling. 'Code Blue, room seven!'

Wide-eyed, Perry backs away, then he suddenly turns and runs.

The nurses calm me down, turn the bells off, and tuck me back into bed. I am shaking all over.

A social worker arrives. She's wearing a cream skirt suit and her ID badge rises and falls with her breathing. She stands there, waiting for the nurse to finish, but before she can approach me, Walshy rushes in and climbs up on the bed. I pull myself into him, my arms around his back.

'What happened? It's okay, Jane. It's okay.'

I hear the nurses instructing everyone else to get out. Footsteps whisper down the corridor and there's the sudden *riiiip* of the curtain being drawn. No one asks me anything, which I'm annoyed by suddenly.

'Perry was here. He's a creep. He stole my knickers. And other women's undies. His shed is full of them!'

Walshy goes horribly still. 'I'll fucking kill him if he did anything!'

I start crying. I feel like a kid that's been messed with. 'He didn't take me to hospital straightaway.' I swallow. 'Water. Please.'

I'm handed water, and I drink it all. Walshy is shaking all over. Behind him, I see a nurse ready to jump in if I need her. 'I remember … I remember something. It's important. Get the police.'

'Jane?' Walshy sounds wobbly now. I grip his waist.

'Don't move, Walshy. Stay here.'

'I'm here. I'm here.'

I need my anchor because I remember something.

I remember a doll.

Chapter 46

Two police walk in, one in uniform, the other in plain-clothes.

'Hi, Lola. This is Constable Jack Davies and I'm Detective Sam Wheeler,' says the woman in a short sleeved-blouse, tucked into her jeans. They both give Walshy a nod like they've met.

'Mind if we sit?'

I shake my head. Jack nods to the nurse, who leaves. He closes the door behind her.

They both find seats, teetering on the very edge, their elbows on their knees. The detective subtly takes out her notepad. 'Lola, in your own time, start by telling us what happened on Friday night.'

I tell them about work, that I'd seen an old friend and went home because I was keen to take another look at Blossom's sketchbook—the only thing she left me.

'Blossom. Mmm. Foster mother?' Detective Wheeler checks her notepad and looks back up. She has clear blue eyes and no makeup.

'Yes. She passed away a few days ago.' They nod and mumble that they're sorry for my loss. 'When I got home, I found the back door broken, and it looked like someone had searched for something. The sketchbook was missing, but nothing else, so I cycled to my neighbour's house and entered the shed.'

Detective Wheeler nods while she writes it all down.

'It was full of women's underwear, including mine—Donald Duck ones, I'd recognise them anywhere.' I look at Walshy. 'Creep must have taken them off my clothesline.'

Walshy's nostrils flare as he snorts in some air.

'Can you tell us how you came to get those injuries?' She indicates my face.

'I flipped my bike on the gravel.'

She nods. 'You said you remembered a doll?'

You could have heard a cockroach cough.

I nod slowly. 'I was hurt, lying somewhere. I believe it was Perry's backyard couch. He was smoking weed, and I could smell it. I was floating and I remembered seeing a doll in the back of a car in a busy carpark. A big one. I thought it was a mannequin at first.'

The two police share a subtle glance. 'Recently?'

I shake my head. 'I was younger. It was in Northam, the night of the school social dance, the same night Lisa Lee was attacked. My caseworker stopped so I could see everyone going in. It was so packed that she double-parked alongside a silver car, and that's when I saw it. I didn't think about it again. But when I was injured, it suddenly came flooding back.'

'It wasn't a dream?'

I shake my head, which hurts. 'No. I remember it like a photo.'

'Can you describe the doll?' Detective Wheeler leans forward, unblinking. 'Did it have a ribbon wrapped around it?'

I shake my head. 'I don't know. It was in the back seat with all these dresses; dance costumes, around it. It was pretty, like dolls are. It had blonde hair.'

Detective Wheeler sits straighter. 'If we showed you a picture, do you think you could tell us if it's the one you remember?'

I nod and get a bit cold as she pulls something out of a folder. 'I'll try.' She hands me a photograph.

The doll is encased in a clear plastic box, smiling, wearing a pink dress with long blonde hair in two plaits. A wide pink ribbon circles its middle. There's nothing sinister about the doll except that its laying on grass and there are water droplets on the outside of the box. 'I think so. I can't say definitely, but it's big like the one I remember. And blonde. It was definitely blonde.'

I hand the picture back and Detective Wheeler takes it, her eyes flickering across the picture. She stows it inside the folder.

'And the car? Could you say what make or model?'

I shake my head. 'I was twelve and fascinated by the kids all dressed up. Cars didn't draw my interest much.'

'Do you remember if it had a boot or was it a hatchback?'

I think for a second. 'A hatchback. There was more stuff over the back seat.'

She nods encouragingly. 'Silver hatchback. Okay. Anything else about last night Lola? Even if it feels minor, do you recollect anything else you want to tell us?'

I think about it and then shake my head. 'That's all I've got. What about the underwear in Perry's shed? I saw him creeping about in the dark the other night, too.' I gave them a quick description. Detective Wheeler noted it in the little pad and then tucked it away and then stood up. Jack followed.

'Lola, how well do you know Perry?'

'Been neighbours since I was nine.'

She nods. 'Ever had any problems?'

'He's keen on Lola, and he's a creep,' states Walshy. The detective acknowledges him before she looks back at me.

'He's awkward. Wants a date with me, but he hasn't really done anything.'

'You've been very helpful, thanks Lola. We sure need a break in this serial rapist case. People need to feel safe.'

'Why would he wait? I mean, if it's the same guy, why does he go so long between attacks?'

Detective Wheeler sighs, holds her wrist in front and widens her stance, and I can imagine her in uniform, gun in holster. 'Lots of factors here, Lola. These kinds of perpetrators can go years between serious attacks. Maybe they're in a stable relationship. Situations change. People get new jobs, move house. But something happens, and they strike again. This one leaves a calling card, a doll, so he wants to be noticed, or he wants a message to get across.'

'You're absolutely sure it's the same one? Don't these crazies get copycats?'

'We have fingerprints, and they match. But unless he's got his paws on record, we got nothing.'

'Perry?'

'We're off to interview him, but don't get your hopes up. Undie stealers and violent rapists aren't the same thing.' She lifts a hand at my expression. 'He'll be questioned, I assure you. Just hold tight and heal up. You've given us a lead—silver hatchback. We have a list of every staff and student that were present at the dance, so we'll see what cars they were driving eight years ago. You've done well, Lola.' She pauses. 'You didn't go inside the hall that night, did you? Could I get you to look over the guest list and see if anyone's missing?'

'No. But I did see some people I knew. I can look.' I shrug.

Detective Wheeler smiles warmly. 'Thanks, Lola. You going to be okay?' she indicates my face.

'Oh sure. I used to get into the odd fight. I'm used to healing up.' She nods.

'Okay. Good luck. I'll get that list to you ASAP.'

Chapter 47

I get home after lunch, having signed myself out when Mary came to see me. She clicked her tongue when I asked if she could drop me home but drove me anyway.

There's bits of wood and tools laying around the veranda, Walshy kneeling in the middle, a determined expression on his face. I go inside and close the door to escape the hammering sound.

Detective Wheeler phones to tell me that Perry's car is gone, and his parents don't know where he is.

That evening, she comes to the Flower House carrying an old backpack with a wave motif on the front.

'Border police will catch him if he tries to cross into South Australia or the NT, but my guess is he's laying low.' She sits on the other end of the couch. 'Are you cold?'

I realise I've done a full body shiver. 'I'm fine. You have that list?'

She nods, takes out a piece of paper and hands it to me. I read the heading; 'Students and Staff York High School Social Dance 1998.'

It has two columns of names. I recognise some immediately.

'Take your time. Tell me if anyone you remember is missing?' She shrugs. 'You never know.'

I spend ages looking through it, and then closing my eyes and trying to see the teens and their parents and the teachers walking around all dressed-up. It's vague, like a bunch of dresses walking around, but no clear faces.

'I'm sorry.' I hold it out to her.

The detective shakes her head. I detect regret in the tightness of her mouth as she shoulders her backpack and stands up.

'You keep that one, Lola. Now, let's just hope Perry makes an appearance so we can straighten a few things out.'

'I can't imagine him doing it. I know it's a weird thing to say, because he's so creepy, but I just can't imagine it. Anything come up about Blossom's sketchbook?'

She shakes her head. 'The break-in and theft have been recorded, but nothing so far. Any chance a relative might have come looking for an heirloom?'

'I suppose. She had nothing to do with her family since she was young though. Never spoke about them. It was like she came from nowhere.'

'Okay, we'll keep you informed.' She winked. 'Just heal up and keep your eyes open.' She looks around. 'Walshy here?'

'Outside reinforcing the fort.' I indicate the hammering sound.

Detective Wheeler taps the doorframe, winks, and leaves.

I do it then, before I lose my nerve. I dial the number from Friday night. A woman picks up.

'Berry Produce. This is Annie. How can I help you?'

I tell her my name and explain that Ned Berry left his number and wanted a meeting with me.

'Oh, sure. He said to direct you to his door if you called.' She gives me directions to his house and tells me she'll call him to warn of my arrival. 'Which will be ...?'

I swallow. 'Tomorrow morning?'

'Sure. He's still recovering from having some surgery done on his arteries last week. Got home Friday. He had a heart attack a couple of years ago and another one since.' She clicks her tongue. 'Keep that in mind.'

I stand there with the phone in my hand even after I've hung up. The *beeps* come out sounding like they're far away.

Chapter 48

I go to bed with a headache. When I wake, the sun is lower, yellowy light on the walls. There is milk in the fridge and a new loaf of bread on the counter. Tomatoes have been added to the fruit bowl. A note is sitting under a glass by the sink.

Back in an hour. Walshy.

There's no time written.

I put the kettle on, fire up the burner beneath the fry pan, and drop two slices of bread into the toaster. As two eggs and a sliced tomato spit and sizzle, I brew tea. The toast pops.

On the table, *The West Australian* newspaper depicts a picture of a war tank and demonstrators waving placards in anti-war protests about US-occupied Iraq. The protests are spread around the world: US, Canada, Asia, Europe and Australia.

'Hello, Lola.'

I jump. 'Shit, you scared me.'

'Sorry. Sorry.' Father Bickley stands outside the screen door, his hands up in surrender. He wears those spectacles that darken in the sunlight, so I can't see his eyes. With his sandy hair, clean-shaven pink face and high collar, he looks like a security guard. But he has the low, soothing voice of someone used to counselling people.

My heart is still jumping around in my throat. 'That's okay. I wasn't expecting anyone. Would you like tea?'

He nods. 'Much obliged. I was hoping to catch you before Blossom's service next Sunday. But I heard you had a mishap.'

He stands outside, hands folded. I open the door, and he wipes his feet and enters. 'Thank you.' He points to a chair and waits for me to nod before he sits. Once there, he settles gently with barely a sound and clasps his hands. His spectacles clear like fog off a lake, and bright blue eyes with blonde eyelashes appear.

'How are you? If you don't mind me asking?'

'I look worse than I feel.' I take a second cup out of the cupboard. 'How do you have it?'

'Just white.'

I pour the tea and take it to the table. Father Bickley takes a sip and sets the cup carefully down next to the newspaper before he speaks.

I sit too, not knowing what to do with my hands.

Blossom always dropped flowers at the church, but we never spoke about religion. The religious ed at school was perfunctory. My best guess about Catholicism is that you have to go to church, confess everything, and be kind to people. Like the church ladies were to me.

'My condolences about Blossom,' starts Father Bickley. 'She had a good heart.'

'Thank you.' We both sip our tea, and the silence sucks in and out of the room until it's unbearable. 'Um, Sunday. How does it all work?'

'After guests and family are seated, I'll read out a little about Blossom in the context of her being a community member and hard worker. Then I'll read a Psalm and mention family. That's your opportunity to speak or give a eulogy, or you can elect someone to read something for you.'

After a moment, I shake my head. 'I wouldn't know what to say. Can you do the talking?'

Father Bickley nods and looks at the table rather than at me like he doesn't want to stare. 'Of course. Then our organ player, Mrs. Pipps, plays 'The Lord Bless You and Keep You.' It's in our Bible, so there's no need for a brochure. You can choose a piece of music Blossom would have liked, or something that sets a certain atmosphere.'

I'm seized by a sudden panic. Brochure? Eulogy? Songs? I hadn't thought about any of this. Thankfully, he keeps talking in his low, comforting voice.

'We find that people with small or no families like us to take charge of the details. I'm happy to do that for Blossom if you wish.'

'Yes, please. Something low key. She wasn't social.'

Father Bickley nods. 'No problem. Would you like to look at the words in the songs, or do you have any questions?'

I shake my head. 'Ah, what about money? I don't know what it costs.'

He gives a brief headshake. 'You have friends in the community, including me,' he says. 'My service will be free of charge.'

'Thank you.'

As Father Bickley opens the door to go, he pauses and turns back. 'After the funeral, please come up to the church. We'll have a chat.'

I raise my eyebrows. He nods quickly and leaves.

I lock the door behind him. I don't know if I want to sit or walk. I hope it isn't concussion making me feel this way. I've lost my appetite, but I force down half the eggs and tomatoes on toast and hear Walshy call that he's back.

Outside, Walshy is already kneeling on the patio, measuring a length of wood. He'd sourced a second-hand screen door, so when I arrived home, the only sign of the break-in were the splinters around the lock. He's now repairing a broken plank from the veranda edge. It's been like that for years, but Walshy has the sudden urge to do it.

The break-in could have been pure opportunity, of course, except that only the sketchbook is missing.

Was there a chance it was innocent? That the thief didn't know anything about Blossom's secret sketches but happened to have an eye for art?

Not a chance.

The replacement security screen is solid, and it darkens the kitchen. We have a new, shiny key, a strange contrast to everything else.

Out the window, Walshy's camping gear is open all over the veranda and out the back door, sheets flap on the clothesline. His work boots stand near the laundry. Nearby, a wattlebird swoops over a brown honeyeater in a bottlebrush tree and clacks its beak. The smaller bird shrills, darting off. I walk out through the screen door at the side of the kitchen.

'I like it like this. It feels normal again.'

Walshy looks up and smiles. 'Any news?'

I shake my head. 'Not about Perry. But I'm going to go see Ned

Berry.'

'But you said he could be the guy messed up with that old murder.' Walshy's face flushes. 'What if you're right, and he knocked off his wife? You're half beat up already.'

'So's he.' I hold my hand up. 'I just spoke to his secretary. Ned Berry only got back from hospital on Friday night. He was in Perth getting his heart fixed. I'm not letting him off the hook completely, but he couldn't have broken in here. I just need to know why he loaned this house to Blossom and whether he really is Ned Del Saur.'

'Are you just going to come out and ask him?'

'I'm not sure.' Walshy shakes his head and exhales hard.

'I can take you next week.'

'I want to go in the morning. I'll ask Mary to drive me.'

Walshy rubs his hand over his face and groans. 'Jane, seriously?'

I walk closer and pull his hand away to kiss him on the lips. He groans, but softens. 'You haven't changed, Jane.'

'I need to know what Blossom is trying to tell me, but I've come to a dead end. I think Ned Berry could be the key.'

* * *

At the inn, Mary offers me food and drink, which I decline. She pours me a glass of water and puts it on a table. I don't sit, indicating my sore knee.

'Worse if I bend it,' I explain. 'You know, I've ordered a copy of my original birth certificate.'

Mary's face lights up. 'Good for you!' Her face sobers and she lowers her voice. 'I heard about Perry.'

'Yeah. I always knew there was something weird about him.'

'You think he might be the rapist?'

I shake my head. 'Honestly, I can't imagine it, but then who knew he crept around at night stealing women's knickers?'

'Right,' Mary agrees.

'Hey, you remember you said there was a portrait here, of Lorrelai?'

'Oh, yes. Ready to check it out?' I nod. 'Come on then.' She heads for the passageway that leads to staircase that leads to the second floor where there are a few rooms for accommodation. 'Let's dust her off!' She climbs the stairs ahead of me.

Feeling woozy, I lean on the wall. The nurse who discharged me said to expect this.

'I'll have to dig a bit,' Mary warns, as she gets to the top of the stairs and disappears.

I take a moment and then follow. When I reach the top, I wipe sweat off my forehead.

Mary is inside a dim room in the middle of stacked chairs, fake flowers, a box with 'Christmas Decos' written on the side, a bedhead, and numerous boxes.

By the wall, Mary skims through a stack of framed prints, most stock-standard inn fare of racehorses, a man in a leather apron pouring beer, a combine in a wheat crop.

Dust rises in the room, the motes caught by sunlight from a high window. Mary stops, makes a satisfied sound, and slides a large, framed oil painting out from the others. She wriggles a bit as she uses the rag from her pocket to wipe it. Then she turns around with it held in front of her.

'There she is!' Mary coughs on the dust. 'What do you think?' Her face drops. 'Jesus, girl. You still a bit peaky from your fall? Better sit down, huh. There's a chair right here.'

Lorrelai is magnificent in a red dress, her dark-red curls covering her bare shoulders, a huge Moreton Bay fig her background.

'I'm okay.' Red, brown, black and gold. Lovely Lorrelai with her slim waist, deep bust, athletic legs, black boots, black stockings and gloves. She gazes out at me with an enigmatic smile. Colour floods her cheeks and there's light in her eyes. *This woman was charged with drowning another woman to get her man?*

'She's gorgeous, huh?' says Mary. 'Probably a natural redhead.' She touches the portrait with the back of her finger. 'Blossom said to give it to you when you asked about Lorrelai. She painted this.'

I get closer so I can see the paint strokes inside the vivid colours on the canvas. 'It's amazing.'

'It is. She was a real talent, Blossom. Kept it to herself, though.' She stands next to me as we admire it.

After a moment, Mary leans the portrait back against the wall and goes to a box on one of the shelves. 'Right, just one more thing.' She searches the box, pulls something out and gets her rag out again. She turns, still dusting a silver ornament, her face a picture of concentration. Then she makes a satisfied noise and hands it to me. It's an old-fashioned candlestick with a decorative silver stem, some black in the grooves.

'We have one of these.' I take the candlestick and turn it in my hands. 'It looks like a match.'

'Well, Blossom asked me to give you those three things: key, painting, candlestick. Don't ask me why.' She indicated the painting and crossed her arms. 'Be worth something I reckon. Or you could hang it on your wall.'

I gaze at the painting and shake my head. 'It's too big, and I'm not sure where I'll be living. Can you keep it here?'

'Sure.' She goes to the door and clicks off the light. I follow her out. 'How'd you go with the house? You able to rent?'

'Not sure. Owner wants to see me.'

'You want to stay now Walshy's back?'

'Yeah. Not just because of him.'

'Yeah? Put down some roots?' She grins encouragingly. 'Nice to have you home again.'

'Mary, did Blossom say anything else to you about this stuff?'

'Nope. But honestly, when she told me she was going to die, I just agreed to do as she asked. I just assumed they were heirlooms. I already knew she was keen on Lorrelai.' She frowned. 'She said something like, "*Please don't ask me something I can't answer. I've kept my promise.*"'

Chapter 49

Berry's Produce is a fresh fruit and vegetable warehouse in Dwellingup, over two hours' drive from York. After she showed me the painting of Lorrelai and gave me Blossom's candlestick, Mary agreed to drive me.

We park at the house directly to the right of the warehouse, as directed by the receptionist. The warehouse is white, painted over with giant, colourful carrots, grapes, apples and eggs, just like their delivery trucks.

'I'm happy to occupy myself in town, or I can come in.' Mary cuts the engine and crosses her arms.

'Ah, could you wait here?'

'Something you're not telling me?' Her eyes narrow.

Doubting my theory, I look at the house. I am glad I said nothing to Mary about the possibility that Ned Berry could be Ned Del Saur. 'No, should be fine, but I mightn't be long.'

My hands shake as I knock. An elderly man with a walking stick answers. Despite his hunched shoulders, he is still quite tall. His blue eyes are bright behind steel-rimmed spectacles. His hair and beard are dramatically white.

'Oh dear, you've been in the wars. Come in, come in.' He steps backwards. 'Lola, was it?'

'Thanks. I'm fine. Just a little accident.'

I step inside, and he locks the door. My heart jumps, although he leaves the key in the lock.

I try to hide my limp when I walk; hard, as my knee has stiffened up on the drive. I motion towards the front door.

'My friend is waiting outside.'

'Good-o. Cup of tea?'

'No, thanks.'

He stares at me for a moment, with a bit of a frown, and then lifts his cane and points towards a sunroom. The furniture is polished blackwood, the carpet thick and luxurious. The light is crystalline, with even more crystals dripping down. I haven't ever been in a house with a chandelier before.

The lounge chairs face an expansive window overlooking a neat hedge, a road, and faint brown paddocks with dense green pine forest beyond.

I take the seat furthest away from the one with two knitted rugs and a foot stool.

He sits there, wincing somewhat, which reminds me about his operation. He's old and sick—the only reason Walshy didn't force the issue of coming with me.

I've memorised the short walk back to the front door, so I can exit quickly.

'Now, young lady, I hear you stayed at the old backpackers with Blossom and wish to rent?' He holds my gaze.

Without staring, I try to assess whether his face is the same as Ned Del Saur's. 'Mr. Berry—'

'Ned. Please.'

'Ned.' I clear my throat to buy time, suddenly lost as to what to say. 'I spent half my life there. I'd like to rent. We could always talk about me buying in the future.'

Ned leans his stick against the coffee table and folds his hands in his lap. The stick is still close enough to grab if he wanted to. I sit close to the edge of my seat, one of my heels bouncing up and down.

'You realise it's a dump?'

'It needs repairs but that's okay. I was surprised to hear it was a rental because Blossom didn't pay rent.'

He blinks a few times. 'It was an arrangement we had. I'll admit I didn't know anyone else was there. You're a dependant?'

This feels like another conversation of tactics. 'She fostered me when I was nine. How did you know Blossom?'

His expression changes. A coldness eases up my spine, and I feel my theory returning. His face is now a maze of deep wrinkles. 'Fostered you? Blossom Brenton?' His lips pull back off his teeth with the words.

I nod, and my ears start to ring. I watch for signs he's going to do something. 'Yes.'

Ned squints, eyeballs me, and then folds his arms. 'You grew up there?'

'Yes. So … you knew Blossom?'

He draws a deep breath, and then slumps as he exhales, as if retreating somewhere internally. 'Yes.'

'How?'

He shakes his head and clears his throat grumpily.

'Okay. Can you tell me why our house is actually your house? Why it had to be sold as soon as she died?' My heart pounds so hard it feels like I'm pulsing.

Ned frowns. His face turns to all corners of the room, as if he is deeply confused. He uncrosses his arms and clutches the arm rests instead. I lean forward onto my toes, placing all my weight on them. He's tall, but he's unwell. And I'm fast.

'Blossom didn't even like children.' He turns back to look me over again. Shaking his head, he sits back. 'How long ago was this?'

'Eleven years.'

Ned's face seems to lengthen. 'Good lord,' he mutters. He stares straight ahead for a few moments, absolutely still. 'So … that's why.'

'Why what?' I wait. 'Ned?'

'She needed a house, something simple. She wanted it right away.' He looks at me curiously. 'It was for you.'

'Blossom asked you for a house, and you gave it to her?'

The old man shakes his head. 'I bought it for the land. Was going to build. House was a dump, but she said she'd take it as it was. Didn't say a bloody word about having a kid.' He stared out the window, his thoughts clearly far away.

'Were you friends?'

When he speaks, Ned's voice is low. 'Blossom and I were definitely not friends.' He glances at me, and then away. 'It's very complex. I'm tired.'

'I have time.'

Ned stares out the window.

'I saw a newspaper article.'

Ned's face falls, but he doesn't look surprised. He takes a moment to answer. 'I see.'

'You lost your son.'

Ned heaves a great sigh and his chin wobbles. 'Yes. I did.'

'Jo?' Silence built around us. 'Ned, did you live in the Northam Caravan Park in 1971?'

Ned closes his eyes for a few seconds. He bends forward and puts his chin on one of his fists. When he speaks, it's a low rumble. 'What did Blossom say?'

'Nothing when she was alive.' I wasn't sure if I should lie. 'But she left me a sketchbook. About a lady called Lorrelai McAllister.' The look on his face stops me dead. 'Are you alright?'

The old man's face has greyed, his expression gone, his hands shaking in his lap. I realise a shock could kill him. 'Um, oh God.' I stare around. 'Can I get you something?'

After a moment, he speaks, but very quietly and with his eyes fixed on the carpet. 'A glass of water.' His lip quivers as he points to a glass on a side table.

His hands shake as I give him the glass. But after a couple of seconds, some life returns to his face. He takes a drink. 'Okay?' He hands me the glass and I put it back.

I needn't have worried about him jumping up. He's slumped in the chair, his hands open and loose on his thighs. He's staring far off again.

'What do you know about Lorrelai?' he asks.

I resume an edge-of-my-seat position.

'I work at the Lion Inn. I'm told she once worked there, as a dancer. I was directed to the Northam Library and found old newspaper articles on the murder.'

Ned slowly turns his face, but his eyes stay down. 'I see. Blossom didn't tell you about it?'

'No. But Lorrelai … you knew her, didn't you?'

Ned nods in a way that suggests he knew her well.

'I read all about the murder —'

'God.' He covers his eyes with one hand. 'I knew this would come up again.'

I wait, but he sits there with his eyes covered. 'Ned?'

He doesn't respond right away. 'I changed my name,' he says quietly. 'I thought I could leave it all behind. Ah, Blossom.' He shakes his head like a parent with a problem child. 'She couldn't leave it alone.'

'Ned, are you saying that you're—'

'I'm Ned Del Saur,' he says with a sigh. 'I knew I'd have to change my name if I wanted any kind of a normal life.' He blinks for a long time, almost like he'll fall asleep, his face long and sad.

For a moment, I'm blank. He's admitted it. I am sitting across from Ned Del Saur. I'm sitting across from Lorrelai's lover, the husband of the murdered woman. I try to imagine him as a big man with black hair and a beard. Adrenaline kicks in, and my veins buzz.

'Lorrelai was accused of your wife's—'

Ned nods and nods, his eyes shut. 'Yes, yes. I know. I was there.'

He covers his eyes again, and I'm struck by how worn his hand looks: a patchwork of liver spots and veins showing through the translucent skin. Lorrelai's lover, now a frail old man. But a man who has lived free.

I can't accuse him of murder. It's just a picture, after all. I thread my fingers and search my mind. Do I mention I've seen a sketch of a man who looks like him chasing a woman who looks like his wife towards a bridge? Do I ask whether he strangled her?

'Blossom blackmailed me.'

I sit back. 'How?'

Ned looks like he's grown older, as though time fast-forwarded in minutes. 'You know, if you ever eat glass, just a chip, a tiny splinter, it stays inside you? It lodges in, and over time, it pierces deeper and deeper until it can actually kill you. Just one tiny sliver of glass.' He looks away. 'The night Dora died, it was like I swallowed glass.'

He spoke towards the window, as if I wasn't there. 'Blossom put it inside me, and all these years, it's dug deeper and deeper. I wake sometimes with a stabbing sensation, right here.' He pokes a finger in the centre of his chest.

I wait a respectable amount of time before I ask, 'How did Blossom blackmail you?'

'She knew I lied. Blossom was outside that night. It was a hell of a storm. She told me she saw me go to the bridge. But I told the police I'd never left the caravan. My son was just a baby, and Dora went out all the time, so they believed it. Blossom said she went down near the river and watched from behind one of those big fig trees, where she used to hide from Peg when they were fighting. She saw Dora head for the river and disappear. Shortly after, I turned up. But by the time I got down there, Dora was gone. Her nightie was stuck to the railing, so I thought the worst. I thought she'd fallen or jumped in. I looked all over, just in case.' His voice dropped. 'But someone strangled her.'

'You lied?'

Without hesitation, he nodded. 'I had to. I'd have been jailed. I had a baby boy to care for. Peggy said she looked out in the night. Something woke her. Thought there were people on the bridge, but she couldn't say who. I don't know who it was. It wasn't me.'

I took a deep breath, unsure whether to believe him. 'You're saying you didn't chase your wife? You didn't catch up with her on the bridge?'

He gave me an odd look. 'Chase? I ran downhill because that was her direction, but, young lady, she had left some time before. I wouldn't normally bother. It was something she did. But it was such a terrible storm.'

'Do you think she was running from you?'

'I doubt it. She left before me. No one was there when I crossed the bridge. No one, I swear.' He stared out the window. 'I thought she must have run off into the trees. She always came back, but when I saw the nightie, I knew she was gone. She never took that bloody nightie off.' He stopped and shook his head, and his breath staggered inwards like he was fighting tears.

'I thought ... I thought, she's finally ended it. She's jumped, from madness or sadness, or something.' He looks at me, and I stiffen. 'And ... for a moment, I was relieved.' His face crumples. He covers it with his hand and cries softly. '*Relieved.*'

Corellas squawk from a rosewood tree across the road. On the grass beneath, chewed helicopter seeds make the ground look like a pub floor on a Friday night. The birds' sleek, white bodies weave in and out of the branches, crawling and gnawing. Some swoop to the ground to eat with delighted, piercing noises—bouncing two-footed, feathered clowns.

'Why didn't Blossom dob you in?'

Ned straightens, pats around in his shirt pocket. He pulls out a crumpled blue hankie, wipes his eyes, blows his nose, and returns it. His eyes are red and watery. I wonder if he's just wiped snot on them. He sinks back into the chair and stares out the window. 'I don't know. Maybe she was too young. Scared.'

'Lorrelai was wearing your wife's wedding rings. Do you know why?'

'I gave them to her because my wife had thrown them away. I explained that to the police. I told them Dora was unwell, dangerous even. They didn't care. I think it only made it worse, made them more suspicious. Ah, but they insisted there was a lot of "evidence" in the end. Lorrelai had been seen wet-nursing our baby. She and I were ... *together*. They said she was obsessed with me, with Jo.' He shrugged. 'She lost a baby, you know.'

'No, I didn't.' Stunned, I ponder that for a moment. 'Was it yours?'

He shakes his head. 'No, she came to the park pregnant — some other married man. It was the reason she'd lost her job dancing.'

He stares squarely at me. 'I did my best for Lorrelai. Told them I didn't think she'd hurt anyone. Told them I gave her the wedding rings as payment for her work. I told them my wife was mentally ill and had hurt our son. I begged them to search Dora's hospital records and consider that Dora had bruised herself somehow and then jumped into the river. She went running around in the middle of a storm, for goodness sake.' His chest rose and fell rapidly.

I chewed my inner lip. 'Any chance it was someone else?'

He blinked, leaned away, took a deep breath. 'It can't help anymore, dredging it up. Lorrelai did her time. She's gone now.'

'You think she did it?'

He gives me a long look and then rubs his eyes. 'Lorrelai was a beautiful, generous woman. She saved my son. I'll always be grateful for the time she spent with us. But she's gone. It's over. The jury gave their verdict. I wasn't there. I don't know what happened. It should be buried for good, the whole sad thing.'

Ned Berry looks so very tired.

I unclench my hands; my nails have made matching half-moon arcs on my palms. 'Blossom left me a bit of a trail. I'm just trying to work out why Lorrelai was so important to her.'

'They were friends.' Ned shrugs. 'Blossom's problems weren't my business. Once she asked for the house, I felt like she had got her favour. I was relieved. Surprised. Hadn't seen her since Dora died. She looked totally different. A tattoo on her arm. Her hair short. Men's clothes.'

'Do you know what Blossom did afterwards?'

'Was meant to be married off when she came of age. She was fifteen or sixteen, I think. Her mother, Peg, was a real battle-axe. But Blossom didn't take to the female role much. She ran away after Dora died. I suspect she joined the hippies or the women's movement.'

I can imagine her running away. Scared or angry about her mother's plans, never to return. Lost and sad after Lorrelai went to jail; a woman near her age, a woman she sketched many times. Maybe her only friend.

'What was she like, before everything happened?'

Ned inhales for a long time. 'Good worker. Solid. Strong. Helped with the gardening and so on. Carried paper around with her all the time. Drew pictures. Pretty good too, from what I saw.'

'Did she have a sketchbook?'

Ned squints, remembering. 'Ah, yes. She used to tuck a pencil behind her ear. She hid her drawings from Peg. She used to holler if she caught Blossom idle.'

He moves to the edge of the chair, pushes himself up, takes his stick and rises. He walks slowly towards the kitchen. Something creaks, but I'm not sure whether it's his bones or the floor.

I follow. 'Did you visit Lorrelai in prison?'

'Ah, I tried, but she didn't want me to keep coming. She seemed ashamed, embarrassed. I understood.'

'Did you see her when she got out?'

'Briefly.' Ned opens a cupboard, then closes it without getting anything. He closes his eyes for a moment. 'I didn't expect it, after so long. She said she didn't hate me, just ...' He shrugs. '... wanted to start afresh.' He opens the cupboard, takes out a jar of teabags and puts one in a mug. He supports himself with both hands on the bench.

'I had someone else in my life then. A stepson, of sorts. Arrived around the time Jo died. He was Dora's first son.' He glances over his shoulder. 'She'd done it before it seems … had a child she didn't want, left him with his father.' He shook his head. He put some water in a tarnished silver kettle and lit a flame beneath it. He blew out the match and placed it in the sink.

'Do you know where Lorrelai went after prison? She died shortly afterwards.'

Ned shakes his head. 'No. But it's a bloody shame. Wasted, wasted years.'

The wind goes out of me. 'I wish I knew someone who had seen her after she got out.'

'Hmm, indeed,' he says. 'Sorry, dear. I think I'll need tea and a kip after that lot. Let yourself out.' He yawns and shudders, his shoulder blades blunt wings.

'Thanks for seeing me.' The silence is a sad one of missed opportunities, of things that can't be put right. 'Ned, why did you tell me who you are? How do you know you can trust me?'

He glances over his shoulder, leaning heavily on the bench. 'Some part of me wanted to tell,' he says gruffly. 'When you change your identity, you lose so much. Old friends, family, connections. You seemed the right person. Maybe it's the right time.' He sounds so utterly defeated.

'I needed somewhere safe to live. Blossom took me to the Flower House. It was a good, quiet place to live. The only place I've ever really belonged.'

After a moment, he turns and leans back against the bench. 'I'm glad, dear. I'm glad. Ties up a bit of a loose end for me, actually. I don't have long to go.' He taps his heart. Then he takes up his walking stick from where it leans against the bench. 'Stay in the house if you want. I'll think about rent, repairs and so on.'

'Thank you.'

He smiles and lifts a hand like he's waving, but he is trembling a lot, so the gesture is unclear. 'All the best, dear.'

* * *

The bitumen hums beneath the car wheels. Mary lets me be silent for a while.

I feel Blossom now, after hearing Ned talk about her. I imagine the young woman, the frustrated artist forced into a role against which she rebelled. Then her friend Lorrelai is jailed. She runs away to avoid marriage, joins the women's movement. She's free ... until she uses blackmail to provide a house for a nine-year-old orphan.

Me.

Now, why would she do that?

Chapter 50

Walshy holds my hand across the front seat, his other hand on the steering wheel. There was no way he wasn't coming, and I'm glad. He looks across and winks.

'Ready for this?'

I nod. 'Yes, I should have found out before this. My caseworker offered to find out about my birth parents years ago. I didn't see the point.'

'Fair enough. You were probably scared.'

'Or I was happy with ending up in the Flower House with you. It seemed so simple after all the drama. Why would I want to stir things up again?'

He squeezes my hand.

Sarah meets us at a coffee shop in Northam, smiling as we walk up together. Apart from more sun damage and that her ponytail is now completely grey, she looks the same.

We all say hello and Walshy introduces himself as Ben Walsh. I'm proud standing beside him, his body solid as a wall.

'Walshy?' Sarah reaches out and shakes his hand. 'Always knew you were special to Lola.'

'No gooey stuff,' I urge. 'I'm nervous as hell. Let's just do this.'

Sarah points at a table almost obscured by plants, and we head over. 'It's a bit more private over here.'

We settle around the small table as a waitress in jeans, a white shirt and a waist apron takes our coffee orders. Walshy holds my hand beneath the table, his thumb stroking the back of mine.

Sarah frowns as she pulls an envelope out of her bag. 'Thanks for involving me, Lola. You've always had a place in my heart.' She smiles briefly. 'Know that this can be difficult, but you have me around whenever you need me. Lean on your friends if it's confusing or confronting.' She places the envelope flat on the table, both hands on top, and gives me a solemn look. 'But it can also be a positive thing. I have contacted a midwife who was working at the hospital when you were born. She's keen to talk, should you be open to it.'

I can't take my eyes off the envelope on the table. 'Tell me.' My heart is drumming like a train accelerating up the tracks, hitting each joint in the metal line. *Boomboom, boomboom.*

Sarah looks around to ensure we're alone and leans forward to pass me the envelope. 'Your mother's name was Lorrelai McAllister. You father is marked unknown.'

* * *

After she left prison, Lorrelai did have time to have a baby. Lorrelai; murderess, dancer, lover, who's been revealed to me in sketches, paintings and newspaper articles, is my mother.

When Blossom came to get me, I wasn't a random orphan, I was her friend Lorrelai's baby.

I've cried and ranted, walked around shaking my head. Walshy has listened without comment, hugged me when I needed him to.

Every brain has a fill line, and I reach mine sometime that afternoon. Small things sharpen into focus. Safe, familiar things relax my brain: the couch sagging beneath my weight, a cushion behind my back. Blossom's crocheted rug across my knees feels too heavy, and I push it off so my skin can breathe.

The light feels softer since we arrived home. The tallest Geraldton wax casts a fibrous shadow on the wall. I focus on the silhouette, pick out the flowers by their five round petals, like tiny clovers.

I have a cup of noodles on my knee. They're cold, but I grip the handle, grateful for something solid. Walshy has called the inn to say he's staying home. He appears at the doorway, hands in his back pockets. His face is simultaneously alert and weary.

'You want something else to eat?' I shake my head, watching him move around and lean his elbow on the mantelpiece. He sees where my eyes go.

There are two matching candlesticks now. A complete set. Like gradually replaced puzzle pieces. I shake my head and look away. I need to aim my anger somewhere, but my thoughts won't land. I'm surrounded by stories and ghosts. I feel like this must be happening to someone else. I keep waiting for someone to call it off, expose it for the crazy joke it is.

Walshy sits beside me on the couch. I like the weight of him there. He is real, warm.

'Jane?' He takes my hand. 'How do you feel? Is your head okay?'

My hand is limp, my energy drained by a spectrum of emotions since we saw Sarah.

'I'm floaty. I can't focus. I don't want to think. I want it to be tomorrow, so I can wake up and … understand.' My chin wobbles again, but no tears come; I cried them all out on the trip home.

'Go to bed, then.' He takes the mug off me. The noodles float, no longer edible. 'Don't shower, just go to bed.' He takes the rug off my knees and holds out his hand. Taking it, I let him pull me up.

'I have to find out everything.'

'Later.'

'Lorrelai was my mother. My mother. Blossom knew everything the whole time.'

Headlines pop up like news flashes in my thoughts, force-feeding my brain. I can't make them stop. I'm so exhausted, but they wrench my attention back repeatedly.

'I need a sleeping tablet.'

'C'mon. I'll take you to bed.' Walshy guides me down the hall like it's somewhere I've never been.

'Walshy, I …'

'Tomorrow,' he says.

* * *

Armadale Kelmscott Memorial Hospital has a limestone façade and archway with its name in brass lettering along the curve.

Walshy and I say little. It's like we've run out of words.

A lady from reception takes us through double glass doors. A sign says 'Maternity' and the air smells of baby powder. A TV is on, and a few babies make high-pitched, kitten-like mewls. She points at someone walking away.

'That's Matron Shirley.'

Striding down the middle of the corridor is a solid lady with white hair in a tight donut bun. She wears a pastel blue skirt, matching buttoned down top, nylons and white shoes.

I call quietly, 'Matron Shirley?'

She turns on her heel and looks me over with clear blue eyes. One black eyebrow is raised. Seeing us, her scarlet lips break into a smile, and then a grimace.

'Ah. Hello, you must be Lola? What happened to your face?'

She walks right up to me, her hands out, and takes both of mine firmly. As she looks me over, she squeezes my hands against her chest.

She smells of perfume and hairspray.

'I crashed my pushbike.'

'Ouch!' She touches the side of my head. 'Everything happens at once, doesn't it?'

We make introductions and she leads us out to the rose garden.

'I'm retired now, just like to drop in and say hello.'

There's a small, grassed section, a cluster of rose bushes and then native bush.

'Sarah, my caseworker, says you were here when Lorrelai McAllister gave birth. I've just discovered she was my mother.'

Shirley's mouth tightens as she nods. 'Yes, I was here.'

'I know she passed away shortly after I was born.' I clear my throat, tightened by emotion. 'It's been a shock. My foster mother, Blossom knew but I've only just found out. She died recently. Sarah encouraged me to come. Thought it might help.'

'Yes. Thanks for the opportunity. I would like to tell you a story.' She drops her voice to a whisper. 'It's a love story.'

Walshy rolls his head left and then right, shakes out his shoulders, and drops his head back. His face lit by the sun, he visibly softens.

I try to absorb that feeling, but I'm too wound up inside. Clouds drift across the sky like released helium balloons. A plane whines, fades. Nearby, a house is being constructed, the bare brick walls awaiting a roof, the sound of the workmen and their radio rattling and singing.

Shirley ambles along the edge of a rose garden, her hand out to touch the flowers. A few petals flutter down. She stops and waits for me.

'Lola, your mother found out she was sick halfway through her pregnancy. She had breast cancer.' She glances sideways. I nod, but I can't speak. 'She opted not to have treatment because she was pregnant.'

A shadow of dread passes over me.

'The disease was aggressive.'

'Oh God.' Tears form and run down my face. A sick woman traded her life for mine. A well of love deepens, bringing more tears.

'You alright?'

I shake my head. 'She died because she didn't get treatment?'

'Let me tell you the whole thing.'

I sniff and nod, wiping the tears from my face. Shirley puts her arm around me and pulls me close.

'Your brave, brave mother wanted a child very badly. She was so happy to be pregnant.'

'Until she got cancer.'

'No, Lola. She was still happy.' Shirley faced me and held on to my shoulders. 'Honey, she was so proud to be growing you, keeping you safe. You couldn't have met a happier patient.'

I whimpered a little. Shirley pulled me beneath her arm and squeezed me tight. 'She sat up there in bed, a pile of pillows behind her back. We waited on her and treated her like the queen. She wouldn't take anything that would hurt you. Oh no, not a chance.'

'Was she in pain?'

'Honey, she was delirious with love.'

'D-did she see me?' The roses beside us go hazy.

'Yes, honey. She saw you. I still remember her face.' Shirley got a tissue out from where it was tucked beneath her bra strap and dabbed her eyes before putting it back. 'You were her joy.'

'How long ...'

'A couple of months after you were born.'

'Oh God.' Waves of grief pull like a current.

Shirley holds me, and then I feel someone behind me. Walshy. And I'm not alone. I'm encased by affection. I cry as I imagine someone sitting up in bed, her hands softly enclosing her bulbous belly. After a while, the tears slow.

'But my father didn't come?'

'She was close-lipped about that.'

A truck from the construction site beeps in reverse and then drives off down the street.

I stagger some air. We unfold like a bud. I wipe my eyes, gaze around. The world seems different. Clearer. Quieter. Overhead, three flying white ibises are silver arrows in a cobalt sky.

I tuck my hands into the pockets of my shorts. Peace settles around me; that low, drugged feeling that follows a good cry.

My mother did not just hand me over. She had no choice. She wanted me. She loved me.

'Lorrelai's friend Blossom visited all the time. She wasn't alone. A priest came regularly too.'

I nod, wipe my face and rub my nose. 'A priest? Was Lorrelai religious?'

'Ah, not that I remember.'

'Do you happen to remember the priest's name? So I can talk to someone who knew her.'

'Oh, gosh love, it was a long time ago. I know he was associated with some charity to do with Breast Cancer research afterwards.' She cocks her head. 'I'll do a bit of digging and see what comes up. Leave me your number.'

Our trip back was almost silent.

The phone was ringing as we walked up the side of the Flower House.

'Yes?' I puffed after struggling with the new door to get it in time.

'It's Shirley. Was easy to find in the end, dear. His name was Father Bickley.'

Chapter 51

I wake and enjoy a split-second of peace before it all comes back. Blossom. Shirley. Lorrelai—my mother. Fragments of yesterday shift like they've been waiting.

'Lorrelai was sweet,' Shirley had told us. 'Blossom clearly adored her. She often slept on a chair in Lorrelai's room. Of course, Lorrelai made Blossom promise not to tell you about her as long as she lived. Because of her past. She made Blossom swear it in front of the priest. Blossom must have kept that promise.'

But I was a living, breathing girl. How could she watch me all those years and keep it to herself? Now, it feels doubly hard. Shocks are coming from all sides like I'm being hit with a shovel and everyone I want to ask questions is dead.

I try to forgive Blossom. Perhaps it wasn't just out of loyalty to Lorrelai but also out of protectiveness for me. Perhaps she had tried to keep me from the weight of this knowledge when I was young, ensuring I was free to grow up without it. Was that why she left the sketchbook? Because she knew she could finally tell me? Because she had kept her promise as long as she lived?

I now understood why Blossom was keen to stop the Lion Inn celebrating the notorious killer Lovely Lorrelai. She knew that one day, I'd find out who I was—the daughter of a convicted murderer. Or, perhaps, the daughter of an innocent woman. Blossom had been there in the caravan park when it all happened. What did she know about that night which made her so sure Lorrelai was innocent?

I get up and head for the garden, where I immediately feel better.

The garden is simple, beautiful, logical. It moves predictably with the seasons. The insects and birds have a purpose driven by instinct. No confusion. No questions. Just life. Simple.

Walshy lies awake on his back in bed, his hands behind his head. He smiles, and a warm wave laps over me. 'I didn't want to wake you,' he says.

I climb into bed beside him. 'You always look gorgeous in the mornings.' He puts his arm around me.

'You feeling okay?'

'Yep. It's still sinking in. But you're here. I've got his place, this garden. That's all I can think about for now.' We kiss properly, and something stirs in me. It is right. It is good. It always was.

He sighs and holds me tighter. I move as his chest moves, and it feels lovely. We listen to the birds chirping, a magpie carolling and the staggered cry of a wattlebird.

'I'm glad you broke up with Shelley.' I roll onto my back.

We watch a wasp build a lumpy mud nest on a rafter above us. It looks like a mini-Uluru.

When we finally get up, we hurry through breakfast, check funeral arrangements with Mary, and then head to the main street. We pull up outside the bakery.

I point at it. 'Remember buying me that first jam donut?'

'Course. You scoffed it like a stray.'

I elbow him before we get out. Inside the bakery window is a handwritten 'Wanted' sign for an apprentice baker. 'Be handy knowing how to make those donuts if I want to open a café sometime.'

Walshy's eyebrows shoot up. 'In York?'

'Where else? This place is paradise.'

He gives me a surprised look. 'Nope. But it's definitely better with jam donuts.'

We walk out with two jam donuts, and a start date.

Walshy speaks quietly. 'Speaking of paradise, I'd like to go to Broome after the funeral. You keen?'

I give him a look. 'I've wanted to go every one of the hundred times you've talked about it.'

He chuckles, hooks his arm around the back of my neck, and kisses me on the cheek.

Chapter 52

I walk into the church in borrowed black pants and a navy blouse with no idea what to expect. Paper flowers are stuck to the ends of the pews, and although they look like kids' craft, they're a relief from the dark wooden pews. A display of fresh flowers stands by the alter. It reminds me of the bouquets Blossom made.

Father Bickley bows slowly and holds out an arm to show me where to sit. I watch him carefully, and it feels like he's watching me too. He knows who I am. He always has. He and Blossom—the two guardians of Lorrelai's secret.

'How are you, Lola?'

'Fine.' I'm wet under the armpits. I pinch my blouse and fan my face.

'I have the piece I'll read out here. Did you want to take a quick look?'

'No.'

He gives me a long look, an expression I've never seen before. Then his expression is composed again. He gestures to the front pew, and I go and sit down.

I look back over my shoulder. Everyone looks different in a church. Sombre and quiet, well dressed, with brushed-down hair.

About half the seats are occupied. I recognise school people, church people, Mary and Con, the Turners, Perry's parents. Perry's father is terribly thin, wears glasses, and has a red moustache. They avoid my eyes and sit far up the back, away from everyone, their knees touching. Perry is still missing. It's been days. I'm surprised they came.

I scan the crowd. Could the sketchbook thief be here? Shelley is three rows back with her mother. Her nose and eyes are red.

When Walshy walks through the door, he catches my eye and heads straight over. He's wearing his black work pants with a white button-down shirt. I turn to face the altar. He slides along the pew, takes my hand, squeezes it.

Walshy sits close enough that our arms touch all the way from shoulder to wrist. I can hear Shelley crying softly. A moment of guilt passes over me.

Father Bickley holds up his arms.

'Welcome, everyone, to the funeral of Blossom Brenton. My name is Father Thomas Bickley, and I'll be leading the service today.' It falls quiet, like we've all stopped breathing.

I focus on the light streaming through the tall vertical windows on either side of the back wall. Up there is the stained-glass mural of the mother and child that Blossom used to look at when we delivered the flowers. It reminds me that my mother died too, shortly after I was born. I haven't been to visit her grave or even found out where it is. I swallow and swallow again, and tears ooze out. A hand squeezes my shoulder. Freda is behind me. She tightens her mouth, nods, and then sits back again.

Father Bickley's voice resonates around the interior of the church. All the right sounding words and sentiments come from him. I can hear throat clearing but no wet sounds of grief. Like me, no one here really knew Blossom.

It feels desperately unfair that I had to learn all about Blossom, about the secrets she kept, after she died.

Then I figure that it seems to fit. She wanted it this way. She planned it. My past is for me to discover, not for her to tell. At least she trusted me with the key to unlock the secrets. She'd always given me the freedom to find my own way, to do things in my own time. It's the way it's always been.

A warm weight settles on my shoulders like sunshine. I see her then, her solid frame and quiet manner, the keeper of secrets as she moved about the garden, letting me do what I wanted in there. I wonder if I was ready for Blossom at the precise time she was ready for me. She trusted me from the beginning, as though I came equipped, whole, and resilient. Even as a nine-year-old, she trusted me to run the house, to know what I needed, rather than tell me. She was fascinated by my knowledge, my skills. She never said no to anything, never doubted me. She let me be free. She found me and gave me a safe place to grow and through guarding the truth, she shielded me.

A new wave of tears leaks out for Blossom, and it's a relief.

To Father Bickley's left is a shelf that contains a long wooden coffin with rose petals all over it. I can't imagine Blossom dead in there. I can't look at it.

Suddenly I am grateful for the beautiful old wooden pews and the melancholy, colourful glass and the hum of people wanting to pay their respects for a woman who never shared much, never asked much, but did at least one very good thing. She took me home.

Walshy pulls me close, kisses my head. There's a drop of sweat running down the side of his face. He swipes his hand across his top lip.

Father Bickley reaches the end of his speech. A tune plays and people sing, and then there's a pause.

The guitar chord twangs out from a stereo set up on the edge of the stage and then John Lennon's voice. 'A Hard Day's Night' shouts from the small speakers but reaches every corner of the church. I'm momentarily shocked I chose it. Then it seems absolutely right.

I see some confused looks and a few smiles.

The Beatles—at least I knew that about her. Blossom. Hard worker. Secretive. Artist. Beatles fan.

Afterwards, we flow outside where food is spread out along trestle tables.

People have dark patches in their armpits, and women are fanning their faces with serviettes.

I was relieved that Blossom was to be cremated, her ashes put in an urn. I hate the idea of a burial: a big dirt hole, a headstone, worms eating through flesh. But I imagine she wouldn't mind being spread over the garden.

When I asked, Mary told me what I was supposed to do with an urn. 'Spread her ashes in her favourite place.'

The sun gleams off dark-chocolate ganache. Icing begins to melt. I recognise church ladies and canteen ladies, and I thank everyone who so much as looks at me, even if I can't remember who they are. It surprises me, suddenly, that I love them all.

Con claps his hands. 'Everyone! You're welcome back at the inn for drinks!'

A cheer goes up.

Shelley stands on the other side of the gathering with her mother, an older, shorter version of her. They have their arms linked and clasp hands like they fear separation. Shelley's lips quiver and her mascara has made dark smudges beneath her eyes. She looks small and cold, although the day is warm.

Seeing me, they approach, hips bumping.

'The service went well,' says Shelley's mother. 'Let us know if you need anything.'

'Thank you for coming.' I shade my eyes and then reach for Shelley's hand. It's limp and cool in my grasp. 'Are you okay Shelley?'

She nods and then sniffs.

'I'm hopeless at funerals.' A little of my guilt lifts.

Mother looks at daughter, and her lips thin in sympathy. 'We're going to go now. Ready sweetie?' Shelley nods and they turn and walk off, conjoined.

Walshy is chatting to a farmer. Both have their arms crossed, their chests puffed out like farm men do. He is suddenly alert, finishing up and jogging towards me.

Detective Sam Wheeler hovers at the edge of the carpark, watching people without trying to be obvious. She catches my eye and gives a slight nod.

'Hey! I'll grab a lift with you.' Walshy catches up, breathing like he's just run a race. He falls into step beside me and takes my hand. I smile at him. We are allowed to do this now. It gives me a buzz every time. I look over at the white Porche Shelley and her mother have climbed into.

'Poor Shelley. I think she was the only one who cried.' Walshy hums in agreement.

'She's a sensitive one, that's for sure. Don't worry, her mother will buy her something nice.'

'Don't be mean.' I elbow him.

'Hello? Lola?'

I turn to find a lady with short yellow hair and an earthy, makeup-free face behind me.

'Yes?'

'I'm Cheryl. I knew Blossom.'

'Oh. Thanks for coming.'

She smiles. 'I live in Boddington. Blossom stayed many times.'

'Oh, her women's group.'

'Yes.' She tilts her head. 'I'm sorry it's taken us so long to meet.'

'Yes,' I agreed.

Cheryl's eyes soften. 'Please come and visit the retreat sometime.'

I thank her again, and Cheryl leaves.

The inn swells with more people than there were at the church. They've lost the weird church tones and sombre faces. Mary and Con have put on a roast and salad, and people are walking around with drinks and plates of food. A weight slides off me.

I order a cider, lean back against the bar, and watch the crowd mingle. Everyone knows each other, one way or another. I hear the occasional whoop when a person sees someone they know. It makes me smile. I feel like part of a big family all sitting round the table together. Me. Drifter, lone wolf.

I look around for Walshy, who darted off as soon as we arrived. He walks in behind the counter, and I twist around to see him.

'Are you working tonight?'

He nods, eyes guilty. 'It's super busy. That okay?'

I shrug. 'S'fine. Long as I don't have to.'

I finish my drink and slip outside. The moon is a huge bright-new pearl in the darkening sky. I rest back against the brick wall, the day's heat easing into my back.

I look for the little window of Lorrelai's old room. *I am Lorrelai's daughter.*

I turn and touch the edge of the Bougainvillea flowers that grow along the old limestone wall at the back of the Lion Inn, obscuring it from the road. The flowers' pink tissue paper petals hide the holes and discolouration and offer a banquet to insects. I love them. I love it all. This is my home.

Then I think of poor Shelley. Her broken heart. She was always there for me when I needed her. I know it wasn't me that broke her heart, but guilt still wells in me. I duck back inside and wave to get Walshy's attention.

'I'm going home soon. Do you think I should check on Shelley?'

He shakes his head. 'Seriously; her mother will take care of her.' He pulls a face. 'Still treats her like a little girl.'

Someone indicates they want to be served, and Walshy nods. 'Get someone to drop you, okay?'

'Yeah. Hey, I might make her a bouquet of flowers.' The thought buoys me instantly.

Walshy pulls me close, kisses my head. There's a drop of sweat running down the side of his face again. He swipes his hand across his top lip.

He's looking away now, keen to work. 'She prefers toys. Stuffed animals and dolls you can't play with. She has a collection of those spooky hard-faced ones in the second bedroom. Night, Jane.' He winks.

'Night, Walshy.'

Chapter 53

Freda drops me home, and we both walk up to the back door. We have new rules now. The porch light is left on and we always lock up before we leave. I use my new key to open the security screen.

'Okay, love, I'm off.' Freda pats my back. 'Close up tight, remember. Walshy might be late.'

The feeling starts as soon as I lock the door. Discomfort. A shift in the air. I look around, but nothing has changed.

Someone broke in here.

It's a horrible feeling. That a stranger was in here. With that in mind, I go into the lounge and grab the new candlestick. *Professor Plum in the Library with the Candlestick.* Clue, the board game. We played it at school.

An owl hoots. I jump and my skin prickles.

A cat fight sounds somewhere close and loud. I look around, shaking out my shoulders, trying not to send myself mad. It'll be two hours until Walshy gets home, three at the most.

I should have stayed at the inn, I think, but my head is heavy, and it wants a pillow.

I go into objective mode, trying to leave emotion out of it. Perry is a creep, but I can't imagine him breaking into our house or trying to grab me. I can imagine him sneaking knickers off people's clotheslines like a stupid fuckwit, but none of the other stuff. I'm sure there are things about him I don't know, weird secret fantasies that probably get him all sweaty and hard. I'm not that naïve. But violent rape? Nope. He's strange, desperate even, but not nasty.

262

But if it's not him, there's someone else out there. Someone who transforms briefly into an evil rapist, then blends back in like Jekyll and Hyde. Or someone willing to travel to commit his crimes. Why here? Why does he go to the effort of buying, then probably concealing dolls, so he can leave a trail? To make it clear that it's the same attacker. What is he trying to say?

I close my eyes, visualising the big doll in the backseat of the silver car. So far, nothing has come from that information. Was it really the same doll which was left at a crime scene a few hours later?

I wander over to the couch and open the top of my backpack, meaning to read the articles about Lorrelai again. The list Detective Wheeler gave me, catches my attention—the names of the people at the 1998 school social dance. I sigh and make myself read through them again and my heart starts pounding. My throat suddenly dry, I get up and cross the room to the phone.

I was outside looking in. He had been too, leaning on a car in the carpark. Maybe he never went inside or didn't even make the guest list. His name is not there. But he *was* there.

Shelley's dolls. The big doll in the car, surrounded by costumes. Shelley's secrets. Oh God! It makes sense.

The paper shakes in my hand. I can hardly dial, my hands shaking with the shot of icy cold adrenaline, my mind jolting with the information. Apart, they're all just little pieces. Together, a complete picture.

I hear the *clunk* of footsteps and freeze still as a mouse hoping it is invisible. Something clamps over my mouth, a stinking cloth.

Too late to scream, I struggle, but he's behind me tightening his arms. His body grips me like a vice. He's solid, unbudging, as I kick my legs back one at a time and feel in my pocket for the candlestick.

My arms pinned to my side, I'm helpless against the fumes. Dizziness comes, and then fog. I can't believe I never thought of him. He'd always turn up, then disappear. Turn up. Disappear. Obvious but unseen.

I go still. No fight left.

He pulls me backwards, his strong arm looped around my waist. I try to move—nothing. My body's no longer mine. My muscles ignore my brain. Ahead of me, on the floor, my legs are out straight, my heels sliding along. One of my shoes comes off, stands up on the heel for a split-second and then falls to the side. Everything becomes hazy. He says nothing, and I can't see him. But I don't need to. I know who he is.

As blackness seeps into my head, his name and face swim across my mind.

Ralph Higgins.

* * *

Car engine. Fumes. He's got me in the fucking trunk of a car! Bastard!

The face that never quite fit, the name missing from the list, the well-travelled dancer who bought an expensive doll for his underage girlfriend.

Ralph Higgins.

I feel sick, travel sick, fume sick, and sick from whatever was on that rag. *Chloroform?* The ancient cricket-bat-to-the-head anaesthetic. My head is thick, and my face is sore not only from my crash but also from having my face gripped. The brake light makes a small red room of the boot. I look around, feel along every edge, find nothing.

I roll to the side and vomit in the furthest corner of the car boot.

Rolling away from the vomit, I take an inventory of myself. My hands are free. So are my feet. He didn't even bother to tie me up. I feel around, the rush of the road and the noise of the engine blotting out all other sound.

I'm unsure how long I was unconscious. Maybe I can pretend I still am when the boot opens.

Something bites into my hip. I tap down my side and remember the candlestick. It gives me a focus, a small lift. Just what I need; something that is mine. I must have slipped it into my pocket when I made the phone call. I pull it out, grasping it with both hands. A weapon.

It's heavy, with ridges up the stem and a wider base. *I can whack him when he opens the trunk. If he opens the trunk.*

I shuffle towards the taillight and poke the edges with the candlestick. I grip with both hands and slam at the centre. A little crack. I try to peer through it, but I can't. I pause.

What'll happen if I get the taillight out? The car will stop, and I'll be silenced again. Maybe forever.

I lie back and try to think. The car doesn't slow, so it's clear there are no streets or give way signs or lights. We're on the open road, out of town. But maybe we'll go through a town.

Which direction? Think, think. Roads go forever out here.

I lie on my side, my knees bent, trying to imagine a map. Roads span out from York in all directions. The worst possibility is straight east. He could drive me to the desert, drop me down a mineshaft. Bodies have been sunk down shafts before. Bikers after a hit. An abducted child. Someone who fell.

No one will know where I am. What will he do to me? What he did to Lisa? Or worse? What's worse? Enduring a vicious rape and surviving.

Fear sets me like ice. With my mind frozen, my body takes over. I roll my head back and forth, moaning and crying. I can't stop. It just keeps going—fear—terrible, terrified waves of it.

Finally, I stop. I can't feel anything except how numb my mouth is, how parched my throat. Slowly, feeling returns. I'm thirsty and sore in all the places I hurt when I fell a few days ago. I lie on my back and just breathe.

I need a plan. If I'm going to survive, I need to get ready to save myself.

The hum of the road doesn't change. I move away from the red light because the car fumes are stronger there. I turn myself around. The other corner is marginally better and further from the vomit. *Should I bang the boot lid? No, there's only him to hear me.* Still, if I leave it too long, I may be too far away from people. At his mercy. Alone.

What does he want with me? Why did he stand in wait at my house? How could he know I worked out it was him?

I should pound on that boot lid, I think. *The longer I wait, the more deserted it will be.* But I can't do it. I don't want to see his face.

Maybe we're headed somewhere: a house or somewhere he can lock me up. Maybe he knows where Perry is. Maybe I was wrong about Perry. Oh God, oh God, oh God.

If he takes me to a house, I'll escape. He has no fucking idea the places I've climbed out of, the window and door locks I can open. *Yes, lock me in a house, Ralph, that would be perfect.*

But he might just kill me as soon as he's far enough from York to find a good ditch.

Was it him who stole the sketchbook? What would he want with an old murder case? How would he know about it?

I try to see a connection. Again, I come up blank. Perhaps it is nothing to do with that.

When I fell and remembered a doll, and the police started buzzing around me. Maybe Ralph got nervous, realised I might work it out?

* * *

The car hits a pothole, and I bounce and hit my knee. I rub it, breathing through the pain. He doesn't care about me back here. He could leave the car and let me rot in the desert.

Murders flood my brain. A body found covered by a branch, thrown in the trees. Naked. Limbs askew. Eaten by wild animals.

I must stop my mind going there. I can't lose control. I must stay switched on. I must be ready.

The engine drones on. I think of Walshy, which makes me cry. I have waited so long to be with him. I imagine his green eyes, his smile, the gap between his teeth.

I think of the Flower House, and all I want is to be inside it, safe. But Ralph was inside the house. How? It was locked.

Then I think of all the holes, all the windows without screens, how those cats sounded so loud. A window jimmied open?

Shit. It would have been easy. Think, think. Stay calm. Breathe. God that vomit stinks.

At foster homes or after returning to care, I used to have a routine. Orientate. Find friends. Check out the pecking order. Learn the rules. Never let down your guard. Work out escape routes. Be ready. Know where the food is. Keep your stuff safe.

It's not going to work here. There are no rules, no friends.

When Walshy was teaching me how to survive, it was all about how to move soundlessly through the dark and seek out the free stuff. How to scale trees and fences and drop into people's yards like a cat. I was a natural. I thought I could survive anywhere.

Did Ralph climb Lisa's fence and drop in silently, like he waited in my house? *What is he capable of?*

He raped a twelve-year-old girl. He dropped the doll, left it there. He is vicious. Muscular. I've seen his body—a dancer's body, but a strong one. A cruel, violent one.

I cross my arms over my chest and hold myself. My right kneecap throbs. I won't be able to run fast if I manage to escape.

I think of the funeral. *Was that today? Will anyone know I'm missing, or just Walshy when he gets in late?*

No one's ever noticed when I wasn't there. I was always an outsider. Never did belong. I came and went like tides on the shore, a bud opening and closing, petals drifting down and blowing away.

I feel around the boot. It's a new-smelling car. All the fixtures are tight. Then I hear something. I go still. Voices. Not radio voices, but two people talking, agitated. A woman. Marilyn?

I roll closer to the interior of the car and put my ear against the felt back of the boot. Everything's muffled, but there are definitely two voices—a man and a woman. My bare foot touches something slimy, and I choke down a gag. It's my vomit. I only have one shoe. *Shit, how am I going to run barefoot?*

If they're both in the car, maybe I can reason with one of them. Marilyn being there gives me a boost. A female, a softer touch, a balance, a neutraliser. Maybe. But she doesn't like me. She hasn't even tried to hide it.

Does she know about Ralph? If she knew about the doll, she'd have suspected him in Lisa's attack. But maybe she never knew about the doll. Maybe she didn't suspect him at all.

I run through it in my head. *Ralph drops in to the social to see the students dance, like he taught them to. But he's distracted. He's there long enough to get glitter on his hands, but he doesn't stay. He wants to see his beautiful girlfriend. He has a gift for her. He's tied a big pink ribbon around it. But he can't find her. Then he finds out she's getting an abortion! He's incensed. He sees a girl in a backyard—Lisa Lee. She has long blonde hair in a ponytail, like Shelley. All his anger boils to the surface.*

I refocus. The road is completely straight. We're likely heading for the desert. They must have a plan or maybe they're arguing and unsure what to do with me now that they have me in the boot.

Did I get in the way? Find out too much? Maybe Marilyn realised I was going to work it out. Maybe it's her I should fear. Two against one. Fuck.

My stomach roils with dread. How can I fight off two adults, with a bad knee while I'm lying in a trunk? I could squeeze myself right up the back to make it harder for them. Kick out, try to scramble past them. I can deal with the pain. Injuries heal. Then I'd run.

Run where?

* * *

When I was a little girl, I went to a foster home in Kalamunda. The school was like kindergarten for early entry to prison. I would run from the bus stop to the relative safety of the school gates in the morning and survive the day. But in the afternoon, I had to run from the gates back to the bus. Those were the few minutes I feared the most. Groups and gangs lay in wait for smaller, weaker, lone kids. Kids got beat up for money or just for notoriety. One girl had her earrings ripped out and her face punched by three bigger girls—a rite of passage.

I learned to run fast, much faster than everyone else, my backpack bouncing against my spine, sweat streaming down it as I bolted beneath the slender lemon gums to the bus stop. I'd listen for footsteps in case I had to veer off or detour down the culvert to the dirty river, which I was willing to run through. I was always primed for escape. I got taunted sometimes, but I never got caught.

Not ever.

Chapter 54

They have to stop eventually. A tank of fuel only lasts three to four hours, depending on the car. And it is a sedan, not a four-wheel drive.

If it veers off-road, it could get a flat tyre or get bogged.

They've stopped talking now. The constant hum of the road and the warmth of the boot mean I'm fighting drowsiness.

Maybe we'll have to refuel. At a fuel stop, I could get attention. I try to calculate where we could be. It gives my brain a focus.

If I'd been unconscious as we passed through Northam, we would still have had to slow down a few times heading north to Toodyay or Goomalling. If we'd gone south, we'd have slowed for Brookton, Pingelly, and turned right for Corrigin. But we hadn't turned or slowed. I scan my internal map for answers.

In my first year of high school, we had an excursion to Bruce Rock. It has a monolith called Kokerbin Rock, Australia's third-largest. No one has ever heard of it because it's just a smooth, sloping granite rock grown over with moss. The guide talked about the flora and fauna, but everyone just wanted to run around and climb rocks. I remembered the views to fenced paddocks and the caves. I hope we're going there, not to Merredin. Lots of kilometres of nothing out towards Merredin.

I think of Merredin. Of the good times, but also of that dark day when Coral didn't saunter through the house with her usual sigh and *clunk* of handbag on the kitchen table. The way the sun moved from one side of the house to the other, and still no one came, and I waited, knowing in my belly she wouldn't come, even if I pretended. No one knew where I was.

I went to bed that night with a rumbling belly and a pocketful of fake pearls. I woke, still dirty from playing with the ants and made myself breakfast, stopping at the tiny sounds I made, sure someone else had made them. I didn't leave the house. The locked door of the lounge both magnetised and resisted me. The phone rang six times. I counted each one.

Coral had insisted I never answer the phone when she left me home alone. But I felt like she'd left me. I knew in my heart I was alone. She wasn't going to breeze through that door—the locked door. I knew because it *had* been open when I came in. I *did* see her body, turning slowly at the end of the rope, and I had pushed the door lock in and pulled the door shut, hoping that when it was opened, Coral would be back to normal. But, of course, that didn't happen. Fantasies are just fantasies. People go and they never come back.

The car begins to slow. I listen for a change of surface beneath the tyres. I listen for voices. I stare at the edge of the boot lid for lights. Nothing.

Then we slow suddenly, and I roll bodily to the right and hit my head on the wheel cover as the car turns left. Not good. We're not in a town, and we've just turned off the main road.

I feel for my candlestick and shuffle back into the deepest cavity of the boot. There's a metre between me and the outer edge, where the boot will open.

I won't think about it opening. I won't think. I'll lie in wait. I'll do what it takes to stay alive, like a trapped animal.

The car accelerates gently. The road whispers and then comes the sudden bump and crunch of rubber over gravel. I can't let them get the upper hand. Will there be time to talk or just to fight? No one throws a threat into a car boot to go bush in the middle of the night for a nice chat. And I'm a threat because I know what he did. I'll have to attack early if I'm to have any chance.

To calm me and give me strength, I think of people I know. My people. The people who made me who I am, who loved and protected me: Walshy, Blossom, even Lorrelai. I think about all the kids who laughed at me, excluded me, chased me, who forced me to be resilient and strong. Then there's Shelley, Mary and Con, Freda, who all took me under their wing. I owe it to them to get out of this.

Candlestick in one hand, feet braced against the boot interior, my head is clear.

Chapter 55

The car stops. I can taste gravel dust. The car doors swing open, and I hear the crunch of shoes near my head. I barely breathe, my eyes scanning left and right. Trying to decide what I might see first. The boot clicks, the lid draws upwards, an endless night sky fills the space.

Every muscle taut, I stop breathing. Moonglow makes things visible —thick tree trunks reaching far up into the sky. The scent of eucalypts, the nocturnal sounds of insects.

Footsteps. I listen with every cell. They're moving backwards, away from the car, closer to the bush. My muscle fibres contract, my heart pounds like a steam train at full speed. Adrenaline screams through my veins and muscles.

'Get out, Lola.' It's Marilyn, a short distance away. Her voice is odd, out here in the trees. She sounds tiny. I wonder if she's wearing high heels. With the handicap of heels, I could outrun her. But it's not her I'm worried about; it's him. Ralph Higgins.

I wait, sucking down oxygen, preparing for a burst of energy.

'I'm not going to pull you out. Just climb out, for God's sake.' She sounds annoyed.

I want to see more, but that would mean sticking my head up, and I don't know how close Ralph is. The ground crunches like someone is walking around. I brace.

'No!' Marilyn again. The footsteps pause. 'Let her get out. Don't touch her.' She's bossing him around. I feel the focus shift from me to their private antagonism.

He clears his throat. He's a short distance away too. They're standing back, waiting. Could they mean it? They want me to get out by myself.

I strain my neck and chin upwards to peer over the edge of the boot. They stand side by side about fifteen metres away. Ralph's hair is short, dishevelled. He wears tight black jeans and chunky boots, like a manual worker. His chest is bare, a softness around the thumbprint of his navel, a wobble of fat around the waist. But above it, his muscled torso gleams like a threat in the moonlight. In one hand, he winds a coil of white rope. I check the other hand for weapons. It's empty, bunched, tense.

My throat seizes. I swallow a couple of times. 'Are you going to rape me?' I demand to know. 'Like you did Lisa?'

Ralph's eyes shift. The corners of his mouth pull down, like it disgusts him.

Really? Could I have been wrong?

'Don't speak!' Marilyn commands Ralph. She turns back to me. 'We don't want to hurt you. We don't. We need to come to an understanding. Get out, Lola. I'm losing patience.' She crosses her arms and stares around like she doesn't trust the bush—like it's scarier than them.

Good. To me, the bush is safety. I'd rather battle a tiger snake or a scorpion than Ralph Higgins.

I keep my eyes on Ralph, on the rope in his hand. So, it's going to be hand-to-hand combat. Marilyn is dressed for dinner, but Ralph looks ready for a cage fight. He's my biggest threat. Strong, fit, agile. An athlete. If he gets hold of me, I'm done. He could crush me in his arms. But I'm small and quick, and evasion is my best chance.

I remember my legs dragging along as he pulled me out of the Flower House. He wouldn't have broken a sweat. I watch his every muscle, his every eye movement, the tension in his body.

'Where's your shirt?' Kneeling on my good knee, I tense, ready to jump quickly. It will have to be tight, no warning for Ralph. The ground is slippery gravel. I'll have to land well, legs wide and bent, minimal scrambling, or he'll pounce like a pigdog on a rabbit. Then I'll have to dart to the right, get inside that thicket. Find cover down low in the underbrush where I can hide.

If I jump, I'll have a few seconds. His reflexes against mine. Even injured, I'll have to be the fastest I've ever been.

Ralph's shoulder twitches, and he looks up through dark, hooded eyes but says nothing.

There's still time to get a reaction, to work out the plan. 'Why did you leave the doll at Lisa's? Was it an accident? Was it meant for Shelley?'

At the mention of her name, the two share a glance.

'Shelley.' I grasp onto it. 'Still love her, Ralph? I saw you kissing after the—'

'Shut up!' Marilyn interrupts. 'Get out for fuck's sake, girl, if you know what's good for you.' She casts me a threatening look, her nostrils flaring. I hold up one hand, the other gripping the candlestick against my leg.

Appeal. Be innocent. Make them doubt.

'Why am I here, Marilyn?' I say as calmly as I can. 'I've never done anything to you.'

Ralph grunts. His eyes narrow. 'Or you, Mister Higgins, have I?'

He stares at me, a chilling, black stare. 'Not yet.'

'Shut up!' Marilyn slaps his arm and then shakes him. 'You're going to have to tie her up or drag her out. Hurry up!'

Shit! Too much. They're angrier. 'You don't want to hurt me? Then tell me what you want.'

Ralph's jaw juts as he glances at Marilyn. He starts towards me and my heart clogs my throat.

Shit! Talk! Talk! 'I'm a threat? I remembered the doll in the car. Your car?'

Ralph's face eases slightly and he stops walking. I feel like I'm off track.

'Or was it about Shelley? She told me what happened.'

His eyes widen.

Good.

I am tensed, ready, but suddenly, I can't jump. One of my legs has seized. I grip the candlestick hard and try to think of more words to stop him coming.

Marilyn snorts. 'None of that is provable, Lola. Didn't that boy next door do something bad? They'll probably blame him. Ralph had a little affair with that dancer girl, but he's a good person.' She sniffs.

Ralph's jaw moves and he starts walking towards me again.

I get the odd feeling there's something bigger behind this. If they genuinely don't think Ralph is close to being discovered as the rapist, why are we here?

He broke into my house—maybe not for the first time. Maybe he took the sketchbook. But why would he care about a bunch of sketches? He probably didn't even know who they were of—unless I was wrong about Ned, and he sent Ralph. My eyes drop to Ralph's boots, workman's boots where there was once dance shoes.

Situations change. People get new jobs, move house.

I grapple for names, and one pops into my mind like a lightbulb. 'How about Ned?'

Ralph is about five metres away. He stops dead. His wide eyes fixed on mine. I feel like a fox in a headlight.

Marilyn makes a low, frustrated sound. 'Don't,' she warns through her teeth.

'Ned.' I say again. They stiffen. Ralph wants to tell me something: I can feel it. 'How do you know him?'

'Shut up!' shrieks Marilyn. 'Get her!'

Ralph surges forwards and then lunges towards the boot. His head is suddenly level with mine, I swing the candlestick, hitting him in the temple. He crumples like an empty costume. Wriggles and flaps, like a blow-up man.

I grab the edge of the car boot, and my body starts working. Ralph humps the ground and drunkenly wobbles to one knee, but his body reels sidewards as if paralysed down the right. Kneeling hand to face, he jerks around, one arm out like a blind person. Blood gushes down one side of his face.

I jump out, bearing my weight on my good leg before stabilising and heading right, towards the bush. Stones bruise my bare foot. I look over my shoulder. Ralph is on his hands and knees, starting to crawl after me. It's the chance I need. I lean forward and run, my bare foot gripping better than the shoe.

Chapter 56

'What did you do to him?' screams Marilyn. A few strides short of the thicket, my injured knee is punched with hot stabs of pain. I hear Ralph's angry grunt, a scramble, a crunch of gravel. Between the jarrah and marri trees, fronds of zamia palm, egg-and-bacon plant, wisteria and parrot bush whip, scratch, and prickle as I force my way into a wall of gnarly Australian scrub. Suddenly, the vines trap my movement, stringing across my waist like rope. I can climb, but the nearest tree is several metres of thick vines away. Then I remember Ralph's arms. He could swing up a tree like a monkey.

I yank a handful of taut vines up and duck into the darkness, on my knees, crawling. But my face is unprotected and sticks tear at my forehead and neck. Sacrificing one arm, I shield my face to avoid a stick in the eye. But coupled with one bad knee, I'm slow and unbalanced, and I lose forward thrust. I have to use my arm, so I close my eyes and drop my head, letting my shaggy scalp take the brunt.

I've made a mistake. I've underestimated the thickness of the scrub. Behind me, I hear the crunch of dead undergrowth, the swish of a branch, the slap of a hand against tree trunk, and a whisper of fern. Then silence.

Neither of us moves.

Predator and prey. One waiting for the other to breathe too loud. It's pitch black in here. I'm blind. But so is he.

Nothing moves under my hands. Nothing wriggles or crawls along my skin. The bush and its critters have paused.

'Should I get the gun?' calls Marilyn.

My spine shrinks, and my guts unspool like I'm going to shit myself. Nothing moves. I have my mouth wide open, measuring each breath in, out. My lungs scream for more oxygen, and lights dance before my eyes. *Answer! How close are you, you bastard?*

Is she bluffing? Do they really have a gun? Farmers use them to shoot rabbits and foxes out here, but guns still aren't easy to come by, unless you trade with biker gangs.

Who knows what sort of people Ralph spends time with? He rapes girls and leaves a doll, like he's mocking them. Has affairs with students. He breaks into houses and abducts people. Yep. He'll have a gun.

I hear an angry exhalation and a movement directly behind me. If Ralph could see, he might be close enough to grab my foot. For now, I'm black as night in funeral clothes.

'Turn the car around, so the lights go this way!' He's not giving up. He's not moving which keeps us both fixed here. Once he can see, he'll drag me out.

'Maybe we should wait till she comes out.'

'This is more fun.'

He's so close. I wonder whether he knows where I am. He just needs light to make it easier. After a moment, the car door clicks, and the engine rumbles. Gravel crunches as Marilyn turns the car to point the headlights our way.

Under the cover of the car's background noise and before my thicket lights up, I sweep my arm either side of me to find an opening. There's one to my right big enough to squeeze into. Silently, I curl back a small way, and then I push into the gap, patting ahead with one hand as I commando shuffle on forearms and knees, crawling into a space cocooned by undergrowth, like a human witchetty grub.

The thicket is strobed by headlights, light finding its way through cracks. A sudden explosion of movement in front of me causes an involuntary scream. A warm mass jumps around, shaking the thicket around me. An animal, a terrified animal that's stayed immobile until I invaded its sleep shelter.

Crack! A different explosion, clean and direct. I hunker closer to the ground. Ahead just a few metres, crunching, twisting, something struggles in the undergrowth.

'It's a fucking kangaroo, woman!'

The space ahead, now wide and empty, gives me a place to wriggle into and an exit into the thick of the forest. Away from the headlights. And that gun. I can hardly believe what just happened. Marilyn fired a damn gun. I'm being hunted by an armed woman.

The tangle of scrub ends suddenly. I uncurl in the strange silence, stay low. The car's headlights are off to one side, and I can't see Ralph behind me in the thicket I just exited.

I keep staring into the darkness, waiting for my night vision to sharpen, so I can choose a path with sparser brush and move fast and deep into the forest.

'Give it here!' Ralph barks. I hear Marilyn slipping and staggering and grunting, making little gasps of effort.

'Where are the bullets?'

'Pocket,' says Ralph.

He was ready. Rope. Gun. Bullets. He was prepared for this. They're not here to talk. They're here to silence me. Out in the bush, dig a hole, bury my troublesome body, go back and play innocent. Like they've been doing it their whole lives.

'Lola!' Marilyn shouts.

I flinch. Then I keep inching forward in a crouching walk off to the left, away from the headlights. I move carefully, heel to toe like a barn dance to avoid crunching. Crashing and swearing back in the thicket tells me exactly where Ralph is. I have about ten metres head start.

He has a gun. I have the dark.

I once heard that when an abductor gets you into his car, your chances of survival drop dramatically. Even with a gun pointed your way, you have a better chance of surviving by running away.

'Lola don't make us do this. We just need you to buzz off again. Stop pointing the finger. We'll pay for your airfare. No hard feelings. Just come out here'.

I hear the bullshit in her voice. She just wants a clear shot. She almost got me already.

I keep my eyes on the canopy, keep my hands out, the secondary light from the car helping me move forwards without tripping or crashing into something.

'You just need to go away again. Save Walshy. Save yourself.' Marilyn pauses. 'If we have to leave you here, we'll go straight back up and get Walshy. We'll make him pay because you won't be reasonable.'

I feel like they've kicked me in the stomach.

Could Walshy save himself, or would they reel him in by telling him they had me?

Walshy has dodged a violent man since he was a boy. But he won't be on his guard. The thought of Walshy walking into the Flower House to be met with a gun, renders me immobile.

After a moment, I move again, slowly. The candlestick bumps against my leg as I stumble. If only I'd hit Ralph harder, put him out cold. I pause behind a jarrah tree, leaning back against it. I am surrounded by trees I could put between myself and a bullet.

I hear them go still and whisper to each other, trying to work out where I am.

They would do it; go and ambush Walshy.

'Sure,' I call out. 'I'll go away. But we gotta talk. And I'm not doing anything until you put that gun down.'

A crackle of twigs alerts me that Ralph is still hunting. I get down low and wait.

A scrabble comes from the right where the animal was. Again, the gun cracks. I drop to a crouch, as if my knees have given way. The shot sends strange reverberations through the bush. Thrashing comes from undergrowth. Ralph pounds away from me, towards the noise.

'Fuck! A stupid roo!' Another shot sounds, and the thrashing ends. 'Fuck!'

A dull, wet thud makes my stomach clench like a fist. He's hit it with the rifle or kicked it. Thank God it was dead. A surge of hatred moves through me. Trembling that starts in my arms travels around my body, until I'm shaking like a nudist in the snow.

That could have been me.

* * *

The poor animal has given me a window. I crane my neck around the tree and see Marilyn in the headlights, halfway between me and the car. She's staring away to the right, where the noise came from, hands by her sides.

I've seen what I needed to see. If I can quietly get to the edge of the clearing, downhill of them, I can make a dash for the car. It is one of those flash modern cars that turns off the headlights or sounds an alarm when the keys are removed. The headlights are on. Bugs dance in the beams.

Next second, the situation flips. Ralph runs, high-kneed to where he thinks I am, which is just metres to my right. I hold my breath, treading carefully around the tree, my arms hugging the trunk. As he walks past, I keep turning, putting the jarrah between us. But if I go any further, I'll be in Marilyn's line of sight. I cling to the trunk between the two of them as Ralph creeps past and stops. Past the stringy bark of the tree, I can see the muscles moving in his back.

He spins suddenly. And I'm staring down a thin metal tube. One thick finger is on the trigger, the gun butted up in the crease of his armpit.

Air hisses from my chest. I can't move.

'Gotcha.' His mouth is twisted into a delighted sneer.

I drop down, scramble around the tree like a child. But he's there. A black boot lifts and stomps down with a *crunch* on my hand. I scream.

Holding the gun by the barrel, Ralph swings the butt at the side of my head. I shift and … *Whack!* A crash of red-black pain smacks the back of my skull. Agony scrapes through my head like a clawed beast.

I sink to the ground—flat, legs out, one arm bent awkwardly beneath my stomach. I want to straighten it, but I can't. I try to move my leg. Nothing. My heart pounds against the earth, a heavy *thud-thud* that echoes in my skull. My face is turned to the side, my mouth open towards dead leaves. Warm, thick drips slither through my hair, trickle down my face. The space behind my eyes is thick, achy, weary.

I've heard adrenaline stops you feeling pain. I wonder when the pain will stop. When I'll be heavy as a carcass melting into the ground. My eyelids flutter closed.

Their voices come through a long tunnel, like the cardboard toilet rolls we sticky-taped together to form long, tubular telephones as kids.

'Did you get her?'

'Course. She's out cold. Get the rope.' An echo follows every word they speak.

I hear Walshy's whisper in my ear. *Hey, Jane.*

I smile, my lips twitching at a leaf in my mouth's corner. *Walshy, I love you.*

Shh. I know. Don't waste your breath. Fill your lungs up. We gotta keep going.

I'm dizzy.

Don't be a sook. We need to get home. Careful. Don't break the eggs.

I can feel the stolen eggs in my shirt, where I've looped up the hem to form a bag. Except they're not eggs; it's my arm.

Chapter 57

I lift my lower back to free my arm.

'Hurry up, woman! She's coming around!'

Twigs snap, leaves crackle. 'I can't come in *there*.'

'Fuck's sake! Here. Throw it in!'

My heart beats harder, louder, faster. I open my eyes. *Legs. Black jeans.* Ralph turns and stomps out of sight, stopping a short distance away.

When fight or flight kicks in, you can still run and then drop dead suddenly. What's there to lose?

I scramble to get my knees beneath me. One foot — *Steady!* — second foot. I'm wobbling, but I'm up.

Ugly, dizzy, messy as a drunk gorilla, I'm running, careening this way and that. I fall on my bad knee, cry out as my kneecap crunches, and roll behind a tree. There, on my knees, I vomit hard, emptying my stomach.

'Stop!' The gun fires, sharp and clean. A slow cracking is followed by a grind, a thud and then an *oof* of effort, like a man's been booted in the stomach.

A few breaths and I'll run. I must get to the car before Marilyn realises what I'm doing. Clinging to the tree, cheek to trunk, I focus on sucking in air, not ants and bark. *Listen. What is that?*

The noises don't match. It sounds like human pain but I'm not making a sound. There's no sound of Ralph stomping around, no crunching of the underbrush, just the echo of a rifle shot reverberating farther and farther away, bouncing between trees.

Someone is screaming, and there's a low keening ... an animal moan.

Concentrate.

I shakily kneel, resting heavily against the tree. When I dry retch again, it feels like my stomach is turning inside out.

Listening, I work out it's Marilyn screaming. The moaning is close. I crane my neck around the tree.

Blood fills one of my eyes, and the vision in the other leaps around like my pupil is a flea, but I see something and begin to make sense of it.

From where I've just come, a dead branch full of ants and dry rot has crashed down. The ugly tear at the top is still attached, while the fork has driven itself to the ground and pinned Ralph Higgins beneath it. I can see his black-clad legs, his bare lower back.

I stand clumsily, still bracing against my tree and look upwards. Then I see a straight slice near the tear in the branch that fell. A bullet's path through wood? *The stupid dickhead brought down a branch!* A bullet fired into the sky to flush me out. But it wasn't just sky. I had trees.

Two against one, and a tree. I look up at the tree in shock and gratitude. 'You little beauty!' I spit some grit out of my mouth.

They've forgotten about me. I give myself a moment to stabilise. I should get away now, but I can't stop myself. I limp towards Ralph and the fallen branch, leaning on every tree I pass, grounding myself. Ralph is pinned like a grasshopper on a display board.

Before me, the scene moves pendulously back and forth, like I'm on a swing—near, far, near, far. Ralph lying face down, the V of the dead branch, chips of wood lying scattered around like kindling.

Next to Ralph, a zamia palm is draped in a dozen necklaces of purple wisteria, like its dressed for an occasion. Ralph emits a low, repetitive moan.

'Ralphy! Ralphy!' In the clearing, Marilyn scrambles forwards and goes down on one knee, bawling.

She was right: the bush is dangerous, especially if you're stupid enough to shoot a brittle branch above your own head.

A wallaby darts off from the edge of the scrub, flash of white along its cheek, and Marilyn screams. I don't know why.

I now know that we have gone south. The western brush wallabies are south, just a pocket of them around Dwellingup and Pinjarra. I look around. An owl hoots. Somewhere, a long way off, a dog barks.

Civilisation.

I breathe in the fresh air and hear leaves rustling in a breeze far above our heads.

Has anyone heard the rifle shots? Will someone come to investigate?

No time to waste.

Chapter 58

I wipe the blood out of my eye and search the ground beside Ralph. I lift my knees high over a low, spiky zamia palm to grab the barrel of the gun with my good hand and hoist it against my hip.

Ralph shivers like he's cold or is about to have a fit. Is that what someone looks like when they die? Did the roo give one last shiver before its heart stopped, prompting Ralph to hit it again?

'Don't hurt him!' cries Marilyn, paused at the edge of the clearing. 'Is he alright? Is he under that tree that fell?'

'Stay there!' I shout back. I bend down to get a better look at where the tree has squashed Ralph. My head swoons. A spike on the end of the branch has penetrated the left side of Ralph's back, splitting him between the ribs. It's an inch thick, like a tent peg, but it's hard to tell how long. He's still making noise, but it's more of a wet, crackling sigh as he breathes out.

Now I just need to get Marilyn under control. 'He's injured! Stay there!'

I head for her, eye to eye. She takes a step backwards. Those fantastic high heels buckle, and she slides backwards, her neck bouncing sickeningly as her bum drops to the ground.

I'm relieved I didn't need to point the gun. Those things can go off suddenly. I throw the gun sideways. It drops, butt-first, into a thicket and vanishes.

I jump on Marilyn, straddling her waist, my knee and good hand high on her chest. Her fingernails bite into the back of my hand.

We roll around. I go down on my side, gravel in my ear, dirt clinging to the wet stickiness on my cheek. She's stronger than I expected. I clamp my legs harder, brace and ride her as she bucks. When she stops suddenly, I push up until she's underneath me. She wriggles weakly, sniffles, coughs against the dirt. I loosen my hand. To my right, a white snake catches my eye—the rope.

Marilyn is flat, and I feel the fight go out of her. Her torso vibrates with sobs. I jerk one of her arms back, pin it with my knee and then get the other arm; they are like two fat dead weights, like lamb roasts.

She's covered in apricot-coloured dust. My eyes are gritty with it. As I secure her wrists, my head pounds, which makes me tie her hands tighter than necessary. Loop over, down, and back, the scouting way, but one-handed. Walshy would be proud of me.

I get up and check that Ralph hasn't moved, risking getting close. He looks like he's asleep, his mouth open, lips loose, spittle bubbling as he sucks air in and out.

'I can't hear anything!' Marilyn yells. 'You killed him,' she sobs into the dirt. 'Ralphy? Ralphy, my love? Oh God, oh God. What am I going to do?'

'Nothing. You're going to stay there, kissing gravel, you fucking cow!' Out comes the adrenaline-fuelled poetry. I feel a hundred times stronger. Feel like I could jump a tree … or lift one … a branch at least. Maybe to release a nasty fuckwit who will need hospital if he's ever going to face court. But not yet.

'You have some explaining to do, Marilyn.'

She whimpers. 'I don't care. Let me die! Ralphy, Ralphy.'

I'd roll my eyes if I wasn't already struggling to see. I cradle my aching hand gently in my good one.

'He's alive, but he needs to go to hospital. Stick through the lung.'

Her head lifts up. Her face is an abomination of makeup, snot and dirt. Mascara has drawn a warpaint of thick charcoal down her cheeks, like a mud-smeared doll.

'He's alive?'

'Only if we get him to hospital.'

Life returns, and she performs a caterpillar motion with her knees and gets to kneeling, wincing and sniffing hard, her kneecaps on the gravel. 'Hurry! Help him.'

'Sure.' I lean against a tree where I can see them both. My hand throbs. 'Start talking.'

She blinks, her watery eyes wide. Then her mouth clamps shut, and she swallows.

I hold up the candlestick. 'Ralph put that poor roo out of its misery. Should I do the same to him? He's badly injured. Wouldn't take much.'

'No! No, don't hurt him! I'll tell you! I'll tell you!'

'HURRY!' I sound angry. I'm proud of myself.

Ralph groans, and Marilyn's eyes track there and then back to me. 'Start with Ned.'

Marilyn clears her throat. 'Ned is Ralph's … father.'

'Ralph's *what*? Don't fucking bullshit me, Marilyn!'

'He is. He *is*! I promise!' Her face changes, the light dying in her eyes. 'Well, his … stepfather, I guess,' she stammers. 'He's also … Ned's also *yours*.'

The oxygen goes out of my fire.

Chapter 59

My arms start shaking.

'Lorrelai was with Ned after she left prison?' I can bloody see it. A visit after she gets out. One kiss, another. Ned—the old man who lied to keep himself out of jail—my father?

'Yes.'

Acid burns my throat. I imagine them: the big, bearded guy from the picture, the beautiful redhead. Her looking older, visiting Ned's house after she gets out, knocking on his door. His face, shocked at first, then the softening in his eyes, their embrace.

I look over at the man on the ground. 'Stepfather? We're related? No fucking way! You're full of shit!'

'Not by blood. Ralph is Dora's son. Ralph found out who his mother was and then about the murder. Perhaps Ned felt bad, or guilty, but he accepted Ralphy into his life after Jo died. Ralph stands to inherit.' She shakes her head, as if there's a fly in her ear. 'Until you turned up! Ned's true child, ready to scoop the inheritance pool.' She glowers at me.

'How'd you know who I was?'

Marilyn wipes her nose on her shoulder. She moistens her lips with her tongue, then grimaces and spits out the dirt in her mouth. 'Ralph and I saw Lorrelai. She came by to see Ned. You could tell there was something between them. Weird to see him like that with anyone, all soft and loving. Never saw him lose a tear or crack a smile. Of course, we didn't know who *she* was then, but Ralph thought he recognised her. He looked her up. Found out she'd murdered his mother.

'Later that year, I had a job in the hospital, Medical Records. There was her file. I snuck into the ward where she was staying and there she was. Having a baby, everyone fussing over her. Curly red hair with a whole lotta greys, but still beautiful. In love with the little beetroot she'd produced. She called it Lola.' She screwed up her nose. 'Couldn't help myself. I looked at the crib. I counted backwards. It was the right length of time to have been Ned's. When I told Ralph, he was furious, flipped his lid. He told me Ned's real name, everything.'

'But nothing happened. Lorrelai didn't show up, so we thought we were wrong, that the baby wasn't Ned's, and Ralph would be okay.

'Then, years later, this beefy thug of a woman comes and demands a house. *A house!* I followed her. What right did she have over Ned's money more than me and Ralphy? When I saw what Ned had given her, I laughed my tits off. What a dump!' She stops, clears her throat and sniffs. 'But it was strange. Why would he give her a house?'

'Then Ralph goes to that shitty town for work, teaching smelly schoolkids to dance after that little bitch at the academy dobbed him in for touching her. Who do I see coming out of that dump of Ned's? You! A scruffy teenager called Lola about the right damn age. Was that why he gave her a house? He knew about you? But you could've been anyone. I wasn't convinced. I got your hair tested.'

I remembered Walshy cutting my hair, the bunches of curls on the ground.

'Argh,' Marilyn groans and drops her head back to face the sky. 'Then, Ralphy goes and gets himself *obsessed* with another dancing girl, gets her pregnant. She's clever enough to get rid of it, but he gets crazy. I don't know how he found out. Probably that stupid mother of hers.'

I remember Shelley telling me her secret. The sadness in her eyes when she was helping me prepare for my school social.

I shake myself. 'So … he attacks a little girl? To get back at Shelley? How fucked up is that!'

'I don't know if he did anything to those girls. But girls like him, you see? They love him at first, then they turn on him and he loses his shit. He loves them. He hates them. He can't stop.'

'He's a monster!'

She gives me a blank, emotionless stare and then blinks rapidly, like she's changing gear. 'Not to me.'

My stomach is sick. How can a sane person explain what he did like it's the girl's fault? But I focus. 'So, you abduct and what … kill me … for money?'

She goes on, like she's talking to herself.

'Ned didn't take naturally to Ralph at first. Didn't trust him. Dora's son, you see. Probably only gave him a job out of guilt. But the old bull has a dicky heart now. He's nearly gone, and we helped him make his will. So, all you had to do was disappear, Lola. And you did … for a while.'

Her voice changes. She levels her face, lifts her chin. 'Ralph doesn't need you as a reminder of how his mother died. And I deserve something after what I've put up with, don't you think? All Ralph's little perversions. You can't take what's rightfully mine! You don't deserve what I've earned. You don't have a right. You never belonged. Just disappear again. Stay the fuck away.'

I can't answer. I'm reeling from her story of Ned and Lorrelai, *my parents*, all of it.

She did visit him. They were together, even briefly.

I was loved. I was made from love, an enduring love that lasted a fifteen-year jail term.

Chapter 60

I'm aware that something has changed with the pervert on the ground. He is still, almost in the same position, but his muscles are rigid. He's awake—I can see it in the tight cords of muscle along his spine. Is he well enough to shove that branch off? Will I have to hit him with the candlestick again? What if I kill him?

'Don't! You! Fucking! Move!' He doesn't. 'Keep talking!' I call out to Marilyn. She sways a little like she's drunk.

'Go away, Lola. Ben Walsh doesn't need the grief in his life. You're the daughter of a convicted murderer. He needs someone like Shelley. She's sweet—broken, but sweet, and on Ben's arm she'd never say anything about what happened with Ralph. She's loaded, you know. That fucking doll Ralph bought her cost three hundred dollars! You don't need Ben like Shelley does. You're a tiny fucking John Wayne. You never needed anyone. You came from nowhere. He deserves better, and you know it.'

The doll. She knew about the doll. She suspected him but still loved him. She's nuts. Why'd I think I could reason with her?

An ache prickles my throat. It would be simple, in a way. Fly back to Melbourne. Escape all this, keep on with my unattached, anonymous life. I don't want any inheritance from Ned Del Saur. And what happens when people find out who my mother was?

Should I let Shelley have Walshy? Doesn't Walshy deserve someone better than me?

Shelley could give him a good, comfortable life, so he doesn't have to struggle anymore. Lord knows Ben Walsh deserves a break.

'So, this is all about money?' Words crawl from my swollen throat like a cockroach.

'What else is there? You don't know because you never had a dime, you little trollop! *You*—a kid who shouldn't even have happened. Lorrelai's scruffy whelp ending up with Walsh money and Ned fucking Berry's money, too? Well, fuck you, Lola!'

She needs to take a big breath. I hope she chokes on a cicada.

I've almost run out of questions.

'Was it you two who stole the sketchbook? So, I didn't find about Ned?'

Marilyn coughs. 'We went looking for documents Blossom may have kept. About the house. Anything you might find that made you ask questions. Ralph saw the book. Recognised his mother.'

My heart is hammering. Ralph twitches and gets his hand up underneath his shoulder. I lift the candlestick in my undamaged had. It hovers mid-air, as if the universe has caught it. Momentarily, it is weightless and so am I.

'Don't hurt him!' Marilyn screeches. 'You dirty, wild girl! See? You see what you are! A clawing, vulgar bastard kid from the system. You'll never be anything else!'

I am a survivor. I can disappear when this is over, knowing I silenced a bad man. Do it for Lisa. Do it because I'm nobody. Just drift back off into safe anonymity.

But I know something, and it's stronger than any reason these people could throw at me.

I am loved. I always was. I am strong. These people are hate and greed. I am not them.

Slowly, I lower the candlestick to my side. Ralph groans for a long time.

'Is he alright? Lola? Lola!'

I focus, which is hard with Marilyn's carrying on and my heart pumping like Phar Lap's.

I start for the car. My legs wobble, and my right knee grinds like a broken bone. 'Stay there!' I try to sound angry. I limp to the car. My one shoe slides. I can't believe I'm slaving over a man capable of such evil.

Then I have an excellent idea.

I back the car as close to Ralph as I can, the dust swirling red in the taillights. Then I go and look for the dead roo. It's a dense shape, a grey dome, then I see the pale stripe on its face. A western brush wallaby, beautiful black and white markings. Bloody Ralph doesn't know the difference.

'What are you doing?' Marilyn stares from where she's kneeling in the dirt.

'It's time that bastard faced up to what he's done. This is the last time he gets away with hurting anything. I want him to remember it.' I get down on one knee, grab the wallaby's long bony hind legs with my good hand and lever it onto my shoulder. Then I stagger out of the bush, the wallaby's head bouncing against my lower back. Blood speckles my shoe. I pitch forwards and flop the carcass unceremoniously into the boot of the car, stand for a moment sucking in big breaths. The animal has left a bloody trail along the edge of the trunk. 'Sorry, fella.'

I glare at Marilyn. Her face is congested, lips moving a little in astonishment but too busy watching me haul the bleeding carcass into her pristine car, to speak.

'You can help me get Ralph in, but don't try anything. I can leave you both out here and he might die.' She nods and I untie her wrists with one hand and pocket the rope alongside my candlestick. We both heave the tree branch off Ralph, Marilyn as strong using two hands as I am using one. She's snivelling and gobbling like a turkey.

We get on either end of him, with me calling out instructions, but he's heavy, his head lolling. The best we can do is push and pull, his bum dragging, his jeans rolling down.

'In there.'

Wide-eyed, Marilyn stares at the dead wallaby. The macropod's head has flopped to the side, its small paws tight against its chest, like it doesn't want to soil its paws by touching Ralph. I sympathise; the skin on my arms, hooked beneath Ralph's sweaty armpits, creeps with disgust.

'He can't go in there,' Marilyn whines. I drop Ralph's top half, and she is forced to let go of his legs. He groans before he sinks onto his side. The gash in his back is bleeding, not fast but the bubbles assure me the stick punctured his lung.

'It was good enough for me. And way nicer than what he did to those girls.'

She crosses her arms, her ugly mouth hard.

'We'll just leave him here, then.'

'No! No!' She grabs Ralph's ankles and lifts his booted feet again, resting them against her hips like the handles of a wheelbarrow.

I wrestle awkwardly with his torso, hissing with pain when my damaged hand touches anything, but the metre we need to lift is too much. He's at least twice as heavy as me, his thick arms flopping around like meaty anchors. I drop him again. He writhes.

'Get in yourself, arsehole.'

Marilyn stares at me, and then at Ralph. She twigs. *Finally.*

She lowers his legs and rushes to his head, stroking the sweaty, grimy hair off his forehead. His skin is a sickly colour, his lips pale. 'Honey? Ralphy? You've got to get in the trunk, babe. We're going to get you to hospital. But you have to help us.'

Ralph winces, bares his teeth, but he lifts one shoulder and the arm that belongs to it. Marilyn guides his hand to the edge of the boot, and we both push from the back, me using my feet, butt on the ground. Ralph grunts a bit, and Marilyn encourages him with soppy words that make me want to puke. With one final heave, Ralph Higgins flops messily into the boot, his head resting on the wallaby's hindleg. His eyelids flutter.

'Safe trip,' I say, slamming the boot shut.

I limp towards the driver's door. 'You'd better keep the fuck away from me and Walshy,' I tell Marilyn. 'You're as evil and pathetic as Ralph!'

I open the driver's door and swing in, immediately hitting the central locking. The whole car clicks. *Hallelujah!* I engage drive and ignore Marilyn's pounding against the window. *Bang, bang, bang,* her furious fist hitting the glass. Her bared teeth, her ugly face smeared, demented.

I turn the steering wheel all the way round and show Marilyn the back of my fist and then my proud middle finger.

The headlights illuminate twin ruts between the trees as the car rolls slowly forward. Marilyn pounds the side panel. The back door handle clicks impotently. I stamp down on the accelerator and surge away.

In the rear-view mirror, I see Marilyn stop running, see the dust swell around her. Hands hanging loose at her sides, she stares like a woman after an explosion. Then she crosses her arms and looks all around.

I follow the dirt road until it becomes sealed, and I find a road sign to give me my bearings.

I am in Dwellingup. We drove down this road the other day. I glance at the fuel gage and see there's enough to get us into the town. My heart lifts so high it feels like it floats the car up with it. Then I see Blossom's sketchbook on the back seat. Of course, they took it, the morons. Probably thought it would be enough to hide the truth. But they didn't know me. They didn't realise I was exactly the right person to whom Blossom could entrust her secret.

We spin smoothly across the bitumen between the beautiful, sentinel jarrahs towards Dwellingup Police Station. More than Ralph deserves, but I think Blossom, and maybe Lorrelai, would be proud.

Chapter 61

I'm alone on the three-hour drive south-west to Boddington. The jarrah, marri and acacia melds into scrubby bush bordering both sides of the road. After a petrol station and street sign, the road is deserted again. I resist the urge to touch the stitches on the crown of my head. That would mean removing my good hand from the steering wheel and leaving only my plastered hand, and I can't afford any more injuries. The stitches necessitated some unflattering head shaving. I look like a beat up clown, curly hair sticking out at the sides.

To the right is a narrow road where an old metal milk pail with BWR assures me this is Boddington Women's Retreat. I wind down the window, suck in a deep breath of air.

The settlement has a pond and rose threaded arch at the front with two long buildings coming off at right angles. A red brick well nestles in a grassed area between the buildings, a small, tiled roof covering the cylindrical structure. Beneath the roof is a bar with a rope and bucket. I wonder if it was ever used to fetch water.

Aware of movement behind some windows, I wander down to the well. Birdcall splinters through leaves and scrub. There's not a breath of wind.

I check the buildings and come to a set of stairs leading up to an open door. I knock, and poke my head in, worried I might disturb silent meditations.

'Hello? Oh,' says Cheryl. She wears beige robes, and her head is shaved. She holds out both of her hands and takes my undamaged one and bows. 'Are you alright?'

'You heard about Ralph and Marilyn Higgins?'

Cheryl shakes her head. 'We aim to cut ourselves off when we're here.'

'We had a … bit of a disagreement in the forest.' The details seem too violent for this place. 'I'm fine. One less criminal on the streets.'

She blinks a few times, her face gentle. 'Are you in need of our help?'

I shake my head. 'I thought I'd come down, seeing as Blossom was here so much.'

She opens her arm to stairs that lead inside a room, an invitation. Inside the room there is colour everywhere. Paintings, craft, woven art, things made of wood, dry leaves and coloured glass. Cheryl looks around too, as though wanting to see what I see. A painting catches my eye. A beautiful red-haired woman holding a baby.

'Ah,' says Cheryl beside me. 'She was proud of that one.'

I'm magnetised by it, blood fluttering in my veins, a huge heat swelling inside my chest. There is no doubt who it is. Lorrelai is wearing a pink lace blouse, resting back against white pillows. Her hair is free of clips, and a beatific look of joy and peace is on her face. The baby is tiny, newborn, all covered except for its face and its tiny, screwed-shut eyes.

A warm hand touches my back. Cheryl says nothing.

I'm suddenly crying. I'm sucking in air, but I can't look away because it's too beautiful.

Cheryl gives me time, and when I'm quiet, she leads me outside and indicates the stairs. 'I'll get tea,' she says.

When she returns, I'm sitting on the stairs, and she's wearing sunglasses which make her look like a badass nun. She passes me a teacup.

My eyes are dry, and I'm staring at tiny avian movements in the grevilleas down the sides of the brick walls. If I concentrate, I can make out silvereyes, robins, splendid fairywrens, wagtails. They're everywhere.

'Thank you.' The tea tastes of cinnamon and honey.

We sit in silence for a while, until I realise she's waiting for me to speak. 'What do you do here?'

'We are open to women everywhere as a place of solace, reflection, and healing. It costs nothing to stay. We run on donations. Even food is donated—only vegan, of course. The food today came from an Indian family, if you would like a meal.'

'I'm okay.' I look at her. 'Is that how Blossom dressed?'

'She was a guest, not a host,' says Cheryl. 'She gardened and did maintenance for the retreat.'

I take a moment, imagining Blossom gardening here, fixing things, painting.

'That painting …' I choke up again.

Cheryl smiles softly. 'It's very beautiful. Our guests often use art to heal. The art here is all donated. But I understand if you would like that one.'

'Did she tell you about me? And Lorrelai?'

Cheryl shook her head. 'She told me about you: that you stayed in the house in York together.'

'Was she sad? Is that why she came here?'

'She didn't seem sad. She seemed peaceful. And she was always busy.'

'I brought the urn with her ashes inside. This is probably the place she'd like them spread.'

Cheryl nodded. 'If that's what you would like. Please come to visit anytime.'

An aroma hits my nostrils, and my mouth waters.

'By the way, the curry is excellent.' Cheryl points at the building opposite, lifts the hem of her robes, and heads back inside.

'Thank you.'

I walk between the trees and upend the urn. Like ashes to dust, Blossom settles to rest back in the earth.

I consider taking the painting back home. But eventually, I drive back to York without it. I know where it is. I can always come back.

Chapter 62

'What's a snowdropper?'

'A man who steals women's clothes off a clothesline, usually underwear, and masturbates into them,' Detective Sam Wheeler says, matter-of-factly.

Phone to ear, I wince. I suddenly feel sorry for my Donald Duck panties and wonder if they're still pegged on the small clothesline Perry had rigged up inside his garden shed. I couldn't believe his parents had never seen anything in that Aladdin's cave of lingerie.

Detective Wheeler escorted Ralph Higgins to hospital in Perth. He has a bad concussion, broken ribs, and a collapsed lung, as well as a long list of charges.

Perry turned up. He'd been hiding in a disused farm shed. He'd hidden his car beneath a tree and survived on water and blackberries. They took him to hospital first, to make sure he was okay, and then he was taken in for questioning.

'Can I smack Perry in the mouth? It would make me feel better.'

The detective chuckles. 'Dwellingup Police told us you gave them a bit of a surprise.'

I start to grin, remembering their faces when they saw what was in the boot.

'They considered locking me up until they got you on the phone. I'll admit, I did look pretty nasty.'

She's laughing. In the background, I hear Royal Perth Hospital's loudspeaker. She goes quiet to listen. 'Ah, Lola, you remind me of that chick in the movie *True Grit*. Leaving Marilyn out in the dark wilderness was a stroke of genius by the way. Never seen someone so glad to be picked up by police.'

'Thanks,' I say with an exhausted yawn. 'Feels like I've been preparing my whole life.'

'We could use you on the force.'

'Nah, too many perverts. I want a simple life with Walshy.'

Bread, pastries and sex. Simple.

'How is Walshy?'

'He's picking up stuff for our trip to Broome.'

'All right, enjoy your holiday. I'll be in touch. Keep safe.'

I hang up and put the phone on the mantelpiece. I have returned the candlestick to the shelf over the fireplace. Despite having been used as a weapon, it's still way shinier than the other one. It needed a wash after its photo session at the police station, and a polish before it got put back. I don't mind. I've developed a strange affection for it. We've been through so much together.

I run my fingertips down the stem, wondering whether Blossom would approve of how I used her last gift. I think she would.

My nail catches in the join at the base of the candlestick, and I can see where it's connected. A feeling rattles through me like a breeze. I compare the two, noticing the shinier candlestick has a bigger gap at the join.

The stem unscrews from the base easily. I don't breathe until it comes apart. Inside, yellowed paper is rolled up tight like a scroll. I carefully pull the paper out and take it into the kitchen. I unroll it, pinning one end with my hand as it fights to curl back in on itself. Using an empty mug to hold one corner, I spread the paper out with my hands.

My pulse stutters in my throat. The missing pages from the sketchbook!

The first page is Blossom's sketch of Dora's face, her hands outstretched, mad as the devil. There're hands around her neck, thumbs squeezing the trachea. Little thumbs. *A woman's hands.* The two people's arms run along each other, gripping each other's necks equally. Behind Dora is a small face, like someone a distance away. On closer examination, I see it's Lorrelai. Down the bottom of the page is the number one. None of the other pages were numbered. A little excitement skims my skin. This is the real secret. Doubly hidden so it was only me that ever got hold of it.

The second page has the number two. It shows two women, Dora and Lorrelai, on either side of a gap in a broken railing. Both are hanging on with one hand, Lorrelai has the edge of Dora's nightie in her fist. Water swirls far below. Dora has one hand raised, ready to strike. Lorrelai cowers, head tucked down.

The last picture, numbered three, starts with a bare bum. It's Dora, falling through the gap in the railing. Her nightie, caught on the jagged edge of the railing, is hitched up to her waist. Like the former picture, Lorrelai is still cowering and gripping the railing. Her other hand encircles her head as if she's afraid of being hit.

Stunned, I sit back.

Blossom has drawn the incident on the bridge that led to Dora Del Saur's death. In the sketchbook, all that remained after the ripped-out pages, was a church.

***

The rectory is an easy ten-minute walk.

The church doors are open. The sun reaches into the entrance, where the black-and-white tiles spread between the doors. It's strange being here when its empty. Blossom always walked the bouquet up to Father Bickley at the altar, then stood and admired the coloured glass before she handed over the flowers, like it was a ritual.

Inside, the paper decorations from the funeral are gone. The wooden pews match the floors, altar and choir area. It smells of polished wood and has its own quietness, separate from the shrill of birds and the purr of a nearby tractor.

'Hello, Lola.'

I jump, although the voice is gentle. 'Sorry, I didn't mean to startle you. I heard footsteps.' Father Bickley is standing off to the right in a doorway, wearing plain clothes; black pants and a blue buttoned-up shirt. 'You'd like to see me?' His eyes go to the sketchbook beneath my arm. He closes his eyes for a few seconds, likes he's preparing himself.

'You said to come.' My heart pounds as I look at him. He nods and gazes steadily back, his pale blue eyes framed by silver rims.

'Let's sit down, Lola.' He gestures towards a pew.

'No, outside.'

I walk out through the doors and lean back against the building. He comes out, stands on the opposite side to me, and pockets his hands.

'You knew Lorrelai didn't you? The matron from the hospital, where I was born, remembers you.'

Father Bickley nods.

'You were there when she died?'

'I was.' It's a whisper.

'You didn't tell me.'

'She made us promise. It was her dying wish that you weren't burdened by her past.' He squints at the rose garden in front of us. The roses are blooming, heavy generous blossoms nodding in the breeze.

'Where is she buried?'

'Her ashes are spread behind the church.'

I start walking that way, and he talks as he follows me around.

'Blossom wanted her where the light from the glass windows shone down in the afternoon. Lorrelai loved how it made colours on the grass.'

We stop at the rose garden at the back of the church. 'And her favourite colour was yellow.'

I'd never noticed before that the roses were all yellow.

I look behind us at the windows Blossom used to stand in front of. It was all intentional. Blossom couldn't tell me about Lorrelai, but she could make sure she had me visit my mother's resting place every week when I was young.

I stare at Father Bickley. 'Did Blossom tell you about the sketchbook?'

He clears his throat and nods.

'Blossom confessed to me. She carried a great burden regarding that night.' I hold the book against my chest.

'Lorrelai was on the bridge that night, but she lied.'

Father Bickley nodded. 'Yes.'

'But there was another person there. Someone who grabbed Dora by the throat. It was Blossom, wasn't it?'

He nods again. 'She said it was self-defence.'

I take a huge breath and let it out. 'The bruises on Dora's neck. A woman's hands.' I shake my head. 'She never drew herself, not once. But she was always there. What I don't understand is, if Blossom loved Lorrelai so much, why didn't she confess?'

Father Bickley leans forward, elbows propped on his thighs. 'Blossom was sixteen. She and Lorrelai had sworn to each other they'd say neither had been there. By the time Lorrelai was charged, Blossom knew it was too late. If they didn't believe Lorrelai, why would they believe her? Lorrelai insisted Blossom go live the life she wanted. No one had seen her.'

'You know, Blossom told Ned that she'd watched from behind a tree. Used it to blackmail him into giving her a house so she could have somewhere for me to live.'

'Yes. A lot of untruths were told that night. But I have something for you. A letter, from Lorrelai. She asked me to pass it on to you when you came and asked. I had planned on bringing it to you when you turned eighteen, but then you left. Please wait while I get it.'

I go back and sit on the church steps, my knee jigging up and down.

Father Bickley re-emerges and hands me a thick envelope. 'Take your time. I'll be inside.' He walks inside, rubber soled shoes squeaking slightly as he leaves.

I look at the envelope in my hands. There's a photo poking out. I slip it out. A woman and a newborn baby, very much like Blossom's painting from the Boddington Women's Retreat. On the back, three words; 'My baby, Lola.'

Underneath she's written her name and highlighted some letters. **LORRELAI.**

* * *

Carefully, I open the folded pages and see the handwritten words.

Lola, my sweet baby. I felt you move inside me every day. I hope you are reading this because you are grown and well and that you had wonderful parents who gave you a good childhood.

You must now know I am your mother and at least some of what happened in 1971 when my world fell to pieces.

Please, if you are scared or sad about this, or angry that details were kept from you, be kind to Blossom and Father Bickley. They have been my closest friends. I did not want you to live beneath the shadow of what I'm about to tell you.

I went to jail for fifteen years for the death of Dora Del Saur. She was the wife of the man I loved, Ned Del Saur. I did see Ned again, just once after I left prison. It was a strange, sad reunion. We held each other, just like I'd imagined so many times while in prison, but some things are lost forever after a tragedy. We parted then and there, on good terms.

Police said I followed Dora and killed her. They said I wanted to steal her baby. This is not true. Dora was a strange woman who was handicapped by her delusions and her drinking. She became a stranger to her husband, Ned, and to her child, and I found myself protecting them from her. I fell in love with them.

The night Dora died was terrible storm. We all lived in a caravan park on the edge of the river in Northam. Blossom was my first friend there, a young woman preoccupied with running away and experiencing life's offerings. Blossom and I were planning to leave together that night, as I had broken up with Ned. If only we had gone a day sooner.

During the night, I heard a scream and opened the door of the caravan. Rain, thunder and lightening pounded and flashed. Wind slammed the door into the side of the van, and the whole thing rocked. At first, I could see nothing in the dark. Then a flash of lightning lit up the world.

I didn't want to go out, but someone on the bridge had screamed. My van was the closest to the river. Wearing my boots, I ran through the mud to the river.

On the bridge, halfway along, were two people fighting. Blossom and Dora had each other by the throat. But Dora was winning.

I screamed their names, but Dora did not let go. Blossom's eyes closed and her hands dropped. I knew Dora could kill her.

I grabbed Dora's shoulders, shaking her hard, and she turned like she was in a trance.

Blossom was down on her hands and knees, on the bridge, her back heaving, still alive!

I grabbed Dora's wrist. She stood there touching her throat where Blossom had grabbed her.

'Dora, Dora! Wake up! What are you doing?'

Dora exploded, thrashing, slapping, suddenly furious. 'It's my fucking show! Give me back my show!'

She was always doing some performance in her mind, dancing, bowing and thanking an invisible audience. Lola, she was mad.

I grabbed the railing along the bridge, but it was the broken section where a branch had smashed it. On the edge, with the wind howling, we were in danger of falling through it.

Dora came for me then and I got down. But then I heard something and looked over.

Blossom was on all fours, crawling away, her boot toes scraping along the wood. Dora looked over too and she stopped hitting me and suddenly all her focus was on Blossom. That's when I grabbed Dora's nightie.

Then it happened so quickly. Dora's heel caught in the bridge, and she stumbled. The momentum sent her swinging against me as I gripped her gown. Around she went, hurtling through the gap in the railing!

I can't tell you the feeling I had! Like I was made of water. The nightie was yanked out of my hands with the weight of her, snagged on the railing. She slid out and down like a newborn baby. The nightie was suddenly empty.

I'll never forget that sensation, Lola. It was hideous.

I don't know how much time passed. Blossom and I craned over the edge to see her, but there was nothing, nothing at all. It was like Dora had not existed.

Blossom was shaking all over, trying to tell me something.

'She-she-she!' I held on to her, tried to calm her down.

'Dora grabbed me! She saw me throw Ma's wedding dress over. She thought I'd stolen it from her!'

We heard Ned calling for Dora, saw the torchlight, so we hid until he passed. And we made a promise: we would never tell anyone that we'd been on the bridge that night.

* * *

My eyes sore from staring, the tip of my thumb between my teeth, I hear Father Bickley come back out. 'You've read this?' I ask.

He nods.

I look out at a banksia. A western red wattlebird is feeding on the splayed flowers. It ducks its beak into a blossom, then swivels its eyes to check for danger. Ducks and twists, ducks and twists—an anxious feast.

'I can't believe you knew all along. I've grown up thinking you were all strangers, unrelated. I was the blow-in.'

'I always kept track of you, wanted the best for you. It was me who told Blossom where you were.'

'You?'

He nods. 'She came to see me. She was still lost, unhappy. You gave her life purpose.'

I sighed deeply. 'Poor Blossom.'

'She loved the idea of you being here, where Lorrelai had been happy.'

I digest it all for a few moments and then remember something.

'Now she's surrounded by yellow roses.'

'Yes. It was such a tragedy. Lorrelai was a beautiful woman with a good heart.'

I listen to the scratchy wattlebird call, and the *pip-pip* of another. A magpie chimes in with a chortle, and a rainbow bee-eater dives with a green-blue burst. Just as quickly, it takes flight, a split-second of apricot flashing from beneath its wings.

'Priests don't normally say that about women, do they? Not that I know the protocol. But I imagine you saying she was a generous or a kind or a devout woman would sound priestlier. And not all your friends get a whole rose garden in their honour, do they?'

Something in his face shows an internal battle. Father Bickley holds his hands in his lap. I watch his fingers thread through each other and out, over and over.

'Was Lorrelai special?'

'Very special.' He swallows.

'Go on.' I encourage.

'Before I entered the rectory, I met Lorrelai. She was a dancer at the inn.' He smiles. 'She was magnificent.'

A swell of pride surges in me. I have begun to own Lorrelai as my mother, to be proud of her.

'We had a relationship when we were both eighteen.' He looks at me and lifts his brow. 'I loved her. I really loved her.' His smile faded. 'When my call-up came, I did not want to go. I wanted to stay with her. I knew she wanted me to stay too. But I had promised myself, and the Lord, all my life. So I went.

'The next I heard of Lorrelai, she was on trial.' He shook his head. 'I felt guilty, like she would have been okay if I'd stayed. If I'd chosen a different life. But that's arrogant. I may have been able to stop whatever led her to that bridge that night.' He swallows.

'I was with her whenever I could be. I visited her at the prison all those years, held her hand, offered comfort. She was happy to have me there, I think. There was still a strong warmth between us. But her heart was with the fellow she'd met, the one whose wife drowned.'

'Ned.'

Father Bickley nodded.

'I was told he's my father.'

Father Bickley takes a breath and nods. 'Quite possible. Lorrelai still loved him after all those years. She went to see him just once. She stayed here, you see, in a room out the back of the church.' He lifts his hand to gesture behind us. 'She was quiet on her return, but she told me she would never go back. Ned had become close to a son Dora had had before she met him. Lorrelai said she saw Dora in his face and could not return. When Lorrelai discovered she was expecting, it was like joy shone right out of her, Lola. When she went to be with the Lord, she was at peace.'

A big lump filled my throat. 'I'm glad you visited. I'm grateful people who loved her were with her.'

Father Bickley pressed his lips together. 'She was loved. And she loved you. I'm glad I've had the chance to tell you that.'

I take a deep breath and look around. 'I like that she's here.'

Chapter 63

Walshy runs up the white shore of Cable Beach towards me. It goes for miles—open beach, hard-packed sand, the shoreline empty and tranquil. Placid waves slide towards the shore and then thin, retreat. Over the water, gulls float and stare down, diving suddenly for fish.

Walshy is grinning hard, his teeth a flash of white. His hair bounces as he slows from a jog to a walk. I can't run to meet him yet. My knee is still tender, my hand still in a splint. My scalp stitches are out, all twelve of them, and I have a spiky patch where they shaved my hair. Most of my scratches are gone; the saltwater is healing my skin.

Mostly, I'm completely at peace. But sometimes, I think of Perry. Other times, I remember the sound of Ralph stomping around the bush with a gun. My heartbeat accelerates, my muscles tense up.

They've questioned Ralph. The attacks were all because of his obsession with Shelley. Lisa was his victim the night Shelley had the abortion. Shelley's mother told Ralph unknowingly when he came by, looking for her. She had respected Ralph, wanted him to give Shelley a chance to return to dancing when she'd recovered.

Chloe had been walking alone just after Ralph was snubbed by Shelley, after she got injured in the Geraldton dance competition. Shelley had warned him she'd tell her parents or the police if he came around again. Incensed, wanting to claw back some control, he'd attacked. He left that doll as a message to Shelley.

Allie was Shelley's friend. Ralph had driven through Northam on the night of Shelley and Walshy's first date and seen them. Enraged, he drove to York to hit closer to home, to hammer the message into

Shelley by attacking her friend. Evil bastard.

I don't know if Shelley knows yet. I don't know how she'll cope. But I'll be there for her, in York, as her friend.

We have swum every day since we arrived. I love floating on my back in the ocean, eyes upward, full of azure sky. I'm part of the landscape, and it is part of me, the red dirt, the endless sky, the perfect Indian Ocean blue. Walshy is determined to show me I can trust him. He promises to stay and face the fire, whatever form that takes. He promises not to run away again, not to leave me. We breathe in the salty air as the ocean's calm rush surrounds us, frees us.

* * *

We flew, rather than drove, to Broome because we have a time limit. It's fourteen days before I become an apprentice baker. I am staying in York, my home, and it's a massive relief. So many things glue me there. It's special. It's home.

Before we left, I went back into Blossom's room and looked at her box of shoes. The lone heeled shoe sent a shiver down my spine. Was it Dora Del Saur's heel, the one that tripped her up? Was it left for me, to prove something? That Dora fell?

I could imagine Blossom, terrified, tugging it from between the wooden slats of the bridge, her sixteen-year-old brain whirling in the storm that night. Had she carried it around all her life, like her guilt, unsure where to leave it, unable to get rid of it completely?

I almost threw it in the bin, but instead, returned it to Blossom's cupboard. You never know. It might just come in handy to prove something one day.

For now, it's over. Blossom is finally peaceful.

I can email the last assessments to TAFE and get to work. I dream of a tiny café in the main street of York, of tourists coming in and finding a place of joy and flowers and excellent food, including jam donuts. Plus, I can keep an eye on everyone. Be the first to notice a new face or something out of step with our little town.

We've been to Gantheaume Point, where colours compete against each other, the red, rocky outcrop against the blue sky and ocean. We walked down to the dinosaur footprints. Walshy bought me a pearl on a leather string, and I modelled it naked for him at the hotel, where there is love and sex and food and sleep. A real pearl: one I will never hide away in a matchbox in the wall.

I have a softness to my hips and belly, dopey, doughy contentment. I sleep more than I ever have. I am addicted to Walshy's skin. He is warm and smooth and mine to touch. I trace him with my fingers, drape my swim-tired, sex-weary body across his on the hammock outside our room.

Walshy likes to be naked in the hotel room and on the beach when no one is there. He spends every possible minute without clothes. It's like he's shrugged off his old life and emerged new and naked as a baby.

The American and German tourists are often sluggish in the morning, so we get the beach to ourselves. One lady is so jetlagged she only wanders out to the pool after lunch. She wears dark sunglasses and doesn't leave the hotel grounds. I feel sad for her. She misses every sunrise and sunset. She doesn't see the camels as they walk in tall lines down to the shore, backlit by vivid orange, casting long shadows. She misses Cable Beach when the sun hides on the horizon and everyone falls silent, caught in nature's cathedral.

Now, on the long, gleaming shore, Walshy falls into step beside me. His hand is cold from the water. I can hear him breathing. Droplets glisten on his brown shoulders. I focus on Walshy—my anchor, my world. He walks slowly, gazing out at the aquamarine depths of the ocean. He stops where it is quiet, crosses his legs, and pulls me onto his lap. We kiss and kiss and kiss.

We hear the Japanese tourists a moment too late. Walshy jumps up and sprints for the water, his neat white buttocks jumping like steamed buns.

I limp after him, laughing. The tourists' sudden high-pitched squeals alert us that they've seen the naked man bolting for the water.

It's low tide; the shore stretches forever. I slow down, stepping where Walshy's footprints glimmer and fade, glimmer and fade, letting the water bubble over my feet as I go to him.

Hermit crabs have rolled hundreds of sand balls that span outwards from their holes; the size of pearls, they dissipate underfoot. Life confetti.

I wade out, and Walshy comes over laughing, and we kiss.

Finally, we are home. Finally, we know how to love each other.

Acknowledgements

I would like to thank Tim and Helen for listening patiently and offering insight and encouragement. For editorial advice, I'm indebted to Karin Cox and Tim Roach.

I thank my parents, family, children, friends, and nurse and fitness colleagues for much patience, faith and cheering on. Nicole and Fiona for forensic knowledge, Lisa for copyright questions, and Teleah for reading the first draft.

About the Author

A West Australian, Kamille Roach lived in nine houses by age five and has a deep connection with the natural world. She has a science degree, is published in magazines, short story collections, recognised in writing competitions, and was winner of the 2013 BJ Paterson Short Story Award and interviewed live on ABC radio. A family woman, fitness instructor and nurse, Kamille lives in Perth with her loves.

Visit: kamilleroach.com

www.ingramcontent.com/pod-product-compliance
Lightning Source LLC
Chambersburg PA
CBHW071848020726
47502CB00003B/661